Rock of Refuge

John Haworth is the pseudonym of an
earth scientist who has worked extensively in
Africa and the Middle East. He taught for
three years at the American University in Beirut, where
he met his wife. After leaving Lebanon abruptly,
courtesy of the Royal Navy (via helicopter
from the beach), they now work in Swansea.
They have two children.

ROCK OF REFUGE

John Haworth

CROSSWAY BOOKS • WHEATON, ILLINOIS
A DIVISION OF GOOD NEWS PUBLISHERS

For John and Mark,
born in Lebanon

In you, O Lord, I have taken refuge;
let me never be put to shame;
deliver me in your righteousness.
Turn your ear to me,
come quickly to my rescue;
be my rock of refuge,
a strong fortress to save me.
                                    Psalm 31:1–2

Wherefore if thou canst fail,
Then can thy truth and I: but while rocks stand,
and rivers stirre, thou canst not shrink or quail:
Yea, when both rocks and all things shall disband,
Then shalt thou be my rock and tower,
and make their ruine praise thy power.
                        George Herbert: 'Assurance'

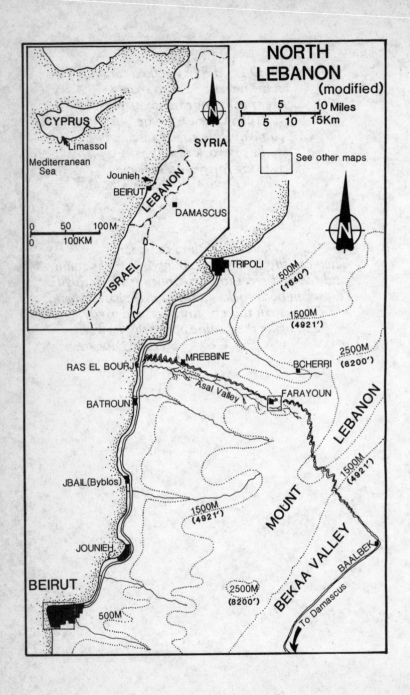

NORTH
LEBANON
(modified)

0   5   10 Miles
0   5   10   15Km

See other maps

CYPRUS
Limassol
Mediterranean
Sea
Jounieh
BEIRUT
DAMASCUS
SYRIA
LEBANON
ISRAEL
0   50   100 M
0   100KM

TRIPOLI
500M
(1640')
1500M
(4921')
2500M
(8200')
BCHERRI
MREBBINE
RAS EL BOURJ
Asal Valley
FARAYOUN
BATROUN
MOUNT
LEBANON
1500M
(4921')
JBAIL(Byblos)
1500M
(4921')
JOUNIEH
BEKAA VALLEY
BAALBEK
BEIRUT
2500M
(8200')
500M
To Damascus

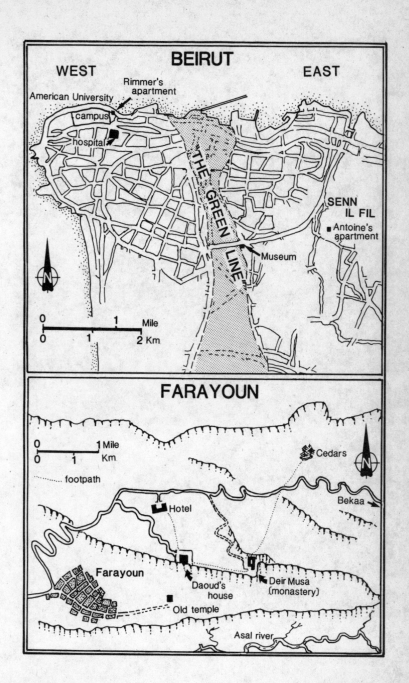

AUTHOR'S NOTE

In writing a fictional work centred on present-day Lebanon a number of problems present themselves. Most of these centre on the relationship of the fictional world to the true one; and unhappily this is a matter of more than literary significance.

With respect to characters, the author wishes to state in as plain terms as possible for the safety of those living in Lebanon that no character appearing in this book is based in any way on a real person, either living or dead.

With respect to geography, I have extended Mount Lebanon for an extra ten miles northwards for the purpose of the story and created an entirely fictional valley. Only those who know Lebanon well are likely to be offended by this, and they are those who will understand most why I did it.

With respect to time I have effectively set the story before the calamitous events of 1989. At least then I more or less understood what was happening.

Doubtless a number of readers will disagree with Henry's stance on the State of Israel; some feeling that he is too hard, others that he is too soft. I hope the criticisms will cancel each other out. For the record, the concerns of this book are matters above – but not immaterial to – politics; and the author happens to believe that the division of the world into saints and sinners does not coincide with political boundaries in the Middle East or anywhere else. I have been very careful to ensure that where Henry talks of historical events, such as the Siege of Beirut, he makes no statement that cannot be confidently substantiated. I have in fact pruned his stay in West Beirut during that time to precisely the period when I was there and can personally testify to what happened.

As many before, I have struggled with the translation of Arabic into English. Literal rendering of even simple greetings produces something faintly ludicrous like, 'Peace be upon you, O father of boys.' Consequently, in the rare places where Arabic is used I have given a free translation.

Finally, there may be those who consider the backbone of this tale to be a fanciful one. To them, I – and others who know the morass of Lebanon – would say only that we wish we had their certainty.

J H, August 1989

INTRODUCTION

This book continues – and concludes – the story recounted in *Heart of Stone*.

Henry Stanwick, Lecturer in Physical Geography at Grantforth University in northern England, is approached by the mysterious Tim Vaughan to lead him through the torturous labyrinth of a pinnacle limestone region of Madagascar. Vaughan also lends Henry a copy of a computer game. Tim's offer to Henry for the trip is very attractive, despite various warnings, as it offers him a chance to postpone making a decision on a request by an old friend, George Roumian, for him to take up a job at a school in Cyprus. Henry's reluctance to take this decision has already resulted in a breach with his girlfriend, Tina Henson.

In Madagascar Vaughan appears to get himself lost in the maze-like pinnacles and his death is assumed. However, Laurent, Henry's Malagasy companion, believes that the disappearance is a fake, a fact which they soon confirm. Vaughan claims to have been working with a secret group, the 'Jezreel project' on global crises which was disbanded because of its ominous findings and its suggestion that only in a world dominated by a single power could a global catastrophe be avoided. He says that the purpose of his disappearance is to allow him to defect to the Eastern Bloc with a critical communication device which would allow them to become the sole world power. In a struggle the device is destroyed and a subdued Vaughan is allowed to make his rendez-vous with the helicopter. On its arrival he is apparently shot and his body jettisoned over the pinnacles.

Henry and Laurent return and Henry decides he can run away no longer. At the embassy Henry is interviewed by the sceptical and cynical J P Lemaire. After a return to the pinnacles it emerges that Vaughan was not killed at all but that this was a hastily arranged further deception. Vaughan is alive and has left the country. Henry and Laurent leave for England as Lemaire continues his investigations.

Back in England Henry discovers that the computer game is a recruiting device for the project. Shortly afterwards Henry takes Laurent and Tina to a meeting with a German television producer in a remote area. He turns out to be Vaughan, who after finding out how much Henry knows, tries, but fails, to shoot him. While leaving the scene Vaughan's car is blown up, killing him. Lemaire arrives and it is revealed that Henry was bait for Vaughan who was indeed working for an independent group, neither East nor West. Lemaire however refuses, for reasons of personal safety, to have anything more to do with pursuing the group, and is confident that a truce between him and Vaughan's colleagues now exists. Henry is disgusted but unable, and unwilling, to do anything other than agree. He and Tina resolve their differences.

Tina and I were sitting together in the Hensons' best room in the early hours of the New Year. Alec and Viv had just left the room to go to bed and we were staring at the dying fire in silence. Abruptly Tina spoke.

'So, Husband-to-be, your New Year resolution is to stay out of trouble?'

'Absolutely. I promised your dad that when I asked to marry you. He didn't quite make it a condition, but he expressed unease about having his daughter marry what he termed was a walking lightning conductor. So I said I'd try my hardest to settle down. Which is what I'm doing. And frankly I'm enjoying it.'

'And you think that is possible?'

'Can but try. But I don't see why not. The wind is set fair. Not a cloud on the horizon and all that. Only the best man's speech. Otherwise all promises a calm sea and a prosperous voyage. Three cheers for peace and security.'

Tina laughed, but then a flicker of concern crossed her face.

'And not the faintest murmur from friend J P Lemaire, or from Tim Vaughan's colleagues?'

'That thing? No, I barely give it a thought. Not the slightest click on the phone lines, or the tiniest probing question from anybody. I heard from Laurent last week and all he had to talk about was the school and the church. So the Madagascar end appears quiet. Jim Barnett is happy in the States. No, I think it's finished and that's just fine by me.'

Tina wriggled a little on her chair.

'But it does hinge on a three way deal between you, J P and Vaughan's people, doesn't it? It doesn't worry you that that might be awfully fragile?'

'No, it doesn't worry me. And it shouldn't worry you. It's over.'

But it wasn't over, not for either of us, not by a long way.

1

The Friday before the start of the Lent term I went into town to do some shopping and met Abie Gvirtzman. He was browsing in what styles itself 'The Recorded Music Shop' but is known to all as 'Albert's'. It's the only shop in town where you can find anything like a decent collection of classical music without being bombarded by Heavy Metal noise.

'Abie, Happy New Year!'

Abie turned and looked at me slightly sideways. It was an odd look with a hint of unease to it. Then he smiled.

'And to you, Henry. Where is your fair fiancée?'

'Back at work; making sure that the flow of paper in the National Health Service doesn't dry up. Anyway, what are you buying? Wagner to take out in a brown paper bag?'

Abie gave me a crooked grin suggestive of long suffering. 'On the banning of Richard Wagner in Israel I agree, but this is Grantforth. No, actually, Schubert I think.'

He gestured to the disc. It was the Song Cycle 'Die Winterreise'.

'Isn't that the thing that is described as twenty-four variations on the theme of despair? The one that is issued with anti-depressant tablets?'

I looked hard at Abie. Beneath the glasses his eyes flickered. Then he shrugged. 'I have heard it so called. But aren't we allowed that? Doesn't the Constitution allow Life, Liberty and the Pursuit of Despair?'

I'm an insensitive soul by comparison to, say, the female Hensons, but I can recognise a troubled man when he flaunts it like that.

'Tell you what; come round for coffee at four. Let's have a chat. I'm probably neglecting my old friends for Tina.'

He nodded.

'Understandable, but thanks, I'd like that.'

A couple of hours later Abie was buried in my old armchair drinking coffee. So far the talk had been mostly inconsequentialities.

'So you're feeling down, Abie?'

There was a very long silence, during which he took a sip of coffee and appeared transfixed by the wallpaper over the gas fire.

'Yes; there are a number of things. There are times when I half wish I had been born a moron, with no feelings or sensitivities. No offence, Henry – you people don't understand – you *Goyim* never do. We always feel threatened, vulnerable. We're always next in line for the chop. We always wait for the man with the big stick. You know they daubed the synagogue last week?'

'Sorry, I hadn't heard. That sort of thing doesn't make the news these days. I can imagine you found it depressing.'

Abie shook his head and snorted. 'It wasn't helped by the fact that they couldn't spell.'

'What was the problem word – "synagogue", "Israel", "circumcision"?'

There was a humourless titter. 'Where do you live, Henry? The problem word was "Jew". Our aerosol expert thought it should have had a "u" in it somewhere.'

He shook his head again. 'And I should continue trying to teach Intertestamental Studies?'

'I can see that could be depressing. Anything else?'

A frown crossed Abie's face. 'At the risk of confirming a racial stereotype I also learn from friends that the University is in bad financial trouble. It is still secret, but it will be in the press shortly. Some very foolish business dealings.'

A vague alarm bell rang. 'That's news to me. What's the problem?'

18

'You know the emphasis at the moment. Every lecturer is to have his own consultancy, every department its own business, every university its own Science Park. Oh, and we are to teach students in our spare time. But we aren't business people. If we were we would be in the city or the banks. Take it from me, and if you are in any doubt ask your future father-in-law, it takes more than enthusiasm and technological innovation to make a business work. Anyway, we've had a fatal mixture at Grantforth; amateur businessmen, heavy investment and too many promises. Too many dreams and not enough reality.'

'So there's going to be a crash?'

'Nothing so dramatic. More a slither followed by a dull thud. But there'll be a knock-on effect throughout the place.'

'I can guess how, but you'd better tell me.'

'Obviously fewer library books, fewer field courses, fewer conferences and probably fewer staff.'

'So that's two good reasons for being depressed.'

Abie drummed his fingers on the arms of the chair and stared at nothing.

'They would be enough. But there's a third thing. It's the old silly irrational business.'

I felt myself stiffen in my chair. 'The old prophetic gift troubling you?'

Abie shook himself slightly as if in irritation.

'It's nothing of the sort, of course. If I believed in psychiatry I'd get it treated and it would be gone. No. Part of the problem is straightforward. I'm writing a course on Apocalyptic literature and reading some weird stuff. Makes your Book of Revelation look like a College News-letter. But....'

He fell silent for what seemed like a long time. Then he appeared to push himself back into the armchair and looked away from me as though trying to outstare something in the corner. When he finally spoke his voice was low and he seemed to be speaking to no one in particular.

19

'But I've been having terrible dreams. Thrones, shrines, blood by the bucketful. Altars, sacrifices, fire too. Darkness thick enough to touch. And the beasts...'

He shivered, and then shook himself as if trying to throw off something sitting on his shoulders. He continued to stare away from me as though unwilling to return my gaze. 'No meaning, no pattern. I can't even remember the dreams fully. I just wake up covered in sweat. They're just full of blackness, emptiness and horror.'

As he spoke his hands trembled and I thought his eyes closed.

I said the only thing that I could say. 'I'm very sorry. Tina and I will pray about your dreams.'

He slowly nodded his head, but still kept his face away from me.

'I think you'd better.' He spoke quietly but firmly. He paused briefly, as if in doubt about continuing, and swallowed. Then he turned his head slowly towards me and fixed his eyes, round and large behind his spectacles, firmly on me. Then he spoke again in a hoarse whisper.

'Yes, I think you'd better. You see – you're in them.'

2

All in all it was a grim little weekend. Abie's dreams hung over me all that Friday night and ruined my own sleep. On the Saturday morning Tina and I went round the estate agents looking for properties more suitable for a married couple than my current end-of-terrace house. Although the wedding wasn't till July there was a general consensus that a new house was pretty high on the list of priorities for the New Year. The area in which I lived was distinctly down market and was beginning to acquire the sort of reputation that makes car insurers think twice about covering anything not garaged overnight behind brick, steel and padlocks. What with two incomes coming in and a hint of generous help from Tina's parents, we were looking for something larger and better.

But in the event it proved a fruitless exercise which just depressed us. We ended up in the coffee shop and I was telling Tina an expurgated version of Abie's bad dreams when Kath Larsen came over and provided some very unwelcome news. Kath taught in the Human Geography side of the department and we'd done some field courses together. In a long round about way she told us that Prof had suddenly submitted his resignation on grounds of ill-health and hinted that all sorts of trouble was about to descend on the department. After she left Tina turned to me.

'I'm sorry to hear about Prof.'

'Not as much as I am.'

She toyed with her coffee cup. 'You like him a lot?'

'Well, yes. He's been getting an old dodderer, but he's got a good heart. But it's what Kath hinted at that worries me. Who replaces him?'

'Does it matter?'

I felt vaguely irritated.

'Yes, I'm afraid it does, in our vulnerable world. Prof's stuck up for me and I'm on a renewable contract. I need all the help I can get. A successor may be much less well disposed.'

'I see. Perhaps we should put our house plans on ice.'

'Frankly it may not be a bad idea. At least till the dust clears.'

Tina had various other things to do so we parted outside the coffee shop.

The news of Prof's illness and early retirement occupied much of my thoughts on the way back to the house. However, I also found time to wonder if I'd been dishonest by not passing on the fact that we were in Abie's disturbing dreams. I concluded that it was such an oddity that there wasn't much point in disturbing the peace by mentioning it.

The mail had come when I got back to the house, depositing three letters on the doormat. Two were the start of the New Year bills. The third was from the United States and postmarked 'Washington'.

Trying to push away a wave of unease, I took the mail into the lounge and opened the bills first. Then I opened the third envelope. It was a single sheet of good quality paper with no more than a paragraph of immaculately word processed text. The address was simply a number in a Washington avenue.

Dear Dr Stanwick,
  J P Lemaire has recently taken early retirement with our agency and I have taken over some of his responsibilities. Among his files I have some paperwork concerning you. My provisional assessment is that there are a number of aspects to the recent events in which you were involved which could be otherwise explained. I was wondering whether you felt that there might be certain things which had perhaps been overlooked? In that eventuality I'd be positive towards a reopening of the case. I'm probably passing through the UK in February if you felt there might be some potential in us meeting together. Either way I'd appreciate it if you would write me at the above address.
  Yours sincerely,
  James K Elweth

The signature was a hesitant black fountain pen affair, starting cautiously, and ending with a flourish and a final decisive underlining.

I closed my eyes for a few minutes, trying to maintain some semblance of calm. The case might be reopened! Elweth might just as well have said that he was thinking of sending me back to the frontline. Yet I realised that in a sense it was hardly a surprise; despite my protestations to Tina, something in the back of my mind since summer had been expecting something like this. That was little compensation and the combination of this and Abie's forebodings made my stomach do unpleasant gyrations.

Then it came to me that I had a choice. I could write and say I agreed totally with J P and that I had nothing further to say. That would do it. There would be nothing that Elweth could do if I refused to co-operate. Vaughan's shadowy colleagues would hardly do anything to me if I wasn't saying a word. I thought of Tina and I thought of my promise to Alec to stay out of trouble and I thought of myself and how I really disliked being shot at. I thought about dying nastily and decided that despite a pretty orthodox belief in heaven I'd be happy to postpone my arrival there. For a few moments, the idea of writing that the whole matter was closed gave me some brief comfort.

Then I realised that it wouldn't work. I couldn't do it. Not now. I'd learned a hard lesson about running away in the last twelve months. That wasn't the way.

So I had a cold, cheerless lunch and then, before my will failed me, took out an airletter form and began to write. It didn't take long.

Dear Mr Elweth,
Thank you for your letter. Yes, there are some things we should talk about. I think we should meet up in London.
Yours sincerely,
Henry Stanwick

It looked lonely and a bit silly in the middle of an expanse of blue paper. I was tempted to throw it away. Then I thought about Lemaire and I added a postscript.

'PS I would be more inclined to talk if you could give me a guarantee that there would be no recriminations against J P.'

That – as he must know – was a bluff. If I'd talk, I'd talk

whatever the situation with Lemaire. Still, I felt for some inexplicable reason that I owed it to J P.

Then I paused and wondered whether I should talk to Tina before posting it. Eventually I decided that there didn't seem much point. I knew what she'd say. 'Henry, you know what to do.' She was right, of course; I did.

So I sealed up the airletter, wrote the address and hurried down to the post box. It wouldn't go before Monday, but I didn't trust myself. After a moment's hesitation I thrust it in.

'So help me God.'

Walking back slowly I wondered whether I hadn't just signed my own death sentence.

That evening I drove over to the Hensons' intending to have a talk with Tina. Alec was looking his usual dapper self, but seemed slightly tired. Viv fussed over me. She seemed vaguely concerned that I didn't eat properly on my own. I pointed out that by marrying her daughter I was taking the most obvious step to remedy the situation. Despite this there still seemed to be concern that I might look malnourished at the wedding and be a sorry reflection of Henson hospitality. So in spite of having eaten already I stayed for dinner.

I ruined coffee by announcing the substance of Elweth's letter and the nature of my reply. Alec looked heavenward, either seeking strength or an explanation of why I should be inflicted on him as a son-in-law. Viv blanched, sighed, said, 'Oh dear, oh dear,' and looked to Alec. Tina put her coffee cup down in a slow, careful manner. Her lips trembled.

'No, you had no other option, Henry.'

Viv glanced severely at her daughter, 'But Tina....' She stopped as Alec reached out and took her hand.

'She's right, dear. Henry needs no reminding that there are some things you can't run from.'

Which was true, but it didn't make the prospect of facing

24

them any easier.

Later Alec caught me on my own in the hallway. His face was thoughtful in a sombre sort of way. He spoke quietly in order that Tina and Viv wouldn't hear.

'You did the right thing, laddie. But....'

I waited for him to finish, but he just shook his head in a motion which suggested unhappiness, an emotion rare to him.

'You were going to say?'

In his concern he sounded more Scots than usual. 'Aye, I may as well say it. See, Henry, this is a big thing and a bad business and I can't help thinking that you got away verra lightly last time. Verra lightly indeed.'

'And this time may be different?'

He pursed his lips.

'Exactly so.'

I could see his point.

'So you're worried about the price to be paid for this?'

Alec just looked at me as though weighing up something. Then he nodded with a faint rocking of his head.

'Aye, Henry, the price. And who will pay it. In life there are no cheap victories. Not one.'

3

I didn't hear from Elweth for a month. Oddly enough I didn't worry too much about it. The simple reason for this was that a far more concrete threat had emerged at the University and I can generally only worry about one thing at once.

Lent term was due to start on a Tuesday. Late on the Monday morning I popped into the department to check the mail and finish the preparation on some lectures. Prof's office was occupied as I went past, so I knocked and looked in. If I'd had any faint doubts about Kath's news the sight of Prof surrounded by cardboard boxes and half-empty shelves caused them to evaporate.

'Happy New Year, Prof.'

'Why Henry! Happy New Year to you.' He coughed nastily, and recovering himself he gestured around the room. He shook his head and coughed again. He looked very unhealthy.

'Good of you to pop in. Twenty-six years and it's all gone. Where, Henry? Answer me that.' He paused and a melancholy expression came over him. 'And to what end, I ask myself?'

He looked up and stared at me. I said nothing and Prof shook himself carefully. 'No point in getting gloomy. I'm glad to be out of it all.'

He picked up a book. 'See this? Sent to me for review; in '68 it must have been. I lost it, didn't I? Just found it today. Too late now, I suppose. Probably blighted some fellow's career. Looks useless anyway.'

He tossed it carelessly into a large box marked in bold felt pen letters, 'NOT WANTED'. The handwriting was that of Ann, his secretary. She was evidently trying to minimise the very real danger of Prof retaining his rubbish and throwing away his valuables. He looked at me again thoughtfully and then a sly expression crossed his face.

'Close the door and sit down, Henry.'

I did as he said. Prof lowered himself down carefully in his armchair, oblivious of the folder buckling underneath him.

'Henry, how long's your contract with this place?'

There was a hint of scorn at the end of the phrase which I'd not heard from him before.

'Two years, I mean another eighteen months or so to go.'

Prof looked thoughtful. 'Thought so. Look, there's a cold wind going to blow around here. I don't really know

26

what to advise. If it was anybody else I'd say make friends with the powerful.'

At this he nodded towards the Administration block. 'But I dare say you wouldn't heed that advice.' A cough shook him. 'For which I respect you. But you're at risk, you know.'

I must have looked puzzled.

'You're a soft target. Like the way you let yourself be pushed around over lecture rooms last term. Don't you understand the way to play things here?'

'Sorry, Prof. I could have out-argued Murray, but it wasn't worth it. I just thought that if he wanted a bigger room that badly, then he might as well have it. I didn't want to fight over it.'

Prof shook his head.

'Henry, being a gentleman is no asset these days. The fact you didn't fight back was noted. Next round it won't be lecture rooms. Remember, Henry, "The earth shall inherit the meek." '

On another occasion I might have defended the original of his misquote, but I didn't feel that this was either the time or the place.

He sighed slightly. 'The place is going to the dogs. Look, all I can say is keep your eyes and ears open. They'll play every trick in the book. Don't say I didn't warn you.'

He sat back and looked around the room as though summoning up past hopes and dreams. 'That it should come to this. All that labour, and some petty accountants end up calling the tune. Demolishing a department just because the Principal wagered our collective shirts on a do-it-yourself Science Park.'

An attack of coughing struck him and took the best part of a minute to subside.

'Well, they've got rid of me. I've not the heart to go on. Drive me out they may, but they're not going to kill me.'

He paused, looking around with a mournful air. I thought I'd try and stave off a further attack of nostalgia.

27

'Any retirement plans?'

He looked at me as though I'd mentioned something totally inappropriate. 'Plans? None really – I mean it's just happened, hasn't it? I suppose I shall sit and watch roses. Read some books. No plans, no....'

He tailed off into a pensive silence. I wished I hadn't mentioned retirement.

Then his eye caught the clock. 'Twenty to twelve! I was supposed to be somewhere at half-past eleven.'

He got up slowly and, picking his way stiffly through the boxes, went out into the corridor in search of his secretary. After a minute or so I decided that the conversation was probably over and left heavy-hearted.

Over the next two weeks things moved quickly in the department and Prof's gloomy forecast was rapidly borne out. The way it all turned out caught me by surprise and made me realise how little I understood university politics. To my consternation and dismay, Administration appointed Murray Lennox as Acting Head of the department within ten days of the start of term. Murray was the senior lecturer in Urban Geography. I'd never greatly cared for him and over the past few months I'd found him something of a permanent antagonist. There was no doubt about his competence or the fact that he worked hard at his research. But he was cynical and ruthless and – worst of all in my book – contemptuous of students, an attitude that was inevitably reciprocated. Indisputable evidence of this was engraved on almost every desk in the main lecture theatre. The gentlest graffiti considered him the personification of urban blight and the worst probed the limits of abuse. (The single scribbling referring to me was a suggestion that I was ignorant of the facts of life.) This loathing of Murray extended to Miriam, the departmental secretary, who had been frequently observed holding his mail carefully by the edges and giving theatrical shudders, as if dealing with something disgusting. But despite his unpopularity, the choice of Murray was far from perverse. Of all of us he had the best business links, with a thriving part-time consultancy. The success of these ventures was demonstrated by his new Audi; their demands by the constant complaints of the students that they could never find him.

In his first few days he moved slowly and carefully. He simply asked us all to submit detailed career profiles within a week. Abie Gvirtzman shook his head knowingly when I told him.

'Mark my words, Henry; a very dangerous man. Note how slow he is to move. This is what you technological maniacs call the data gathering stage. He's looking for cracks in the armour. Once he has the information he needs he'll study it carefully, say for a week. Give him a couple of days to clarify the plans with the Principal, then he'll pounce. A divide and rule policy, of course. Nothing so stupid as a staff meeting to discuss it. No, he's a man of private deals. And private threats.'

I stared gloomily at the rain running down the windows. 'Abie, I hope you're wrong. But how can you be so confident?'

Abie grinned at me. 'One: I've been on committees with him. Two: this sort of thing is what history is all about. If Herod the Great had been alive and a geographer, the Principal would have picked him. He's neither, so Murray Lennox will have to do.'

Abie's guess proved accurate. Murray called us all in one by one. Few would reveal what was said in those meetings, but in due course my turn came. I had viewed the meeting with dread and as it turned out I was fully justified.

Murray gestured vaguely to a chair and, opening a file, began immediately in smooth, amicable tones. 'Right, Henry. Some good things and some bad things in this.'

He paused. I remembered that he was fond of meaningful pauses. He glanced up at me. It was not a kindly look.

'You realise the situation, of course?'

Of course I didn't; he hadn't told me. He just wanted to build up a strong points lead.

'To a limited extent.'

He gave me a faintly scornful look. 'Well, you should. The writing's on the wall. These are tough times. We're coming up to a review in Geography. We must get the ship in order. It's my job to see us through. We mustn't lose Geography.'

Murray's thin face peered at the file. 'You're going to have to change your research. Redirect it at least. We've got to talk products and consumers now. Basically you're not marketing a product that anybody wants.'

'I'm sorry, I hadn't seen research in that light before.'

The temperature dropped by a few degrees.

'You'd better. Your record with industry is very poor.'

'I had 5,000 dollars worth of helicopter time from an oil company in Madagascar.'

He shook his head. 'We're not talking non-accountables. We're talking cash input to the department. Sponsorship, grants, salary cheques – preferably yours.'

The temperature dropped a few degrees further. I was tempted to ask what he thought a 'non-accountable' was, but decided in a rare flash of common sense to stay silent.

'I thought I'd heard of some German TV work. What happened?'

My heart sank. 'I didn't hit it off with the client.'

Slightly misleading, I thought. The truth is he tried to kill me.

Murray winced visibly. 'That about sums it up, doesn't it, Henry? It's got to change.'

Then he fell into a carefully measured pause that was heavy with significance. King Herod would have loved it. I expected to be thrown out there and then and it seemed that anything less would be an act of the deepest clemency. Finally Murray spoke, slowly and carefully with a hint of reconciliation, so that I realised how generous the offered lifeline was.

'Tell you what. You like carbonate geomorphology? Write up a proposal on, say, "Limestone and Leisure Activities". An analysis of utilisation of resources – waterfalls, cliffs, caves, climbing, scenery, all that stuff. Conflicts of interests. Opportunities.'

Unbelief battled with outrage and horror for the post of dominant emotion. Murray continued, his tone now gently encouraging, 'I'll do the costing. We'll float it round the tourist boards. Perhaps the EEC. Leisure's a growth industry.'

He stared at me. I think he expected a delighted response.

'Don't look so stupid, Henry. You do *want* a job, don't you?'

I very nearly said no, but didn't dare. Murray closed the file slowly and looked up at me.

'Four weeks' time, please. Thanks, Henry. I knew I could rely on you to understand.'

I recounted the interview to a sympathetic fiancée that evening.

'So you were less than enthusiastic about "Limestone and Leisure Activities"? I'm intrigued. Why?' Tina looked at me searchingly.

'You're concerned I'm just an intellectual snob who doesn't like getting his hands dirty? I thought of that. I don't think it's true. You see, Murray didn't present it as a scientific problem. Just a way of earning cash. Whether it was interesting or relevant or helpful was totally irrelevant.'

A vaguely mischievous look came over Tina's face. 'Like sex?'

I shook my head in mock disbelief. 'Sorry, where did you get that from?'

'Well it sounds like prostitution to me.'

'An interesting illustration. Yes – I'd prefer to do pure science of my choosing. Or alternatively, if I must work to someone's brief, then I'd prefer it to be on something of more value – the pursuit of truth or problem solving – not just the generation of paper.'

Tina was silent for some time. Her thin fingers played on the arms of the sofa in time to the background Mozart. 'Is he serious? I mean, is it possible he's simply trying to drive you out?'

I thought for a bit. 'Yes, I'm afraid you're possibly right. We *are* overstaffed. He's already muttering about slimmer, trimmer departments. It would save him a lot of trouble if I simply handed in my notice.'

Tina's fingers stopped beating time and she pointed them together under her chin in what was almost an attitude of prayer. It was a gesture, common to her and her father, of concentration and thought.

'Next question, Henry. Would you do that?'

It was my turn to think hard. 'Two weeks ago I would have laughed at the idea. Now I'm not so sure. It makes me sound defeatist, but I'm afraid I can easily see a situation arising in which I might simply not wish to be part of the department.'

Tina nodded ever so slightly. As I thought it over I felt a wave of insecurity and unease.

'I'm sorry, Tina. It's a lousy thing to say with the marriage coming up, but I'm not sure you can assume that I'll be a lecturer here for all that much longer.'

Tina said nothing, stood up, walked round behind my chair and put her hands down on my shoulders.

'I would have been very, very silly to take that for granted.'

4

In the first week of February Elweth got in touch with me by telex, and through a brief exchange of messages with a final change of venue only the day before I arranged to meet him in London one Saturday at the end of the month. As I took the train down on that wet and grey Saturday morning I spent a lot of the time staring out into the mist thinking about what I should say. Only the Hensons knew of my visit and I'd half thought of bringing Tina, but in the end this seemed a thing I should bear myself.

The address I had been given turned out to be a rather shabby hotel near Euston, apparently staffed entirely by non-native speakers of English and decorated throughout in faded browns. It seemed to take an extraordinary time for the receptionist, a charming French girl, to understand who I wanted and to call his room.

"E says 'e is expecting you. Room five three five.'

I took the creaking lift, walked down a drab corridor impregnated by a vaguely organic smell of decay and knocked on the door. There was a pause and a faint sound from inside.

'Who is it?'

It was a female voice. A shadow flitted across the security viewer in the door.

'Henry Stanwick.' I wondered if I'd got the wrong room.

'Come in.' The door was opened abruptly by a short dark-haired girl with a sullen expression.

'I'm Jim's secretary. Could you hang your coat up please, Dr Stanwick?'

33

The voice seemed to have no identifiable accent and was flat and unwelcoming. It seemed to be the personification of the hotel. I went in and looked around as I hung my coat up and the door was closed firmly behind me. It was the standard small cheap hotel bedroom with the bed removed. An extra table took its place, supporting a portable computer and a printer which appeared linked to the phone wires. Beyond, and to the side of the table, was a door in one wall indicating another room. The girl sat down gracelessly at the desk and stared at me. I began to feel distinctly uneasy.

'I hope you don't mind, but just a few security checks. Stay standing and empty your pockets on the side table over there, please, and then turn round slowly.'

The thing about staying standing was a bit theoretical as there wasn't another chair in the room.

'What happens if I protest?'

'Just turn round, please.'

It was the sort of cold, authoritative voice that kills stone dead any desire to make conversational pleasantries. As I turned round I noticed, with a tingle of fear, that she had her right hand in an open desk drawer. I felt I could make a reasonable guess as to what she was holding and how fast she could fire it. Any vestigial idea of this meeting being a cosy chat evaporated.

Clearly she saw nothing to attract her suspicions because after a moment she spoke again.

'Now open your briefcase slowly. Very slowly. Assume I'm the nervous sort.'

I did, and opened it very slowly, revealing a couple of books, a newspaper and a folding umbrella. Her eyes flickered between the case and me – she wasn't giving me any chance to jump her. She gave it a final glance and seemed satisfied.

'One final thing. Give me your date of birth and three scientific journals you've published in.'

A small amount of admiration crept into my annoyance as I gave the names. This time her eyes flickered between me and a small piece of paper cupped in her left hand.

'Fine. Pick up your things and go through the door. Jim's waiting for you.'

I muttered, 'Anytime,' with as much dryness as I could manage and went through the door. It was a similar but slightly larger room with a bed and two armchairs. A suitcase lay half open on the bed. In one armchair a man was apparently reading a thick book. As I walked in he slammed it down and seemed almost to leap out of his seat to meet me.

I had an immediate impression of youth and vigour. He stood with his hand out as we both scrutinised each other. He had a tall muscular body which seemed to be dominated by limbs, a clear unlined face and blue eyes. He almost looked like a film star, but his arms and legs were definitely too long and his face had a naive openness to it which suggested he might have problems with more subtle roles. He was wearing a creased leather jacket that seemed too short for him and rather striking ornamented leather cowboy boots. By London standards they were quite eye-catching, but I suspect by some American tastes they were probably fairly discreet. A broad grin spread over his face.

'Henry, great to see you! Jim Elweth.'

The accent was a rich American one, possibly mid-Western, and the voice sounded open, transparent and honest. He gripped my hand firmly, very firmly. I winced and tried to smile back.

'Er, good to see you, Jim.'

I'd been rather caught off balance; I'd expected a junior Lemaire – slightly less ravaged by cynicism, cigarettes and Bourbon perhaps – but not the youthful Mr Clean that I saw here. He motioned to a chair and went over and closed the door behind me. As I sat down I caught a glimpse of his book which looked to be a solid work on 'Computer Technology and National Security'.

Jim looked at me with the air of satisfied curiosity that the more exotic zoo animals probably get faced with all the time. 'Yeah, great to see you at last. Look, sorry about the security. Boy, does Angie take it seriously.'

He slumped heavily and comfortably in the other armchair. I felt I should make some sort of comment and there wasn't much point in being too rude.

'Somewhat deficient in the old grace and charm. But better to be ruthless than dead, I suppose. We too have intimidating secretaries.'

But not quite like that, I thought. Security or no, that check had been a foolish move. I had come along fully prepared to co-operate and now I was busy trying to soothe my trampled-on nerve ends. Doing my best to ignore my nervous system I felt I had to make an effort to try to help the atmosphere. I nodded at the book.

'Business or pleasure?'

'Business I guess. Although it's kinda fun. I like to keep on top. It's tough though, keeping one jump ahead.'

As he said it the smile seemed to drain away slightly as if he'd remembered something unpleasant. Then he wriggled his large frame in the chair and smiled harder. 'Anyway, now we know you are really Henry Stanwick. We've authenticated you.'

It was a happy, confident smile. It was slightly unnerving. I was finding it hard to come to terms with Jim Elweth, despite realising that we must nearly be contemporaries.

'Well, I'm delighted. But at the risk of starting an existential debate, how do I know who you are?'

He nodded slightly, confidence unabated. 'Good thinking. You don't. However, I have a letter for you.'

He pulled out a pale envelope from his inner pocket and handed it over. It had simply scribbled on it 'Henry'. I opened it and found a single sheet of cream paper, written on in a crabbed, spidery hand.

Henry,
    You probably don't recognise my handwriting, but this is from your old friend, J P. I suppose no one else in the world

36

knows that in the seismic camp I told you I'd lost three friends in Beirut in a day. Last time we met I asked you not to break a truce. I guess it's been broken, but not by you. Jim Elweth has gone over the whole story with me and I've been straight with him. Thanks for suggesting a no comeback deal. He now knows the lot.

The bearer of this letter should be Elweth. If it's not, you're in trouble. Probably are if it is. Tall guy, your age, looks like a farm boy. No distinguishing features, to my eyes – leastways not what you'd call unique. Unhealthy interest in this new technology. Jim's bright, confident and ambitious and obeys orders. I guess they wanted a change after me. Can't blame them. He may learn, but I wouldn't give him life insurance. You might hit it off with him.

If you're ever passing through St Pete, and not in trouble, come and visit me. Florida does a good line in orange juice for your sort.

Best of luck; you're heading into deep water.

Yours,
J P Lemaire

I folded the sheet up, carefully replaced it in its envelope and tucked it away in an inside pocket. It sounded genuine, but it was difficult to be certain; the letter didn't prove anything. However, J P was right on one point. Whether this was the real Elweth or not I probably was heading into trouble. I looked at Jim. Now Lemaire had pointed it out it wasn't difficult to see him as a farm boy, even as a bit part actor in a 1950s cowboy movie.

'Doesn't prove much, but it sounds like you may be genuine. J P gives you a fair character reference.'

'Good; I had a couple of heavy days with him down in St Pete. Boy, his files were a real mess. When I received your letter I got the orders to talk to him. After a bit he told me the lot.'

'So now you know everything.'

'Well, not really. Just starting in fact. But we will. Oh boy, we will. We've got a couple of us mobilised on this. First things first. I've got a couple of pages of statement from J P. I'd like you to read them through.'

He got up, opened a briefcase and handed me the sheets.

'While you're reading those I'll order some sandwiches for lunch.'

He got up and went through to the anteroom. It didn't take long to read Lemaire's sparse account. I could just see Elweth prising it out of him line by line. Jim came back and picked up his book on computers while I read on carefully and thoughtfully to the end.

'Yes, basically accurate. A bit short on interpretation though.'

Elweth put down his book and looked at me. 'Suits me. I don't take to second-hand interpretations. Prefer to make my own.'

'And your own interpretation is what?'

He looked at me carefully and folded his arms. 'Probably the same as yours I guess. A renegade group that sprung off a defence programme.'

'So Vaughan didn't lie, at least on that.'

'Maybe. A further question for you first. Have you had any further contact with anybody connected with Vaughan since then?'

'No; categorically.'

Elweth stared at me again as though weighing up what to say.

'OK. Well, Henry, I've got permission to tell you some things. It's not really a gamble. Basically we still know very little about the original project, which may, or may not, have been called Jezreel. Some guys even doubt it existed. Anyway, the idea is that it did exist and the few people who were involved were apparently very careful to erase all the files. Every darn last one. The best model is that when the project started to get out of hand it was wound down and all reference to it deleted by us. But some folks reckon that anything that was left after that was removed by a later round of deletions by them.'

He paused momentarily, a slightly worried look on his

face. 'Well, we'd prefer not to buy the second hypothesis, of course. But recent events.... Anyway, we've recovered some fragmented computer files that we think may have belonged to the sort of project you described, but they're useless. It looks like it was climatic data, but we can't be certain. It's lousy evidence for sure.'

He shook his head. 'The whole thing's just amazing. A massive project and nothing of it exists. Like my boss says – one of the old timers, "It's what you get with computers. Erase paper and you leave an imprint on the page. Pull out the page and you leave a gap in the book. But delete a computer file and it never existed." So that avenue is closed.'

At this point there was a knock on the door. Angie entered with a large tray of sandwiches and an assortment of soft drink cans, ignored both of us and put the tray down on the table. She then turned and left the room with the look of sullenness still set on her face.

'Help yourself. At any rate we tried another approach. My idea. We got a listing of all the service personnel and all the government employees, who had died over the past five years. Then we filtered it. We made certain assumptions about the people on any such project; like they'd have a degree or two, have been given high level security clearance and be above a certain rank and so on. That eliminated a lot of names. Then finally we went over the records of everyone left. It was a lot of work.'

He paused to take a large mouthful of ham roll. Jim Elweth seemed to have the sort of hearty appetite associated more with haymaking than interviewing.

'Let me guess; to see who'd died without leaving the mortician any business?'

There was an approving nod. Eventually Jim cleared his mouth. 'Not bad sandwiches. I like this brown bread. Yup; died without leaving a body. A lot of paperwork. Then we cross-checked. By last weekend we ended up with ten main suspects with common characteristics. They all had high qualifications, all had different expertises. Kinda interestingly too – none had heavy personal insurance; just as if they wanted to avoid any investigation from that source. Those guys get mean. Above all, they all had career patterns that had striking similarities.'

He took another bite.

'In what way?'

There was a pause as he chewed. 'Five years ago they all had an abrupt career change. Almost all were relocated or shifted. Australia, Buenos Aires, Montreal, Paris, Moscow, Diego Garcia, China, Cairo; I forget the others, but it looked like they'd been deliberately dispersed. When you looked hard there was a further odd thing. The year before, their records showed they'd done exactly the same as they had the twelve months before that. Basically just ditto marks. Looks very much like a cover-up. And four years ago they started dying.'

Elweth stood up, took another sandwich and went over to the desk. He came back munching hungrily and waving a folder.

'So it sorta fits. The project runs for a year. Long enough for preliminary results. The project starts to go off target so they kill it. Press the big red button. Disband the group and post them all to the ends of the earth. Within a year they have started to regroup unofficially.'

He sat down and tapped the folder.

'Scarey, Henry; real scarey. These guys have been running something big and covert for four years. But what and where?'

I said nothing; I was too busy taking it all in. Elweth wiped his lips on a paper tissue and opened the folder. From it he pulled a sheet of printout.

'Let me read you the list of names first and then you can look at the photos. Here goes.

'Tony Beard, oceanographer. Boating accident off Bermuda in winter. Just wreckage. No body.

'Duane Carter, ecosystems modeller. Whatever one of those is. Lost in a single engine plane over the Andean foothills in Western Brazil. No body.

'Simon Dyer, military intelligence. All we can find out is he was trying to find some MIAs in 'Nam.'

'Sorry?' I felt awkward about interrupting the impressive list.

'Missing in Action. Anyway, either the jungle or the gooks got him.

'Alan Gencher, agronomist. Boat lost in heavy seas off Australia. Lots of hungry sharks, so they never really expected a body. Didn't get one.

'Terry Scanlon, epidemiologist – I think that's how you pronounce it. Fatal road accident in India. Car crashed and caught fire. Identity of corpse confirmed on dental records by a local dentist. The dentist incidentally is now doing time for fraud on another matter.

'Mike Hempton, economic forecaster. Drove off a bridge into a flooded river one winter's night in Alberta. No body.

'John Hays, expert in counter terrorism. Lost in covert operations in Lebanon; no ransom demands. Believed dead.

'Arthur Kauffman, theoretical climatologist. Interesting one this. Died of a coronary in the boondocks of Argentina. Local hospital's morgue wasn't working, so they had him cremated real quick.

'Gerald Roeder, nuclear weapons proliferation expert. Lost with his wife mountaineering in the Himalayas. They found a pack just below a crevassed glacier and drew the obvious conclusions.

'Shirley Vachette, geneticist, plants. Car broke down on an interstate in Montana. Witness going the other way thinks he saw her picked up by a Buick. They found her bloodstained shoe a few miles down the road. No body.

'There's a few other probables that we are working on, but these look the definites so far. What do you think of it?'

The expression on Elweth's face indicated that he expected a pat on the back. He looked like a farmhand that had personally found ten lost sheep. I couldn't blame him for looking smug – he'd got some very interesting information.

'I'm impressed. Seriously. It really does look like the core of a global problems group. And you've checked on all these people from their colleagues?'

'Sure, we're working on it. It takes time. We don't want to raise the alarm. The pattern is pretty common. It's impossible to find anybody who can actually tell you what these guys were doing six years ago. People say they think they were apparently on sabbatical, temporary foreign assignment, seconded to the State Department or something like that.'

'Can I think for a minute?'

'Go ahead, I could use another sandwich.'

I ran over the brief descriptions as far as I could remember them.

'I can think of a few other expertises that might be lacking: a pollution expert, a political analyst. The absence of a computer or communication man is significant.'

Elweth, chewing heavily, nodded enthusiastically. 'Vaughan.' He spoke with his mouth half-full. He hastily cleared it and spoke again.

'Yeah, that's what we thought – and you're probably right about the other two. We just haven't pinpointed them yet. You missed out a sociologist and a population expert of some sort too. Maybe they are still alive – if you follow what I mean. They haven't disappeared yet.'

I got up and walked to the window, noting as I did so that Jim's eyes followed me carefully. It was still raining and the world looked the same. It just didn't feel the same. There seemed to be a big shadow somewhere. I turned to Elweth, who was pulling the tab off an orange juice can.

'You mean no one noticed?'

'Noticed what, Henry?'

'These guys dying off, I suppose.'

'Of course not. That's the beauty of it. These people

42

were deliberately drawn from a dozen scattered departments in the first place. Probably only two, three people knew the full make up of the team. It would have been an outrageous chance if they had noticed even a couple of the obituaries. Like my boss says, "When a mystery happens to a secret, no one's going to shout an alarm." ' He shrugged dismissively and started on a chocolate bar.

'Why are you telling me this?'

A vague look appeared on Jim's face. He swallowed hard.

'Simple. You apparently saw the man who met Vaughan at the pick-up point. You got a decent look at him. That's what you said.'

'Well, yes, but I don't have a good memory for faces. And it was through binoculars which distorts perspective.'

'OK, but run through these photographs and tell me if it was any of these.'

I sat down again and Jim handed me a large sheet with ten photographs mounted on it. I ran through them once quickly and again slowly. I squinted, trying to conjure up again the man with the gun in the middle of the pinnacles.

'No, he's not one of these. Unless they've had plastic surgery.'

Elweth made a clucking noise. It was muffled, as he had a mouthful of sandwich. He'd obviously started on lunch all over again. Definitely an agricultural appetite.

'Aw, pity. I was hoping we might have a definite identification. Could have used that.'

He put the files and the sheet of photos carefully back in the folder. There was a moment of silence. Elweth wiped his mouth with his tissue and looked at me.

'Henry, I'll be honest. We have a problem. These names don't help us much. We can't prove anything. The trail was well hidden in every case and it's now very cold. We don't even know what happened to Vaughan from the pinnacles to the time he tried to kill you. These guys have new names, new faces, new bank accounts; and they could be anywhere

43

in the world. In fact – right now – I've even got a problem proving that this is a real threat. I mean, as my boss says, "It's right off the traditional East-West intelligence axis." Heck, if we only had Vaughan alive. I need results, hard data.'

'Meaning that without it you'll run out of funds pretty quickly?'

'On target. How did you guess?'

'Budgetary problems aren't confined to intelligence.'

'I guess not. But I could use some progress.'

Elweth seemed a little uneasy and something of the open, innocent expression had oozed away. A nasty feeling stole up on me and nudged me in the ribs.

'Do I perhaps figure in your plans to find out more?'

He gave a little start and looked unhappier still. 'Sort of. Look, originally this meeting was simply to confirm your story and to show you the photographs, OK?'

'So what happened?'

Elweth shifted in his chair. He looked uncomfortable, rather as if he was going to have to tell the cattle boss that the prize steer had fled the ranch.

'Since I heard Lemaire's story – and especially the bit about the computer game – the boss and I decided that the data on this project needed special security. So I put all the files on one machine, isolated entirely from the outside world and almost entirely from the office network. I got a lot of software and hardware devices on it for security. I'm trained in that.'

He nodded at his book as if for confirmation, then seemed to run out of words. He fidgeted with a paper tissue.

'Two days ago someone broke into the machine.'

The prize steer had indeed fled the ranch.

'Physically?'

'No, through the phone lines. We think. They were good, almost unbelievably good. I mean just the best. Logged on to a machine in another part of the building and used that as a remote terminal to browse through the files on my machine. You spot the classic pattern with these guys? They always keep several links in the chain. They had the entry password and had reset the program that logged all access to the machine. What tripped them was that they needed a password to exit the system. That rang the alarms. Too late for us, of course. But you see the implication.'

An ill-defined worry began to coalesce in my mind. I said nothing.

'So, Henry, they know what I know; or at least what I had in those files. They know that I'm talking with you now.'

I felt as if the floor under my feet was beginning to give way.

'Oh.'

I didn't like the look on Elweth's face at all. It suggested that there was further bad news and he was now for some reason locked on to telling me about it. Not only had the prize steer broken out, but it looked as if they'd found it dead.

'So it's, well, kinda likely that they may try, in the most subtle of manners, to find out from you what we have discussed. If they do that, we'd like you to tell us as soon as possible.'

The ill-defined worry suddenly came into clear focus as a feeling of horror and dismay. 'Look, the last time they did that they tried to kill me!'

Elweth had the grace to look even more uncomfortable. 'We consider that eventuality to have a low probability. My boss thinks that the original attempt was an anomaly.'

I had other words for it.

'See, Henry, they know I'm desperate for evidence. A body would give it me. It would guarantee me funding for a long time.'

I felt coldly angry with Elweth and all he stood for. 'I'll try to console myself with that thought as I'm being shot in your low probability scenario.'

45

Elweth gave me a rather sheepish look. It was probably meant to be reassuring, but he needn't have bothered.

'Look, I'll be straight, Henry. You know you're safe. If they were going to eliminate you they'd have done it before we met. In the last forty-eight hours.'

5

I tried to tell myself, that while a gripping fear and a compelling desire to hit Elweth in the face were understandable emotions, they weren't either right or especially helpful. The anger I felt just became colder and fiercer.

'Thanks. Yes, thanks a lot for the warning. And next time you write your ideas up I suggest you do it in a little notebook and put it in a safe. And remember to lock it.'

The sarcasm seemed to wash over him, but he had the grace to look even more unhappy. The day wasn't going well for him.

'Sorry, but we felt a negative action towards you was unlikely.'

He paused for a moment and tried to smile. It didn't work. 'Look, I'll order some coffee.'

He got up and left the room, leaving me trying to put out the brushfire of panic that threatened to overwhelm me. I decided that the only tactic was to go on the offensive. There now didn't seem to be much to lose. What a mess!

Elweth returned and sat down on the edge of his chair. He looked unhappy.

'And you want my co-operation, Mr Elweth?'

'Call me Jim; er, yes.'

'Look, I've got some questions that I want straight answers to before I'll even think about co-operating.'

46

'OK.'

He looked vaguely relieved, doubtless due to the fact that we were still talking.

'What are you doing about the game?'

He looked at me dumbly.

'The computer game that Vaughan was circulating to recruit people. That game.'

Comprehension dawned on his face, but it brought with it another look of faint unease. 'Yeah that; well we've moved against it in the States.'

There was a look of evasiveness in his eyes that made me push the matter further. He was a lousy actor.

'How do you mean?'

He hesitated. At that point Angie came in with a tray of coffee, put it gracelessly on the table and left. I wondered briefly what had brought her to her present state of misery, then I returned to my own problems.

'Jim, you were going to tell me what you were doing about the game.'

'Yeah well. We took over the mainframe involved two weeks ago. We removed the program.'

I nodded faintly, trying to encourage him.

'It's a university machine in New England, shared between five campuses with 5,000 registered university users alone. We have no idea who put the program on. There was no trace of anybody running it. It just modified the programs and stored the names and addresses and scores....'

I nodded again.

'Apparently, every so often someone called it up and downloaded the data. They probably called from a public phone too. We learned very little.'

Elweth was fidgeting with a paper tissue again. There was something more about the game and I thought I knew what it was.

'Why haven't I seen anything in the press about it, warning people that this game is a recruiting agent? It would be a big story, even over here.'

He made no answer.

'Jim, it wouldn't perhaps be because it's too useful an idea to lose, would it?'

Elweth seemed to be biting his lip. Then suddenly the tissue he was holding disintegrated into fragments.

'It's sorta complex. I mean the boss felt it could be used under some circumstances, for good.'

My heart sank. Indeed, why alert the world to the existence of an ideal recruiting medium? I wondered whether they were already working on the new revised government approved model to test for intelligence, acceptable politics and patriotism. I felt it was time for a change of subject.

'Why do you want to nail this group?'

The switch of topic produced a visible look of relief, coupled with puzzlement. 'Henry, isn't it obvious they're a threat? If they are what we think they are then they're big. These guys have lots of data and ideas; they could do damage. They're probably still running those simulations and models. Maybe even intervening in things. They could be a real destabilising influence.'

I nearly told him how destabilising I thought the continued arms race and unconstrained corporate greed were, but I thought I'd better not.

'OK. What's your objective with these guys?'

He looked at me with a mixture of incomprehension and disfavour. 'Bust the outfit, of course. That's the order.'

'Your brief is to destroy the entire thing – people, programs and data?'

'No, no. A definite negative. We want the people alive, and the data and programs intact. Some of us consider it possible that these people have probably the most sophisticated climatic and economic models around.'

Then I'm afraid I was rotten to him. 'So you'd like that data, Jim? I guess it would be real useful to predict certain things. To use it for good, of course.'

He fell for it although I honestly wished he hadn't.

Lemaire was right; in one way we could have hit it off. For one thing Elweth was no dissembler; I think he'd have had a job to tell a white lie to save his mother from the electric chair. For another he had a naivete which, in almost any other job, I'd have found charming. Here, playing with lives and possibly more, it was dangerous. Whoever had pushed Jim Elweth into this job needed his head and his morals examining.

'Yeah, that's the idea. I mean if these guys can really help us predict the Soviet grain harvest a year in advance or give us the price of oil in ten years' time.... That'd be neat. Real neat. We'd sleep a lot easier.'

It's odd really; he wasn't stupid. I just don't think he'd considered that there might be any other point of view for me to hold but his own.

'We?'

'The US, well, I mean the West.'

'Not the world?'

Then he saw where I'd been leading him and his face fell. 'But our interests are those of the....'

I cut him off. I was too angry and disappointed to care about letting him finish. 'Let's get this straight. You want me to co-operate with you. But for what? You guys don't care about the issues involved. I don't mean Americans. I mean your grotty little intelligence community. Ours is probably the same. Lemaire was only interested in saving his own skin. You lot seem to be interested in nothing much else.'

Elweth's mouth opened a little. I think he realised he was supposed to be doing the interviewing and he made an attempt to regain the upper hand.

'You're out of line, Henry, right out of line.'

'Doesn't it strike you that for these people to make this sort of sacrifice there might be a real problem? Something so big and terrible that unless you and your clones in Moscow, and here, and everywhere else, stop playing games we're in big trouble. You know how many habitable

49

planets there are round here? One.'

I ran out of steam. Elweth plodded on lamely.

'Henry, I'm under orders. The project was presumably authorised by the United States Government and evaluated by them and their verdict was termination of project. I work for them. Under oath. What can I say?'

'And they said to you, find this project if it exists, salvage what is strategically useful and then destroy it?'

He looked so miserable, I almost felt sorry for him. He had nothing to say.

I sighed, downed the last of my coffee, picked up my briefcase and stood up.

'Sorry, Mr Elweth. I don't care for what I know of Vaughan's group. But I don't care for what I know of your group either. A plague on both your houses.'

He rose to his feet, a picture of confusion. 'Stop. Look, I'm sorry. I guess I hadn't appreciated how you felt. I'm new to this business. I gotta obey orders or I'm on the street.'

He reached into the pocket of his leather jacket and pulled out his wallet. For an incredulous moment I thought he was going to bribe me, until he produced a business card and thrust it in front of me.

'Henry, take this and give me a call if you change your mind, or if you get into trouble.'

I looked at the card briefly, then took it and put it on the table. 'There's no point, Mr Elweth. I know this isn't entirely of your making, but no deal. Sorry.'

He began to protest. 'Hey, I thought you were on our side, not theirs.'

I opened the door to the anteroom and turned to him. 'Who said there were just the two sides?'

Then I went over to pick up my coat, trying to nod pleasantly at Angie whose face seemed even more fixed in sourness, and walked out. As I closed the door there was a despairing exclamation or muffled expletive from Elweth.

It was only as I walked out onto the unfamiliar wet

streets in the already fading afternoon light that the import of what I'd done hit me. War had been engaged and I had apparently become an enemy of both parties.

Later as I stood in the overcrowded railway carriage I realised how vulnerable I was. Anyone might be an assassin and there were so many ways to kill; a gun, a knife, a poisoned needle, the push under the oncoming train. Then, as all the good books recommend, I spent some time reminding myself that God reigned and my life was in his hands. After a bit I felt better.

But when I changed trains at Derby the observant watcher would have noted that I still kept well clear of the platform edge.

6

At church next morning we had a visiting preacher. Normally Dave makes sure we get good people, but this one had slipped through the net. Starting off with an apparently straight exposition of Christ's statement, 'Heaven and earth will pass away, but my words will never pass away,' he started to drift, and was soon informing us of his conviction that these were 'the Last Days'. The Second Coming, we were assured, must be within a few years at the most. As to 'no man knowing the day or the hour' he agreed, but he seemed to hint that he might be persuaded to make a fair stab at the year. As he had clearly departed from his notes, the evidence he marshalled for this was rather disordered and coupled with a great deal of incoherence. To my relief he spared us the interpretation of modern Middle East politics usual to such preachers and resisted the temptation to play 'Name the Antichrist'.

What was striking, however, was that he seemed to base his conviction of the imminence of the Return of the Lord on such things as the apparently unstoppable growth of pollution, population, military weaponry and the inequality of global wealth. He tried to bring his argument together with what was meant to be a prophetic thundering.

'Can you not see where these things must end?'

However, he had neither the voice nor the manner ('or the text', said Alec when we discussed it later) to pull it off. Nevertheless, the parallels between his emphases, and the things that Tim Vaughan had talked about as being central to the Jezreel project, were striking and gave cause for thought.

Unfortunately, he was long on doom and short on hope, and his application, such as it was, seemed to be that there was consequently nothing worth doing now, but praying and preaching. With half the youth group currently involved in job applications or college or university interviews, I hoped that they'd take his message with a large pinch of salt. He ended up in a real mess and, in a manner reminiscent of one of those finales Dvorak obviously wrote with indigestion, tried to end five or six times before finally slithering to an abrupt, ignominious stop.

I'd been invited for lunch at the Hensons' that day and over food I made a few rather noncommittal remarks about the meeting with Elweth. I think both Alec and Tina saw deeper, but they didn't pursue it. They seemed to have something else on their minds. At the close of the meal we moved on to the sermon. The Hensons are the sort of people who rarely either praise or discuss preachers while still at church. However, open season is generally declared at Sunday lunch, although it's as often commendation as condemnation. Today I was witness to the dissection. After a few preliminaries Alec warmed to the job.

'Man, I feel sorry for yon fella. He's seen his feet hanging above the void and hasna realised that he's a rope round his waist. "Feed my sheep," the Lord said; not scare them wit-less.'

Tina joined in. 'I thought you would have been more worried about the "end of the world is nigh" bit.'

'There was so much awry that I was finding it hard to know where to begin, if you must know. No, you're right, Tina. The world may indeed be drawing to an imminent close with the Second Coming and with it a new heaven and a new earth (which incidentally got short shrift today), but we do not know it for certain.'

As usual Viv Henson was self-appointed counsel for the defence. 'I think you're being over hard on the poor man.'

'Probably so, my dear, probably so. But, Henry, you're not so intimidated by us as to stay quiet. Comments?'

I struggled with my thoughts for a moment. 'Hardly intimidated by the company, but perhaps by the topic though. I agree with what you've said, except that he touched on some real problems. I think he had the wrong diagnosis and certainly the wrong prescription, but these problems of the world remain. What do we do if, as it seems to, the world scene darkens?'

Alec looked hard but sympathetically at me. 'Mmm, fair point.' He looked around at Tina and Viv as if to invite comment from them. None came; they knew it was his question. He sat back in his chair and steepled his hands.

'Well, it would seem to me that the orders we have to be salt and light have not been rescinded. That we should continue to build hospitals, or honestly administer their funds,' at this he looked at Tina, 'or build universities and search for truth,' he gave a nod in my direction, 'seems part of that mandate. To give up that, unless called to, would be verra wrong. In other words, I'm aware of no special commands for dark days.'

Then he gave an elfish grin and looked at me. 'Unless of course you want to adopt Paul's injunction in 1 Corinthians, that in view of the present crisis it might be better not to get married.'

53

Tina jabbed him playfully in the ribs with an elbow. Viv smiled at both of us and turned to her husband.

'Thank you, Alec, but as for your serious point about giving up good works I wouldn't have thought anyone could have believed that.'

Viv spoke in tones that suggested she was deeply distressed at the thought of having to give up compassion out of theological conviction.

Alec beamed at her. 'No more you would.'

Then he turned to me. 'But I sympathise, Henry. The problems of the day do not deserve simple answers.'

The conversation drifted to other things and then the sun peeped timorously through the clouds and Tina and I decided to go for a walk. Gathering my coat I noticed Tina and her father pass a few quiet words together at the end of which Tina seemed to be getting permission for something.

We drove down to the park by the lake and wandered around looking at the ducks and the bare dripping trees. My priority was to tell her more about what had happened with Elweth. She listened carefully and sighed at the end of it.

'I'm sorry to hear your news, but it's difficult to see how you could have done anything else.'

We walked on in silence. She turned to me again.

'And how do you feel about it yourself?'

'I feel vulnerable, as though I'm totally exposed.'

'I could imagine that. Are you going to do anything about it?'

'I've thought about it. I can hardly see anything to do. I don't really know I'm in danger. There is after all some logic in Elweth's crass point that if I was going to be killed they'd have done it quicker. Anyway, where would I run to? What precautions can you take against unknown foes? Where do you take refuge in situations like this?'

I kicked a dead stick along the path. 'No, hopefully I shall now be ignored by both sides. I hope so, we've enough planned this year without getting involved in that.'

'Indeed; which raises another matter.'

There was something in her voice which made me look up in some alarm.

'Relax! It's not that serious. No, it's just that Dad has been talking to me these past few weeks about his future. Well, Mum and Dad together. Anyway, he's given me the go ahead to tell you of his plans. In confidence.'

As she spoke I felt the vaguest feeling of unease. I tried to shrug it off. 'So that was what you were talking about. Fire away.'

Tina seemed to take a deep breath.

'It's quite a big thing. Basically Dad is thinking of retiring.'

'That'll be bad news for the weeds in your garden. If there are any.' Alec's mercilessness to uninvited vegetation was notorious.

'Ah, but that's the thing. Or one of them. He has not the slightest wish to retire to prune roses. He has other plans. You've heard him speak of Stuart Macleish's church at Queen's Road, Glasgow?'

There was the intimation of something going on here that I felt sure I wasn't going to like. I was beginning to wonder whether marrying into this family was going to be that good an idea.

'Er, yes. He lent me some of his sermons. It's his old church, isn't it?'

'Right. Anyway, Stuart has a lot on his hands; he has a younger man working with him, but he could use another assistant. They are very active in the community and are doing some exciting things. There's a lot of scope for Mum and Dad. No preaching load either which suits him. Just lots of pastoral work.'

Of course when she said it I could see him in it. He'd love it. But there were a lot of implications, which we were doubtless coming to. However, I voiced my support.

'Sounds great. Very worth while. And it's a good time to do it. Now we're going to get married and Debbie seems settled. I'm surprised he kept it so quiet though.'

Tina gave me a slightly sideways look.

'Well, I'm glad you approve. The secret is because of the firm though. "You have to be a wee bit canny in business," he says. But that's the other thing.'

A little nagging doubt circled around.

'You see everything has come together. Dad's just had a review of the firm done and it's a bit negative. In fact downright brutal actually. In order to survive Henson Textiles has to lose staff, increase productivity and put in a major investment programme. It'll take six to eight years, and with no guarantee of success at the end. Needless to say, this is the confidential bit; he's been keeping his cards close to his chest.'

'I can see why. Anyway, so now is a good time to leave.'

I nearly said 'to take to the lifeboat', but it just didn't seem to be an appropriate thing to say about Alec Henson. And anyway Glasgow was no lifeboat.

'Actually, it's deeper and more complex than that. He doesn't want to fire faithful workers, he doesn't want to borrow millions and he doesn't want to commit himself to a programme that will take him well into his sixties. You see, he would feel responsible to see it all through.'

'I could see that. So what's he going to do? Tell me the worst.'

Tina gave me a curious smile. It didn't disturb the nagging unease one bit.

'It's not that bad. He's letting his Financial Manager buy the firm.'

I'm afraid to say the first thing that crossed my mind was that it was quite welcome news; a father-in-law with a cash surplus just when we were getting married could be pretty useful. But there was something that began to trigger alarms.

'Jeremy? That's a good move from what I've heard. Nice chap. But I didn't know he had access to that sort of money.'

I tried to keep the unease out of my voice, but Tina was giving me the sort of look that suggested I was in for a shock.

'Ah, that's the point. He doesn't have it. So Dad is basically going to give it to him.'

I stopped dead. 'He's going to do *what*?'

It wasn't quite a shout, but I got funny looks from two squirrels and a courting couple.

Tina seemed to find it all rather funny. 'Well I think it's sweet and good stewardship.'

I wasn't so sure and told her so. However, after a quarter of an hour of explanations I could see her point. Just. Alec wanted the firm to survive, as much for the sake of his employees as for anything else. To sell out to another company could mean the entire firm being broken up in some brutal corporate rationalisation. Jeremy, however, who had the brains and energy to carry out the overhaul, could be relied on to keep the enterprise going in a reasonably humane manner. But he couldn't afford it. So Alec had calmly decided to sell the whole enterprise to Jeremy for a nominal sum and some guarantees, thus freeing him to borrow the money for the investment. Apparently Alec felt he'd done well enough out of the firm already and that was that. And of course the Glasgow job paid nothing.

We sat down on a nearby park bench and I tried to put a brave face on it. Tina turned to me. 'Apart from the unfortunate financial repercussions for us, and the fact that it's unorthodox, I don't see any objection. Mum likes the idea; I think she was meant to be a pastor's wife. What do you think?'

I tried to collect my thoughts and kill a few of the more unworthy ones in the process.

'Still a bit stunned, really. No, I suppose I think more or less like you. In fact I admire your dad's guts. That takes nerve.'

Typically Alec in fact, I thought. Decide what's the right course and then full steam ahead and never mind the consequences. In fact I should have expected as much knowing Tina. The one was just as bad as the other. There was only Viv, Debbie and the cat sane in the entire family. Tina peered into my face.

'You aren't too bothered about the financial thing, are you?'

I thought for a moment, trying to find honest words. 'Not really but, well, I suppose with all the job uncertainty I'd always thought that if it came to the worst, your dad would bail us out.'

Tina looked sympathetic. 'You mean that if your contract wasn't renewed at Grantforth you could always get a job with your father-in-law?'

One of Tina's rare, and covetable, skills is her ability to be blunt without being offensive.

'Well, I suppose it had crossed my mind.'

'Don't worry, Henry; that sort of security isn't worth bothering about.' She held my hand tightly. 'Anyway, half the world gets married on nothing.'

'I had hoped that we might be in the other half.'

Tina looked thoughtful and scrutinised me again, her face full of concern.

'What's all this sudden concern for security, Henry? I agreed to marry the guy who'd spent years in the Middle East and got into trouble like dogs get fleas.'

She had a point. She generally does. I thought about it all for a minute.

'Yes, you're right. I am concerned about security. I suppose it's because for the first time I'm worried about providing for you, for us, and eventually for a family. Not just for this year, but for years ahead. And on top of it all the bottom keeps progressively dropping out of my world with an appalling rapidity.'

'Unhelpful hyperbole. If I thought your job was the bottom of your world I wouldn't be marrying you.'

'Sorry, I know that. It's just that unlike you I've grown up with insecurity. As far back as I can remember Mum and

Dad were always arguing and threatening to split up. Incidentally, it was mostly over money. They'd been having a row the night they hit the lorry. That simply replaced one sort of insecurity with another, till they eventually found one relative who would take both Andy and me. But she was always telling us in the nicest possible way that she wished she hadn't. I suppose going to university helped, but I still didn't believe I belonged anywhere. Anyway, you know all this.'

Tina was looking very sympathetic. 'Yes, but not from this angle. Go on.' She spoke quietly, even tenderly.

'Then I did three years abroad. I still haven't worked out why I did that. I think I felt I was condemned to be adrift for ever. A sort of geomorphological flying Dutchman....'

I ran out of steam. Funny, I'd never really seen it all like this. Not put it all together. But it all made sense.

'So why the change, Henry? Hardly me. You came back before meeting me.'

'No, actually I felt it was time to come back; maybe that I'd worked it out of my system. Since then I suppose I've been putting down roots. And know what?'

Tina smiled and shook her head. 'No.'

'I like it. I like having my own house and a monthly pay cheque. I like being settled. I even like this place. I love its dullness. Well, most of the time.'

She said nothing.

'So now I'm getting ready to build my new stable, fixed life with a nice sheltered girl from the most solid home ever. And what happens? The rock turns out to be quicksand. So that's why I'm uptight about security.'

There was silence for a moment.

'I see. Yes, I hadn't thought of it all like that. Well expressed.'

'So, Tina, I hope you know what you've let yourself in for.'

She gave me a slightly odd, vaguely amused, look. 'Given your concerns I'm astonished you're not worried about

59

what you've let yourself in for. Didn't you find Dad's decisions surprising and unexpected? Outrageous? Even shocking?'

I felt a fresh spasm of alarm come over me. What had I missed?

'Well yes, I was a bit taken aback by what he was planning. In hindsight not illogical, but a bit breathtaking.'

She grinned at me.

'Well it's an hereditary trait. I'm just as bad.'

7

February slipped into March, along with gales and frost. There was silence from Elweth and no indication of anything from Vaughan's colleagues and I began to breathe a little easier on that front. Alec's ideas for the firm began to take shape and the company lawyers were busy. Tina and I quietly decided that perhaps my house wasn't too bad after all and gave up visiting estate agents. Besides, the wedding began to loom high on the horizon and our plans began to harden into invitations.

But in the department things began to go from bad to worse. I dutifully prepared my proposal for Murray Lennox on 'Limestone and Leisure Activities', but my heart wasn't in it and he knew it. Then one day we clashed openly. It was a petty thing, but I felt that it was symptomatic of what was going on. It also had repercussions.

What happened was that I had promised to talk to the Grantforth Sixth Form College about Madagascar. It was to be a slide show of the pinnacles with emphasis on the science. Certain aspects of my last trip were, of course, not going to be mentioned. However, the day before, Murray stood up at the end of morning coffee time and announced an urgent staff meeting to discuss industrial grants at precisely the time I'd scheduled the talk. Such impromptu meetings had become a new feature of the department, although they achieved little beyond establishing that Murray had a right to call them. The real decisions were made elsewhere.

The staffroom was full with almost the entire department; academics, technicians and the two secretaries. After making the announcement he went over to the sink to wash up his cup. I followed, partly on the same errand and partly to give my apologies.

'Sorry, Murray, I won't be able to make the meeting. I've got a prior engagement tomorrow.'

He looked at me in a severe manner. 'Really? I hope you can cancel it.'

Conversation ceased either side of us.

'I'm afraid I can't. It's a long standing invitation to talk to the Sixth Form College. About geography.'

The circle of silence spread rapidly outwards in the crowded room.

'Our meeting is very important, Henry. I think you should be there.'

Although Murray spoke quietly there was an implicit threat in his voice. It was also said in a tone and pitch which suggested that he wanted other people to overhear. As he spoke total silence fell over the room and everyone turned to look at us. I tried to keep my anger in check.

'I promised.'

There was a moment's heavy silence and Murray spoke again, his voice filled with controlled tension. 'Make an excuse, man. Tell them you're ill.'

I must have glared at him because he stiffened slightly. I thought at the time that he'd realised that he'd said the wrong thing. Later, as I went over it all in my mind, I came to the conclusion that he'd decided to try and irritate me. If so, he succeeded. Murray shook his head slightly.

'Well, I can't help but note your priorities.'

He spoke firmly and very clearly. At that point I suppose I should just have shrugged my shoulders and left. I didn't.

'Look, I'm sorry, but I happen to think that encouraging students about geography is important. My understanding is that universities are about students. And the pursuit of truth.'

I turned to leave. I suppose I was half hoping for a burst of applause or a chorus of, 'Well said, Henry!'

Nothing happened. If anything, the silence merely deepened.

Murray gave me an anaemic smile. 'Fine words don't pay salaries, Henry.'

Then he slowly swilled his cup out under the tap and walked out. I stood there wondering what I'd done as the conversation drifted back to where it had been before. As I left the room I noticed that no one was looking at me.

The results of that confrontation were very depressing. True, Murray said nothing further about it, but then neither did anybody else. No one phoned me up that night to say I'd voiced the general opinion. No one stopped me in the privacy of the library to offer support. No one said anything.

By the middle of the following week I'd had enough. I was getting into the van one evening when I saw Kath Larsen coming over to her car which was parked next to mine. I went over to her.

'Hi, Kath! Got a minute?'

She started.

'Henry! Well it depends. I've got to pick Anthony up. We said we'd go out this evening. He's been so busy lately that we haven't done a thing together....'

I interrupted bluntly. 'Sorry, Kath. Look, am I the only one who thinks that the line that Murray's taking is a disaster for the department?'

Kath bit her bottom lip in evident consternation. For once she was slow to answer. Then she looked over at the lights of the department. It was an unfortunate gesture; it reminded me of how people in Damascus looked around before they said anything about the government.

'Maybe not, Henry. But you're the only one to stick your neck out. And, Henry, let me warn you, the knives are out. Murray holds all the cards too. Yes, he's a swine – off the record. But, Henry, this is the real world. Students and truth are nice, but frankly count me out. Anthony and I are planning to move house this summer and we need two salaries. And anyway, "Factors in Supermarket Siting" isn't too lousy a research topic.'

'You find that satisfying, Kath? Supermarket siting? I thought you were interested in the great questions. Why cities are where they are, that sort of thing.'

She looked miserable. 'Well, that would be nice, but I've never believed in science being about truth anyway. Now our masters don't either. There isn't any truth, so we do what we can to pay the mortgage. That's it. Pragmatism rules – it's that, not truth, which pays salaries. Murray was right on that count.'

My heart sank and I felt desperately sorry. For her, for myself, for the department or for all of them? I don't know. She fumbled in her handbag.

'The others?'

'The same. Sorry, Henry. The lifeboat's pretty small and the Captain's a stinker, but there are sharks in the water. Between them and Captain Murray I know what I'm choosing. Look, must dash. Be pragmatic, right? Sorry. Goodnight.'

I walked back to the van and kicked a tyre. As usual it didn't help.

After my confrontation with Murray things in the department quietened down. I think he was clever enough to realise that there had been little spirit to oppose him in the first place and that his public victory over me had put out any remaining sparks of rebellion.

He was also smart enough to realise the importance of the carrot as well as the stick. The few senior tenured staff who might have posed a threat he soon neutralised. He made a point of inviting them into his office to meet visiting industrialists and civil servants in cordial, profitable meetings where the sherry flowed. The existence of an 'inner circle' was soon apparent, although there was no suggestion that it was a club of limited membership. Indeed, in hints and nods and careful words, it seemed to be suggested that any might join. In fact the solicitations were openly made – as though they were intended to be overheard – which doubtless they were.

'George, I was wondering if you might join the Principal and me for lunch today with this fellow from the Department of Industry. You might get a chance to push your regional trade pattern models.'

'Andrew, I gather you're not funded to give that paper at Moscow. It's a shame. Call around this afternoon and we'll see if we've really exhausted all the avenues of funding.'

And George and Andrew went to lunch and Moscow respectively, and subsequently made only very minor noises of dissent at staff meetings.

In view of what was going on, it wasn't too surprising that when it came to the Easter field trips, I found myself swopped with George and taken off the Single Honours trip to Majorca. Missing Majorca was bad enough. Getting lumbered with running the Joint Honours field trip, twenty unmotivated students and a cheap, underheated hotel in one of the wilder extremities of Scotland was worse. The fact that all I had got for my rebellion was a week on the Gulag Archipelago didn't go unnoticed among my colleagues.

8

Not too surprisingly I spent much of the Easter weekend in bed with a cold. After Easter Monday the weather improved markedly and, shaking off the remains of the cold, I decided to go and do some fieldwork in the Dales. I'd been working up there on and off for a couple of years looking at details of some of the limestone solution features. In summer I'd normally spend a week camping, but at Easter I tried to get bed and breakfast for a few days. Spring tends to be a good time for my sort of fieldwork as the grass hasn't grown up to hide everything. It's just often numbingly cold.

This year, as in the past, I was staying at a farm in Nunnington, within easy distance of Malham. It was a pleasant spot, remote and conducive to work. I came back from the field late on Friday afternoon and was standing in front of the parlour fire trying to unfreeze when Mrs Thwaites, the farmer's wife and a lady built on a monumental scale, came in with a piece of paper.

'Careful, lad; tha'll burn tha'sel. Bert took a message for thee this morning. Phone call. Nowt serious it were, otherwise he'd a tried to find thee in Malham. I hope tha can read his writin'.'

I came away from the fire and went over to her.

'He'd have had a job finding me. Still, a nice thought. Thanks.'

I took the proffered paper out of a massive pink floury fist. It was an old envelope with the message scribbled on the back in ragged pencil.

Henry,

Dr Hammond called. Would like to meet you tonight at 7 about research work. Will take you out for a meal. Please confirm by calling the Craven Heifer at Calversdale ASAP.

Yours,

Bert Thwaites

Mrs Thwaites stood there looking at me, an apparently immoveable mountain. She was friendly, helpful and cooked marvellously, but was inquisitive to the point of being nosey.

'Dr Hammond? Never heard of him. You're sure that Bert got the name right, Mrs T?'

She put her head slightly on one side and looked at me. 'Oh it's not a "he", Luv. It were a lady, Bert said. He thought it were your fiancée. Sounded a reet nice lass, he said. Then she talked about jobs and he reckoned as it weren't.'

I returned her gaze. 'No, never heard of her. Well that's a mystery. Sounds like I'm not eating in tonight then. Unless she takes one look and realises I'm the wrong man.'

'That'd be a pity. Well, it won't take long to do thee an omelette.'

I called the Craven Heifer. Dr Hammond wasn't in, but she was expecting me to call, so I left a message and retired upstairs to smarten up and try to scrutinise my brains to find a Hammond. Eventually it crossed my mind that one likely solution was that she was a student of mine who had married. Whoever she was, I thought I'd better try to make a good impression. Fortunately, I had a jacket and tie I'd brought for Sunday, so the end result after I'd showered didn't look too bad.

Around six forty-five I positioned myself downstairs in Mrs Thwaites' parlour and waited for my mysterious visitor. I passed the time glancing through the paper and tickling a large sheepdog which had taken a fancy to me. At five past seven a car drew up into the farmyard and a few moments later the doorbell rang. Near to the door as I was, I still couldn't beat Mrs Thwaites who was conveniently polishing the brass at the other end of the hall. She padded rapidly down the stone flagged floor and opened the door. Her bulk was such that I could see nothing of whoever it was.

'Dr Hammond, is it? Come in for a moment; it's a cold night. Certainly I'll get Henry.'

She turned round and saw me.

'Oh, here he is now. Well, I'll leave you both.'

She made her way back down towards me and as I stepped back into the parlour to let her pass she gave me a knowing look. Oh well, I thought, there goes my reputation for piety and clean living in this town.

'Thanks, Mrs T. I've got a key.'

I pulled my duvet jacket off the hook on the wall and went to the door.

I looked hard at the girl standing cautiously just inside the hall. She was in her late twenties, tallish and well-built; not plump, but I felt she could be if she wasn't careful. She had light brown, even gingery, hair, tied at the back and short at the front. Blue eyes heightened by discreet makeup were set in an angular face with a clear complexion. She was undoubtedly pretty; not perhaps stunningly so but enough to make you sit up and notice. She was dressed in a smart long padded blue cotton coat. Large plain gold rings hung on her ears, adding a certain exotic tinge to what might have otherwise been a homely elegance. She certainly wasn't any student I'd ever taught and there was no wedding ring to suggest a name change due to marriage.

The girl must have followed my train of thought. 'No, we haven't met – at least I don't think so. I'm Nickie Hammond, from the Philip and Alice Houten Foundation.'

A pleasant southern English voice; confident but at the same time slightly awkward. The foundation name she mentioned was totally unfamiliar to me, but then that wasn't surprising. There's a lot of them about.

'Welcome; I'm Henry Stanwick. No, I don't think we have.'

We shook hands.

'Let's go shall we, Henry? I have a table booked for seven thirty and it's a few miles away.'

With Mrs Thwaites still palpably hovering at the other end of the hall I readily agreed.

Nickie's car was a new but nondescript Japanese saloon. She had driven out of the farmyard, carefully avoiding the hens, before she said anything further.

'I booked us in at Knighton Hall. Ever been there?'

'No, but then I'm just a visitor to the area.'

'The foodies recommend it. Do you have any good restaurants in Grantforth?'

'A few. Expensive though. Do you mind if I ask how you found me?'

'Called the departmental office last week. They gave me your address. It was on my way so I thought I'd catch you.'

'That was nice of you. I'm very grateful.'

I meant it. I found being driven off to an expensive restaurant by a pretty female who had travelled miles to see me on account of my research an idea of considerable charm.

'Not at all, we're interested in your work.'

I thought for a moment. 'Who were the people you worked for again?'

'The Philip and Alice Houten Foundation – dreadful mouthful, isn't it? I'll tell you more about it later. Why did you ask?'

'I wanted to know whether you were in the Physical Geog field yourself.'

A rabbit ran across in front of the lights and Nickie swerved a fraction to avoid it.

'Me? No, far from it. I'm a marine phycologist by training. I now do some management and dabble in genetics.'

'Phycologist? Ah, algae. Interesting little things; they are greatly under-rated.'

Nickie turned to me. I thought I could detect enthusiasm on her face. Then she turned quickly back to peering down the winding dark lane.

'Excellent! I'm so glad you agree. I'm always saying it. I'm curious why you say it though.'

'Self-interest, I'm afraid. There would be little limestone without them. And no chalk at all. Academic tunnel vision, I'm afraid.'

She laughed. 'Better than no vision at all – I should have known you'd say that. Anyway, you tell me about your academic background. Oh, and keep your eyes open for the signs – we should be there soon.'

For the next few minutes I filled her in with my PhD research. She just nodded or asked a few straightforward questions. Then I mentioned that I'd done post-doctoral work in the Middle East.

'Speak any Arabic?'

It seemed a casual comment thrown out to keep the conversation going.

'I speak Colloquial after a fashion; Classical – the written stuff – I'm very poor at. Ever been to the Arab world?'

'No.'

It was said so quietly but firmly that it stuck in the mind, although at the time I thought nothing of it. She spoke again immediately.

'We must be nearly there. Don't forget to watch out for the signs. Tell me about your current research.'

As I did so the signs duly appeared and we turned off the road into a narrow drive lined by trees whose skeletal branches could just be made out against the near blackness of the sky. As we drove slowly over the gravel a large, well lit house came into view. Nickie pulled into the full car park and slipped neatly between a Jaguar and a BMW. She turned to smile at me.

'Great! I was worried we'd get lost. I'm so awful with

maps. How you're supposed to drive and read them at the same time is beyond me.'

I decided that I liked Nickie. I've a soft spot for self-depreciation. That wasn't to say I felt anything more than that she seemed a pleasant enough person to spend a couple of hours of conversation with. Especially with the hint of a possible job offer around.

She switched off the ignition and turned to me. 'Henry, there is something I've got to tell you before we go in.'

There was an edgy note in her voice that made something cold and sickly turn in my stomach. She was looking ahead and her hands were holding the steering wheel. An ear-ring caught the light from the hotel.

'The foundation that I work for is linked to a group. You've already met someone from that group.'

In a flash I saw it all. Jim Elweth had got rid of the gloomy Angie and recruited Nickie to handle me. No, more likely still, Elweth had bungled it so badly they'd appointed Nickie to replace him. Or passed it over to MI5. Whatever way, I'd been had.

'You've probably guessed, haven't you?'

I shook my head angrily. So much for the research interest. 'Yes, I probably have.'

Nickie sighed and bending her head over the wheel stared through the windscreen. She drummed a hand on top of the dashboard.

'They said it would be difficult after what had happened. After what Tim did.'

It took a full second for the critical consonant to register.

'Sorry, you mean Jim?'

'No, Tim, Tim Vaughan. I'm part of his group.'

9

For a moment I could think of nothing at all. Fear reigned supreme although part of my brain was trying to raise the issue of culpable stupidity. I felt for the door handle. Then, as the panic subsided, I paused. Nickie didn't seem to be about to shoot me.

'I see,' I said rather stupidly. 'I hadn't realised that.'

Nickie looked over at me.

'Yes, I suppose after what happened with Tim it must be a shock. We certainly don't mean you any harm.'

She waited for a moment. I began to calm down. It seemed death was not immediately imminent. Nickie spoke again in matter-of-fact tones.

'Feeling better? Good. I've got a lot of things to discuss with you and time is short. I have to be in Scotland tomorrow. It was my idea to contact you, and it was backed. The first thing is to give you an explanation.'

'Go ahead; I'm listening. So why did you – I mean, your group – try to kill me?'

'You're jumping the gun. Sorry – unhappy phrase. It was Vaughan who tried to kill you, not us. That was an unauthorised action. You can only take my word for it, of course.'

'Of course.'

'See, Tim was his own man. So they say. I never knew him well. I mean he was only ever part time with the group. Except for the last few weeks when he was in trouble for bungling Madagascar. No one really liked that stunt I'm told, even in the planning stages. But everything else had been done and we had the contacts to do it.'

'By "everything else" you mean plane crashes in New Guinea and boating accidents in the Bahamas?'

I think, in saying that, I was trying to show her that I knew something and to reassert some sort of control of the situation.

'Yes, of course, Elweth told you all that. I'd forgotten. Anyway, let me continue. We need to go in soon, but I'm giving you the chance to cool down. Relax! Well, Tim blew the whole thing entirely in Madagascar, as you know. Then he panicked and had the pilot killed in Paris. He got disciplined for that; that was the sort of thing we've been against from the start. But he'd caused a leak – the first – so the pressure was put on him to try and sort it all out. So he organised your monitoring and then vanished. Now one of the troubles with the group is that it's largely self-running units; sometimes communications aren't that hot either. That has largely been fixed. Next we heard was from one of the German branches saying they hoped we had authorised him running off with a fully equipped Mercedes because they hadn't and he was in a funny mood. I was around in the London office for this, so that's how I know what happened and how I got an interest in you.'

I thought about asking questions, but I didn't feel like it. I'd never expected to hear the other side of that story and this, if it was true, was it.

'Then they realised what he was up to and that he was in Grantforth. But they only knew vaguely where he was and they couldn't be sure. He wasn't answering his phone. They found out he'd got hold of a gun. Not from us – at least I don't think so.' She gripped the wheel tightly, apparently bringing back unhappy memories.

'So we had to stop him. But how? Then someone pointed out that because of all the communications gear with all the codes, there was a self-destruct set-up in the car and that we could trigger it by remote control. They thought about it, but we didn't know where he was. Could have been a crowded street. Finally he called through, and sounded in a bad way. He was muttering about killing you, but he sounded so deranged that it was difficult to know whether he had done it or was going to do it. So they asked where he was and he gave the locality. It was open space so they pressed the buttons.'

She paused and shook her head in forceful regret, then she continued in a flat tone.

'There was just a crackle. And silence. That was it, we didn't speak for minutes. It was horrible.'

She made a noise of disgust and shuddered.

'I'm supposed to believe that?'

Nickie turned to me, but the light was too poor to make out any expression.

'We'd like you to. We abhor violence, Henry. For moral reasons and because we are pragmatic. We want good people in the group. We are also aware that being secret, there is a danger of turning into the Mafia or worse. We recognise the temptation.'

Away from the memory of Vaughan's death she sounded competent and believable. I said nothing.

'If you don't believe me ask yourself why Lemaire made it into early retirement alive. We let him go. We knew that there was a real risk that his replacement would smell a rat and squeeze J P for the truth.'

She turned round and picked up her handbag from the back seat.

'So that's it. Vaughan had gone completely out of control and was homicidal. That's why we had to have him removed. We were all sorry. He was good; we still miss him.'

She opened the door and cold air came gushing in.

'Anyway, let's go and eat, shall we? That is if you can stop worrying about whether you're on the menu.'

I thought about it. I'd largely recovered from the shock, I had some further questions and I was hungry. More conclusively, I didn't have a better idea.

'All right, Dr Hammond, let's eat. I'm still thinking over

73

your story. I'm not sure I buy it, at least not yet.'

Nickie had done her homework on restaurants well. The room we ate in had clearly been the main hall of a large Victorian country house. The tables were well spaced and the lighting subdued. They gave us a table in a corner and left us well alone with the menu. It was classy and impressive without being either obscenely expensive or laden with culinary pretentiousness. It did cross my mind that if Mrs Thwaites could have seen us I think she would have felt her suspicions were confirmed.

Nickie looked over the menu. 'You OK, Henry? You still look a bit like a frozen chicken.'

'Sorry, Nickie. It was the sudden expectation that I might be lying in the morgue tonight. It has that effect. Still, I'll try to thaw out enough to eat a hearty meal.'

'Incidentally, you are probably wondering why I'm taking the risk of telling you so much.'

I looked up at her. 'It had crossed my mind. Let me guess; you're going to kill me after all?'

She kicked me gently and threw her hands up in mock horror.

'Stupid! The answer is simple. We know your options. There's no one you can go to. Most roads would lead you to Elweth. Others lead you to people who are certainly worse. They'd all know a good thing when they saw one. They'd have the group broken up and take the spoils. In fact some of the things we know, some of the things we can do, could be deadly in the wrong hands. You're already aware that Elweth's crowd have got their hands on the computer game?'

'Yes, I must be to blame for that.'

Nickie nodded firmly, a thin gold chain around her neck catching the candle light.

'Yes, I think Vaughan was particularly anxious about that. It was supposed to have been his baby. But it had served its purpose. Sooner or later it would have been

74

uncovered. Where was I? Yes, I'm afraid there is not a lot you can do. Besides, I'm giving you no current names, no locations. Nothing that can be traceable.'

I didn't like the implication of that. 'So the Philip and Alice Houten Foundation doesn't exist? That would be a lie in your first sentence to me. Lies tend to be gregarious. Like starlings.'

Nickie just looked at me slightly sideways with a faintly amused air. My attack, such as it was, had left her unperturbed.

'Sorry, it does exist. It's totally above board. Albeit a bit secretive. There are four fellowships and six PhD projects being run by it at the moment. About half of them are following my own research interests. Actually we'd better order; the waitress has been hovering over there for the past five minutes. Remember the bill's on me.'

So we ordered and, the waitress having disappeared, I raised a question. 'With all due respect, I thought the group was concerned about more serious things than marine plankton?'

Nickie tossed her head in mock annoyance and flapped a hand dismissively.

'Oh, those silly little green things. I exclude the seaweeds, of course, which aren't little. Yes, and I'll come back to that point. Don't confuse me by dragging me off my agenda, Dr Stanwick. I don't want to forget to tell you something important.'

It was said with such plain good humour that I found myself more than thawing out, but actually warming to her. Not my sort of girl, even if I hadn't been engaged, but as Bert had said 'a reet nice lass'.

'Right, well then, you continue with your agenda.'

'Thank you. I gather you know the origins of the group – the very negative initial findings of a top secret global problems unit some five years ago.'

'The Jezreel Project.'

'Ah, yes. That reminds me. That's not a term we use. In

75

fact the group has no name. We use euphemisms like the Steering Committee, the Management Team and so on. The reason is obvious.'

'Not to me. It must be cumbersome.'

'We get round it. No, but I'm told intelligence suffers from a surfeit of data. In theory the CIA, or whoever, could listen to every phone conversation in the world and map every square metre by satellite. But's that's too much data. So they have machines that look and machines that listen. But they need something to search for; a word, or a name, or a pattern. So we don't give it to them. No machine will flash a light when it hears about the Research and Development Team. So we drop project names. We hide in the background of the world. It's actually rather neat. All these intelligence people are so locked on to each other that they don't give us a thought. Long may it last. Anyway, not having names is a bit less sinister too, don't you think?'

I agreed. In fact there was nothing very sinister about Nickie. It was difficult to conceive of her looking sinister under any conditions. She wasn't being totally open, but she seemed no worse than some of the people I've talked to, say, in the oil industry. There was also an air of natural self-confidence that I liked.

'Sorry, I got side-tracked again. Well, the original program is still running, with continual improvements and better data. The original thesis unfortunately seems to hold. Basically, when you have a complex interlocking system, such as the world economy, and you increase that complexity, then you also increase vulnerability to disruption. There is an interesting proviso that if you could manage the system then you would add increasing safeguards as complexity grew. As in the animal kingdom when you start to increase complexity over a few cells, then you develop a circulatory system to ensure that no cells are left deprived of oxygen or nutrients.'

She paused and looked at me, toying gently with the chain around her neck.

76

'And our global economic system isn't developing the equivalent supporting systems?'

'Not at all. It's an unmanaged mess. To change the metaphor, we're like a bunch of savages that have inherited, say, a medieval cathedral. But we're not leaving it alone. We're just adding a load here and an extension there.' At this point she gestured with her hands. 'In places we've even removed the odd flying buttress because it doesn't seem to do anything. And eventually... crash!' And her hands flew apart.

It came over as a disturbing image. Nickie was just getting warmed up when the waitress came over to ask about drinks. I settled on fruit juice, Nickie on water.

'I can't risk a drink driving charge. Besides, I might let something slip. Where was I? Oh yes, cathedrals. Of course that's not the worst of it all. There are forces that would actually want to bring the cathedral down. So that's the predicament. What do we do about it?'

'Try to reform the system; teach the savages what a flying buttress is?'

'In the real world most of the people doing most of the demolition are the best educated. No, Henry, a lot of people have tried that; we don't think it works. I certainly don't have the faith to believe it will work in time – not with greed and stupidity so endemic. So we have given up on the system. We are working outside it. Our goals are simple: a world that is stable, sustainable and secure.'

The final phrase had a slightly worn feel to it, as though it were a motto or a slogan. Nickie paused for a moment. As she did something she had said earlier came to me.

'Sorry to interrupt the train of thought again. I gather you know that I met Elweth?'

Nickie clapped her hand to her head in mock dismay. 'Oh yes, I should have said it earlier. We decided to talk to you after your interview with Elweth. You did such a nice job on the poor fellow that we thought it might be worth talking to you again. Personnel called me over to listen to it. We were impressed.'

Consternation turned to anger.

'You were listening in on it? That's a bit much, isn't it?'

'Henry, believe me, *we* didn't tape it. Jim Elweth did – it was all on orders, of course. In fairness we gather he had to be persuaded very hard. No wonder, in view of his performance. Didn't you notice he wasn't taking notes? When he got back he ran the whole interview for stress analysis to see if you were lying. Which was when we acquired a copy.'

I was spared from saying something very rude about Elweth by the arrival of the waitress with the soup.

10

I turned to Nickie. 'So what are you going to do about Jim Elweth?'

'Nothing; he's unlikely to find any more evidence. What he's got is unconvincing and he's going through his budget horribly fast. We sent him to Sydney last week on a total wild goose chase.'

She took a mouthful of soup. 'This is good. Yes, it was a pity that they caught on to us hacking into his computer files. But the novelty of that has worn off and, after all, it could have been anybody. But it does sort of prove our case, doesn't it, when a man like that is responsible in even a small way for keeping the West safe? I mean he's doubtless a decent sort, but he's got the makings of a national disaster.'

'But look, I agree Elweth is a pain, but that raises a serious point. You broke into his files; that's illegal. You've stolen his tape. Your whole foundation is built on deception and lies.'

Nickie put her spoon down and toyed with her chain again. She nodded gently. 'Ah, the ultimate put down argument. We're immoral. It's actually never bothered me, but I could see that it might you. In fact there is a simple response to that. I presume you believe in what I gather is termed a "Just War"?'

For a second I was caught off balance. 'You mean that under carefully defined circumstances it is morally legitimate to wage war? Well, cautiously, yes. I've never really analysed it – my generation hasn't really had to. None of the wars I've ever been in fitted into that category anyway.'

I had a nasty feeling I was going to be outmanoeuvred. Nickie smiled, not maliciously, but with a certain gentle amusement.

'And that therefore under the circumstances of a "Just War" it is permissible to use lies and deception? Even force? Exactly what we feel, although we do not resort to violence. Although I have no doubt, Henry, that if governments knew we existed and where we were they would use force against us if they felt they could get their hands on what we know. But to go back to the point, we accept we are involved in the occasional deception, but that is only a very small part of our operation.'

She played with her spoon a moment and then gave me an intense look. When she spoke it was with passion.

'But what is that, Henry Stanwick, when we see millions die painfully in Africa because of corruption, because of the degradation of their land, because of stupid wars? And we may have seen nothing yet. Sorry. My conscience rests easier knowing I'm taking a stand for them than that my hands are covered with the odd lie. If what we are engaged in is not a just war, then what on earth is?'

I felt curiously disorientated. Ever since I was told who she worked for I'd felt confident of one thing. They were bad and I was right. Her sudden outflanking movement, with its apparent seizure of what the politicians call the moral high ground, was devastating. I thought about making some pat reply, but I didn't think it would do justice to the occasion, and certainly not to millions of dead Africans.

'Hmm. I'm prepared to admit you may have a point. I'd need to think hard about it.'

'Don't spend too long setting up the terms of reference on your working party; we may not have that much time.'

I had some more soup to cover my confusion.

'Henry, I didn't mean to raise the temperature, but we are morally defensible.'

Something came back to me that Jim Barnett had picked up from some people who seemed to belong to the group.

'Nickie, I'd heard your people have what is called a "No Holds Barred" policy on these problems. What is it? That morality shouldn't be allowed to get in the way of a solution, so that if the answer to the world's ills lay in wiping out the population of Africa then it should be done? Something like that?'

She looked very briefly nonplussed. It made a change for me to have caught her off guard, even for an instant.

'Oh that. That's just a debating trick. You can discuss it, but we'd never carry it out. Would I work for them if I thought that sort of thing might be carried out?'

I shook my head. It was hard to believe Nickie would get involved in something like that.

She continued, 'But in the process of unrestrained free debate we might find some idea that could be usable; that otherwise we might have eliminated.'

It seemed a reasonable answer. At the time.

'OK, Nickie, let's talk about something else. How can you hope to do anything? There can't be more than a handful of you.'

'Ah well, we have a pyramidal structure. There's a co-ordinating committee at the top. They are mostly people from the original project who have reappeared. They know everything. Then we have sub-committees. I'm on Maritime Projects, for example. We are all what we call high level appointees. We know what's going on – at least broadly. Then below that we have research groups. That's a tricky one because some workers know more than others; it's a mixture of high and low levels. Below them are projects and studies to answer specific problems. This is the largest level in terms of numbers by far. The people on those know nothing about the group; they're all low level. So it's big and getting bigger. The problem is recruiting at the higher levels, where people have to be aware, if only vaguely, that there is an overall co-ordination above them. That's partly the group the computer game was targeted at recruiting for. We've had some success with that, but I don't think we can use it any longer.'

'I see. That partially answers a question on how you are structured. But what do you do?'

She took a last mouthful of soup and put down her spoon.

'That was good. Well, I don't know the whole picture. Even at my level there's a lot of separation between projects. Until recently it has been data gathering and perfecting the model. That's fun. You realise, Henry, that we are the people who know best how this planet functions as an entirety? How the atmosphere and the seas affect each other? How the climates function and how the whole thing interacts with people? And then on the human side how the economic and political processes interfinger and how the whole lot can be integrated into a single whole. I'll be honest with you, apart from the value of the work the science is marvellous. I can call up whom I like, can have access to whatever data I want. The computer modelling facilities we've been borrowing have been mind blowing.'

Her description made 'Limestone and Leisure Activities' drop still further in the hierarchy of desirable science projects.

'Sounds fascinating.' I meant it.

'Yes it is; incredibly relevant science, with a dimension of urgency. And now we are working on doing things. For example, gently boosting areas of the economy and making others less profitable. I heard the other week we had wiped out a company.'

'That doesn't sound very nice.'

'This one was cutting corners on marine waste disposal. We thought of tipping off one of the environmental groups, but the company was financially overstretched, so it was an easy matter to get them wound up. And the job was taken over by a firm that's a lot more responsible. Anyway, that's just a small example of a rather negative action.'

'Neat. Sorry, I'm all questions, but this one is obvious. Your budget must be at least a million a year. Say a couple of million sterling at least. Where do you get it from?'

There was a pause while the soup bowls were taken away.

'You are out by at least one, and possibly two, orders of magnitude. In its entirety I don't know. But a lot comes from careful investment. Remember we have the finest economic predicting facilities on the planet. I gather from loose talk that we made a lot on the oil price fall, for example. Where the initial capital came from I don't know, but we probably put most of the money back in selective investment. We recruited some good people, too, to manage the finance.'

I sat quietly for a minute or so just reviewing all that I knew so far. What Nickie had said had cleared a lot up – if she was telling the truth. Or if she knew everything. But it was difficult to believe that she personally was involved in any large scale dishonesty. She just didn't seem that sort of a girl. At length she broke into my silence.

'So you understand a little about what we do. In fact our conversation has highlighted the cloak and dagger stuff. It's unfortunate but essential that we work away from a restrictive state control, but ninety-five per cent of what the group achieves is through the low level research work. That's all above board. Any further questions?'

'Not for the moment. I'm waiting for the catch. I'm

82

repeatedly warned there is no such thing as a free lunch.'

She gave me a smile. 'This one is. OK, let's talk algae, which will incidentally root and ground the thing in practicalities. You presumably rate the rising atmospheric CO_2 levels a fairly serious hazard?'

It wasn't quite an insulting question, but almost.

'Me? Pretty high. The whole global system is beautifully balanced, but there is only so much muck you can throw in before you exceed the design specifications.' There was the faintest lifting of an eyebrow at the word 'design', but she let me continue. 'The evidence seems unequivocal. The carbon cycle is complex, but it does look like a lot of the oil and coal we burn is ending up in the atmosphere as carbon dioxide. The rising levels are fairly well documented. It's probably one of the few global environmental problems on which there is general agreement that it at least exists.'

'It does. It's not helped by the fact that deforestation is putting the CO_2 that would otherwise be locked up in vegetation in the jungle back into the atmosphere. But it's the greenhouse effect we don't care for. For one thing it's already started. Our people have modelled various degrees of global warming on the machines and we don't like it one bit. On some scenarios the higher sea levels and climatic disruption could be the trigger for the HD event.'

'HD event?' I tried to ransack my scientific vocabulary.

'Slang for the unthinkable; the Humpty Dumpty Event.'

'I see – "all the King's horses and all the King's men..." '

'"Couldn't put Humpty together again." Yes, when the whole global economic and political system crashes. It's worth briefly thinking about that event while the next course is served.'

So as the waitress delicately served our orders I sat thinking about the sudden, abrupt and inevitably bloody end of the civilised world and I didn't like it one bit. I've lived in the contained anarchy of Beirut, but even there if you had money and the right passport you could say, 'What the heck,' and get out to Cyprus or Paris where people don't need to sleep in their basements. The prospect of seeing it writ so large on the world that there would be no escape was enough material for a lifetime's worth of nightmares.

The waitress left and I decided to speak.

'OK, Nickie, so it's a problem. We know that. Even our government admits it. But tough. You can't do anything about something as enormous as global CO_2 levels. The standard answer is, "If you don't like it, then get nuclear power stations," which is no answer.'

Nickie surveyed her plate with some satisfaction and then flashed a smile at me.

'Henry, that's defeatist talk. Let me rehearse some marine chemistry for you. Those algae that have calcareous skeletons produce them by taking calcium and CO_2 out of the seawater. When they die the skeleton sinks to the sea bottom, and if we get enough of them in time we get a bed of limestone or chalk. Which eventually, courtesy of geological uplift, gets up to the earth's surface to be studied by people like you before it dissolves away again. Correct?'

'In essence.'

'But in making those skeletons they are removing carbon dioxide from the seas; and ultimately the atmosphere. In fact it's the best way we know of doing it. Nature's way.'

I was beginning to be puzzled by the trend of the conversation.

'So you're going to persuade them to work overtime?'

She faked a grimace. 'This is serious stuff, boys and girls. I'll ask questions later. Now a key point is that not all of the marine algae produce carbonate skeletons. In fact very few. We don't really know why. I've got a girl working on it at Woods Hole. However, if as seems likely we can identify and isolate a genetic sequence that causes the production of carbonate in some algae, then we have the makings of a solution. We can transplant it using standard recombinant DNA techniques and make a lot more species do it.'

She looked at me in a vaguely triumphant manner as if to say, 'How about that?' My fork stopped halfway to my mouth and then descended slowly to the plate. I vaguely remember wiping my mouth carefully and taking a drink. What she was saying was so big, so enormous, that I found it difficult to take in.

'Nickie, in ten years of listening to people come up with scientific propositions I have never come across one that came within light years of that for being....'

I stopped and thought about what to say, trying to ignore Nickie's grin.

'For being, well, lunatic, dangerous and the rest.'

There was silence as I ran over the idea again in my mind.

'All right, it might work. I mean, on the back of a beer-mat that sounds fine, but to make any impact you'd have to release them into the oceans. No one's dreamed of doing that sort of thing. The release of genetically engineered organisms into the environment is banned, isn't it? I mean it ought to be.'

As the significance of what she had said sank in further I found myself just staring at her. Her face had a fixed, vaguely amused look on it.

'Go on. Sound off.'

'Yes I will. I just hope you've done your homework, that's all. There are all sorts of implications – even if it's possible. For one thing it's a gross oversimplification to say that once the skeleton is formed then the carbonate is removed from the system. Look, take it from me, I've just done a whole chapter on the dissolution of carbonate for my book. The main thing is that below a few kilometres' water depth the carbonate dissolves again. Faster in cold water than hot too. And that depends on whether it's aragonite or calcite. But of course, it's probably too simplistic to think of a single particle....' I stalled. 'Sorry, I'd have to think and do some reading. The oceanographers have done more on it.' I realised that I was getting excited about the whole thing. Nickie gave a nod of acknowledgement and she tapped a finger on the table.

'Excellent. Now do you see why I need a research team?

In theory it is brilliantly simple. It could be done by a small lab the size of this room. Smaller. The modified algal cultures would be dropped off from a boat around the world and that would be it. There would probably be no noticeable effect on global levels for ten years, but it should work. And it's the sort of thing that only we can do. No national institution would dare to try such a thing; they'd be paralysed by fear of lawsuits. For a global agreement for, say, the UN to do this, we'd be talking decades. As you gather, the legal side doesn't concern us. We signed no treaty.'

I found myself marvelling at the whole concept, half in wonder and half in fear.

'Nickie, you realise what you're talking about is planetary engineering? You're playing God.'

'Henry, someone's got to.'

'Really? I wasn't aware the post was vacant.'

'Oh, sorry. I forgot. I was warned to watch what I say.'

'How thoughtful of them.'

'Anyway, eat your food. The hotel will think there's something wrong with it.'

If they had thought that it would have been a shame because it was excellent. After a few minutes Nickie spoke again.

'I think I can tell you why I came here now. The work is expanding enormously on this project. In fact it's the tip of the iceberg. You see once we understand how to make the bugs produce skeletons, and once we are assured that the whole thing works, we can do other things. Imagine getting them to bond on lead or cadmium, or even some of the radioactive elements to the skeleton? We'd bury pollutants with the carbonate. But the solution problem is critical, as you suggested. We don't want these skeletons to form at the surface and dissolve again at depth. So we are prepared to make you an offer. In terms of your research interests you are on the edges of the field, but we think you are sympathetic – at least from your interview with Elweth.

86

Besides, we don't lose very much by talking to you. You already know enough to be a nuisance if you chose to be.'

Things were indeed taking a most curious turn. I wasn't sure which was more peculiar, them offering me a job or me seriously thinking about it. Nickie looked expectantly at me.

'Go ahead. I'll do you the courtesy of listening.'

'I hope so. It's a serious offer, although you're not the only candidate. Wc'll fund you through the foundation to run a research project on the solution of carbonate particles in the marine environment. You can choose your university or science park. Stay in Grantforth if you like, but there are better places. We'll give you a research fellowship. Get a research assistant with some marine biology and a couple of students, and get moving on the problem. You said it yourself, "I hope you've done your homework." Well, I'm giving you the opportunity. It's got to be done and we know you'd do a good job. True, it's peripheral to your main research so far, but we've checked your background and your track record. You'd soon master the field and maybe bring in some insights.'

She paused, fiddling with her gold chain, and letting it all sink in.

'We need to know fast whether it can work. We can guarantee you a budget for five years. Total figure for the five years would be about half a million sterling. If you need more for equipment and you can justify it, then it's yours. You'll report to me or anyone I designate. Any papers or seminars would need clearing through me. Now a key point. You won't be required to do anything illegal. Indeed, you'll be required to keep out of trouble and not flash your budget around. You'll also be expected to keep silent about what you know of the group. We can only work if no one knows we exist. Once our existence is widely suspected we will probably not last long.'

I thought hard and long. It would have been an attractive research project at the best of times, but with the current crisis in the department it had taken on an extraordinary charm. It was a project of supreme importance, intellectually fascinating and came with all the funding you could want. It would also allow me to say farewell to Murray Lennox and I'm afraid that was not the least of its attractions.

'Frankly, it's intriguing. Very much so. What happens if I say no?'

'OK, this is the deal. Really it comes down to two questions. Will you work for me? To all intents and purposes you can forget the group. It's me you'd work for.'

I could easily think of worse bosses. Very easily. Nickie's competence was impressive.

'So, question one: Do you accept my offer? If yes, then the foundation will contact you inside a week. If no, then we move on to the second question: Will you promise to keep quiet about the group? If you say yes then we forget about you. Only if you break that promise do we have problems.'

'That second one. My fiancée and I have a "no secrets" deal. In fact I'd have to talk to her anyway. I'm planning to be down in Grantforth late tomorrow night and I can talk it over. But it wouldn't go beyond her.'

'OK, count her in, but don't talk about it too openly. If Elweth's unit gets to know of this meeting he'll be very unpleasant, and we won't lift a finger to help you.'

'So when do you need your answer by?'

'Forty-eight hours. I'll give you my answerphone number in London. Just say yes, or whatever, but I can't discuss the matter beyond tonight. We don't talk on phones, and anyway I've a lot of other things to do.'

'And if I say no to the offer and no to the promise of silence. What then?'

'That's the problem in high level recruitment. It's a risk. But I think you should realise from what I've said that we aren't as bad as we've been painted. Anyway, who would you tell? Not Elweth, that's for sure. The press? We could probably contain it. I don't think you'd be harmed physically. Our friends might have to paint you as being unbalanced. It'd be a mess, Henry, but I make no threats. We're not that sort of people. Really. So unless you've any further questions let's leave it at that and talk about anything else.'

So for the rest of the meal we talked about the academic world, travel and lots of other things. Much of the time my mind kept coming back to the extraordinary offer. In spare moments I couldn't help contrasting Nickie with Tina. Nickie was charming to be with but by no means as stimulating or as well read as Tina. She was, however, better travelled and apparently much more at home with the big wide world. But most of the time I thought about the tantalising proposal.

Eventually they offered us coffee in a different part of the house, possibly a one time study, where a log fire blazed, casting flickers of light onto Victorian prints. I sat there and stared into the fire while Nickie went to powder her nose or whatever. Trying to focus on the offer, I threw out a brief prayer asking for wisdom and guidance on what to do.

And it was an answered prayer because I didn't even need to wait to talk to Tina. Next morning I dialled London from a frosty call box and spoke to the tape recorder.

'Nickie, this is Henry. No to the offer and yes to the promise. Thanks and, well, all the best.'

11

'So what decided you, Henry?'
Tina stared intently from the other side of the kitchen table. She'd come round to Sunday lunch and had

listened with the greatest interest to the details of the conversation with Nickie Hammond.

'It was an odd thing. Very odd indeed. Unmistakeably providential. The manager was called away as we were leaving so I played the gentleman bit and got her coat. It was a very nice coat – long, thickly-padded cotton and pale blue. Sort of delicate Wedgwood thing. Matched her eyes.'

'I hope this is relevant, dear fiancé.'

'Every least word, my dearest. Now pay attention. As I pick up the aforementioned coat my eye is caught by the label because on it is scribbled something in pen. I stare at it and suddenly recognise four Arabic letters. So I stand there and go "H", "M", "N", "D", and pat myself on the back that I haven't entirely forgotten how to read Arabic.'

'Her name, Hammond, in Arabic – no vowels.'

'Right. Easier to transliterate than Stanwick by the way. So it registers that she's taken the coat to the cleaners – I suppose a dry cleaners, but that's irrelevant. So I put it on her and then suddenly it clicks. Flash of light and the rest.'

'That she said she'd never been in the Arab world. I wondered why you had regaled me with that bit of conversational trivia half an hour ago.'

'It was all part of a carefully controlled and sustained narrative. Anyway, my mind goes into overdrive and a scheme of subtle cunning and unparalleled deviousness occurs to me.'

'Can we stay with the controlled narrative please? I know you enjoy telling me how clever you are, but I already know.'

'Oh, all right. So I say to her, "Nice coat, suits you, but doesn't it pick up dirt a lot?" Well fortunately she's miles away. "Yes, that's the trouble, only had it a couple of months and I've had to have it cleaned once already." Then she looks down at it and says, "Don't say it's dirty again, it was cleaned only a fortnight ago." I hastily changed the subject and said a little "thank you, Lord" for answered prayer.'

'I should think so. The fact she'd lied on that point rendered her offer distinctly suspect.'

'Exactly what I thought. I don't see any other conclusion, but that she'd lied about not having been in the Arab world. So the deal was off.'

Tina scrutinised me carefully. 'Was it ever on?'

'Not without talking to you first. Even then I think it was doubtful, but she made a strong sales pitch. It was a tempting offer.'

'Thanks for thinking of calling me first, but it sounds like it was a tough decision. I can imagine how attractive you must have found the project. Still, it's a shame, I'd like to have been married to a Fellow at an Oxford College.'

'Sorry.'

'But I'd rather be married to you.'

Some time later as we were washing up Tina raised a point. 'Do you draw any other conclusions about Nickie's coat? I mean it being a thick coat rules out a lot of the Arab world, doesn't it? It was April when she had it cleaned.'

I leaned back against the wall. 'That aspect had not escaped me, Watson. Indeed I think you will find it a profitable avenue for speculation. In other words, good thinking, Tina, and continue.'

'Well, there is one place that immediately springs to mind, but then I've seen your slides so I'm biased, but there must be other places in the Arab world.'

'A few; the Atlas Mountains of Algeria and Morocco. Northern Syria; just perhaps Jordan apart from the obvious.'

'Lebanon. Is it likely?'

'After careful thought – yes. Given her line of business I think the chance of her doing much travel in a country with a strong, dynamic and inquisitive police force, to use a euphemism, seems unlikely. There's also the slightly curious fact that it's her name and not anything else.'

'I don't follow. You are ahead of me, Holmes.'

'It's not a room number, so the cleaning probably wasn't done in a hotel. She must have taken it in herself. Taking it all together I deduce that the lady is a liar, albeit a charming one, and that she was very recently staying at a private house in an Arab country. Probably on business or why hide it? And that country was, in all probability, Lebanon.'

'Sorry, Henry. Sounds convincing, but the higher you build a tower, the broader the base needs to be. I'd prefer more evidence.'

'All right, try this. Vaughan had a contact in West Beirut whom he was going to get to announce my elimination. I'm not going to forget that in a hurry. He also had Syrian ammunition for his gun. That also was, in a word, memorable. And there was an interesting statement by Nickie that they had to work away from restrictive state control. When you think about it it's perfectly feasible. Even obvious. Lebanon is about the only place I can think of that's accessible, where there's no law and no state, but is developed enough that you can still set up a scientific outfit. There would be no problems getting decent technicians, for example. All they'd have to do is pay off the local warlord. They'd have everything they wanted. If they kept well away from the Israelis or the Syrians they could basically do what they wanted. I wouldn't even rule out working in those areas. After all, there are factories openly processing cannabis and heroin. One producing modified algae isn't going to cause too much trouble.'

'But with all these virtues they get insecurity thrown in.'

'True. But that's a risk that could be minimised; there are some towns and villages where things have been pretty much untouched since the start of the Civil War. There would be a subtle irony in having a base in Lebanon. What they are trying to do is prevent the world disintegrating into a larger Lebanon. What better place to start?'

Tina picked up a tea towel with a determined air. 'Well I

think you'd better keep your all-too-convincing speculations quiet. I hope you're not proposing to do anything about it?'

'Not at all. I've signed off. No, if the group is as innocuous as Nickie says it is, then I wish it well. I have my doubts, as you know, but I've promised not to do anything to threaten them and that's a deal I intend to keep. I trust you agree.'

'Well, as this Nickie pointed out, it's difficult to see what we can do about it without falling into the hands of Elweth and his bosses. No, I agree. Treat it as a closed book – especially as we have the wedding to plan for.'

'Very well; a closed book it is.'

12

The trouble with closed books is that they have a nasty tendency to open themselves when you least expect it. This particular one, however, gave every impression of being very firmly shut indeed. For the next couple of months all I did about it was occasionally to wonder what Nickie and her group were up to. Interestingly enough, I now preferred to think of it as Nickie's, rather than Vaughan's, group. Sometimes I'd wonder, as Lebanon came up in the news, where in the mountains, valleys and towns they were. But I did nothing and talked to no one about it.

Alec and Viv's plans gradually crystallised and in May the transfer of the firm was made swiftly over to Jeremy Atcliffe and – as was intended – caught Grantforth by surprise. The Hensons made plans to put their house on the market as soon as the wedding was over and were already making regular trips up to Glasgow.

After Easter the run up to exams began to dominate the department. Paradoxically this produced an easing of tension as energies were dissipated in areas other than internal scheming. In addition, Tina and I were kept busy in our spare time in redecorating my house. Although the immediate aim was to have something 'halfway decent' to live in after the wedding, another, less spoken objective, was to have something sellable if needs be.

And so spring passed into early summer and the countdown to the wedding became measured in days not weeks. The wedding day was set for the first Saturday in July and, on the Wednesday before, my brother Andy arrived from Cyprus. Having missed a couple of flights he was a day late, a fact that had given cause for concern because he was the best man. He arrived full of excuses. George Roumian, the head of St Paul's Evangelical School, had postponed preparing timetables for the coming year until the last possible moment. But despite the delay Andy now lay stretched out on my sofa, feet dangling off the end, drinking a mug of tea.

'Andy, why doesn't someone tell George that enthusiasm isn't enough?'

'You said it, brother. But we all love him. The man has such a vision too. Know what his latest dream is?'

'Look, kid, when George Roumian has a dream it's time to find your passport and plane ticket. He should have a health warning on him. I'm not sure that I want to know what his latest dream is. Begin by telling me I'm not involved in it.'

'You're not involved in it. You know he's now got ambitions to do something in Lebanon?'

'To be fair to the blessed George, I'm sympathetic. Rationality goes out of the window for a lot of people over Lebanon. Besides, he comes from there – Bourj Hammoud, the Armenian quarter of East Beirut. Still got a small part of his family there, although I don't suppose he can have more than thirty aunts and uncles left now. But I thought St Paul's was about a quarter Lebanese anyway?'

'Something like that. It's dropped a bit since your day though. It's partly financial. The Lebanese economy having disintegrated, most of the parents are finding it expensive to send the kids over. Most people would say, "Tough, let's get Jordanians." Not George; he dreams about a Lebanese branch.'

'He *is* crazy. Not in Beirut?'

'No, even he admits that's too hot. Besides, there's a more serious point; property is too expensive. So he's looking for somewhere north of Beirut.'

He shook his head in affectionate amusement and continued, 'But as you can imagine it's more than that. He thinks he can help rebuild the nation. Someone said that part of George's uniqueness is that no one taught him to be cynical.'

'I think it was me, kid. But he may have a point. Lebanese schooling is notoriously effective at teaching Ali to be a good Muslim and Pierre to be a good Maronite, but to neglect the more important matters of the law: justice, mercy and faithfulness. But that's some dream. There are times, Andy, when I worry about letting you work with that man. Anyway, who is he planning to head this up?'

'Fuad.'

I had to think for a moment.

'Fuad Attiyah?'

He nodded. I knew Fuad well from my own brief stay at St Paul's. A tall, gangly, extrovert Lebanese in his early thirties who ran the Biology department. Although instantly likeable he wasn't the obvious choice, but then George rarely dealt in the obvious. As I'd found out before.

'Fuad's a good chap, but he left Beirut in '75 to go to the States. The place has changed. I used to tell him war stories and he wouldn't believe them.'

'Well, he's keen. You know his father has gone back to pastor a church in East Beirut?'

'Now wait a minute. Yes, Philip Ringwood told me

about that. Achrafiyeh or Senn il Fil? '

'Sorry, brother, can't remember. Just names to me.'

'Never mind. I haven't met the father, I think his name is Antoine. I did hear about the background though. The whole family left in '75 right at the start of the Civil War and Fuad's mum died in the States in '81 or '82. I remember him hearing about it. That was the father's last tie to the States, so eventually he left to go back. An elderly fellow, I think. The story sticks in my mind because Philip said everyone was praying that he'd be the first of many going back. The flow has been pretty much all outward since the start of the Civil War.'

'Sounds like what I heard, brother. Any more tea?'

'Just this once, I'll get you some. Talking of Philip Ringwood, he's coming to stay on Friday night. I thought he'd better have the spare bedroom then, so you'll have to sleep on the sofa. So it's nice to see you're getting some practice.'

'No problem. I guess he's your age, so he probably needs a bed for his rheumatics. Actually, skip the tea. I'll go and unpack.'

A few minutes later he came down clutching a thin brown envelope.

'George asked me to give you this. It's your wedding present from him and Sevan. He said I was to guard it with my life.'

I took it from him. Needless to say, it had been used before, the old address crossed out and 'Henry and Tina' scrawled above it.

Without much thought I opened the envelope and out came a sheet of paper, a card and two Cyprus Airways plane tickets.

A minute later I was upstairs with Andy.

'Kid, did you see what he sent?'

Andy emerged from behind his open suitcase. 'He warned me what was in it. What does it say in the note?'

I read it again.

Dear Henry and Tina,
   Sorry Sevan and I can't be with you on the big day. I don't
think you'd want Krikor and Ara anyway. We wish you every
blessing. *Shnorhavor!* (Henry will tell you what that means,
Tina.)
   My travel agent was thanking me for all the business I put
her way. So I said how much we'd love to see you both and the
Lord laid it on her heart to give me two tickets. Hallelujah! But
you must use them before the end of January. So come and see
us for Christmas, yours if not ours. Our house is free for you.
   Yours in Him,
      George, Sevan, Krikor and Ara Roumian

Andy chuckled. 'He haggled with Anastasia for twenty
minutes over those tickets. Made her work out exactly how
many thousands of pounds the school spent through her
travel agency. It's very difficult to refuse George anything.'
   'Don't tell me that; I learned that last year. Still, that's
quite a present.'

Tina came round briefly in the early evening to see Andy.
She was as delighted with the tickets as I was.
   '*Shnorhavor?*'
   'Congratulations in Armenian. It's a full five per cent of
my Armenian vocabulary, so look after it.'
   'I will. The reference to Christmas is that they keep the
Eastern Christmas?'
   'Yes, January 6th.'
   Andy looked up from the sofa where he was horizontal
and reading the newspaper.
   'Hey, sister-in-law pending, do you know why George
celebrates Christmas on the sixth of January?'
   'I give up, Andy.'
   'So he can buy his presents in the January sales.'
   'Excuse me while I hit him, Tina.'
   But he fled upstairs before I could get him with more

97

than a cushion.

'Henry, my biggest qualm about Saturday is your brother's speech.'

'Mine too.'

'You think we can make Cyprus for Christmas? I don't see why not.'

'No, I don't either. You'll have to be careful with your holidays, but I'd guess we could spend two weeks with them. If we're still around in Grantforth, that is. It would make a belated extra honeymoon'.

'You know, Henry, it'd be nice to meet George and his family. Perhaps he'll offer you a job again.' She smiled mischievously at me.

'Tina, don't even joke about that!'

She left shortly afterwards to perform her part in the many and mysterious chores that have to be carried out on the female side in the days before a wedding. Andy came down again and we had a long chat which went on to nearly midnight. The conversation drifted over the relatives that were coming and whether they would speak to each other, marriage, my job, Cyprus and his teaching. Andy had made himself very much at home and was somehow managing to lie on the sofa while keeping his feet on the table.

'It's hard work keeping up to date with what's going on in biology in a backwater like Cyprus. I'll have to use your library while I'm around in town. Some of the kids do "S" level and need to know some of the current issues. Medical topics are bad.'

'Cover genetic engineering much? I suppose that's university level theory.'

'No longer the case. They need to know some of the concepts and issues at "A" level. Anyway, gene splicing is a pretty standard technique in most university departments at undergrad level. Just do it on bacteria, of course.'

'I hadn't realised it had become so widespread.'

'Thinking of going into the business?'

'No, no. It's just that some of the ethical and moral issues have been raised recently.'

'Ah, Henry's famous paranoia. No sweat, brother. It's all controlled. Rules and regulations. Don't worry. You're just getting old.'

His attitude vaguely jabbed my pride. 'I don't know about paranoia. I mean, what's to stop some renegade outfit somewhere out of the way dabbling around with, say, a bacteria?'

'Weird ideas you have. Well, it requires a certain amount of technology and knowledge. But I mean, brother, there's not a lot of market for these things, is there? I mean shady characters hardly sidle up to you in pubs and say, "Psst, want the latest in bacteria, Guv?".'

'No, that's true. But then I haven't been to a pub lately. Anyway, you're probably right.'

'I reckon it may be a problem for your kids. Not for mine.'

'Why not?'

'Because I'm not stupid enough to get married.'

I had to hit him again.

Philip Ringwood arrived on the Friday. He was fresh from Jordan where he was currently involved in an Anglican project with the Palestinians. We spent a lot of time talking about things and he showed me some of his latest photographs of Jordan which were up to his usual exacting standards and I felt it was a pity Tina wasn't around to see them. Andy was working on his speech on the kitchen table and popped in and out every so often when he got bored.

Eventually the conversation got round to Lebanon and old friends.

'A lot of people gone since your time. A few new faces. Raji and Sanaa Abdul-Malik send their best wishes. They're still clinging on up in Ain Mroueh.'

'Andy was saying about Antoine Attiyah being back in Beirut.'

'Bless him. Yes, the edge of Senn il Fil. A great encouragement. Small independent Evangelical church. Doing very well. You never met him, you said?'

'No, I worked with the son for six months at St Paul's.'

'Antoine is a very striking man. Elderly – sixty plus I should think – but made of iron. Preaches well. He's openly denounced some of the local militia for their involvement in drug pushing and other things. That takes nerve. It should have been done years ago, of course.'

What seemed like a good idea came into my mind.

'Say, Phil, what are the bad guys up to in Lebanon with the economy down the drain?'

'Most things. The pattern's changing a bit. With something like a million Lebanese abroad there are lots of international deals being made. You know in the past they used just to counterfeit dollars. Now it's thirty-five other currencies as well. The usual copying of computer software and tapes and faking watches, perfumes and clothes. That's hardly new though. North of Beirut there's some nice marine insurance fiddles being done. On one deal ships that are claimed sunk in storms off Spain suddenly surface off Jounieh, Batroun or Tripoli, with different names. The other one is where they secretly offload the cargo in Lebanon and then sink the ship on the high seas.'

'So in both cases you get the insurance payout and the cargo.'

'Just so. Of course there is all the archaeological material that is going out. Illegality, of course, isn't a meaningful word in Lebanon. I heard a fascinating story of a great eagle made out of solid gold found in the Bekaa and shipped out. Presumably Roman. What a find that would have been! I wonder who has it now. What else is new? Drugs are big. Hashish is almost the only crop in the Bekaa north of the Damascus Road now. Having said that, heroin pays better so there's a lot of that going on. The processing as well. Everything that can be imagined and some things that can't.'

He shook his thin face in a gesture which left no doubt as to how much he deplored it all.

I gently tossed out my carefully prepared question.

'I suppose it would be the ideal place to set up some little high technology cottage industry that was totally illegal. Let me think – say, some little biomedical outfit.'

He stared at the ceiling in thought for a moment. 'But of course. I think I know what you mean. Copying the expensive pharmaceutical drugs, or some of the fancy illegal drugs that need more elaborate chemistry. That's big business. Probably is being done. If there's money in it they'd do it.'

'Phil, supposing I was going to set up something like that. Say copying silicon chips, or genetic engineering. Something hi-tech that I wanted to keep secret. From everybody. In case they wanted a cut. A long-term, high investment programme. Where would I put it?'

He looked at me hard, but said nothing. Phil doesn't ask questions a lot. 'What an interesting suggestion.'

He closed his eyes briefly as though visualising a map. 'Well, you'd want to be well clear of the Israeli border because they or their proxies keep a close eye on what happens in that area. Their regular detailed photoreconnaissance covers up to the Beirut to Damascus Road, so I think that rules out the south. Anyway, it's desperately fluid. Things are a bit more fixed in the Syrian areas, except that you can never tell what Damascus is going to do. And you'd have to pay a lot. So that really eliminates eastern and northernmost Lebanon. Anyway, you'd want to be near the coast to get people in and out. And of course you'd want to be rural rather than Beirut or Tripoli. Both circuses. Actually there's only a few places for your factory. The Maronite areas – East Beirut northwards to Batroun would be the best bet. But if you were putting investment in, that might be tricky – there's tensions there, different groups jockeying. Hmm. The other problem these days is the power supply. West Beirut is the worst, but it's bad all over. Could get a generator of course, but that means oil to be shipped in, except in the few places where they have hydroelectricity. Hmm.'

He closed his eyes again and then spoke slowly.

'Actually, what you want is somewhere where the old feudal thing holds sway and you can get the patronage of one man. Frangieh's area at Zghorta would be neat, but the Syrians are too jolly pally with him. But....'

He stopped, opened his eyes and a smile lit across his bronzed face. 'Ah yes. Actually I know the ideal place. You and I have been there.'

'We have?'

'Yes, we took your Beetle up to Farayoun and the Nahr el Asal. That day. Elias Daoud's area. Nearly ruined the suspension, if I remember. That little Roman temple of Adonis.'

It came back to me suddenly.

'Yes, of course; I remember it well. We went to look at the temple in spring. That day; quintessential Lebanon I think you called it. Why do you say it would be ideal?'

'Elias keeps the valley under tight control, but he's an independent fellow. On cool terms with everybody and his own security is paramount, but the valley is near enough impregnable and he's a useful buffer zone between the Syrians and the Maronites. He has his own free port on the coast too, of course. At Ras el Bourj. The Syrians allow him that, as long as he brings everything under the Tripoli Road. Nice, quiet, stable spot hid from the eyes of the world. He also has a small hydroelectric power station in the bottom of the gorge by Farayoun. Or had. I don't know whether it's still working. Could do anything there, as long as Elias Daoud would let you, that is.'

'Hadn't thought of that. It's a pleasant spot too. Well, just a wild speculation.'

Phil gave me a funny half stare.

'I see. Well I've heard the academic world is tough these days, but if whatever you want to do can only be done up the Nahr el Asal you are in trouble.'

I thought it time to change the subject. Phil's no fool, but I didn't think I'd broken the promise to Nickie.

13

We all got to bed (or the sofa) just after midnight. Not surprisingly, I couldn't get to sleep. As I lay awake in bed that night trying to think – and not to think – about the wedding, I diverted my thoughts back to the conversation. As I ran it over in my mind it came to me with increasing conviction that Farayoun or its environs was the place, or at least one of the places, where Nickie's group was based. It wasn't a place I had thought seriously about for several years, so I put the light on and tiptoed to the bookshelves in my bedroom. I had no trouble finding the fat blue guidebook I wanted. Although out of date by almost fifteen years (and what a fifteen years!) when I'd picked it up in a bookshop in Beirut it was still a useful guide to the country. I read carefully through the entry on the Nahr el Asal and Farayoun.

17 km (11 m) north of Batroun the Beirut-Tripoli Road crosses the Asal River. The Asal River flows into the sea by the headland of Ras el Bourj where there is a small fishing village and a ruined fort of unknown date. Immediately after the bridge a road to the right leads into the rugged and isolated valley of the Nahr el Asal (the River of Honey). The Nahr el Asal is a picturesque valley with much of interest to the tourist. In general, however, it must be said that the Qahdisha-Bsherri area is not only grander but is easier to visit. The main road to Farayoun winds steeply upwards for 8 km (5 m) to Mrebbine, a pretty village of about 1,200 inhab. (mostly Maronite) at 2,230 ft. It

is a market centre. From Mrebbine a minor road descends with bends and gradients of increasing severity to the small hydro-electric plant on the Asal River below Farayoun. The main road continues for another 24 km (15 m) through mulberry and apple orchards to Farayoun. *Farayoun* (Hotel Splendide 25 rooms) a picturesque town of roughly 5,000 inhab., mostly Maronite. Lying at 4,529 ft and overlooking the Nahr el Asal at a perpendicular angle, Farayoun has several churches and a monastery. One of the churches, the Church of the Saviour, is possibly very ancient. To the east of the town near some grot-toes lies a small Roman temple, probably dedicated to Adonis. The monastery (Deir Musa) is perched on a rock ledge another 300 ft above the town and has spectacular views. It is very old and probably goes back to Byzantine times. Renan visited it and noted that its 'charming atmosphere was very conducive for contemplation'. Nearby is the Hotel Barakat (20 rooms). A little road leads beyond the monastery and the hotel past a small group of cedars. These are some way between those of Bsherri and Baruk in numbers and size. In summer the road continues some 56 km (35 m) to Baalbek, crossing the watershed at around 8,100 ft.

It was the sort of description that seems to be the topog-raphic equivalent of an obituary and which if you've been to the place concerned you find profoundly inadequate and even vaguely depressing. I put the book back, switched the light off and got into bed, feeling ready to go to sleep. But as my head sank into the pillow I realised that from now on I wouldn't be able to leap around heedlessly putting the bedroom light on in the middle of the night. And that started me thinking about the wedding and all the rest of it. So in an effort to still my mind and to exorcise the guidebook I thought over the trip Phil and I had made to Farayoun.

It had been early spring. The Nahr el Asal had been almost in flood and dark brown with mud as we'd crossed it on the Tripoli Road and reached the first checkpoint. It had been Elias Daoud's militia, identifiable by their posters and their badge, a cross surmounted with a triangle like a north arrow that was their particular tribal version of a stylised cedar. Then we'd started to climb on the narrow bruised road through five miles of almost continuous bends. The last part was past terraced orchards as we'd climbed high along the north side of the gash of the valley with frequent hamlets of stone-built, red-tiled buildings. And if you dared to take your eyes off the road for a moment you could see the blue of the Mediterranean below with the dark smear as the topsoil flowed out into the sea from the river mouth. When you looked again the other way the high ridge of Mount Lebanon, the snow dazzling white in the sun, loomed ahead of you, appearing almost cut out against the sky.

Finally, the road flattened out along a narrow plateau perched between a higher scarp and the gorge. Here there was the first decent sized village, Mrebbine, with its potholed streets, and we'd stopped to let the engine cool down and had coffee in an empty restaurant with a faded Lebanese flag and a bad poster of Elias Daoud on the wall. And the bored lads in the militia had come in and asked us to play table football. It wasn't an offer sane men refuse, although they were all pleasantness and kept the safety catches on. We also lost without having to pretend to.

Then we'd motored on, climbing now more slowly between small farms, mixed deciduous and pine woods and fields with half-melted snow drifts at their edges. On upwards we'd driven till we'd rounded a bend and there was Farayoun, perched like a seabird on a cliff, breathtakingly on the edge of the gorge. Without a word we'd stopped for photographs. And as we got out the air was clear and sharp and sweet and tasted as it must have done to Adam. The sky was a deep perfect blue and you could hear the flowing water of the melting snow and we had sat and stared.

To the south of Farayoun a thin white ribbon of water plunged over the lip of rock and tumbled down sheer to the gorge bottom, hundreds of feet below. In the town itself the eye was caught by the elegant old red-roofed grand houses with their gardens and withered vines, and skipped over the creeping virus of new grey dead buildings made out of slabs of concrete. And rising above them were the spires, towers and domes of the half dozen or so churches. But behind them, as if to have the last word, rose further gaunt tiers of cliffs, broken screes and snow-covered hillsides, that swung round the town in almost a semicircle and then passed eastwards into the flanks of the great crestal range of Qornet Es Sauda. The effect was almost that of the rock forming a pair of hands around the town as if in protection.

From the edge of the buildings a narrow road ran up across the first of the higher cliffs into a patchy woodland. Here three buildings could be identified. The most easterly, sited precariously on a rock promontory and seeming to merge into the cliff, was clearly the monastery. A small square tower seemed to rise in front of it like the prow of a ship. A lesser building to its left was a large balconied old house which seemed to teeter on the cliff. Further still to the West and somewhat behind these buildings, as though standing at a discreet distance, stood a low undistinguished building that we had decided was the Hotel Barakat. The road continued south-eastwards beyond the woods over progressively higher rock benches towards the retreating snow and still upwards until the eye could faintly trace it crossing the skyline. Just before the road started its ascent up these final cliffs it was just possible to see, not far above the monastery, in the very shadow of the hill, a smudge of dark green. There the Cedars of Farayoun formed the last local remnant of the once great and awesome cedar forests.

An old man had come over to us, his face dark and wizened and his Arabic accented and gutteral close to the point of incoherence. He jerkily pointed out the sights with his stick: the waterfall, the town, the monastery, the home of the Daouds and the road over the mountains.

'That is the road to the Bekaa, Baalbek. And the Syrians. But here we are safe. Thanks to the Saints.'

Much to my relief we'd found the temple, half-hidden by trees and almost underneath the monastery, just east of the town and hadn't had to take the Beetle up the mountain track. By the colossal standards of Baalbek the temple of Adonis was as a garden shed to a mansion, and little more than a plinth of massive oblong blocks of limestone, the edges still sharp after twenty centuries, survived. But it had charm and oozed history and, where the snow had melted, the cyclamens grew.

So we'd driven slowly and happily back to Beirut in the spring sunshine, minds echoing with the beauty and glory of all we'd seen. Then on the outskirts of East Beirut, we found they'd shelled Jall ed Dib and the road was covered with glass, smoking metal and blood.

Quintessential Lebanon.

As I ran it over in my mind it was curious to think that quite possibly somewhere in that lonely valley of the Asal River lay a house where people were sitting around trying to make the future of the world secure.

But then a more mundane thought occurred to me. As Phil and I had talked the kitchen door had been open and Andy – who lived so close to Lebanon – could have heard every word. Then I thought how unlikely it was that he would have made anything of the conversation and that, anyway, he would have been far too busy working on the speech. And on that topic I turned back to thinking about the wedding and Tina, and eventually fell asleep.

14

And the next day was the wedding.

The church was full of friends and relatives and familiar and half-forgotten faces and despite apparently malevolent ushering an almost millennial peace seemed to break out. Abie Gvirtzman was seen smiling and talking to Ahmed Husseini, formerly of Nablus; Darren and Cynth, the unmarrieds with the matching green hair dye from next door turned up and sat next to Ann, the pastor's wife who has doubts over the morality of moisturising cream; Stan, the research demonstrator who sells *Socialist Worker* was affable to Freda Lewis who has two sons in the army and one in South Africa; Murray Lennox turned up with his wife and was pleasant to all, and Stanwick was heard to speak to Stanwick. As Alec said to me drily, one almost expected the lion and the lamb to be lying down together round the corner.

And Dave, the new pastor, took the wedding service and seemed to turn it inside out and upside down, so that all that was trite and traditional became alive and new and fresh and even awesome. And all the hymns and prayers seemed newly minted and had point and purpose and, in what seemed a brief address, Dave blended solemnity and humour in a rare mixture and was rewarded by the sort of intense attention that normally only newsflashes get. And Alec looked venerable and wise and was (I'm told) cheered by his ex-staff when he left the church, and Viv looked overwhelmed throughout it all and shed lots of tears and completely forgot to be concerned about everybody else, which – just for once – didn't hurt her. And Debbie was bridesmaid and looked so pretty that Andy nearly forgot where he'd put the ring and whose wedding it was. And Tina looked beautiful and happy and everything a bride should look and more, and the word 'regal' came to mind and stuck there. And no one garbled their words and the deed was done in the sight of God and Man.

The only thing that was even briefly sad was that I thought of Mum and Dad and how they'd messed it all up and said to myself that by the grace of God I'd try to do better.

And the reception at the Hensons' went perfectly and had the sort of carefree spontaneity that only comes from months of precision planning. Here the numbers were fewer, but the atmosphere was more relaxed and less solemn, and everyone forgot they were in suits and jackets and their best dresses and hats and had fun. All the presents were marvellous, appropriate and overwhelming, and there were only two cheeseboards. And eventually we spilled out onto the lawn and ate and drank in the warm sunshine in high good humour and everyone seemed genuinely delighted to see everyone else and probably was.

There were messages of goodwill from many places including Antananarivo, Beirut, Damascus, Los Angeles and (to loud cheers from some) Glasgow. And Alec gave a little speech of mellow wisdom and wry humour, and Andy spoke clearly and wittily and most of the time in sentences, and everybody got all the jokes and he seemed no longer to be simply a kid brother, and I didn't have to hit him at all.

And oh, it was all laughter and tears and there was much joy and it seemed then, and seems now as I think of it, as if for those few sunlight hours the curse on the world had been lifted.

And at length we changed, and with kisses and hugs and handshakes slipped off in Tina's car for two weeks in Scotland. And, as we had planned long before, evening found us in Durham where, as sunset retreated into twilight, we looked out from our hotel window at the silhouettes of the cathedral and castle, defiant and proud on their river-surrounded rock.

And then, at length, we drew the curtains and I turned to Tina.

'Happy, my Queen?'

'Indeed so, my King. Shall we go to bed please; at last?'

'I thought I was supposed to ask that?'

'Ah, you've forgotten that I promised to surprise you.'

And as night fell everything was good and right and complete.

15

The next few months saw the beginning and end of many things. We started married life together by trying to knock the house out of its bachelor semi-squalor into something more like a family home. On the whole we succeeded. In October Murray called me in and told me that this year would be my last at Grantforth and that unfortunately he saw no likelihood of extending the contract beyond its present expiry date in twelve months' time. Although he did say he was sorry, and pointed out it was a long time away, he held out little hope beyond the fact that a final decision wouldn't be made until February. Everyone was sympathetic in the department, but you could feel the relief because they all knew that they were now more secure; the sacrificial animal had been chosen. In a curious way too there was a certain relief in the Stanwick household; at least we now knew where we stood. Besides, in some ways I was glad. Murray's idea of what a Geography department should be was a long way from mine. From then on the decorating was very definitely with a view to sell.

Then Alec and Viv sold up and bought a house in Glasgow. I went over to the old house on the day Alec left, Viv being already up in Glasgow and Tina being busy at work. The removal men had gone and Alec was walking round the echoing house checking to make sure that everything had been left that should have been, and nothing taken that shouldn't have been, and that it was all tidy for the new owners. I followed him at a slight distance, not wishing to disturb his last moments in his old home. Eventually he went into what had been the best room, sat on the window sill and looked around the bare boards and bookshelves, passing the door key from one hand to the other. I stood nearby, wondering if I trampled on too many memories and looked away out of the window where every so often the wind would pick up a handful of brown leaves and blow them across the lawn.

Eventually I couldn't help saying something. 'I'll miss it too, for what it's worth.'

Alec nodded gently and gave a smile tinged with nostalgia. 'Aye, I remember the evening you came here first. You've grown a lot since then.'

'Thanks. Well you helped a lot, all of you. I shall miss your advice very much.'

He looked thoughtful for a moment. 'Nice of you to say so, but in fact I don't think I've given you any lately. You can both well manage without me to prod you. In fact moving away is no bad thing; it removes the temptation for you both to be lazy. In fact, isn't that near the heart of marriage? "For this reason a man will leave his father and mother and be united to his wife...." You have your own family now. Besides, you'll have responsibility for the next generation soon enough.'

There was nothing to say. After a few moments Alec stood up. 'Well, I'll be off. It's a long road.'

He looked around again. 'It's been a good house. A quarter of a century. The only house Tina will remember. I wish the new owners as much joy as we have had. I won't come

111

back. And if they grub up the roses I'll be grateful if you don't tell me.'

I suddenly felt rather nostalgic and blurted out a question. 'Are you sorry?'

'Sorry?' He gave me a look of affection. 'Of course I am. I *am* human, Henry. But you can never take anything with you. And houses are the biggest snare in the world.' He tapped the wall. 'This apparent solidity; you think it's security. And it's not.'

'But don't you feel insecure going up to Glasgow, leaving so much behind?'

'Aye, I get pangs of it. But you know, Henry, I'm helped by thinking of the Lord's covenant with us. On our side we have to repent, believe and obey, but on his side he promises never to fail or forsake us, and to see us eventually safely home. The one side goes with the other. Only he keeps his side a good deal better than we keep ours. And that's the cure for insecurity. That's my view of it all.' He paused briefly. 'But it's times like this you have to make an effort to remind yourself that it's so.'

Then, ushering me before him, he left the room, walked down the hall and out of the front door. He locked the door with a final, deliberate action and handed me the key.

'Right, drop it off at the agent's straightaway, won't you? Good lad. I'll ring you both tonight. Thanks. Give my love to Tina.'

Then, without turning to look back, he walked down to the car and drove away.

Autumn slipped gradually into winter. We decided to leave worrying about job hunting until after the February decision. Near Christmas, a day or so before we were due to leave for Cyprus, Abie Gvirtzman came to see us one cold blustery evening. He'd been away a lot during the term and I'd seen little of him. What I had seen had given cause for concern. Tonight the apparently palpable aura of gloom seemed to have gone. The three of us sat down over coffee round the gas fire.

'You look better than I've seen you, Abie; at least since the wedding.'

'Thank you. I thought I'd better tell you about it. I've had a very difficult couple of months.'

There was silence and he swallowed some coffee.

'Ach, where to begin? Since my youth I have been a modern man, if you follow. Science was the basis of the only truth there was. The religion of my ancestors had been tried in the fire and unlike Shadrach, Meshach and Abednego no fourth stood with them and they perished. But I studied the creeds and the writings and I made my contribution to the study of the religious beliefs of my ancestors.'

He paused again, but we said nothing. The burning intensity in his voice warned against interruption.

'But increasingly as I came to think about things I asked myself whether it was worth it. For what did I study? And as I examined everything I could find no purpose for it. We don't learn from the present, let alone from the past. So I searched for something that I could trust, for something – anything – that could supply a meaning to it all. And one by one I sought for rocks. I put my foot on them and they crumbled away. As I looked, even morality became meaningless because there was no standard for judgement. If my philosophy was right then I had no basis for condemning even Hitler. If he too acted simply according to his passions and desires, how could I judge him if there was no final truth?'

He seemed to balk at this thought and stared at the fire for a moment. 'Well finally even my rationality became suspect; the very brain that I was using to judge truth was an instrument that was itself the product of blind chance. And love was just instinct and chemistry. And in the light of time, everything was nothing. Art, the greatest music, civilisation, even the history of the world itself, was just noise and the briefest and most temporary and insignificant of disturbances in the cosmos.'

113

His tones were those of dreadful awe. 'So everything, just everything failed and I found myself suspended in a void of darkness. It hit me most at the Jerusalem conference. I hired a car and drove into the Negev with a bottle of aspirin and turned off the road into a place I would not be found.'

Abie talked distractedly, almost as if to himself. I turned momentarily to catch a glimpse of Tina's face, pale and distraught.

'Then night came as I stood by the car just wondering whether I had the courage to do it. Then I looked up and saw all the stars in their thousands as Abraham must have seen them. And I just realised how stupid we were and I said out loud, "My God, we know nothing." You see I realised that here we were as insignificant beings sitting on one grain of sand on an endless beach, passing judgement on the meaning of the universe. And it all seemed folly. I realised exactly how weak was the basis upon which my scepticism stood.'

He was silent for a moment.

'It also came to me that there was much in my life – art, love, humour, friendship and those precognitions of events that I had – that my worldview had never been able to explain or accept. So I suppose I had a crisis of belief, or maybe unbelief. And it occurred to me possible that love and justice and truth and meaning did really exist and that the folly lay in the denying of them. So I threw away the aspirin bottle and drove back to Jerusalem. And before I went to bed I said something that was probably the first prayer I'd ever said since I was six.'

Silence fell. Eventually it was Tina who broke it. 'Well, we have been praying for you.'

Abie nodded slowly, as if in acknowledgement of something. 'Yes, I know that. Thank you.'

He picked up his cup and downed the last of his coffee. He put it down on the side table, carefully and even thoughtfully.

'That was four weeks ago and I'm still evaluating everything. I'm not sure where I stand now, Jew or Christian. But not atheist and no longer agnostic, and certainly not sceptic

114

any more. I'm working my way through the Bible now and I may well get into the New Testament.'

We talked with Abie a lot more that night and he had changed. For the first time there was something that you could identify as hope in his make-up. As Tina said later, it was a start. Eventually, with the hour approaching midnight, he said his farewell. I reminded him we were going to be away for the next two weeks.

'So, Abie, no gloomy prophecies about our trip, unlike Madagascar?'

'No, and it's curious. Since I have turned around in my thinking, that sort of thing has gone. The future for me and for you now is just blank, just a closed book. It is almost as though it was a gift, or a sign, that has now served its purpose. I trust you will have a good holiday.'

But I wasn't going to let him get away as easily as that. 'So you no longer attach any importance to the lurid dreams you had at the start of the year about us?'

He looked vaguely startled, then puzzled. 'Those? No, that is odd. At the time I felt I should warn you, but it seems to have been a good year for you. I think I would forget about it. Probably those dreams have passed their expiry date. Maybe it was about a path you avoided.'

Later, after he had gone, I thought about Nickie and her offer and wondered whether Abie's warning would have been fulfilled if I had taken it up. If so, then I was very glad that that was all over with and that no more had been heard from either her or Elweth. In fact the subject was now barely even discussed in the Stanwick household. Almost the only exception had been that once when I'd gone through a photo album and come across some prints from that day in Farayoun. I'd mentioned to Tina that I felt that was where the base was and given my reasons. And that had been that.

Two days after Abie's visit, on December 23rd, we arrived in Cyprus to catch the tail end of a sunny winter's afternoon. To my surprise Andy wasn't at the airport. George was there instead, but surprise darkened into concern when I saw the worried look on his face and the droop on his shoulders. He looked a lot older than he had when I'd last seen him, only three years ago. Some of the change could have been predicted, the slight accretion of fat on his once angular frame and the thinning of the fine brown hair, but the posture and expression were disturbing. The greeting, however, was as warm as ever with kisses on both cheeks for all and the grip of the large hands still strong. If you hadn't known his normally dynamic and outgoing personality you mightn't have noticed anything was wrong. But I had known it and I did notice. I looked him in the eye.

'What's up, George?'

He said nothing for a moment, until he had drawn us out of the mêlée with his hand. Then he turned and spoke in a low voice, full of concern.

'It's Fuad Attiyah; he's missing in Lebanon.'

The cosy happy world I now lived in seemed to shake a little.

'Where, George? You didn't send him south of Beirut, did you?'

He looked at me, as though puzzling over the intensity of my question.

'No, that's what puzzles us. It was north. We think he may be being held by Elias Daoud in Farayoun.'

The shaking of my world suddenly became a complete disintegration and the abyss opened before me.

16

We sat in the back of George's battered old Mercedes and as he drove out of the airport he filled us in with all the details. They didn't help my state of mind. Although

Tina didn't entirely understand why I was so worried she seemed to catch my unease and sat quietly, holding my hand tightly.

'Fuad was checking up on contacts for the new school I was thinking of starting in Lebanon. You know about my dream?'

He turned right round to look at us as he spoke and the Mercedes began to drift obliquely to the flow of traffic. Tina held my hand tighter. George turned round leisurely and corrected the course.

'Vaguely. Andy told me. Anyway, where is he?'

'Ah. He thinks he was responsible – something he said to Fuad. We heard yesterday morning. He hasn't said much since, but he wants to see you about it. And there has been something else, so I confined him to his room.'

It got worse and worse – there could be no doubt that in some way I, through Andy, had sown the seeds of the disaster. I felt myself sinking into a pit of silent misery. Tina spoke, I think as much to break the silence as for any other reason. 'You were saying about your school plans, George.'

'Yes, thank you, Tina. I was looking for somewhere north of Beirut. Somewhere where I could have independence and relative security. The idea would be for the students to board during the week. That was the idea....' He shook his head and I noticed a faint bald patch. He continued, 'So Fuad had been working northwards and was about to return to Jounieh.'

I broke in. 'Hang on, George. You didn't send him alone, did you?'

It crossed my mind as I said it that I was probably trying to pass the blame onto him. Blame that was almost certainly mine, although how it had all happened I couldn't be sure.

'Oh, Henry, I may have wild ideas sometimes, but I try not to risk lives!' It was said with jovial good humour, but there was a hint of terseness underneath. 'No, I sent him with Ramzi Najjar, a Lebanese brother. All I know is from

117

phone conversations, and the links are not good now. They went to Batroun. We had discussed Farayoun and that was an option, but the stories about Elias Daoud are not good. You know much of him?'

George turned round again and we nearly hit a motor-cyclist. The joke used to be that George had two guardian angels when he drove: one to protect him and the other to protect everybody else. I forced myself to speak as conversationally as I could.

'Not a lot; he was never a big player. The little I know is coming back rapidly. So what happened?'

'You know the situation along the coast road, I think. North of Batroun there is the last Lebanese Forces, Phalangist, Maronite militia – call them what you want, checkpoint. Then a few hundred yards away is the river. What's the name?'

'The Asal, Nahr el Asal.'

'Right; it's years since I have been there. The road between Farayoun and the coast runs under the Tripoli road by the river at Ras el Bourj, and you drive off the main road and go onto it. But if you don't turn off then, within a few hundred yards you're into the big Syrian checkpoint. Well Ramzi doesn't like being anywhere near the Syrians, he was stuck in Zahle for the couple of months when they used it for artillery practice. So when Fuad said he wanted to go to Ras el Bourj and at least have a look round, Ramzi said he'd prefer to sit safely in Batroun and wait.'

'Understandable. And Fuad didn't come back?'

'No trace of him since then. Ramzi started enquiries going and the Lebanese Forces – I still think of them as the Kataeb, but I'm told it's incorrect – say they are fairly certain he passed out of their checkpoint. Look, you can't miss him. His Arabic is a little rusty and he has an American residency permit in his passport. Next day Ramzi drove around down to Ras el Bourj and there was no obvious sign of him, but he didn't ask any questions for fear he'd join Fuad. He said it was full of Daoud's militia and pretty unfriendly.

118

There was no car in the port either. So we don't even know whether he is held by Elias or not. It could be he missed the turning and ran into the Syrians, but they have no reason to hold him.'

Tina spoke again. 'No ransom demands?'

'No. So we aren't even sure whether he is being held hostage. One of the many problems is that the economy of Farayoun is apparently largely drug smuggling – hashish, maybe heroin. They are a bad lot and ransom money doesn't mean too much to them. We just pray and prefer not to think about the other possibilities. He's probably worth something though, so we like to think there will be a demand one day....'

I interrupted. 'So what's being done?'

George turned round again. 'Lots, Henry, lots. Ramzi is trying to chase up some contacts with Elias Daoud, but it is very difficult. Antoine, the father, is doing his bit. We are trying to keep it low key as far as we can. I have contacts here in the US Embassy and they say to keep it quiet and keep them informed, but that there is probably nothing they can do. Their view is that he shouldn't have been there anyway. I'm planning to go over on the evening of the twenty-fifth to Jounieh if there is no news. Time is important, but we need to have some leads first. But it would be easier if Elias Daoud kept on better terms with his neighbours. He sometimes seems to think he's running Albania.'

Silence fell in the car. Then suddenly George turned round again, nearly sending the car off the road. For the first time he spoke with something like his old enthusiasm and sparkle.

'Oh, Tina, I am *so* sorry! You can't believe me when I say how sorry I am. Look at me! Your first visit to Cyprus, your first visit to my family, to our school and we have this crisis! Besides, this thing is not your problem and I just hope that you and Henry can forget about it.'

I felt like saying that there wasn't much chance of that, but I kept silent. Tina looked at me, sensed trouble and bit her lip in concern. Eventually she seemed to feel the need to try to change the subject.

'Do you like Cyprus, George?'

'Very much so, Tina. We've been here for over ten years now. We find it home. But I still struggle with Greek.'

Trying to forget my dismay I rejoined the conversation. 'George knows Armenian, English, French and Arabic. His difficulties with Greek must be put into perspective.'

'It's a fourth alphabet. And your husband has told you about us Armenians?'

'Of course. He made me read up on the subject. Your culture and the tragedy.'

' "Those whom the Lord loves he disciplines." It applies to our people, we think. But maybe we brought it on ourselves by our pride, I do not know. Anyway, we claim to have had the first genocide of the twentieth century. My family fled from Turkey in 1915 to Aleppo, in Syria. Then to Anjar in the Bekaa and then to Beirut. Then the new troubles and we are here. For how long? The Lord knows. "Here we have no lasting city." '

Eventually we arrived at the school. Old Costas opened the gates for us and let us in and we parked round the back. Four years hadn't improved the school's overindulgence in concrete. For a man who believed that indeed 'here we have no lasting city' George was uncommonly fond of solid buildings. However, it was clean and tidy and the palm trees had grown up. Sevan, still short, thin, dark and pretty came out to meet us from the Roumians' apartment and greeted us with hugs and kisses.

'Welcome, both of you. Please excuse me. I am feeding Ara and Krikor. Come in please.'

We followed her in to the main room to meet the two boys, both changed beyond recognition, Krikor now a big, gap-toothed seven-year-old and Ara a thinner-framed five-year-old. Krikor got up and came over to greet us while Ara remained preoccupied with his food. Judging from the debris of plastic on the floor they were neither short of toys nor destructive potential. True Lebanese I thought. Sevan motioned to the table.

'You must be hungry. I will lay the table now if you wish?'

I looked at George who had just come in with a suitcase. 'George, if it's all right with you and Sevan, I'd like to have a talk with Andy.' I caught a look on Tina's face. 'Actually, we'd both like to.'

'Go ahead. It can keep. Anyway, Krikor and Ara should clean up their mess before we eat. I'll put your bags in the guest room.'

As we walked over to the staff accommodation Tina turned to me.

'You seem particularly struck by this. What's the problem? I know you were a friend of Fuad's, but you seem to be taking this as though you sent him.'

'I'm afraid, terribly afraid, that I may partly be responsible for this. Anyway, Andy will perhaps explain.'

Andy was sitting on his bed looking morose. 'Hi, brother, welcome back to the Middle East. Hi, Tina.'

He got up and gave her a kiss, shook my hand limply and flopped down on the bed again.

Tina and I took the only chairs in the room. I spoke first. 'So we lost Fuad.'

'My fault, brother.'

'I think I share it, Andy.'

He shook his head.

'I wondered why you had that bee in your bonnet about genetic engineering and then when I heard you talk to Phil about Farayoun I put two and two together. Then Fuad mentioned he might be going up that way and that he'd heard it was pretty. And like a fool I said that you suspected there was something brewing up there. Probably literally. Well Fuad got all excited about that—you know what he was like.'

I put my head in my hands for a moment. 'I wish you'd

talked to me about your deductions. I'd have warned you in no uncertain terms. But Fuad was hardly stupid enough to walk into the port and ask questions, or was he?'

'Oh, brother, he was. You see he had this great idea. Absolutely brilliant. He reckoned that the reason why the whole mess kept going on in Lebanon was that the superpowers don't care enough. Sorting it out is too much trouble. But if it could be shown that what was going on was a threat to them... Well, then they'd act.'

It was just awful. I looked at Tina. 'Two Stanwicks who can't keep their mouths shut and a crusading Fuad lights the fuse. What a combination. Look what you married into!'

Tina looked at me with concern. 'It may not have been that, Henry. Perhaps he got lost, missed his turning and got involved with the Syrians or whoever it was.'

Andy shook his head emphatically. 'Sorry, sister-in-law, it won't work. You see there is something else. George told me about it. Yesterday someone called the school claiming to be from Immigration. Spoke in good Greek apparently, according to the secretary. They had a query about me; could she supply information? Well this is Cyprus and she didn't worry about it. So she gave all the standard details such as name, date of birth and asked if that was enough. Then the caller asked for name and address of next-of-kin and then they rang off. When George found out he was furious and phoned around Immigration trying to find who'd made the call. No one had. So that's largely why I'm confined indoors.'

It was remarkable. Every time I felt I had reached the ultimate bottom, everything gave way and I dropped down even further.

'Just marvellous; marvellous! Fuad is now firmly linked to Henry Stanwick of Grantforth.'

Tina got up, came over and put her hand on my shoulder. She said nothing. After a moment or two I realised that I'd probably done all I could with Andy.

'Look, Andy, stay here and don't even stick your head

out of the window. Try not to worry about it. I take the blame. See you later.'

We walked out of the building and along the path. Night had fallen and it was starting to get chilly. I stopped Tina when we were well clear of the buildings.

'This is terrible, Tina. Even by my standards. I honestly thought it was all over. Your dad called me a walking lightning conductor. You see what it could look like from the group's point of view?'

'It looks like you have declared war on them.' She spoke quietly.

I felt terribly tired and close to despair. 'It may be exactly what I will have to do.'

17

George was sitting by the phone when we came in.
'I was just about to call round some more friends for ideas. But let us eat first.'

So the four of us sat down at the table and George gave thanks in Armenian with an apparent clause about Fuad, and we set to. I realised how hungry I was, although my mind was on other things and the eating soon became mechanical. Ara and Krikor played noisily on the floor nearby and sometimes crawled under the table and interrupted everything. George and Sevan said nothing, but then in the Middle East you generally don't. Relegating them to their bedroom would have been virtually equivalent to child abuse. One view of the origins of the Lebanese Civil War which does not appear in the textbooks says that the country would be alive and well today if its leaders had actually been disciplined as children. While a little simplistic it deserves more consideration than it has been hitherto given. At the end of the meal I thanked Sevan, asked to be excused, and made my way to the guest room.

There I threw myself on the bed and prayed, hard and seriously. As I did, a conversation with Laurent came into my mind from over a year ago; a conversation where I had said that I felt I wouldn't pursue Vaughan's group, because I didn't feel called to, and I didn't have a mandate for it. And Laurent had pressed me and I'd said that I would if I had to. How had it gone? I tried to remember. Suddenly and effortlessly, as though they had been ready waiting, the words slipped quietly into my mind: 'I've not been called up for that. Not yet.'

And after I remembered that, there didn't seem much more to pray about because the road was clear. All too clear. The next sixty miles of it especially so.

I got up and went downstairs and called Tina away. I looked at George. 'No news?' He gave that little cluck with the sharp vertical bobbing of the head which the Lebanese use for an emphatic negative.

Once in our room Tina sat down on the bed, looking tired and drawn.

'So you see what I've done?'

'I see, but I don't hold you entirely responsible.'

'But you see what I've got to do?'

She paled a little, as well she might. 'Can't anybody else do it? It's not your country.'

It lacked conviction – I don't think she believed it.

'There are lots of answers to that. One of them is that I should try and do it precisely because I do not live there. If I do make enemies then at least I can walk out of the country. No, I shall go to Lebanon and see Elias Daoud in person, and I feel scared sick at the thought. I'll go as soon as I can fix it.'

Tina bit her lip and looked as if she was going to cry. But she didn't say anything. Then, just as she was going to speak, there was a knock at the door and the sound of George's voice. It had an urgent tone.

124

'Henry?'

It crossed my mind briefly that he'd heard that Fuad had been released, but when I opened the door his face told me otherwise. He smiled weakly at Tina and drew me away from the door which he closed. He looked unhappier than ever.

'Henry, what's going on? Costas, the man at the gate, says that a man was watching us when I drove in and the same man came back and tried to start talking with him. He wanted to know who the foreigners were who arrived today.'

Once more my spirits descended abruptly to a new low. 'Costas told him to clear off, I trust?'

'He doesn't think like you, or even me. He told him exactly who you were. Even your name. Then he realised that there was something suspicious and came to see me.'

'Any ideas on the man? Cypriot or not?'

'He thinks maybe Lebanese or Palestinian. He spoke Greek badly.'

George looked at me, the gentleness in his eyes for once seemingly dimmed. Frankly, if I'd been in his shoes I'd have been furious.

'You heard of this phone call about Andy? Now this. Henry, what is going on?'

So after a moment's thought I told him that I thought there was some sort of conspiracy centred on Farayoun and that it was big and that they knew my name, but that Fuad and Andy and the school were only involved by accident.

And I realised that if I'd had any doubts about where I was going to go, they had now gone. The trail had to be led away from here, from George and Sevan and the school.

George spoke. 'Well at least we probably know where Fuad is and why he is there. So that may be some help. But....'

'Look, George,' I said. 'I need to talk to Tina and then I'll come down and tell you what I'm going to do. In the meantime, could you put sheets on a couple of beds in the staff

125

block – without making too much fuss about it? I think we want to move out of the guest room tonight. Could you maybe get the police to cruise by once in a while as well?'

He looked at me for a moment as if wondering why he'd gone to the trouble of getting me the plane tickets.

'I will do it.'

Then I thought of something else. 'Don't tell anyone that we know where Fuad is. I don't want anyone else to be drawn in. I'll explain later.'

I went back in to Tina who looked stern and resolved. Without a word I switched the light off then moved along the wall to the window where I pulled the blinds down and closed the curtains. Then I went and switched the light back on. I turned to Tina.

'Further seasonal tidings of comfort and joy, I'm afraid. Our arrival is known, as is our identity, to men who do not appear full of goodwill and who probably do not bear gifts. At least not the sort you accept willingly.'

I sat down in the chair and looked at my wife. 'Frankly, Tina dear, I'm inclined to put you on the next plane back.'

Her head gave a sudden decisive shake. 'I can think of several reasons why you won't do that. First, all the flights are full for the next two days. Secondly, I might not be safe there, bearing in mind the events of last summer and thirdly, I'm coming to Lebanon with you. I feel I should do. Please.'

'You aren't serious?' From her face and tone of voice I felt I knew the answer to that already.

'I am. I can't be left and I can't go home, so I'd better go with you. I'll try not to get in the way.'

I stared hard at her, hoping for any sign of a bluff or a weakening of resolve. There was none. She really did mean it. There are times when I wish I'd married someone with a bit less determination, but they aren't frequent. This was, however, one of them.

I got up and walked to the door. I thought about banging my head on the wall; it would at least have expressed how I felt. In the end I opened it, and without a word walked away

126

down the corridor agonising over what to do. Of course it was foolish to think of her going and I tried to list the reasons. There was a good chance that neither of us would come back, or even worse, I would and she wouldn't. But then our deaths could be just as easily arranged here, or in Grantforth. If she was taken hostage herself I would be in a very bad negotiating position. However, they already had Fuad. She didn't speak the language or know the culture. That though was curiously counterbalanced by the fact that she would patently not be a spy. So the negative points all seemed to be balanced out. On the other side there were a number of things that came to mind in favour of her going. It would be useful to take a companion, and who better? She might be able to charm where I couldn't persuade and there were few cases of women being held hostage. Lots of them being raped and murdered of course. But she might indeed be in little more risk than being here. And she wanted to go. Curiously in the end it didn't take long to decide which was the lesser of two evils. I turned round, went back in and closed the door behind me.

'Your last chance. You seriously want to go? You've thought about all the news footage you've seen and you realise you might be – I only say might be – in the middle of that?'

She nodded, still looking pale. At least she wasn't glibly snatching at the idea of going.

'You know there's no police, no authority and no law? That if I say jump you'll have to jump?'

She still nodded. 'I'll do my best. But when you were in trouble last year I did help.'

'I'm not forgetting that. If I didn't think you might be able to handle whatever happens I wouldn't be taking you.'

I shook my head. I seemed to be out-manoeuvred on every side. 'OK, you're signed on, but there's one condition. You write a full letter to Mum and Dad saying you are going of your own freewill; the letter to be left with George. Just in case.'

127

She got up and flung her arms around me as though I'd offered her a further honeymoon instead of a potential death sentence. Eventually she said, 'Thanks, Henry. I'll write it straightaway.'

I peeled her off me.

'Leave it for now; we have to set things up with George.'

George and Sevan were sitting downstairs in a slightly quieter room. The boys had apparently just gone to bed. I didn't beat about the bush. I wanted a good night's sleep as soon as possible.

'George, this is my business not yours. I want to go to Lebanon and see if I can get Fuad out.'

George threw his arms about in a manner that made me glad he wasn't driving.

'This is crazy! Henry, you don't have to.'

'Don't argue, George Roumian. I have decided. Tina wants to come too, so both of us will go.'

I don't think Sevan could believe her ears and she said something in Armenian to George, who appeared to explain something to her. Then he turned to us.

'So you are both crazy. To take your wife – that is not right. Leave her....'

'Leave her here, George? One of these people nearly killed us last year near Grantforth.'

George thought a bit and there was some further whispering between him and Sevan in Armenian.

'Fine. Well, of course, it's not fine, but you try it. Elias Daoud is an odd man. Maybe he likes crazy people. Anyway, he will have no love for an Armenian like me, or a "priest" as he will no doubt think Antoine is. We have no better plans.'

He shrugged his shoulders and looked up to heaven as if handing over responsibility. People seem to do that a lot with me. Then he sat down and pulled his pad of paper over to him.

'What do you need?'

128

I nodded at Tina, first hurdle over.

'First, we'll go in by boat through Jounieh, so I'd prefer visas, although I'm sure we can do without. I'd like to have an entry stamp of some sort in our passports.' George nodded.

'Secondly, the boat passage to Jounieh needs to be booked – with a berth preferably. That's not just for comfort, it's also security. I'd prefer to sleep going over behind a lockable door, OK?'

A further nod and a scribble.

'Then I need a contact in Jounieh, to lend me a car. With papers. Nothing too smart or covetable.'

'Covetable? Fine. I follow you. Yes, I have friends that will do this. Fourthly?'

'Fourthly, I need to talk to Antoine Attiyah first. He may be able to help and I want to talk to him. Fifthly....' I hesitated.

'Fifthly, you want money. How much?'

'Sorry, George, 2,000 dollars and a couple of hundred dollars' worth of Lebanese notes.'

He stared at me for a moment. I thought he was working out how many envelopes he'd need to recycle to recover that, but I did him an injustice.

'Ransom payments start at ten times that now.'

Curiously I found a slight feeling of frivolity creeping in. I suppose it's my character; I can't be too serious for too long. 'Then if we are in that position I'll take him on hire purchase. Seriously, I'm not running round Lebanon with a suitcase full of money.'

'True, my accountant is going to love this as it is.'

'Well, I'll see if I can get a receipt from Elias Daoud. And I need a few smaller things. Everything written you can get me on Daoud. If it's in Arabic I'll need a translation unless it's very simple. And one more thing: a dozen photographs of Fuad – preferably more, if you have them from a different angle. Clean, sharp, preferably colour. I presume you Armenians control the photographic trade here too?'

'More or less. We are working on it. But I have done this already.'

Then Tina spoke in a quiet voice. 'Warm clothes?'

I looked at her. 'Thanks, you are earning your keep. How did you know that?'

'I saw the altitude on the map, over 4,000 feet.'

'George, that's a good point. We'll need to go to a ski shop and get something. Discreet but not camouflage.'

'OK, I'll get Sevan to take you. What else?'

'Do you know anybody at any of the airports or airbases? Say, RAF Akrotiri?'

He nodded cautiously.

'Can you get them to give you a seven day weather forecast? Say you've got friends sailing off Lebanon, which is true. I don't want to be trying to get out of Farayoun in a hurry with six foot of snow around.'

George scribbled it down. He was going to be a busy man tomorrow.

'I have many friends in the military. Maybe I can fix it for them to talk to you? They may be able to give you maps, tell you how many soldiers Daoud has, that sort of thing.'

It didn't take long to refuse that offer. 'How long has the world's mightiest military power had its citizens hostage in Lebanon? No thanks, I'll pass, George. "Put not your trust in princes" and all that.'

'Fine. Just an offer. I can get you these things, Henry. Nothing else?'

'No, that will do. Except this.' I caught his eye to try and add emphasis. 'I don't want anybody else to be involved. No one. We could go through all the church contacts and push on lots of doors, but that would involve innocent people. So when we go, I'm going to avoid all my friends and all your friends, even though they may be useful and I'd like to see them. I'd like to talk to the Abdul-Maliks, for example, but they won't know anything about Farayoun, and they have problems enough. So try not to get the search cranked up any more.'

He sighed and shrugged. 'This is your wish? Fine.'

He glanced at his wife who looked unhappy. Then he brightened.

'Henry, Tina, I thank you for what you are doing. Maybe it will not be needed. Perhaps the phone will ring.'

He looked at it as if willing it to ring. It didn't.

'But in the meantime, let us pray.'

Soon afterwards we went to bed in a spare staff room. Maybe the heating wasn't on, maybe there weren't enough blankets and maybe it was something else, but I felt cold from head to toe and lay awake for hours. And when at last I did sleep my dreams seemed overshadowed by an intangible and unfocused dread.

18

Christmas Eve, although it was hard to think of it in those terms, was busy. George woke us early to get the passports. We dressed and ate breakfast with Sevan and the children. Sevan revealed that James Erickson was coming in today and would show me the files on Lebanon. James had originally been Head of Biology before taking up the post of Vice Principal with responsibility for science on Fuad's promotion. It had been James' family problems the previous year which had precipitated my crisis over whether or not to take up the job with the school.

Immediately after breakfast we went to see Andy who was still wrapped in profound gloom. This only deepened when we told him our plans and he was as miserable as I've ever seen him. We tried to cheer him up and largely failed. After only ten minutes we gave up and made our way over to the office where James Erickson was waiting.

131

After greetings and introductions James showed me a series of box files on Lebanon in a room next to the library. He was a tall, silver-haired man in his late fifties, slow to speak but quick on the uptake, honest and warm-hearted. He looked the sort of American from whom you expect a leisurely southern drawl and when he spoke – which was only when necessary – you got one. The one anomaly was that he hated being called Jim. He gestured to the box files in the room attached to the library.

'Ah guess George started dreaming about the Lebanon school at the end of summer 1982 when things looked real good. So it kinda dates from then. I guess it's most in English. Some French. George dun't like to read Arabic much so there's little of that. It's mostly about places he's interested in, East Beirut up to Tripoli.'

'Any order to it?'

'Order? Henry, where you all been? George ain't got time for no order.'

It was good humoured, but there was more than a faint suggestion of personal suffering behind his bland comment.

'You jest starts at one end and goes through to the other.'

So I cleared a desk, pulled out pen and paper and started at one end. George had arranged for Tina to be shown round the school by James so they both departed, leaving me in solitude with my task. I reminded myself of my goal: to find out anything that might suggest an avenue of approach to Elias. I wasn't at all sure I'd find it or even what it looked like.

The bulk of the material in files was press cuttings of ephemeral interest – some of them cruelly so; predictions for the new year, the long-term plans of a politician whose life was to end bloodily only weeks later, the chances of peace. There was strikingly little about Elias Daoud, although if I remembered things correctly this reflected the general political verdict, rather than being simply George Roumian's selective filtration of events. In general the Lebanese papers were of small help, most of the comments

132

on Elias being neutral to the point of useless, but you can hardly blame journalists for being little interested in a critical analysis of anybody with his own militia. As someone from the BBC had once said to me, 'Lebanon isn't the place for investigative journalism.' I struggled with the French cuttings from *L'Orient, Le Jour*, ignored the rare Arabic or Armenian clippings, searched in vain for a report from Farayoun by a non-Lebanese source and ploughed on.

It was mid-morning before I hit on exactly what I was looking for. It was a three page interview with Elias in *Monday Morning*, the Beirut English language weekly that would bizarrely juxtapose the latest car bomb deaths with photographs of the doings of the 'beautiful people' of Beirut and Jounieh. 'Elias Daoud, Lebanon's Silent Leader, speaks' was the title and much was made of it being a rare interview. There were three photographs. The first was of a besuited Elias reclining on a sofa being earnestly interviewed by the elegant female reporter and the second was a file photograph of Farayoun. The third made me catch my breath because I knew who it portrayed well. The image was of a man in late middle age with a mane of ill-kempt white hair set over an angular face. He was sitting at a desk surrounded by piles of paper and an old manual typewriter. A wine bottle peeped naughtily out of the background. Underneath was the caption 'Professor Charles Rimmer – Elias' co-author.'

'Rimmer!' I said out loud. What was he doing in an article on Elias Daoud? I looked at the date of the article. It was only a year old. I scanned through to find the relevant passage.

Interviewer. 'You rarely leave Farayoun. How do you spend your time here?'

Elias Daoud. 'I am very busy with the administration of Farayoun and the Asal Valley. Despite the security situation we are trying to maintain programmes on roads and schools. I also have other interests. I am currently collaborating with Professor Rimmer of AUB on an anthology of Arabic, English and

French poetry about Lebanon.'

Interviewer. 'You have known Professor Rimmer a long time?'

Elias Daoud. 'Yes, certainly. I was his pupil in 1972 and '73 at the American University. I did an MA in English Literature; the subject of the thesis was "Orientalism in the poetry of W B Yeats".'

At this point either the tireless interviewer or the editor had decided they preferred blandness to esoterica and we passed onto a vague, neutered statement on the Middle East peace process.

I picked up the journal and, in a mood of some elation, went down the corridor to where the main office was. As I had expected, James and Tina were there. Tina was sitting down with a long list of names and figures and James was peering over her shoulder with what appeared to be a frown on his face. As I came in she looked up, but kept a finger clearly marking her place on the list.

'Hey, everybody, a ray of hope. Elias Daoud is a big friend of Charlie Rimmer. And Charlie Rimmer I know. I've spent an evening in a basement with Charlie Rimmer among other things. We were the only sober people.'

Tina looked up at James and then grinned mischievously at me.

'Gosh, Henry, that sounds extraordinarily exciting. To think I married you without even knowing it.'

James' mouth wrinkled a little; he found it funny too.

'So you kinda reckon this Mister Rimmer would give you a reference to our friend Daoud? A letter of introduction?' James was no fool.

'Should do. He's quite a character though. Downright odd.'

That was a statement that you could have had a lot of people agreeing to. Charlie Rimmer was English – a fact he exaggerated shamelessly – but I think the Ambassador frequently wished he wasn't. Although Rimmer had made it to the status of full Professor of English at the American University of Beirut they'd never, even in the worst days of the Civil War, let him be even acting Head of Department. Everyone agreed he was odd and even a bit wild, but his parties were widely gatecrashed and he was a not unwelcome gatecrasher at others, and gatecrashing is a serious pursuit where the men on the door can have machine guns. His fame in large measure derived from an apparently total lack of fear, which had resulted in him maintaining a high profile when everybody else was trying to lower theirs. Journalists frequently brought him into their articles about 'war-torn, mainly-Muslim West Beirut'; it was good copy and he was safer – and easier – to write about than either the unfathomable fighting or the warlords behind it. Charlie Rimmer loved it all, rarely failed even appalling students and wrote bad poetry from his flat in Ain Mreisse on the seafront. The only reason he'd been in the basement that night at the Dales' party that everything broke loose was that the shelling was so bad that there was no one upstairs to talk to. Or so he had said.

But in fact there was another side to Charlie. When you watched carefully you saw that he took only calculated risks, that he ensured any drunkenness was apparent rather than real and that he always made sure he had at least one powerful friend in every camp. He was also careful never to insult anybody of influence and never to do anything more than outrageously flatter their wives or daughters. Smarter still, if the conversation turned to matters military he would politely vanish or feign total ignorance, thereby avoiding any suspicion that he was a spy. As the joke went, Rimmer was the last man in West Beirut to think that Kalashnikov was a dissident poet. He was a survivor, but a survivor with style. Despite a few reservations, I had a good deal of admiration for Charlie Rimmer.

Tina broke in on my recollections. 'Sorry, Henry, how does your friend Charlie help you? I thought you were just going to ring Elias' doorbell?'

As I thought about her question I began to worry a little

135

that I was going to have to explain everything to her.

'Good point. Lebanese and Arab society generally has lots of virtues, but it isn't democratic and open. It's hierarchical. You can't just walk up to the big boss and say, "Can I see you?" You need an intermediary – a go between – someone who will give you an introduction, as James says. We didn't have one. We may do now.'

'OK, I see. Well that's encouraging. Where does he live?'

An awful lot of my exultation disappeared very rapidly. 'Ah, I'd forgotten that. A charming little flat in West Beirut. Maybe we can do it all over the phone. I'd prefer not to go there.'

James made a faint sucking noise. There was no doubting his opinion on the matter.

My enthusiasm somewhat dampened, I was about to return to the library when I saw Tina's finger still glued to the column of data.

'Looks serious stuff; you auditing the books?'

Tina gave James a non-committal look and turned to me. 'Sort of. Tell you about it later.'

So I went back to the room and ploughed through a few more boxes, with little to show for it. Then Tina called me for lunch. On the way over to the Roumians' apartment I asked her how her morning had gone. She paused a moment before answering.

'Very interesting; in fact a very striking operation. I need to see more.'

The way she phrased it, coupled with the cautious tone of voice, told me enough not to question her further. Midday meal was with Sevan and Ara alone – Krikor being out with friends and George still running round on business.

After lunch we went shopping and bought some warmer clothes. The assistant – who had good English – seemed to think we were off up to the Troodos Mountains, and we didn't argue with her deduction. Then it was back to the paperwork.

At about four I had finished and I scribbled down everything I knew on a piece of paper. I would have learned a lot more from the Middle East reporters who were based in the area or even from using their files, but they were the last people I wanted to talk to. Taking everything together I felt I had a fair picture of Elias Daoud, but the picture was the official portrait and I still knew little of the real man.

To my surprise Tina was still going over lists with James. A sheaf of papers, with scribblings on them in Tina's dense handwriting stood on the table next to a calculator. In fact, Tina was so engrossed in what she was doing that she put a hand up as I came in and I had to stand by quietly while she finished off a sequence of figures.

'Sorry, Henry, I didn't want to lose my train of thought. Anyway, James and I have just about finished. At least I think so?'

'Ah guess so, Tina. Many thanks; sure given me a lot to think about. Talk to you some more when you get back from your trip. Henry, I'm about ready to go now so I'll just wish you all every blessing. Y'all take care now.'

He shook hands and left.

'I like his confidence. So what have you been up to?'

Tina got up and closed the door. 'Henry, did the Armenians help run the Ottoman Empire?'

'So I've heard them claim. Why?'

'Because I now understand how it collapsed. Do you have any idea how badly run this place is?'

'I've always said organisation isn't George's strong point. You think it's bad, eh?'

Tina shook her head.

'I was intrigued to see how it was run – professional interest and all that – so for starters I asked James how many students they had. He said they had the enrolment figures for October 1st somewhere, so I said, "But we are at the end of December. What about the late arrivals and the departures?" "We are working on it," was his answer. Charming and honest but....'

'I did warn you. But that's just the numbers game thing.'

'Henry, "just the numbers game thing" is what profit and loss is about. The administration here, if I can dignify it with that term, is like that all the way through. For example, there is no breakdown of where students are from. Ask whether the numbers of Jordanians are rising or falling, it's hopeless; it's all done on guesswork. There's a student enrolment list. I say to him, "For example, how many students are Jordanian?" "We could pull out the application forms," James says. How can George plan? I looked at the schedule of fees and I noticed that it's the same fees for all "A" levels. So I asked, "How much does it cost to teach biology per student as opposed to English literature?" It had never occurred to James, and presumably George, that it could or should be done. Basically, George seems to run this school like he drives his car.'

'I see. Well he always hated paying for administration. You'd better have a word with him about it. Gently, of course.'

'Sorry; he is a nice man, but cheapness gets expensive at times. He could do so much more if he'd only plan it better. Careful computerisation would be one solution, but he'd need to get it set up properly. Anyway, I'll have a chat with him.'

George was back for the evening meal. He had done all he set out to, although it evidently hadn't been easy and he looked tired. He handed over the passports and a brown envelope full of US currency, which I signed for without too much reluctance. I had a feeling that any worry about having to do the accounts at the end of the trip was going to be relegated to a minor concern very soon.

'I've booked your berths. Seven thirty tomorrow night on the "Levant Star" out of Limassol. Israeli gunboats and Syrian artillery permitting.' I noticed that Tina blanched slightly, but George kept going regardless. 'It gets you in at dawn the following day. The weather should remain good for five days or so, then there is a front coming in. It should

138

hit Sunday, or Monday. Probably get thick snow up in Farayoun. My memory is that it gets cut off badly up there. Up to a week in recent years.'

Tina looked at him. 'Is it that bad?'

George looked solemn. 'Don't underestimate the mountains, Mrs Stanwick. They claim the Syrians had a hundred soldiers on the Mount Lebanon killed in a single storm a few years ago. Maybe.'

He shook his head and recounted his fingers again. 'Ah yes. The car is fixed up and I've talked to Antoine. He wants you to stay with him the first night. Sevan says you've got clothes. Money, photographs, papers and weather we've covered. Good.' Then he turned to me. 'So tell me what you now know about Elias Daoud.'

'OK, pen portrait coming up. He's just forty-five. Elder of two brothers; younger one is Butros and he lives in France. Father was Sheik Boulous Daoud. Maronite family, although the father married a Greek Catholic. That, and other things, rather lowered his status among the Gemayels and Chamouns and the rest. Elias was AUB educated, rather than Universite Saint Joseph – apparently the mother's influence. Degree in English; MA in English Lit. He is friendly with his thesis supervisor who is still around. And whom I know.'

'Good.' George was listening carefully.

'At the outbreak of the Civil War he backed his father. Nothing I have talks about his war record, but then it wouldn't. Father proved to be an independent sort and rapidly became isolated. The old man died in '81 of a coronary and Elias took over running the Asal Valley. Now what is interesting is what happened. Elias adopted a much more up front position than his dad for several months. There was even talk of him taking the leadership among the Maronites and of presidential ambitions.' I paused, wondering if it was worth trying to explain the Lebanese constitution to Tina, but she had jumped ahead.

'So what happened?'

'His wife, their only child and his mother were blown up driving into Beirut one day.'

Tina grimaced. 'That's terrible. Who did it?'

George shook his head. 'We all know the story. No one in Lebanon asks who did it, although most of us can guess. Why bother? There are no courts, even if anyone would give evidence. We cannot judge them, God will. Anyway, it was a thousand atrocities ago.'

I spoke again. 'Well Elias got the message. Since then he virtually never leaves the valley. The only political pronouncements he makes are bland to a very high degree. He talks about "a Lebanese solution in an Arab context" to please Damascus and the "necessity for respecting the unique character of the communities of Mount Lebanon" to please the Maronites. But he maintains certain intellectual and cultural activities and he likes poetry.'

George gave a slight sigh. 'Poetry? That's Lebanon. One leader can't write his own name. Another reads poetry in three languages. Both will happily feed you to their dogs if it pleases them. Anyway, that fits with what I know about Elias, and at least you have a mutual contact. Perhaps Antoine and your friend may give you some more information, but....' He fingered his moustache abstractedly for a moment, 'But everyone says he is tough.'

He looked at Sevan and gave a final smoothing to his moustache.

'Very well. Unless there is anything else to do I suggest we spend the next twenty-four hours doing something else rather than worrying about your trip. Given that it is the twenty-fifth of December tomorrow perhaps we should celebrate Christmas for you. Of course, if you are still around on the sixth we can celebrate it properly.'

It crossed my mind to point out that, all being well, we would be back in the UK by the sixth. But, given where we were sailing tomorrow, I didn't have the confidence to say or even think anything about where we would be in twelve days' time.

That evening I thought I'd better try to give Tina a crash course on survival in Lebanon. It wasn't easy. Where did you start?

'Now, you know there are no good guys. It's the Wild West and there's no sheriff.'

'No cavalry?'

'There've been a number of volunteers for that task. They either left in a hurry or joined in the brawling and became as bad as everybody else. Or like the UN, sat in dugouts and counted tanks going past.'

'Sounds like the sort of quagmire where you keep moving on or you sink in.'

'Right. Preferably never get into. Let's see, you should know that every Lebanese is labelled at birth according to religion; inscribed unchangeably on his identity card.'

'I think I'd gathered that. So whether he is actually an atheist or whatever it doesn't count. He is still labelled as a Maronite or Muslim?'

'Exactly so. The term Muslim and Christian says more about your background than you. It has nothing to do with conviction or belief. So people use the term "believer" to describe someone with a personal faith.'

'Not a bad idea for England. Go on while I'm still awake.'

'Where next? OK, so it's not a country, not in any real sense. As I understand it, it's a collection of families, clans and religious groups brought together in an artificial country with an artificial constitution. There has never been much of a national identity – everyone thinks of themselves as belonging to their family first, then to their religious grouping and finally to Lebanon.'

'So what's George?'

'Ask him tomorrow. He's an Armenian first, always has been. He will justify that by pointing out his unique culture, his long persecuted past and his distinctive faith. Just like a dozen other groups in Lebanon. The Armenians do have their own language – which does make them slightly different. The Maronites used to, but it's all but gone now. He's Lebanese only second, a very distant second.'

'Keep going. My brain is still functioning. Just.'

'Look, I'll save the Civil War for tomorrow. While I remember though, don't be fooled by all the Arabic. At least where we are going, in the Maronite areas, it's spoken after a fashion, but there are vast differences to, say, the Gulf. Elias Daoud will be called Sheik, but that simply means clan leader and he'll probably have the best of French tailored suits on his back. If you turned up in Jounieh with flowing white robes then they'd probably die laughing. Before they shot you. One final thing.'

'What?' She sounded half asleep.

'There are no camels. None.'

19

By all accounts the first Christmas Day of your married life is always memorable and ours certainly was that, although in fact by the standards of the following days it was serenity itself.

George and Sevan had put up decorations after we had gone to bed so that at least there was some sort of Christmas feel to it all. We had deliberately not brought most of our presents, partly because of the weight and partly because we knew that it wouldn't really be Christmas in the Roumian household. So what we had for each other were token gifts. I had a small pendant for Tina and she had a nice tie for me which, as I remarked, would be useful for job interviews. For Andy we had brought a newly published book on the birds of the Middle East which I was assured wouldn't have made it out to Cyprus yet, and that lifted the gloom off him for at least five minutes. We gave George and Sevan their presents, but they decided to keep them for what they jokingly called the 'real Christmas'. They did, however, allow Krikor and Ara to open their toys, on the fairly safe assumption that they were going to get plenty on the proper day.

George took us down to a nearby Anglican Christmas Day service and that was good, although we left smartly because we didn't want to get involved in conversations which might raise awkward questions.

Back at the house we all tried to laugh and be merry, but the atmosphere was at best beleaguered and at worse depressed. After lunch George and I sat down with Tina and gave her some tips on how to survive in the Arab world. She did her best, but I think we probably scared her. I tried to sum it all up.

'Don't smile at the men until you know them. Just remember that everybody is a persecuted minority. In terms of politics there's no good guys, there's no true and no false, no police worth the name, no legal and illegal, the posters of murderers on the walls are the political leaders. Everyone's had a rough deal. Don't say, "*Salaam aleikum*" to the Christian militia or "Happy Christmas" to the Muslim militia if we get that far.'

She winced.

'Try to look stupid and innocent at checkpoints. Be polite to men with guns. Don't give them the impression of being afraid. That just encourages them. Smile and enjoy it.'

She didn't look at all convinced. 'I can but try.'

I caught George later on my own.

'Do you think we overdid it, George?'

He stroked his moustache thoughtfully. 'Henry, she overdid it marrying you in the first place. But rejoice, it's too late for her to change her mind on that. I don't know, but it's better she is on her guard.'

Then we called Glasgow just in time to catch Alec and Viv before going to church. We kept it short deliberately and hoped that Alec would assume that the reason was purely economy. Tina spoke first and after a few sentences began to trail off and look very sorry for herself.

I took over the phone quickly to get Viv. 'Henry, is Tina all right? She's not homesick, is she?' I was able to reassure her truthfully that that wasn't a problem. Then I said it was likely that we'd be 'travelling around for a few days' and might be out of touch for a bit and had a brief word with Alec. He sounded as though he was becoming more Scots by the day.

'So ye'll all be off travelling for a few days, will ye? I trust you'll take care. The roads are supposed to be fearful nasty. Ye'll no do anything silly?'

I swallowed. 'Silly? Of course not. This is Cyprus. No, nothing that you wouldn't do yourself. I can promise that.'

As I put the phone down afterwards I thought of Alec and Viv starting up again in a less than glorious part of Glasgow, and was fairly certain that I'd made a promise I'd have little trouble keeping.

There were a few final things to do. We went through everything we had and removed things we didn't need and then we went through what was left to make sure there was nothing that could incriminate the innocent, such as address books and letters. Then Tina and I scribbled two separate notes to Viv and Alec and, having sealed them, left them with George in case of the worst.

Andy stood by the door looking miserable as we left.

'Brother, I should be going. I'm so sorry.'

'Rejoice, it's Christmas. Nothing to despair of. It'll probably be dead simple.'

Then George said a prayer and we kissed Sevan and the boys goodbye and set off in the car for Limassol port.

The 'Levant Star' was a better sort of boat than the three or so other vessels I've done the trip on in the past. It is true that in the UK she wouldn't have been allowed to do anything more than fairweather trips round the coast, but at least you didn't have to sleep in the hold. In addition, the whole procedure was a lot slicker than in the early days when the Christians still used to use the airport a lot unless it was closed by shelling. It now had very much the appearance of a routine operation. It was good too to have a small but adequate cabin where we could leave our holdalls in relative security under lock and key. The other good thing was that today the boat was almost half-empty, the twenty-fifth being Christmas for many others beside ourselves. Most of the passengers appeared to be harmless: frail little old ladies with boxes, children and their mothers and businessmen with expensive briefcases that they never let go of. So I decided to take the risk and stay up on deck as we left Limassol harbour. We stood near the bow. As we cleared the shelter of the harbour we watched the spray rise up along the sides of the boat and gradually the lights of Cyprus were lost behind us, leaving only the stars and the ship's lighting.

After a while I broke the silence. 'Well, Happy Christmas, anyway. I bet you wish you'd married a chartered accountant after all.'

Tina answered quietly, 'Not at all. It could be a lot worse. I could be back with the Roumians wondering about you. Thanks for letting me come.'

'It's my pleasure. I couldn't trust you there, could I? You wouldn't be safe. Not the way George drives.'

Tina gave a faint little laugh. I think she was feeling overawed by everything, as well she might. I thought I would try and change the subject.

'Which reminds me, did you say anything to George about the school?'

'No, I didn't have the heart. James knows some of the suggestions I've made. I'm still thinking of the best solution, so when we get back I'll tell him.' There was an awkward pause. 'If we do.'

I put my arm round her.

Gradually the deck cleared as people made their way down

to cabins and the bar, and we were left on our own. The breeze was blowing strongly now and there was something of a swell, although nothing to what it might have been, or would be when the front came in.

'You promised to tell me more about the War.'

'Yes, I did. I'm still thinking about it.'

I ran it through my mind in all its tangled woefulness; the impenetrable interlocking of politics, economics, religion and culture, the incessant interweaving and unravelling of alliances, the hopes and the treacheries and the blood and the bungling and in the end I came to a decision.

'No, I won't. I'd probably get it all wrong. Lead you fatally astray. It probably wouldn't help you anyway. Besides, I don't feel like it.'

'But don't I need to know something, Henry?'

I caught a glimpse of her concerned profile against the deck lights.

'Well, yes. The main thing for our purposes is that most of the trappings of civilisation have disappeared. There are no treaties, no laws. Power is money and force of arms alone and there is no higher authority.'

Tina shivered. 'That's scary enough.'

I hugged her tightly and wondered whether bringing her was the right thing. Yet strangely it seemed to be. Then a thought seemed to strike her.

'Henry, am I going to understand anything that goes on? I don't understand the language and frankly the way you describe the culture I'd be better off in deepest Africa.'

'I shouldn't worry about the language. The three key people, Antoine, Rimmer – who hopefully we won't need to meet – and Elias are all fluent in English. Lots of people are, and failing that you've got French. Which reminds me, at checkpoints I prefer to speak slow English or bad Arabic. Arabic of any competence makes them worried you're a spy. As for the culture, well it's alien, but not that much so. Everybody is human and their needs and problems are ours, just writ large.'

'I see.' But she didn't sound convinced. After several minutes she spoke again in a subdued voice.

'Henry, what do you think our chances are?'

I said nothing for a moment, wondering if she could stay on the boat and return to Cyprus, but Tina interrupted me before I could speak. 'Henry, promise me you'll be honest. I want the facts. They may scare me, but I'd rather you didn't hide anything.'

'Very well. Our chances of getting Fuad out? Low, but not impossible. He should have been released by now if it was a mistake.'

She was silent for a moment. 'And of us?'

She did ask the most dreadful questions.

'I've been thinking about that. Part of it depends on how malign the group is. I still live in hope that it means well and the incidents with Vaughan, and now with Fuad, are simply aberrations. It may be that we can walk up to Daoud, make some pleasantries about Farayoun and get Fuad back with apologies all round.'

'But if the group is bad?'

'Then we have a problem. We have something big, powerful and ambitious that no one knows about, and in that case....'

I didn't finish the sentence. I didn't want to. After what seemed a long time Tina spoke quietly.

'In that case, *what?*'

I wished I hadn't said anything, I wished I hadn't brought her, I wished I'd kept silent about the group, I wished a lot of things. Finally, I spoke quietly.

'I think it is up to me to try and destroy it.'

There was silence apart from the wind, waves and the distant engine. I collected my thoughts and continued: 'So if it is bad, and I do hope it's not, then I don't give much for our chances. We got off very lightly last time. Your dad insists that there are no such things as cheap victories in life.'

'I'd hardly disagree.'

It was a faint voice.

147

Then it occurred to me that I might have been a bit gloomy, so I tried to cheer her up.

'Anyway, Tina, today is Christmas Day. I take that to be a guarantee that we win in the end.'

The voice that replied was cautious but firm. 'True, we've read the script, but it's the bit in the middle that's tough.'

I set the alarm on my watch for six o'clock and we piled the luggage against the door. To my surprise I slept well and didn't wake before then. I gently woke Tina.

'Time to get up and see something.'

Say what you like, the jet may be faster all the time, that is if you don't get kidnapped going out of the airport, but it's difficult to beat the view on the overnight ferry to Lebanon in winter or spring. When we got on deck it was still dark, although a waxing moon gave a pale light over the sea and caught the spray from the bow. And we stood and peered ahead in the darkness till gradually the eye could make out pinpoints of light on and above the horizon. Above and behind them you sensed rather than saw a fathomless something that seemed to reflect the moonlight. Then, infinitely slowly, the sky began to lighten ahead except along the bottom where the darkness, now sharp edged, still prevailed. As we watched, chilled and eyes running, we realised that we were not alone and that other people, wrapped up against the wind, had come alongside us. Ahead, the indigo turned to grey and then a pinky blue and below it the now crisply demarcated blackness seemed to gain solidity and height. Then the sun began to rise above the black and it became impossible to look directly at it for long. Turning away for relief, the deck was full of people staring and pointing and some were crying. Then as the sun rose clear of the ridge you could see that black mass of the mountain begin to pale rapidly as though the dark was being drained out of it and then in minutes the sun was shining clear on the snows of the great rock of Mount Lebanon.

The woman next to Tina spoke to her in emotional

French and I couldn't catch most of it as it was blown away before reaching me. Tina seemed to understand it and answered back carefully, in what sounded adequate French. Then, the woman leaving, Tina turned to me.

'She asked if it was my first trip here and said wasn't it the most beautiful view in the world and that she lost two houses here, but that she still had to come back. "There is nowhere else I can live. This land is my home." '

Tina smiled softly.

'Thanks for getting me up early.'

As we came in and the coast became clearer, I pointed out Batroun to the north and Tina looked carefully, apparently hoping to see something of the town I did not name behind it. To the south I gestured to the smudge of Beirut. Gradually, the buildings of Jounieh and the sprawl of flats and houses behind it became clearer and we could see the Casino du Liban, the great statue of Mary and the Walt Disney Gothic cathedral behind it. Then we went to pick up our baggage, but we needn't have bothered because no one beats homesick Lebanese at getting off a boat quickly and they'll only queue at gunpoint and even then it's tough work.

We disembarked almost last of all and had to stand for some time at the end of what was a fluid, jostling wedge of people. This gave Tina a chance to get a good look at the bored but heavily armed militiamen standing by the boat and the equally bored but unarmed militiamen reading the passports, checking sheets of paper and writing down names on lists in the quayside office. The only decoration to the office was a portrait of the President and two flags; one, that of the State, of horizontal white and red bands with a vaguely realistic cedar and the other, that of the Lebanese Forces, with a similar cedar in a red circle.

Tina turned to me and whispered. 'Is this unofficial or official?'

'Not really a meaningful question. Consider it as the end

149

product of unwilling privatisation. It's the Maronite militia.'

The endemic boredom persisted through the examination of our passports, although if the man at the desk had seen my old one with its Syrian visas and stamps he might have thought twice. I practised my stupid but innocent look and that seemed to satisfy him. The trivial enquiries were conducted in accented but grammatical English, then he handed the passports back.

'Welcome to Lebanon. Free Lebanon.'

'Thank you.'

I was standing outside the exit looking for George's contact man when my arm was caught. I turned to see a dark, rather plump, well-dressed Lebanese in his thirties.

'Doctor Stanwick? Mrs Stanwick? Welcome, I am Ramzi Najjar.'

I shook hands and returned the greetings.

'You have come from where?' He was checking, of course.

'Cyprus, St Paul's School and George Roumian. Any news of Fuad?'

'None, we are thinking it must be that Elias' men have him. I'm afraid I have no fortune in trying to talk to any contacts of him. Your car is here, anyway. I have been here since two hours.'

He seemed uneasy and in a hurry, but then maybe he didn't like being so close to the militia. I couldn't blame him.

The car was more or less what I'd wanted. A fairly recent Peugeot saloon with reasonable bodywork and good tyres. I just hoped the suspension and the engine were in good condition. I checked the papers and at least one had my name on it in Arabic. So I thanked Ramzi, wished him well and watched him go round the corner. Then I looked under the car and around the engine, searching for suspicious packages. I found none, put our luggage in the boot and we set off.

150

I drove carefully northwards through the centre of Jounieh, gradually trying to ease myself into the state of alertness necessary to tackle the rush hour into Beirut. It must have been thirty years since Jounieh was a pretty town and the last decade hadn't been kind to it. There were a few older buildings still left, but the dominant architecture of apparently randomly strewn concrete breezeblock flats and houses, most with strands of rusty steel protruding from the flat roofs, was depressing. Nothing seemed to be built with any thought for outside appearance or a life expectancy of more than a few decades. The litter and the potholes didn't help. I reminded myself that this was now the best maintained area in Lebanon.

Tina looked around attentively, asking a dozen questions a minute. She looked interested, disturbed and finally puzzled.

'I thought Beirut was the other way, or am I just disorientated?'

'No, you're quite right. I want to give the impression, if anybody is watching us, that we are heading north to Farayoun.'

In a minute we came to the north – south autostrade and I swung right towards Beirut.

If I'd wanted to test the car it was the wrong time. The rush hour was on and it took us over an hour to do the ten miles to Senn il Fil, although we did stop for ten minutes at a bakery to get breakfast. It was nerve-racking to get back into Lebanese driving. Every so often the traffic would make a fast, desperate weave either to the right or the left to avoid a pothole. Cars would suddenly nose in front of you, heedless of your approach. Indicators were totally extinct and brake lights an endangered species. The cars were older, more battered, but no less numerous than I remembered. From the silence next to me, broken only by sudden intakes of breath, it was plain that Tina was not enjoying it one bit. Finally she spoke, after I'd overtaken on the inside.

'Do you have to drive like this? No criticism meant.'

'If I did it any other way I'd probably cause an accident. They expect me to drive like them.'

'But aren't there any rules?'

'No, this is Lebanon. Well, there are some: watch your front, ignore the rear, don't argue, and if they pull a gun after they drive into you, apologise for reversing into them.'

'Oh.'

I glanced at her – a dangerous manoeuvre in itself – and saw she looked very unhappy. I reflected that driving is so much part of modern everyday life that it is perhaps the area in which a breakdown of law and order is felt first.

As we passed the Dog River I pointed out where I'd got into trouble for trying to look at a cave system. At the time it had been spectacular, but as I thought about it and compared it to the present mess, it didn't seem that big a deal.

Then we were into East Beirut with its supermarkets, blocks of flats and solid traffic jams. I thought it looked much shabbier than I remembered and it seemed that there were a higher number of bullet holes and shrapnel pock marks on the buildings. A new generation of political graffiti had appeared, although the general thrust seemed much as I remembered it. Eventually, I found the block of flats that Antoine lived in. It was a rather run down, densely packed area of town overlooking the Beirut River, which is now contained, at least for the time being, in a concrete channel. The volume of cars around made parking a problem. I eventually found a pavement that I could get the car onto.

'On the pavement?'

'The last legal court case over driving in this country was spring 1975. Anyway, where murderers are politicians, parking on the pavement is no big deal.'

I looked at Tina. She had stiffened and was staring behind me.

'Well, why is that guy in uniform and carrying a machine gun coming over to us?'

'Ah. Well spotted. It's the local law and order. Try to

think of him as a policeman, not a spotty youth who might want to kill you. We've probably nicked his parking place and he's better armed, so I won't argue. Remember, smile but go easy on the eye contact. We don't want him fancying you.'

The acned youth in dirty combat fatigues and the casually held Kalashnikov was clearly coming towards the car. Pre-emptive action was called for. I wound down the window, trying to look innocent and called out to him in English. It was the cheeriest and most affectionate 'Good morning, my friend' I could manage for what might, with considerable justification, have been held to be really a rather offputting specimen of humanity.

As it generally does, it caught him off guard. He put his head in the car and smiled at Tina in a manner calculated to offend any sensitive female. In return she gave him the sort of smile that the Prime Minister gives the Leader of the Opposition. It shouldn't have given him any cause for encouragement.

'Hello, who are you wanting?'

I stuck with the slow English. 'We are visiting Pastor...' No, that was no good. Try the Arabic and hope he doesn't notice, 'Er, *Assis* Antoine Attiyah. Do you know his house?'

He thought. 'Yes, I will take you.'

'Well thank you, that is kind.'

'Pleez, I must see inside your car.'

So we got out and took out the holdalls and I made sure that our friend had a good chance to see that the boot held no suspicious packages. Then I locked it up carefully and we followed him to one of the flats.

There was no lift, so we climbed slowly up the tight, dusty stairs. There were smells of cooking and washing and a hubbub of children, babies, radios and chattering. In the background you could hear the muffled roar of generators from the street. The electricity was clearly off. Finally, we stopped at a door on the fifth, and apparently top, floor and

153

our guide hammered on the newly-painted brown wood panelling with a fist. I took some comfort from the fact that it was his fist rather than a boot or gun butt.

The knocking brought a shadow to the security viewer and the door opened cautiously. A voice spoke in soft Arabic.

'Ah Elie, thank you. You are kind.' Then it shifted to English. 'Dr and Mrs Stanwick, I believe? *Ahlan wa sahlan.* Welcome. Come in please. I am Antoine Attiyah.'

20

Antoine Attiyah was tall by the standards of his generation of Lebanese, and the initial reaction was that he was thin – even gaunt – to the point of almost appearing a husk. But he was anything other than burned out. That impression was belied on every count. The handshake was firm and strong, and the eyes, behind thick metal-framed lenses, looked us over as if memorising our faces. His face was lined and his white hair thin and receding. He spoke in careful, neutral English with little trace of his years in America. It wasn't the accent, however, that struck you, rather the gentle but firm tone of his voice.

'Please come and sit down. I must just talk to Elie here for a moment. It is so good to see him.'

I wondered whether even Elie's own mother thought that. Tina and I put our holdalls in the corner and sat down on the iron-framed sofa. At the door Antoine talked, quietly and persistently, in Arabic to Elie.

I looked around the small neat room, tiled but with a rather worn rug covering the central portion. A window and a balcony door lay on the north side and you could see the sun shining on the balcony through the lace curtains. There were two small sofas and a chair around a small coffee table with its ubiquitous ashtray, but, unusually for Lebanon, no cigarette packs. In a corner stood one of those mobile heaters that work off bottled gas. There was a chest of drawers on which three photographs stood. One was of a large congregation and a church building which had been in colour, but had faded in the sun. It looked as though it was somewhere in America. The second was not a very good portrait of an elderly woman sitting in a garden chair. Everything about it said, 'This is the last photograph we ever took of my wife.' The third was a formal, posed shot of a student in an American graduation gown and hat.

Tina gestured to it, 'Fuad?' I nodded and looked away, finding it too painful.

There was one other thing in the room that caught the eye. It was an Arabic text on the wall, beautifully drawn. For once you felt that the calligraphy helped rather than overwhelmed the words. It looked worth the effort, so I struggled with the classical Arabic. In the end I recognised it rather than translated it all. I murmured to Tina.

'Got it, the end of Psalm twenty-three. How does it go? "Surely goodness and love will follow me all the days of my life, and I will dwell in the house of the Lord for ever." '

The conversation at the door ended. Antoine put a thin hand on Elie's shoulder as if to encourage him. Elie came into the room looking vaguely embarrassed and held out a hand, the machine gun slung awkwardly over a shoulder. I got up, shook his hand and thanked him, and Tina rose and did the same. 'Bye bye,' he said and left after shaking Antoine's hand again. The older man stood at the top of the stairs and waved him on down with some words of encouragement. Then he came in, closed the door after him and took a seat.

'Do excuse me. I know his family well, but Elie gets into trouble so easily. I'm afraid that.... No, it wouldn't be fair to blame him entirely. Now tell me, have you eaten?'

155

He looked us over carefully, his eyes, brown and large, dancing and scrutinising. He was somewhat older than I had first thought, possibly in his mid-sixties. But there seemed no concession to age in his manner.

'It's good of you, but yes we have eaten.'

'Good, well, coffee then? I'm afraid it is just instant, but one lives with it.'

'Please, but let me help,' said Tina.

'No, it's no trouble at all.' Antoine disappeared into the little kitchen.

'I had forgotten how formal and courteous the society was,' I said quietly to Tina. She looked ill at ease and shook her head.

'I'm more impressed by the fact that Elie is law and order here. He looked as though he wouldn't think twice about killing someone.'

Antoine had come in quietly behind her.

'Sorry, I overheard. Yes, that is precisely the problem, I'm afraid. He has something of a reputation. I haven't enquired into the details of the deaths. Some at least were, I think we could say, unnecessary even under the circumstances.'

Tina looked hard at him for several seconds, clearly waiting for the punchline or the smile that would tell her it was a joke. It didn't come. Her face took on a very disturbed look.

'You're serious? I was just joking. He's a murderer?'

Antoine nodded. There was deep sorrow in his face.

'But define murder for me, Mrs Stanwick.'

Tina was quick with the reply. 'The unlawful taking of life.'

'Correct, but where there is no law and there is no distinction between military and civilian, or really between war and peace, the term becomes difficult to apply, although the sin exists.'

Tina just stared at him blankly and said nothing. Then she looked at me with a face of bewilderment before looking back at Antoine. At that point the kettle whistled and

156

Antoine turned and went into the kitchen, returning after some minutes with cups. As we took our coffee I knew the time had come for business.

Antoine began. 'I am so sorry that this meeting should have been under these circumstances.'

It crossed my mind that with almost anybody else I know, under these awful conditions it would have been merely formality to say that. Somehow, Antoine seemed genuinely to mean that he really was sorry that the pleasure of meeting us had to be under a shadow. He continued. 'George called last night, so I know that you have no news of my son. I suppose I have to say that I have no news either.'

His face gave nothing away, but the eyes flickered towards the photograph as if to reassure himself that it at least was still there. Then he turned to me with a penetrating look as if to give me a cue to begin. As I gathered my thoughts I had a funny feeling of being exposed, of being examined – indeed almost of being judged. If I'd been uncertain about whether or not to tell the truth then Antoine's gaze would have settled it. He seemed to be the sort of person who had little time either for lies or liars. I swallowed and began.

'We have no real news, I'm afraid, but I think we can shed some light on your son's disappearance.'

Then I thought, what can I call this man? Hardly Antoine. 'Pastor' would do.

'Pastor, it is probably the result of an accident, but I must take a lot of the blame. You see last year I ran away from a decision, I did some stupid things and I found out about something that is very big. It is a group that are very concerned about some of the paths the world is taking; military, political and environmental.'

'I see. What sort of group?'

So I told him in a shortened form a lot about what had happened. But in my brevity I tried not to hide anything. He said nothing, but watched me. Eventually I wound to a close.

157

'...so your son got hold of the story that they were doing something in Farayoun.'

'What sort of thing?'

I thought for a moment. Explaining genetic engineering was one thing, but to try not to make it sound like a work of the devil was harder still. Some of these Arab pastors are super people, but can have a pretty jaundiced view on science generally, let alone tinkering with DNA.

'It appears to be what is called genetic engineering. Er, that is to say that....'

The stern gaze broke into a little knowing smile and Antoine raised a finger.

'Henry, I pastored a church in California where people worked in biotechnology for a living, and where their neighbours talked about whether they should have tissues preserved so that they could be cloned in the next century. Besides, Lena, my wife,' here he gestured to the second photograph, 'was a diabetic in the last years of her life. We did hope the new genetically engineered insulin would help. It didn't, but that's not the point. So I know a little already about it and also about some of the ethical issues.'

I felt rather silly and not a little rebuked, although it seemed Antoine was not in the business of scoring points over anyone. He continued, 'But what exactly are they up to in Farayoun?'

'I don't know. The one case I heard of involved the possibility of making algae take up excess carbon dioxide from the air. But there may be other things. I heard from my brother that Fuad felt that if it could be proved that dangerous genetic experiments were being undertaken in Farayoun, then the superpowers might intervene to make peace in Lebanon.'

For a moment Antoine looked away out of the window as if to hide any emotion. Then he spoke slowly, trying to conceal his feelings, but doing it badly.

'Yes, that is Fuad. I can hear him say it. He loves this place, and he dreams of a short cut to restoring it. But in one sense he is right, Henry, and Tina. The devil has a free hand here.'

He stared out of the window again, where the mountains could just be seen through the lace. Then he turned back to me.

'Thank you, especially for your honesty. So that is the story.'

I felt I had to interrupt.

'Yes, but I have to say, Pastor, that it is my fault. And I have come to do what I can to undo my mistake. If it can be undone....'

Antoine bowed his head slightly.

'Thank you again. We shall see. We at least now know where to look. But, Henry, where do you think Elias Daoud fits in to all this?'

'I think perhaps he is simply the landlord for this group. His background doesn't seem technical enough.'

'Perhaps. I know little of him. The few people who do know him I don't have much to do with. I have had a little information from some of the monks and priests who are friendly with me.'

I think he caught Tina's expression.

'Yes, not everybody is dead within the old churches, and not everybody is alive in the churches that came from the Reformation. Thankfully, in places there is life and the gospel is preached and the word is read and studied, but not everywhere and there is a lot to do. Still, it is better than it was when I left. That at least is a mercy. But Elias Daoud....' He shook his head firmly and sadly.

'I'm afraid the reports are bad. A hard man, callous, brutal and with a streak of cowardice. With cunning too. He has emptied the old monastery, although that was probably no loss. He harasses the priests. Of course, much may be his militia and his captains, but a man should surely be responsible for his dogs, yes?'

He shook his head again. 'Do you plan to see him, Henry?'

Hopefully I can get an introduction.'

Antoine looked encouraged.

'That would help a great deal. As George has told you, we have so far no contacts with him. He is not an easy man to get to see. In fact, it is said he is scared and he rarely sleeps in the same bed more than one night running. He claims this is to foil Mossad and prevent them from assassinating him, but I think the Israelis have better things to do. No, I think he has enemies closer at hand, but it makes him difficult to deal with.'

Tina put her coffee cup down half finished. I noticed she seemed distracted. Antoine observed my glance.

'I'm sorry, you probably want to clean up after your journey. Now perhaps I can show you to your room and the facilities, and you can unpack. I assume you are here tonight. Then maybe we can sit down again to discuss plans. But thank you both for coming.'

The bedroom was a small room looking west, with two beds pushed together. I closed the door and looked at Tina, who seemed at a loss for words. I gave her a hug which I felt she needed. Then I went to the window and looked out. Beyond lay the Beirut River valley and behind it the hill of Ashrafiyeh. To the south you could see beyond to Mazraa and West Beirut. Almost everything was houses and flats.

'He has a good view. Come and look.'

I opened the window.

'Over there is the museum and behind it West Beirut. That's probably the only crossing point at the moment.'

'How far away is it?' The voice was distant, the question formal.

'Maybe two miles, probably a bit less. It helps explain a lot. People like Elie. For these people that's where the Islamic Empire begins; their backs are against the sea. They feel that they are sitting on a rock and the tide is coming in around them. It's just a question of how high it will go. If it goes too high, or they slip, then all they can hope for is their own Dunkirk – if they are lucky – and then they will become

160

the Armenians or the Palestinians of the next century, condemned to wander the world despised and rejected.'

Tina spoke as if in a trance. 'Is that true? Would that happen?'

'True? I don't know. But they think it's true and here that is what counts.'

You get out of the habit of thinking like a Beiruti, and that is dangerous. I'd been admiring the view for a few minutes when it occurred to me. I leaned out a bit further.

'I'm stupid. I missed the important thing. The view is too good.'

'Too good?'

'A clear line of fire from West Beirut. Sorry, didn't mean to alarm you. Just look at the wall below the window.'

The wall below us had once been smooth concrete; it now had a considerable population of craters of various sizes.

'Oh!'

'No problem, that's probably many years' worth. They mostly look to be the product of bullets at the end of their trajectory.'

What I didn't tell her is that it's that sort of bullet – yawing and spiralling wildly – that is the most lethal if it strikes.

So I went and shaved, and then looked and felt a bit better, and came back to find that Tina was sitting on the bed staring at the wall. She hadn't moved since I'd left.

'You all right?'

She shook her head. 'No, not really. I can't believe this place. I can't put it into words. It's not the danger, I don't think. It's just....'

She broke down in tears and I put my arms around her.

'Tell you what, lie down. Try and relax. What has to be done I can do.'

'OK, but don't go out and leave me.'

'Of course not.'

I pulled the door closed gently. The balcony door was open and Antoine was standing there watering an azalea. I went over and he must have caught my expression.

161

'Your wife is all right?'

I paused, thinking that this man had troubles enough of his own, but he seemed to be the sort of person that you couldn't tell even a white lie to.

'No; to be honest. She's finding it all a bit much. Culture shock I suppose.'

Antoine looked over his glasses at me. 'What is her background, if I may ask?'

'Tight, loving family, totally secure in a quiet northern town. Never travelled abroad before. Lots of faith, lots of guts.'

Antoine gave a kind little smile. 'Clearly, but I see from your description of her that you know what the problem is.'

That caught me a bit off balance, but as I thought about it it became clearer.

'You mean that it's the fact that there are no rules; that it's all one big swamp here, that murderers wear uniform. It's totally anarchic.'

'I'd guess so. It happened to a friend who came. "I knew it was a zoo, Antoine, but it was the fact that there weren't any cages that threw me." I liked that. I think you will find that she has nothing to latch onto – all the cultural supports she expects: law, order, rules, are all gone.'

I had a strong suspicion he was right.

'It may pass. If it does she will be stronger for it because she will have grounded herself in something deeper than culture. As she already believes in that, I am cautiously optimistic. If you like I'll talk to her.'

I thought about it for a minute. 'Yes, I think that would be a good idea, Pastor. You are from here, it will help if she can identify with you. Please.'

He held another pot plant up, looked at it and put it down delicately. Then he turned to me.

'Right, I'll go and have a few words with her.'

21

When Antoine had gone to the bedroom I stayed on the balcony feeling sorry for Tina and wondering why I'd let myself be persuaded to bring her. Here I was supposed to be helping Antoine and already he'd had to help me. It wasn't an auspicious start, yet what he had said was wise. The place was crazy. Perhaps Tina's reaction of shock was more rational than my acceptance of it.

After ten minutes or so Antoine came over and put a thin hand on my shoulder.

'She'll be fine, Henry. But it will help if she has no further excitement today.'

'Thanks, Pastor.'

'Please make it Antoine, or else I shall call you Doctor.' There was the glow of a faint smile on his face.

'An irresistible bargain. Antoine it is.'

We stood on the balcony for some moments saying nothing.

'Henry, why did you bring your wife here?'

Antoine spoke in a tone of curiosity rather than rebuke. It was not an easy question to answer honestly. Yet he seemed to have that greatest of all pastoral gifts, the ability to draw out answers.

'I've just been asking myself that, Antoine. In part, because she asked to come; in part... I'm not sure. Because I felt it was right for her to come. Maybe it was an excuse to show her Lebanon. But why did you let your son come here?'

There was a gentle smile, but it overlay suffering. 'Ah, good. Because he asked to come and because I love this place and these people enough to risk the one I love most on earth.'

I thought for a minute. Then I spoke slowly and hesitantly as the answer was pulled out. 'I can understand that, because perversely and inexplicably I love this place and these people, you Lebanese. And I wasn't born here. Quite illogical.'

Antoine looked at me and there was understanding and affinity in his eyes. There was a bond between us.

Then, somewhat to my surprise, Tina came out of the room and walked over to us, her face a little taut. She sidled next to me and caught my hand. She spoke quietly.

'Sorry, Henry, it was just a mood. It was stupid of me. I thought I'd come back and join you. Antoine helped me to see beyond it all.'

I moved along the balcony a bit to allow room for her and put my arm around her.

'Welcome. We had just been saying that it takes time to adjust to the situation here – as has been doubtless truly observed, Beirut isn't Grantforth. Come and look at the view. It's not as good as it was unfortunately.'

Tina smiled rather thinly and squeezed next to me, but she hadn't relaxed very much.

The view had certainly deteriorated. A clearly visible brown-grey pall hung over the city and only the foot of the mountain, beginning to rise two or three miles away, could be seen. High up to the right I could just see the top of a snow-capped ridge.

Antoine broke the silence. 'The smog is much worse than it was, now everyone has his own generator and the cars are getting old. You see that there is nothing green to be seen – no parks, no gardens, just these pot plants. Everything is built up, or parked on.'

I thought for a moment.

'Antoine, can I ask you why you came back from California?'

He leaned on the balcony rail and spoke out slowly and

thoughtfully ahead of him. 'I left for the States when things got bad in the first days of the Civil War and everything seemed impossible. You say *you* ran away last year?'

'Sort of.'

He looked sideways at me, then turned to stare away.

'Well so did I, so I can understand. I shouldn't have – but who can put the clock back? Oh, if only we had worked harder in the sixties, preached more urgently, built bridges between the communities and spoken out against the rot. But we thought it would last for ever and it didn't. We were Lebanese, cultured, civilised and rich. Suddenly the house of cards fell about us and it was too late. So we left. We said we had the boy and I suppose it's true – Fuad was at the age to be called up for the militia and I didn't want him to turn out a *zoraan*, a thug, like Elie.' Tina pressed harder against me, her body still stiff. Antoine continued, speaking as though he were thinking it all out for the first time.

'And Lena wasn't well. We loved the States, but we always wanted to come back here, but Lena was never up to it. Then after the Lord took her I found myself free to come back. And I had a debt to repay to my land. My church in California was very helpful, although of course they wanted me to live up the hill.'

He gestured eastwards to where pine forests could just be made out in the haze on the flanks of the mountain.

'In Mansouriyeh, or even Broummana, and get a big flat and breathe clear air. But I thought about it and it seemed to me I had no children and I could always drive up if I wanted a change, but that here was the need. So I am here and the extra money went to rent the church. And now I don't have to drive to my parish, which is a blessing.'

He made a gesture at the noisy traffic jam that had formed below us. Then he broadened it to take in the drab expanse of concrete walls and wires, broken only by the green shutters and multi-coloured washing on the balconies.

'So here I am. Normally I would be very busy, but for the moment much of my work is taken by Nabil, my assistant.

165

He is running things at the church. There are a lot of problems in the congregation.'

Antoine paused and looked at Tina, as though wondering whether to continue. 'Today is quiet, but at any minute the shelling could start, or any of the cars below could explode.'

I could feel Tina becoming even more rigid, and I wondered what Antoine was playing at.

He continued, 'But you have to face it. So I have to emphasise certain things constantly: true security, assurance, peace and hope. Fear is so destructive and corrosive. As someone said, "Perfect fear casts out love." But after all, things are not so different from California; traffic accidents, coronaries and cancer took many in my old church. They only thought they could escape death. Here we have no such delusions. We are reminded too often of it.'

As if to highlight his words there was a rolling boom that echoed and re-echoed round the flats, vibrating the glass. It was followed a second later by another. Tina jumped and looked at me. I pointed upwards. High in the blue sky two thin lines of white were being cut northwards.

'So they still do it, Antoine?'

The noise had made me shudder. It had brought back various recollections, all unpleasant and some terrible.

'Still they cannot rest secure.'

Tina looked at me. 'What are they?'

'Israeli photoreconnaissance planes. They keep watch on most of Lebanon. People in West Beirut used to say that they had no need to break the sound barrier, but that it was a useful reminder.'

Antoine spoke. 'It's probably still the same. Don't forget, we came once, we can come back again. Bad memories, Henry?'

I turned to Antoine. 'Yes, I was in West Beirut for the first part of the invasion in 1982. It's not something I like to talk about much. I left West Beirut after the first two weeks or so.'

Antoine said nothing, but I felt he expected more.

'Why did I leave?'

'I didn't ask that. It would have perhaps been more surprising if you had stayed.'

'It was difficult, Antoine. You see at the start of the invasion a lot of us thought it was terrible, but that at least it would be the end of the Civil War, and within weeks at that; that it was a price worth paying, a necessary evil; that out of the blood a new Lebanon would be born. Sorry, Antoine, we can all be naive.'

He was silent, but listening. I caught Tina's concerned look. She realised that this was something of which she had heard virtually nothing.

'So when the Israelis started bombing and shelling, everyone thought there was a plan; that they were being subtle. Then gradually we realised that it was effectively indiscriminate – that there was no purpose to it and that these things were being done simply to terrorise the community into forcing the Palestinians out. Anyway, as it progressed I found I could do little and I was scared, and gradually I found myself on the verge of hating the Israelis. So I left and drove out to Mansouriyeh; to the Hagopians, if you remember them. When I got there they said, "Guess who's staying in our garden?" and it was half a dozen Israelis and a halftrack.'

I paused as I thought about it. 'The sheer psychological shock was enormous. In Syria and West Beirut they were invisible, almost alien, figures whose machines rode the clouds dispensing death. You never saw them, but their spies were everywhere. Maybe, maybe not. And finally here I was face to face with them. So I was going to tell them what I thought of their wretched airforce. But they were all conscripted kids who hadn't a clue about where they were or what they were doing, and all they wanted was to get back to their families in Tel Aviv and Beersheva. They thought the whole of West Beirut was full of mad Arabs with headdresses wanting to kill them. And I realised that they were people too and I couldn't hate them. Of course, when I came

167

back I saw what was left of Sabra and Chatila, Ain el Helwe and the rest of the camps and I was angry. Still am in a way, but not hateful. So their planes still make me feel lousy. Sorry, you didn't ask for that.'

'I think I did. I was interested to hear it.'

I shrugged. I hadn't liked even talking about it. Then I realised that there were things I had to do.

'Antoine, I need to call someone if the phone works. May I?'

'Go ahead. I shall ask your wife to help me in the kitchen, if she would. Cooking is not my strong point.'

I looked at Tina. I couldn't think of any better therapy.

'Yes, why not? A good idea.'

It wasn't easy getting hold of Charlie Rimmer, especially as I didn't have his number. It wasn't helped by the fact that on December 26th he almost certainly wouldn't be in the office at the university. However, Antoine had a venerable and rather greasy brown telephone book that went back many years and a 'C M Rimmer' was in it at the same address I remembered. It took half an hour to get a line on the phone and then there was no answer. I rang again, and to my surprise and elation a distant, formal voice intoned, 'Charles Rimmer here.' The elation vanished as it became apparent that he couldn't hear a word I was saying. I put the phone down and tried again, but this time there was no line.

I went into the kitchen where Antoine and Tina were finishing off making a salad.

'Incredible. Rimmer is in his flat two miles away and I can't get to talk to him. What's the deal on driving over, Antoine?'

He shook his head forcefully, 'Don't, unless you absolutely have to. No recent Western hostages have been taken, but you can't tell. The radio says there is internal tension and the camps are a mess again. The Syrians just about keep the lid on, but I don't know. I haven't been over since '84, so I can't tell. Try the phone again after lunch.'

After we had eaten Tina went to lie down and I followed her into the bedroom. While we were talking there was the sound of someone at the front door. A minute or two later Antoine called me out and I saw that Elie had turned up. I managed to greet him affably. Antoine put his arm on my shoulders and led me into the kitchen.

'Henry, Elie has brought an invitation for you and Tina to go and talk with a friend of his, a man called Eduard.'

I looked at him, puzzled. His face was troubled.

'This Eduard is – what shall we say – a man who deals in things and people. He does not talk to me; I have spoken against him before now. I do not care for his trade. I believe the people in charge over here do not care for him either. He belongs to the past, the older part of the Civil War. However, he apparently has an offer to do with my son.'

'And he feels he might be able to deal with us?'

'Perhaps. If you wish, you can refuse to meet him. It might be the best thing.'

He was silent. I thought rapidly and found the answer all too easy.

'I will meet him if he has information, but must it be both of us?'

'Apparently.'

'Then I'm sure Tina will come.'

'Thank you. I should say that....' He paused, a mixture of emotions crossing his face. Then they hardened into resolve. 'No, there are prices for my son that I will not pay, and I would wish that you do not pay either. No further evil must be involved. Categorically. Money, maybe we can arrange in time, but I will be surprised if it is money he or Elias wants. Do you understand?'

'Yes. How do we get there?'

'He has an office nearby. He has his own men, but I think you will be all right.'

I didn't want to say that I had the very strongest reservations about the whole business and that I felt Eduard was going to be a very nasty piece of work indeed, but if there was the slightest chance that meeting him would get Fuad out I had to take it. Besides, it might spare me a trip to Farayoun.

Tina barely saw it that way.

'Do we have to?'

'They may be just fine. Probably just want to drink coffee with us. We have to go for Fuad's sake. Try not to be frightened, that only makes them worse. We're supposed to show them love too.'

She bit her lip. 'All right, but I'm not going to enjoy this, and Elie doesn't make me feel any more secure.'

'It isn't my idea of a fun afternoon either, but there's no need to be prejudiced against Elie just because he's a proven psychopath. Let's go.'

I won't say Tina was tense, but I had nailmarks in my hand for a long time. It didn't take long to walk down to the office, which turned out to be an old warehouse, unobtrusively but heavily guarded. Once inside we were ushered very carefully past an assortment of anonymous crates and sacks that I guessed were a mixture of drugs and weaponry. In an inner room we met the bulk of Eduard's 'men'. I suppose I had wondered where all the old thugs had gone when they'd tidied up the militias in East Beirut and made them do training and fill in forms. Eduard's private army supplied something of an answer for at least half a dozen. These were militiamen of the meaner sort, just as I remembered them. This lot were frankly ugly, in every sense of the word. All of them were large, most had paunches and a number had heavy untrimmed beards. Most were wearing filthy combat fatigues. One or two stood and argued while others sat in armchairs, or in one case lay stretched out on a bench. A glance at the faces suggested that between them they had gone through every crime in the book several times over and had the scars to prove it. In fact it was difficult to find any in the room to whom some synonym of the word 'thug' wouldn't have been appropriate. There was shouting and cursing, much of it in the sort of so-called English that occurs in the worst sort of American drama. As background to the hubbub the radio played loudly. The place smelled of beer, cigarettes and what I remembered as hashish. On the walls, scarred by squashed mosquitos and the odd bullet, were a miscellany of posters. Bashir, Pierre and a few half dressed film stars I recognised, but there were a couple of others I couldn't name. Near the door had been posted a number of the small black margined sheets with photographs that announce a death. In a corner, propped up as casually as if they were old umbrellas, were a number of machine guns. That, and the fact that everybody was wearing Cuban heeled boots suggested only a limited military efficiency. The whole effect was of a seedy malevolence that looked ready to explode into general mayhem at any moment, with only the slightest prompting.

As Elie led us in, there were ribald shouts of recognition, jeering and – towards Tina – pretty explicit lust. Tina coloured and looked away. At least she hadn't understood the Arabic. I tried to look harmless.

'Where's Eduard?' Elie shouted over the noise of the radio in a high squeaky Arabic. Someone laughed and gestured into another room.

Eduard was polishing his boots when we came in. I can't think why he bothered, everything else was sloppy or dirty. He was middle-aged and overweight, and his office was a smaller, more compact version of the larger room and in no better shape. It smelled of sweat and worse, and his desk was covered with cigarette packets and small plastic cups full of the sooty black dregs of Arabic coffee and cigarette butts. Here, too, the inevitable radio was on. There were, however, subtle differences. There was a yearly calendar on the wall that was current and well marked, and on the desk there were sheets of paper and a well used calculator. When you looked at Eduard carefully you saw that there was a good deal of intelligence, or at least craftiness, about the eyes. He looked the sort of man who had not only sold his grandmother, but was interested in negotiating over yours.

Elie introduced us and we shook hands. He apologised for his English and I said that we'd understand slow French, but he preferred to struggle on with his English. As so often, it seemed to be something of a point of pride. He sent Elie to bring in coffee and sat back in his chair. He seemed interested in checking who we were, so I let him glance over our passports. He perused them carefully and then handed them back.

'So, you have come to help about Mister Fuad?'

I nodded and spoke slowly and used my hands as much as I could. 'I am an old friend. When I heard he had gone I decided to come.'

He looked at me inscrutably. I couldn't fathom whether he was smart, and was playing me along for answers, or whether he was just out of his depth. I decided it was safest to assume he was smart.

Eduard looked craftily at me. 'We think Elias Daoud have him. Elias is a coward, is scum, is garbage, is trash. Elias is bad man. Very bad.'

The coffee came in and produced a break in what looked to have the makings of a tirade. Any hope that Eduard would provide a means of access to Elias had vanished. Then he continued.

'No good man. Friends with Syrians. No honour. In former times he fought with us. Now nothing. Elias does nothing. He is a dog and the son of a dog. Your friend Fuad is with a bad man. He kill a friend of mine.'

I thought I'd better try and say something before we got the visceral details.

'Awfully sorry to hear it. But, Mister Eduard, how do I get my friend out?'

'Is very difficult. Maybe he is already dead. But I have an offer.'

All was beginning to come clear.

'We know man from Daoud's family. Staying near here. Not nice man. We make a deal, yes? Private deal. Secret

172

between you and me, no one else. My boys catch him. Then you go to that donkey in Farayoun and you make exchange. Then we work out cost.'

The local economy *was* in a bad way. Tina looked at me with horror as what was being planned sunk in. I gave her hand a squeeze and thought hard. I now understood why he hadn't wanted Antoine with us, but it was a tricky situation. I needed to be able to back out of this particular example of the great Lebanese entrepreneurial spirit without giving offence. I also felt sorrow and anger at what he was proposing. I knew that Antoine would have taken him to task for his suggestion and I wondered whether to do the same, but decided that it wasn't my job. My job was to help, not hinder, the rescue of Fuad.

So I reigned in my annoyance and answered slowly and carefully, 'Thank you, my friend, you are making a very kind offer, but no thank you. My friend Fuad is a good man and he would not like this. He is honest. But thank you for your kindness, for your help.' I repeated my answer in slow French to be sure that he understood the meaning of it.

Eduard sat back in his chair, clearly somewhat disappointed. 'As you want. But Elias is dangerous man. You may lose your friend.'

He made the universal slitting-the-throat gesture. I thought I would try to risk a departure, so I caught Tina's eye and rose to my feet.

'Thank you again so much. And for the coffee.'

Tina spoke for the first time. 'Yes, thank you for your help. And the coffee.'

It was well done; not exactly overflowing with gratitude, but without the quaver of fear I had dreaded. I extended a hand. I made a little prayer that Eduard would respond or else we could be stuck here. There was a pause. Then he shrugged his shoulders, stood up, shook hands and led us to the door. Elie seemed to have left and one of Eduard's men hauled himself out of a broken armchair and led us out of the warehouse and into the brightness of the street.

173

'Wave goodbye to him,' I whispered as we walked away. Tina did as she was told and then turned to me.

'Henry, I'm not sure I can take much more of this. I'm serious.'

From the tone of her voice she wasn't joking. I thought for a moment and squeezed her hand again.

'You did very well in a very unpleasant situation. I know exactly how you feel. Let's get back to Antoine's.'

So we set off up the hill past the shops and flats and weaved our way through the parked cars. Then I made what turned out to be a very memorable comment.

'If it's any consolation, Tina, you are most unlikely to get anything worse than that.'

You feel a little miffed with life when such bold pronouncements get falsified within seconds. For as I spoke I noticed that we had nearly drawn level with a new Volkswagen van which had the sliding side door open. Then I heard a step behind me. Instinctively, I half-turned and my hands were grabbed roughly. I twisted and pulled, desperately trying to work out whether to fight or surrender. As I did so I saw someone grab Tina. She squealed as a hand went round her waist, but was abruptly silenced as a second hand covered her mouth. I was being forced towards the van by the man behind me. I tried to wriggle my hands free, but I couldn't. Then there was a curse and the hand over Tina's mouth was pulled away sharply. I realised that she was putting up a fight, so I cancelled my surrender policy and swung a foot back very hard, hoping to hit my attacker. It connected with flesh and bone, and there was a pained exclamation. At the same time I threw myself as hard as I could against the van side hoping to catch my opponent off balance. It worked and for a second I was free. I turned round, pressing my back against the metal, ready to try to help Tina.

As I did, the only thing that registered was that the man facing me had pulled a pistol out. I glanced at Tina who was still struggling – but there too a pistol was emerging.

Well, there's only one thing to do in a situation like that. 'Tina, stop it.'

She gave a final kick and did so. I was able to get a better look at the attackers. They were in their early twenties and wearing neat jeans, pullovers and leather jackets. I think my attacker had worn strong aftershave of some sort. They just gestured to the sliding door with the guns. I motioned Tina over. She looked sick with fear.

'Ladies first, Tina.'

I noticed that the one who had attacked Tina was sucking a hand which looked to be bleeding. I wasn't exactly overcome with sympathy. Then he made a rather insistent, bad-tempered motion with the gun that I thought I'd better obey, so I followed Tina into the blacked-out interior. As the door slid shut I noticed that a handful of people were staring from along the pavement. As is customary in these cases they were doing nothing but staring. But then it was too late to call the police. Years too late.

The door slammed and we were in darkness. Then the engine started and with squealing tyres the van pulled off. I reached out for Tina, who was shivering, and held her.

'You OK?'

There was silence for a long time before a faint voice emerged from the darkness.

'I suppose so.'

I tried to evaluate the situation, but nothing helped. On the basis of the past hour kidnapping was clearly a current growth industry. The people who had taken us could have been from a number of sources, but they weren't expecting any local trouble with just pistols. In the meantime, there was no way of breaking out of the van, so I thought I would try to cheer Tina up.

'Well, my wife, you could look on the bright side. If they wanted to kill us they could have done it there.'

There was silence. Then she spoke in a low, tired tone. 'Any other cheerful thoughts?'

That encouraged me enormously. She hadn't given in yet.

175

I held her in the darkness and after a moment I thought of a reply.

'Well, just think, a week ago we thought getting my contract renewed was our most serious problem.'

22

The driver of the van seemed to be in something of a hurry, even by Lebanon's standards, and we swerved round corners and bounced over potholes. It was all very unpleasant in the back. At first we seemed to be going downhill then, judging from the change in tone, we crossed a bridge before taking a steeply winding road upwards. I wondered whether this vehicle was used frequently for this sort of thing. Not a crack of light entered from anywhere and the floor seemed covered with stale smelling sacking. I tried to think what might be ahead. I would have preferred to think about almost anything else, but it had to be done. Eventually I spoke.

'I think we have to remember that whatever we do or say, trying to improve Fuad's chances is a priority.'

'I'll try,' came the answer in a small, rather stifled, voice.

At last the van stopped and there was the noise of steel doors being slid open. Then it was driven slowly but steeply downhill followed by a few tight turns. I thought it was probably an underground car park, but that didn't help. Then we stopped and one person at least got out of the cab. After a few seconds the side door opened slowly.

At first it was difficult to see because of the darkness we'd been in. A voice said, in bad English, 'Slowly, please mister, over to wall.' My eyes began to work in what at first seemed to be a bright light in which a gun barrel glinted. There was the smell of car fumes, damp and oil. I went over against the wall slowly, half-expecting to hear the sound of the gun and feel the bullet. I was trying to work out any possible preventative action, but it wasn't easy. Then a pair of hands searched me thoroughly. They weren't gentle, but it was vaguely encouraging – you don't search men you're just about to shoot. The voice spoke again.

'Now you, Madame.'

Nothing happened. I realised that the light wasn't actually that bright, but that we were in fact in a gloomy underground garage.

'Please the same.'

I interrupted, 'I think you'll find she's not armed. If you'd thought about it you'd have realised we would have pulled out guns earlier.'

'Shut up.'

Very slowly Tina came over against the wall. She stood there eyes closed and trembling as the man ran his hands over her. He seemed to take his time. The temptation to try to do him an injury was very strong, but the gun barrel was pointed at Tina throughout and I had no idea where the other man was.

Then to one side a door clanged open and more light came streaming in. It wasn't daylight, but it was brighter than what we had in the garage. One of the people coming down was vaguely familiar; he looked to be the one Tina had bitten. Behind him was another man, young and slimly built, in jeans and talking Arabic in a loud voice. He was being coarsely rude about the fact that the other had had his hand bitten by a woman. It registered that the Arabic was slightly curious, then as I listened more carefully I realised that the dialect was strongly Palestinian or at least that of southernmost Lebanon. It struck me as being a puzzling feature if we were still in East Beirut, where the last thing a lot of people had ever done had been to use the faintly different Palestinian word for tomato.

The two came over and the puzzling voice changed to an

177

accented, almost East European, English.

'Follow me.'

It wasn't hard to obey. I took hold of Tina's still trembling arm and led her over to the door. There were steps up beyond it to another door and, beyond that, a larger room. The man, who was, I noted, unshaven and wearing an old sweater and grubby jeans, leaned against the wall to let us pass.

'Keep going. I must close the door.'

As we went past I noticed that it wasn't just shaving he had missed out on recently. He smelled badly. Then it occurred to me that if that was the sum total of his unpleasant habits we were probably going to be all right. As we climbed up, the door behind rang shut and there was the sound of a key turning in a lock.

The room we entered was a substantial improvement on the garage, but it left a lot to be desired. There were no windows, the paintwork was peeling and the central part of the floor was covered by a carpet with a whole collection of stains and cigarette marks. The furniture could be rapidly listed. There was a central wooden table, which had behind it two steel office chairs and in front of it two cheap folding ones. The illumination was a single buzzing fluorescent strip. Behind the table there was a closed door. The room smelled as though they were having trouble with the sewers.

There was another man in the room, sitting at the desk reading a folder. He looked up as we came in and, closing it firmly, put it down by a pile of magazines. He was a much older, balding man with a florid white moustache and tufts of white hair above his ears. He stood up to display a spreading waistline which a thick blue pullover barely covered.

'Please take a seat.'

The accent was curiously ill-defined, but the English was confident. We sat down carefully on the rickety chairs. He looked at Tina and then at me.

'Is your wife all right?'

I looked at Tina who had stopped trembling but still

looked very unhappy. I reached out and held her hand.

'Actually, no. She has a strange dislike of being manhandled by thugs, thrown into darkened vans and then being groped at gunpoint.'

I suppose I should have been grateful for the first non-threatening action towards us for over an hour. The older man turned to the young one who was just closing the door of the room behind him and there was quite a bit of arguing. I caught the name of 'Eduard' in it and decided he had probably been involved at some level. As I listened closer it took me a few seconds to realise that I couldn't understand anything else and a few more to surmise what the language must be. I peered at the magazines on the desk and my heart sank. The language was indeed Hebrew.

As the realisation of who held us dawned, it also became apparent that there wasn't any love lost between the two men. I caught Tina's eye and leaned over to her.

'Now we *are* in trouble. It's the Israelis.'

The older man saw me whispering and stopped, apparently in mid-sentence. Then, with a glare at his colleague, he gestured angrily to the chair.

'I'm sorry. Zvi tells me there was trouble with the pick up.'

Zvi, who'd sat down sulkily, shrugged. 'You're alive and not harmed. Your wife bit the boy bad. Anyway, it's local labour.'

As a placatory answer it had its deficiencies.

'Local labour. You're still responsible, you know. Or have you forgotten what happened in '82?'

It wasn't, in truth, a very nice answer on my part. The older man sighed.

'Dr Stanwick, I remind you that the Israeli Defence Force investigated the events you allude to and punished the guilty. Please, I think it is in all our interests to finish our discussions quickly and get you and your wife back to where you are staying as soon as possible. With different drivers.'

He looked meaningfully at Zvi who was taking out a

crumpled cigarette packet. Zvi shrugged and lit his cigarette.

'Now, can I get you some coffee? European style.'

Tina spoke quietly, 'Please.' I nodded. The older man, who clearly had rank as well as age on his side, spoke to Zvi who drew on his cigarette, nodded, then got up and left by the rear door. As he left I got a glimpse of a brightly-lit room, filled with electronic equipment and cables. The older man shook his head and opened the folder.

'Dr Henry Stanwick?'

Here we go again, I thought. The same old stunt with the folder. Perhaps I should try and get global rights for it. I had a bizarre vision of it rolling round the world for ever, gradually accreting pages. I seemed to be the only person who never read it. I nodded as pleasantly as I could, which wasn't saying a lot.

'The same we picked up in Majdal Shams at end of '82.'

Ah that.

'The same; hopefully older and wiser.'

I turned to Tina. 'These good people having run amok over the south in '82, I thought it was a good time to go and have a look at Mount Hermon. So I drove down to Sidon and cut across country. I got all the way round into occupied Syria before they stopped me. It was a lot of fun.'

The older man sighed. 'I should quibble over your use of obsolete geographical terms, but I, at least, have your wife's interests at heart. Last year your name came up before us. J P Lemaire asked us what we knew of "Henry Stanwick" and a "Jezreel Project". Unfortunately, we knew very little about you beyond the fact that you were a friend of all sorts of odds and ends. But the project name puzzled us and then it worried us.'

He paused to root through the folder. It was all on flimsy, rather shiny paper. Of course, they'd fax it all up, it would save having Hebrew telex machines.

'They never told us what "Jezreel" was. They said they didn't know themselves. Unfortunately all too credible. But the word "Jezreel" worried us. You see someone remembered a verse in the prophet Hoshea – Hosea I think in English – and we were very worried it might have been the inspiration for the codeword. Ah, Zvi with the coffee.'

It crossed my mind that they might have put something in it, but the older man was no fool.

'There are four mugs. Perhaps you would care to choose two, Henry?'

The use of the first name was a little careless on his part. It takes more than a mug of coffee to put me on first name terms with anybody who's had my wife assaulted. I suspect I may not be alone in that.

'Yes, here we are, had it faxed up to read to you. "Call his name Jezreel, for yet a little while and I will punish the house of Jehu for the blood of Jezreel, and I will put an end to the kingdom of the house of Israel. And on that day, I will break the bow of Israel in the valley of Jezreel." Familiar words no doubt?'

I sipped the coffee to play for time. This looked as though they had the wrong end of the stick with a vengeance, but did I want to explain to them what the real nature of the project was alleged to have been? The best guess about the reason for the name had been Alec's happy little thought that Jezreel was the valley leading to Armageddon. But I wasn't going to kick that idea around, not here.

'I know the words, but I can honestly say it's the first time I've associated them with the project.'

'But you see our worry – "breaking the bow of Israel"? So we put it on file and worried. We have to worry.'

He took a sip from his mug and looked reflectively behind me.

'You just don't understand how threatened we are, do you? You've seen our army and our airforce, Henry. You think we are powerful, all seeing, all knowing. You see us as the Arabs see us and, as Zvi would say, we want them to see us.'

Zvi nodded in agreement.

181

'We are just three million people; by the year 2000 the population of Egypt alone will be ninety million. Then we have borders with Jordan, Syria and Lebanon as well. We are like a little island surrounded by a vast sea. We are only dimly aware of what is happening in its depths and we live in fear. Every so often something does crawl out and menace us. Car bombs, terrorists with hang gliders, new explosives we cannot detect, longer range missiles, the uprising. So we have always to watch, to peer through the muck for anything that will indicate a new enemy or a new threat. That is why we are here. As you may guess we are close to the Green Line. From this building we can watch and listen to West Beirut.'

Zvi grunted. 'Watch and listen and never act. This is Operation Rooster where we sit on the dung heap and watch. We should act.'

The older man muttered something to Zvi, who simply shrugged, then he turned to me.

'We keep an eye on many people, particularly those who travel from Cyprus to this place, this "dung heap" of my colleague. Particularly we watch for anyone in a hurry, anyone travelling at odd times. Like Europeans travelling on Christmas Day. So one of our people there ran your name through the computer and the lights flashed. And we remembered you. So we rang Lemaire to find what was up, but Lemaire had left and they had a replacement. So we tracked him down and worried him at home on Christmas Day. He wasn't amused, about us or about you. He said we should probably try to talk. He's probably over the Atlantic now on his way to visit. So you see why you are here? We want answers.'

I looked at Tina again. She looked a lot better than before, but was still clearly distressed. It was hard to feel anything but sympathy. I looked at my watch – five o'clock. It was less than twenty-four hours since we had left Cyprus. She caught my glance, returned a faint smile and gave my hand a squeeze. The older man spoke again.

'I should say, Henry, that standard interro... interviewing techniques suggest that we should separate the two of you and ask the questions independently. I am waiving that for a variety of reasons.'

He glanced at Zvi, who pouted. I think the younger man would have gone straight for the thumbscrews if he'd had the chance. I can take a hint as unsubtle as that. Speak, or I'll let Zvi have a chance. So I spoke, trying to radiate honesty, innocence and confidence, with just a dash of naivety. 'Try and look like a cross between Bertie Wooster and Mother Theresa,' Phil Ringwood used to say at checkpoints. Well, I tried.

'Actually, it's a simple matter. An old friend of mine, Fuad Antoine Attiyah, a Lebanese, now with US residency, used to teach with me at St Paul's Evangelical School in Cyprus,' I gestured to the folder, 'and is now missing in north Lebanon.'

The older man wrote the name down and nodded for me to continue. It struck me bizarrely that his pale eyebrows could be described as tufty as well. I thought carefully about what to say next.

'Probably kidnapped by Elias Daoud, so the evidence goes. So, as Fuad is an old friend and as I know one of the few people Elias Daoud still talks to, I volunteered to come over and to try and sort it out. That is my only interest. Whether it has anything to do with a so-called Jezreel Project I do not know. You should talk to Elweth about that. But I can say this: nothing I have ever heard about that project poses any threat to the State of Israel. You have my word on it.'

Zvi snorted. 'Big deal. We risk our necks on the basis of your word.'

There was something that might have been a sigh from the older man. I thought through cautiously what I was going to say next.

'Anyway, I ought to remind you that the single source for the word "Jezreel" is what one man said to me, under difficult circumstances in Madagascar. You may be putting far

183

too much weight on it.'

That too was true. Lemaire had never tracked it down, Elweth had made no mention of it and Nickie had effectively denied all knowledge of the name.

Zvi spoke quickly, 'We judge that. So you believe Daoud is kidnapping now? That would be new. I thought he was getting fat on heroin, hashish and smuggling. But let me tell you, in the dung heap Elias is a very small worm.' He stopped and muttered something in Hebrew. The older man seemed to give him a single word reply with some reluctance. 'No, not a worm, a maggot I'm told. A worm is useful.'

Another fine character reference for Elias Daoud, I thought. There soon won't be an animal group left that they haven't used to describe him. Then there was some dialogue between the two men in Hebrew. It concluded with the older man turning to Tina.

'That is all there is? A simple kidnapping? By Elias Daoud?' She looked straight at him. 'I'm hardly going to contradict my husband when he's telling the truth. Yes, we think so, although I gather that there is no signed ransom note from him yet.'

The voice was tonally flat, but sounded alert. There was even a hint of exasperation in it. The older man turned to me.

'And Jezreel is just the name of this project? There is no link with Daoud?'

This was a nasty one. Putting these people onto Daoud would ruin any chance Fuad had. Then I had a glimmering of a strategy.

'As to the first part you'd better ask Elweth. He's the man responsible and also he knows what you should and shouldn't know.'

'You mean you know more, but you aren't telling?'

'A little, but nothing of relevance to your security, as I said. But I made promises to Elweth and I don't wish to reveal anything more that he may have told me. I don't know whether you have the right to know.'

Zvi shook his head in annoyance. The older man continued quietly.

'Very well. And the second part. Is there a link between Jezreel and Elias Daoud?'

'I am not certain. I refuse to say any more because it is a breach of confidence with Jim Elweth and it may damage the chances of getting my friend free.'

'I see. Excuse me.'

Then he got up and motioned Zvi to the door where there was some discussion. I breathed a sigh of partial relief. Then the old man came back and sat down and Zvi disappeared behind the other door.

'We have possibly overlooked our friend Elias. I have a recollection that in our index it says, "Daoud, Elias; see under Franjieh." Zvi's view of him being a rather small maggot is a cruel exaggeration of that viewpoint. More a jellyfish in a pool of sharks. So Zvi is going to call up head office and ask for some details. He will also check if there has been such a kidnapping reported.'

He settled himself down in his seat and began to wipe his glasses with a clean handkerchief. His pale eyes turned to Tina.

'How are you doing, Mrs Stanwick; Tina, isn't it?'

'I'll survive.' There was a pause. 'But thank you for asking.'

'Sorry, it's a bloody business. Is it a stupid question to ask you what you think of Beirut?'

Something approaching a smile crossed Tina's face. The first for several hours. 'No, but it would be stupid of you to attach any importance to my answer. I've only been here for a few hours.'

Good for you, I thought. Show him you're on top of it all. Then I thought of something else.

'You say you found out about us two days ago, presumably when we booked the tickets and got the paperwork done. But someone was making enquiries about us earlier in Cyprus. Wasn't that you?'

185

There was a flash of unease on his face and I realised I'd asked the wrong question.

'Not to my knowledge and we keep good records. We have too few intelligence agents to be able to afford needless duplication or risk them shooting each other. Tell me about it.'

So choosing my words and trying to play the whole thing down I mentioned the phone call about Andy and the visitor who had asked Costas about us. I concluded that eventually we had thought that they were probably Daoud's men.

There was a moment of silence. 'Just so. I would watch your step. You think Zvi's thugs were bad, his are worse. Be warned – even jellyfish can kill. He has a linkman, a business manager in Cyprus. So he could have done it. He ships everything he wants from there to Ras el Bourj, a sort of mail order scheme. It avoids him having to go to Tripoli or Jounieh where his life would not be safe.'

For a few minutes none of us said anything. Then suddenly there was a dull, heavy ringing thud that seemed to vibrate the floor and the walls. Tina grabbed my hand and turned to me. The Israeli spoke.

'They are starting early tonight. We are very close to the Green Line. We hear everything.'

He caught Tina's look. 'It's nothing; just rhetorical artillery. That was probably only a mortar round. This is the theatre of the absurd.'

He shook his head and looked at me. I realised he must be near retirement. I wondered how many years he'd fought for his country and what he'd done, or whether he'd volunteered, to end up in this hole with Zvi on the edge of a war zone just counting shells. He stared down at the desk and started to try and score a line in it with a finger nail. He spoke quietly and reflectively, half to us – half to himself.

'The futility of it all – not just what they do, but what we do. The whole thing is depressing. Infinitely depressing. The mess is just out of control. They started this with knives and shotguns, now they have tanks and rockets. And I

186

know, Henry, before you say it, that we armed both sides at different times. We've tried controlling it; the Syrians have tried. We have both failed. But they are better at it than us. Those that shout "Sabra and Chatila" at us don't shout "Hama" at the Syrians.'

He fixed his sad eyes on me. 'Probably only people like you even know where Hama is.'

'A town in Syria where Assad killed thousands of his own people in putting down a rebellion.'

He shrugged his shoulders slightly. 'But you see that depresses me. We were supposed to be "a light to lighten the Gentiles" and we end up defending ourselves by saying we are no worse than our lousy neighbours. For this we fight? I have lived, and I may yet die, in the battle for the security of the State of Israel and the ideals of the Jewish people.'

He looked briefly over his shoulder and sighed.

'People like Zvi worry me. I'll be honest and I'm too old and too honoured to care and he knows it. Besides, I'm due to retire within a few months. For him, security has become an end in itself; he says we must survive at any cost. But that is the spirit that leads to making pacts with the devil. Will the land that Zvi gives to his children be the State of Israel our fathers dreamed of? Hetzl and the other Fathers dreamed of a garden, but it has turned into a fortress.'

There was silence. There was something pathetic about this man's words. It crossed my mind that it was just an act to elicit sympathy and squeeze me further. Then I regretted having thought it because he seemed so genuine. I tried to formulate an answer. 'If you mean that, and I believe you do, then I have a very great sympathy with you.'

He nodded quietly. 'Thank you.'

It was almost a peace treaty.

Then the door opened and Zvi came in carrying a couple of sheets of paper with him. The older man got up and went over to the door where they looked at them and muttered together. There was another echoing thud and Tina gave a little jump. Then the two of them came back to the table and the older man looked at first one, and then the other, of us.

'We have confirmed that Fuad Antoine Attiyah is reported missing just north of Batroun, so that bit matches.'

He looked at the fax and screwed his face up. 'But something is odd about Elias Daoud's operation. I think we have overlooked him for too long. These faxes come from different branches of our operation. One report says that contrary to general opinion he is not that big a dealer in drugs. Another lists some of the things he has been importing through Ras el Bourj, and they indicate a lot of money. A third, from the air photo people, points out he has been engaged in building projects at a monastery, a hotel and a hospital. Things don't add up. It could be he is just shipping these things through to the Syrians over the ridge. But why?'

He sat down and talked to Zvi for a moment and the younger man bent over the list following his finger and giving what appeared to be a negative all the way down. On one or two they looked at each other. After a minute the older man turned to us.

'This is a list of a shipment we intercepted nearly two years ago. We thought it might be arms for Tripoli. It wasn't. It was all medical supplies and we looked stupid and forgot about it. But...it doesn't fit. Somehow.'

He looked at Zvi, who shrugged. Then the older man seemed to think of something. He picked up the folder that had my details in and ran down it with a finger. This man was clearly no fool and I wondered what he was going to produce. What he did come up with caught me by surprise. He turned to Tina.

'Ah, perhaps you can help us. You work in hospital administration. The list is in English, copied from the cargo manifest I suppose, with a Hebrew translation. But some of these names mean nothing to me in either language. For example, what are "autoclaves"?'

We must be truly married, I thought; she's made it into my folder. Tina stirred.

'They are for the heat sterilisation of surgical equipment, glassware, anything that might be contaminated by bacteria or viruses. Any hospital would have them.'

The older man looked at her a moment and then nodded. Then he ran a finger down the list and spoke again. 'Lots of chemicals, a chromatography outfit; Elias must be paranoid about his health, but I suppose he would be dead on arrival by the time he got to Jounieh. They'd see to that. Yes, here Tina, I quote, "equipment for setting up a negative pressure ventilation system". Very helpful. What is that?'

I agreed, it didn't mean anything to me. There was a further rumbling nearby. I hoped we weren't going to get stuck here – staying overnight would be awful. Tina thought for a few seconds.

'It's a system where you have a laboratory under reduced air pressure. You have them in university labs or hospitals where you are dealing with pathogens or biohazards. If there is a leakage, then nothing escapes because the air flows in, not out. It's pretty specialised.'

I suddenly stopped worrying about whether I could stand sleeping in this room and realised what she was saying. A glance at their faces showed that they were hanging on every word as well.

'What is a biohazard?'

'Something like a bacteria or a virus, something especially dangerous to man. Such as....'

But she tailed off because they weren't listening. They were looking at each other and the older man's face was the colour of clay and had on it such an expression of fear and horror that I felt the hairs on the back of my neck rise. He looked as if he was reliving the worst nightmare of his life.

Without a word they got up and walked over away from the table to near the door. There they talked. And the talking was very different from what had passed between them before. I couldn't understand a word, of course, but they had the earnestness and concentration normally attributed to condemned men.

I turned to Tina. Her face was pale.

'I'm afraid we may have made the job of getting Fuad out a lot more difficult. You realise what is worrying them?'

She looked puzzled and ran her fingers through her hair. 'No, not really. I gave a straight answer. I don't understand.' Then a sort of light appeared to dawn and her lips quivered.

'I see. Oh dear. I'm sorry, I'm just not myself. You mean that they are worried that Elias or someone could be deliberately producing harmful bacteria or viruses? Biological weapons? That would be a scary thought.'

Zvi left through the back door. The older man came over and spoke to me. His face had no colour in it at all and his voice was full of fear and uncertainty.

'I think as you realise, something your wife said has opened a possibility for us. A possibility that, in all its implications, I would prefer not to think about, but it is my job to do so. There will be a lot of work done on this. Hopefully we are wrong.'

He sat down and put his head in his hands, almost as in despair. Then he shook himself as if trying to shake off a memory and lifted his head up. He stared at me.

'I have decided that we are finished with you. Zvi is going to get you taken back to where you are staying. With our own people. It is something of a breaking of rules. You will find it of no advantage to tell anyone where you have been. We will have to get in touch with you again, probably at the pastor's house. In order to avoid the unpleasantness of the pickup today, please leave a note or a message to... shall we say "John"?, about where you are going. Whatever you do, don't go up to Farayoun or warn anybody there before talking to either us or Jim Elweth.'

He paused and sighed deeply.

'Let me spell it out to you. These supplies may be normal. Maybe Elias has taken up microbiology for a hobby. Or they may indicate what we have always dreaded. Even in that case we may be able to solve the problem speedily and quickly. Even without bloodshed. But if in that case – God forbid – Elias panics and tries to move things....'

He swallowed hard. 'Elias is ten minutes' drive from the Syrians. He is half an hour from the Palestinian camps at Tripoli. He is an hour from Hizbollah at Baalbek. If he moves these things out before we can destroy them neatly, then we will have to do terrible things to stop them. Very terrible things. Things more terrible than all our wars put together. I shall say no more.'

Zvi came back in and nodded in affirmation of something to the older man, then went and opened the door to the garage and disappeared from view.

'Zvi is going to open the van up. If you could go down, get in and let him close the door. Then the driver and his companion will take over. When you get out, do not look at the driver. Just get straight out, close the door and look ahead. That is my condition.'

He paused and I looked at him again. He seemed to have aged. Then he continued, 'One final question. What do you think, Henry? Have we just become paranoid?'

I thought hard, still wary of being trapped. 'I think you are wrong and I think what is being done presents no danger, but I have to admit that I know little and that I could be badly mistaken. I think you may be right to keep your powder dry, but please, don't fire until you are certain that it is what you fear.'

He stood up slowly and stiffly. 'Thank you, I will try to remember your words, but this is now outside of my control. The message went with the very highest priority. They will be meeting in the Defence Ministry within minutes. Good luck in getting the young man out.'

There was an awkward pause while we wondered whether to shake hands. Then there was a whistle from below.

'Goodbye, Henry and Tina.'

'Goodbye,' I said.

Then I felt I ought to say something else because I respected this man, although I would never be on the same

191

side of the wire with him.

'I wish you a long and peaceful retirement. And *shalom*.'

He gave what seemed a solemn bow of his head and spoke quietly.

'Thank you. *Shalom* for us all.'

Half an hour later the side door of the van was thrown open to allow us out by Antoine's block of flats. It was dark, but at least the electricity now worked. Antoine almost wept as he hugged us, but I couldn't help noticing that as he gathered us into his room there was a brief, forlorn look for a third behind us. Finally he spoke.

'It has been a terrible couple of hours. The neighbours told me you had been taken. Elie was apologetic and blamed Eduard. I just prayed. There was nothing else to do.'

I sat down in the chair and Tina next to me. I had to break him the news.

'Antoine, what can I say? Thank you for your prayers. We've had an awful afternoon and, I'm sorry to say, we are no nearer to getting your son out.'

Tina went to bed shortly afterwards, having just taken a bowl of soup and some bread. I soon joined her. In the distance there were episodic noises from the Green Line, but they sounded fairly harmless. Before she fell into sleep, Tina turned to me and spoke in a tired but worried voice.

'Have we really made it worse for poor Fuad?'

'I'm afraid so. If the people we met check with anyone who knows the hospital – and they will – they will find out that that equipment is not there and never will be. I suspect, too, they will find that those chemicals will be over and above anything other than a research hospital would use. When they do that I think we are looking at a very brief period before they find exactly where the equipment is and destroy it utterly.'

She looked really miserable. 'And Tina, when they do that I want us and Fuad to be well clear.'

23

Despite the fears and traumas of the day and the distant noises of half-hearted war, I slept well and woke to hear Antoine moving about in the kitchen. Tina lay sleeping deeply while I washed and shaved, but woke slowly as I dressed. I sat on the edge of the bed to see how she was. She opened her eyes, reached out a hand and held mine.

'I suppose this is still Lebanon, isn't it? I had the most horrible dream last night. I dreamed I was in Beirut and was leered at and assaulted by rough men with guns. Now I've woken up it's all true. Still, I feel better for the sleep.'

I kissed her, greatly relieved. I'd half-expected her to be screaming for the next boat out.

'Extraordinary dream, Tina; can't think what brought it to mind. Anyway, better get up, we've got things to do. It's a thick pullover morning this morning. At least for a bit. You know, Tina, with a stroke of good fortune or two we should be up in Farayoun tonight. Or even....'

Tina sat up in bed, hair dishevelled, but still as pretty as they come.

'Or even what, my dear?'

'Actually, it's wishful thinking. Well, it's just two hours' drive to Farayoun, we might even be back here. But that's too hopeful; this is Lebanon. In the meantime, why don't you get a bath if Antoine can spare the water? Then we'll have breakfast.'

I went into the kitchen and caught Antoine unawares, sitting at the remains of a frugal breakfast and sipping at coffee and reading an Arabic New Testament. He stared at me for a moment and I had a vision of a tired face etched with lines, the face of a man under a great burden. Then his expression changed and he smiled and we exchanged greetings in Arabic before lapsing into English.

'Your wife – how is she?'

'Seems fine. She's able to joke about yesterday.'

'That's encouraging, although these things go in phases. If we can avoid any further stress....'

'Then, Antoine, we'll be very lucky. Anyway, have you got water for a shower or a bath for her? I think that would help. She was too tired to take one last night.'

'I'll put the heater on for her. But it will take half an hour at least for warm water. Maybe in the meantime you'd both better come in and have breakfast and we can talk.'

So I went and had a word with Tina, who dressed and came through to the kitchen where I introduced her to the breakfast of flat bread, cheese, olives, jam and labneh, the mainstay of much Lebanese cuisine that lies midway between cream, yoghurt and soft white cheese.

Antoine seemed quiet over breakfast and said little. Towards the end he spoke quietly. 'I have a favour to ask. I wonder if you would both pray for me about something?'

I looked at Tina and then back at Antoine. 'But of course; what?'

He seemed awkward. 'It is this. It is that even if we get Fuad back I will have the courage to stay here.'

'I see,' I said after a moment of silence.

'Yes, I'm afraid the temptation is very strong, Henry, just to leave. To take the ferry out to Cyprus.'

He stared at the kitchen cupboards.

'It's not fear. Well, not just that. It's a draining of the will as well. The thousand little battles against corruption, hatred, prejudice and superstition. And despair. We get good men in the church, and I feel there is hope for the future. Then they decide to go to America. And who can blame them? My church in California wants me back. Everyone here would understand. I've served my time and this incident with Fuad, however it ends.... It would be

194

seen as the reason.'

I said nothing. After a moment he continued.

'And at times I too am scared and I ask to be let out, to be relieved of this duty.' Here he glanced at Tina who, catching his look, suddenly found her plate of interest. 'But I know I am to stay until I get further orders. But it is still a temptation and the past few days have made it worse than ever. So I ask you to pray for me. I can hardly share it with my people, can I?'

Tina spoke first. 'Antoine, we will pray that you are strengthened.' I agreed, wondering as I did so how I could have assumed that he could stay here without a struggle.

'Thank you both. Thank you.'

Something of the weight hanging on him seemed to have gone. He smiled faintly and spoke again.

'And now to business, I suppose. What are your plans Henry?'

'Well, Antoine, I'm going to try and call Charles Rimmer again. Hopefully this time I can get through. I've got to talk to him.'

Antoine nodded. I didn't pursue the possibility, in fact the probability, that I wouldn't be able to get through to him. I tried to change the subject.

'Is there anybody else I should see or talk to?'

Antoine scratched his pointed chin in a thoughtful manner.

'I think your friend is a key man. There is one other person I was hoping to hear from. Perhaps you know him? Ghassan Halibi – he is a doctor at the American University Hospital.'

'Sorry, the name means little. No, wait a minute. Syrian?'

He nodded in his economical way. I knew who he meant.

'Yes, then. But not well. Big fellow, met him in Damascus at one of the churches. From Homs, but he's not stupid.'

195

Tina looked puzzled and Antoine, seeing her expression, gave a faint smile. 'Homs is a Syrian town just north-east of Lebanon. The Homsies are allegedly the most stupid people in Syria.'

'I see. I've learned something useful already today.'

'Antoine, how do you know him?'

'I met him in '84 a couple of times in West Beirut before it got really a bit too difficult to go over. Of course he can't come here. Since then we have kept in touch and we met in Cyprus recently at a conference. We have a few things in common. He has decided to stay in the area rather than go to the States. So we are both rare creatures.'

'Has he done his military service yet?' I caught Tina's eye. 'That's three years of your life. It's compulsory. They send you to the desert in summer or to the mountains in winter. It's pretty tough.'

Antoine spoke again, 'No, he hasn't. But apparently he is going to do it. The amazing thing is that his father is a Colonel in the army. They want no strings pulled to get an exemption. The father is an elder in one of the Damascus churches, incidentally.'

Tina looked like she'd misheard and looked at me. I wasn't surprised at the response.

'Well, my wife, why shouldn't he be an officer in the Syrian army? By all accounts he's not on his own either.'

She swallowed a fragment of bread. 'I suppose you're right. It had never occurred to me, that's all. It must be tough reading about Israel in the Old Testament and then having to be prepared to fight a modern state under the same name. But then they are by no means the same thing. Is anything simple here?'

I shrugged and Antoine smiled gently.

'It would be nice if it was all black and white. But it's not. Anyway, Ghassan was going to ask his father to see if the Syrians in the north knew anything about... about our problem. But I suspect from what you say that he will have no information.'

He paused for a minute and seemed to be thinking of something else.

'Fuad wanted to be a doctor, but the competition was so strong that he didn't make it. Perhaps Tina doesn't realise that every boy here wants to be either a doctor or an engineer. I suppose almost every Arab biology teacher is a frustrated doctor. In fact Lena and I wanted him to go into the ministry, but it would not have been right to force him. He would always say, "Not yet, maybe later." Well maybe if....'

He broke off suddenly under some deep emotion and forced a feeble smile. Tina did the only thing that could be done and reached out and held his veined, thin hand. Then he brightened. It seemed as if sorrow and gloom had no lasting hold on this man, but passed over like fleeting clouds.

'I'm sorry. On occasions it gets on top of me.'

After breakfast Tina disappeared to have her bath and I moved a chair into the sun and picked up the phone. There was no line. I kept waiting and listening, endlessly rehearsing the number in my mind and the words I was going to say to Charlie Rimmer. After ten minutes I began to despair. It was already half-past eight. If I couldn't get a line now it was going to be impossible when the shops and offices got going. It was useless, there was nothing but an empty crackly silence. What was I going to do?

The doorbell rang and Antoine answered it. It was a small elderly Lebanese woman, well dressed in black and with her hair elegantly set. She seemed slightly out of breath. I nodded as politely as I could and turned away to concentrate on the distant crackle on the phone. I was vaguely conscious of Antoine moving onto the balcony with the woman. Then he came over and tapped me on the shoulder. I looked up and his face was serious. I put the phone down quickly.

'Henry, this is Mrs Salibi from the Khoury building opposite. Let me introduce you.'

We made the introductions in Arabic and she started to ask whether I knew Brighton where her sister was.

Antoine interrupted gently. 'Mrs Salibi was in George's shop opposite, just below her apartment, and two men came in and asked for the pastor's flat.'

I made the mistake of asking her in Arabic whether this was true, thereby getting a very much longer account. I was only listening with a limited attention as I was still worried about how to reach Charlie Rimmer. I couldn't understand why Antoine had seemed to find her story so important.

'...then they said, "And the English couple are staying with him?" Well, I was surprised. You had only been here since yesterday....'

I suddenly had a feeling it would repay me to take an interest in the conversation and to start preparing for the worst.

'Excuse me, Madame.'

I turned to Antoine who was hovering nervously nearby. 'Tell Tina to get out of the bath and dressed as quickly as she can. Please. Without alarming her unduly, tell her it's life or death.'

Antoine nodded in agreement and moved quickly towards the bathroom.

'Continue please, Madame. Then what did they do?'

'They went to their car and are sitting there with a newspaper. I didn't see which paper it....'

'The car, what sort of car is it?'

'A blue fast one, a BMW I think. My son-in-law in Jounieh has one like it... he drives too fast....'

'The men, where are they from?'

'Well not from round here, of course, or I would know them, and anyway they would know the pastor's apartment, although why he should have chosen to live five floors up....'

'What part of Lebanon?'

'The north, Tripoli perhaps. The son of my neighbour has a wife from Tripoli and she speaks like that....'

198

'Are they armed, do you think?'

'That sort of young man always is these days. Even Pierre, the son of my sister Marie, the one who lives in Bikfaya, not Brighton....'

'Thank you, Mrs Salibi, you have been very helpful.'

Antoine had come back into the room and I saw him walk over to the balcony and look down on the road before retreating with a plant. He came over to me.

'They are still in the car. Some youths from the party are putting up posters on the walls below. Maybe they are waiting for them to go. Mrs Salibi thinks we should call the militia.'

I thought hard. 'No, I think not. I'm fairly certain these are Daoud's men. I was warned to expect them. So we have a few minutes yet.'

Tina came in with her hair in a towel, but at least she was dressed. Poor girl. I wasted a few seconds thinking about my track record. For the ultimate in adventure tours marry a Stanwick; go to strange exotic parts of the world and be chased by a selection of thugs at the most inconvenient moments. Then I switched back to the real problem.

'Tina, Daoud's people are outside. We're going to go visit Charles Rimmer. Maybe see Ghassan too.'

She just closed her eyes briefly and turned and ran back into the bedroom. If it had been to bury her head under the pillow I couldn't have blamed her. But we had to get out.

'Antoine, do you know the people on the ground floor?'

'The Chehabs, yes moderately. The husband is abroad. Why?'

'If we went downstairs with you do you think we could leave by a back window or door?'

He thought hard. 'Probably; that might work, if....'

Tina came back in. I'd misjudged her. Her hair was still wet, but she was carrying her handbag. I caught her arm.

'Great. You've got your passport? OK, grab a coat. We're off.'

I tried to think ahead.

'Antoine, if someone calling himself John turns up tell him we are in Ain Mreisse talking to Rimmer. We'll be back as soon as we can. Hopefully by tonight.'

We moved towards the door. I grabbed my anorak and checked for my passport and car key. Then I caught sight of Mrs Salibi who was looking at Tina, so I made the introduction as we were leaving through the door. They assume the British are rude anyway, so I probably just confirmed a stereotype.

'Oh, Mrs Salibi, my wife; Tina, Mrs Salibi. Bless you, Mrs Salibi. *Toujours la politesse.*'

'Now silence.' It was Antoine.

We descended the enclosed staircase as quietly as we could. I tried not to think about what would happen if we saw the men entering the stairwell below. We tiptoed down as fast as possible, but the steps seemed to stretch out for ever. Finally we were on the ground floor.

Antoine knocked on the door. I was sure they could hear it across the street, but there were a lot of other noises around. After a few moments there was the sound of feet shuffling towards the door and a voice cried.

'Who is it?'

'Pastor Antoine, Madame Chehab; there is something very important. Can I see you? Now.'

'OK, one minute.'

So we waited for long seconds in the open stairway just twenty yards from the men. Then there was the sound of the turning of keys, the drawing of bolts and the slipping of chains and at last the door cautiously opened. For once Antoine dispensed with his usual courtesy, got a foot in the gap, and pushed it open.

'Excuse me, Madame, this is an emergency.'

I made for the kitchen. Tina followed, with Antoine closing the door behind him and explaining as quickly as he could to a perturbed late middle-aged lady with a lined, sagging face. I had a brief impression of a fussy, over-crowded room with a glass chandelier, vases of plastic

200

flowers, a synthetic Madonna, a calendar with a bad drawing of St Maroun on it, a large, appalling 'Last Supper'
dominated by iridescent reds and purples surrounded by a
baroque gilt frame and, carefully positioned on every one
of the four ornamented chests-of-drawers, large numbers
of small decorated boxes of various styles. I was thinking
rude things about Lebanese aesthetic tastes when I entered
the kitchen.

If Mrs Chehab had known what I was thinking she
couldn't have got a nastier revenge. The window was barred from side to side and the glass panelled kitchen door
had a steel grid of extreme functionality over it. It was
held in place by a formidable padlock. I pulled at the lock,
but it didn't move a fraction. I turned on my heels and
almost collided with Tina as I ran back into the living
room.

'The key, Antoine, the key to the kitchen door! Where
does she keep the key?'

He blinked and began the translation. I wondered if
there was room under the sofa. Mrs Chehab beamed mildly
at me.

'The kitchen door key, is it that you want? It's the times.
The security situation. I keep it locked. Certainly I keep it
in one of those boxes. That one, no, not that. But which
one? Perhaps it is in the bedroom?'

I tried to keep myself calm. It was not easy.

'Antoine, check through the window carefully. Please.'

I looked around. At a glance there were over two dozen
small jewellery boxes and caskets.

Then Antoine spoke in a whisper, 'Henry, they are coming over. I think they are armed.'

I tried to concentrate. No point in panicking. I tiptoed to
the door and waved him and Tina over to follow. I peered
through the inevitable security viewer to catch a glimpse of
the two pass by up the stairs.

'Antoine, in a few moments Tina and I will slip out.
Hopefully they will not see us. Call the militia afterwards

by all means. We don't want these people around when we return.'

I turned to Tina; her hair was still wet. 'We are going to tiptoe out. Avoid the stairwell. Then we walk as fast as we can to the car.'

She nodded hesitantly. I opened the door inch by inch waiting for the chains to rattle. Heavy footsteps could be heard going slowly upstairs. There probably isn't a single fire escape in the whole of Lebanon so they must have felt fairly certain that we were trapped. Then I gestured to Tina and slipped out and tiptoed to the foot of the steps. There was the whisper of Antoine's voice.

'God be with you.'

He'd better be, I thought. Then we were out of the doorway and along the street. I could hear Tina just behind. There was no shout, no firing and we walked rapidly along the road trying to avoid the rubbish, the holes and the parked cars. I didn't look back. Then we were at the corner and the car was visible a few yards away.

There I made the mistake. I turned and looked at the block of flats. There was a head and shoulders at the small window at the top of the stairs and as I watched an arm came out and pointed at us.

'We've been seen. Now run if you can.'

I reached the car first and pulled out the keys. Which one was it? For once I got the right one first time. I slid in, sat down and slammed the door closed and let Tina in on the other side. As I turned the ignition I realised I was hemmed in tightly both front and back by other parked cars. There appeared no way to get the car out.

I looked around, noting with some relief that there was no one close at hand. Then I backed the car until it firmly hit the bumper of the one behind. That car didn't move. I turned the steering to full lock and went forward till I hit the car in front. This rolled away a few inches. It was a gratifying feeling. I reversed the lock and repeated the procedure. The second time the car in front rolled forward a few more inches

202

and I was able to pull free and we headed off down the road.

A small voice beside me said, 'That's not in the Highway Code.'

I tried to grin. 'If you say things like that I'll begin to think you're enjoying it.'

'With wet hair?'

Then we drove into a busy street and I decided to turn right. I weighed up all the alternatives. I could hammer the horn and drive like mad, but that might lead me straight into being stopped by someone with a gun. Far better to try and get lost in the traffic.

'Put your seat belt on if it works and then keep an eye open for a blue BMW with two men in leather coats inside.'

'OK. Why don't you pull into a militia office?'

'I thought of that. They might be made a higher offer by Daoud's men. A thousand dollars and a crate of beer for each of us. No, we're off to West Beirut. I've put it off, but we need Rimmer and we may be safer there.'

A junction loomed ahead. I made a quick decision and turned left down the hill towards the river and the dual carriageway that leads into West Beirut. At least it used to. I just hoped that it wasn't being dug up or had been cratered beyond repair. The traffic seemed to thicken, but at least it was still flowing. Progress wasn't helped by the fact that Beirutis habitually drive as though they are being chased by armed men. Still, it did mean that we blended in with the crowd. I weaved in and out of the traffic using the horn liberally.

'Don't they object to you using the horn?'

Typical of Tina, I thought. Here we are being chased by armed men and she is concerned about making unnecessary noise.

'No, why should they? As they don't use a rear view mirror, they wouldn't know you were there otherwise. It's the accepted convention to let them know you are coming.'

Then we were down to the dual carriageway and I began to breathe a sigh of relief. Suddenly Tina spoke and her tone of voice said it all.

'Oh, they're behind.'

I glanced in my mirror. I could see them filtering in off another road. They must have outguessed me.

'Keep telling me how many cars behind they are. We have only a mile to the museum. That's the last turn off. Beyond that we have at least one checkpoint on this side, then the Green Line and then the Syrians. I don't think they will follow us beyond the last turn off. How far are they away?'

'Eight cars.'

I took a risk and accelerated on the inside of the lorry ahead; for a moment I had one wheel on the road and one off into the dirt and debris. Then it was back onto the tarmac as I got back in, just in front of the lorry.

'Still eight.'

I tried to overtake an old Renault ahead, but suddenly a massive pothole loomed so I had to pull back in.

'Seven.'

Traffic was peeling off to go up to Hotel Dieu and I realised I was too close inside. I pulled out, but our lane was slowing.

'Seven, now six. He's gaining.'

The road was starting the final swing up towards the big junction at the museum; we would be there in a minute. But the surface was deteriorating as we approached the Green Line. Every few yards there was a crater in the road, mostly only a few centimetres in diameter and the larger ones were generally filled. But then I had to swerve to avoid one that could have taken off a wheel. Everything – buildings, lamp posts, signs – began to show bullet holes to the extent that in places it appeared as if they were just crumbling away.

'Five. Oh, they're going fast, three.'

In front of me two old Mercedes seemed to be invisibly tied side to side. Together they totally blocked any possibility of going any faster.

'Two. Henry, he's waving us in to the side.'

I could now see the old museum ahead, with its sandbags

and the peppered colonnades. It was now perhaps only 200 yards, but the traffic ahead appeared to be solidifying. The blue BMW was now just a car's length behind.

'Let me know if he starts waving any weaponry about.'

At least these days there's not much temptation to try to duck below the car window. Most things used in Beirut are supposed to be able to go through anything short of an engine block. Then as I watched in the rear view mirror he roared out wide and overtook the man behind. He was now alongside.

'Pointing a gun and waving.'

She sounded as scared as I'd ever heard her, but it hadn't stopped her doing what I'd asked. The junction was coming up, and ahead I could see traffic crossing our road. The last road off before the checkpoints was just over a hundred yards away. If he was going to force us off the main road he'd do it here.

'Hold on, Tina, just a few yards. He may try to ram us.'

I tried to keep my voice flat. I mean there's not much point in panicking, is there?

The road was a mess here, torn, ripped and pitted. Then as I expected he pulled ahead slightly and began to edge over in front of us. I glanced in my mirror. I had a space behind.

I touched the brakes gently. As we fell behind, the BMW swerved across to come directly in front of us and began to slow. A hundred yards to the junction. I could feel my heart pounding.

'Now let me puzzle him.'

It sounded calmer than it had any right to. I turned on the indicators to show we were turning off onto the side road. They seemed to work. Ahead, the passenger spoke to the driver and they began to drift slightly towards the side road. My hands were clammy with sweat on the steering wheel.

I changed down, glanced over my shoulder and decided there was just enough space if I timed it right.

'Hang on tight.'

Now! I stabbed the accelerator pedal down to the floor. I

almost overdid it, and with tyres spinning wildly, slewed out. As we shot past them on the outside I regained full control. The driver realised too late what was happening and swung out to ram us, but by then we were past him. Then the traffic was crossing ahead of us and I was just able to get through a gap between a school bus and a lorry. Behind there was a squeal of brakes.

Tina was staring back down the road. She didn't say anything for a moment and when she did speak it was with a voice full of suppressed emotion.

'Henry, they've turned off.'

Breathing heavily and saying a deeply felt mental prayer of thanks I slowed down trying to pretend to be just any other Lebanese driver. As we rolled towards the final Lebanese Forces checkpoint, Tina spoke again.

'I hope you realise how much better I feel knowing that we are now going to make it safely into West Beirut.'

24

The militiaman waved us through from his sandbagged post. We drove along past the temporary Parliament building and, almost as irrelevant, a Lebanese Army checkpoint. Again we were waved forward. Forward into the line.

In its own macabre way the Green Line is one of the world's most awesome places. Technically, dryly, geographically, it is simply the no man's land between East and West Beirut, where the militias face each other and give episodic, and futile, battle. But it is more than that. It has a life and a potency of its own. It is a river of desolation, a stream of anarchy, that flows northwards down from the hills beyond the airport through Beirut to the sea, gradually broadening as it flows. At the port where it debouches into the sea with its rusting half sunken ships, it is fully two miles wide, but crossing it by car on a warm day, waiting for the crack of the sniper's rifle, it can feel like for ever. Indeed, for many, eternity begins on it.

The banks of the Green Line are not as fixed as men would like, and without warning the stream of disintegration will suddenly overflow, now to the East and up the hill into Achrafiyieh; now westwards into Zarif or Basta. As it over-flows it empties streets of people and forces those remaining behind doors and into cellars. When the Line retreats (if it ever does) it leaves behind a flotsam of smoking cars, broken windows and shapeless corpses. In 1982, for a brief spell, the Line all but dried up and people were able to promenade again in the Martyrs' Square or ogle at the disintegrated cafés and shops of the Rue de Damas. Then it began to flow again.

As befits this tributary of the Styx, crossing points have been limited since the river began to flow. Each turbulent ford, each precarious bridge has, or had (for some are long swept away) its own protocols, hazards and names; names unwritten on any map, but scored on many minds and graves: 'The Port', 'Fouad Chebab', 'Sodeco', 'The Museum' and 'Galerie Semaan'.

During the day the Line, away from the crossing points, is quiet and sleepy, especially in the long hot humid summer, and lizards scuttle over spent cartridge cases. The grass grows long where fractured pipes ooze water or sewage to the surface. Now young trees grow through holes in roofs and catch the sun in this most parkless of cities. Perhaps some day the Line will live up to its name. But in the dark-ness of the slits of each fortified emplacement men watch each other in perfect, unsleeping symmetry. Towards even-ing, as the broken shadows of the Green Line thicken, merge and flow along the channels of pitted buildings, there is a stirring of life. Cigarettes are lit behind walls, weapons are cleaned and cocked and eyes strain in the darkness. Then without warning the silence is ruptured by the bullet, the mortar round or the rocket-propelled grenade and the Martyrs on their statue are pierced again.

Then those beyond the banks, the sandbagged levees, lie awake and wonder whether tonight will be the night that the river of dissolution will overflow their house and their Ali or their Mary.

And some dream more darkly that one day the Green Line will overflow the world.

This time, the line was quiet and nothing but rubbish stirred along the road beside the old race track. Which was just as well because the traffic just stopped completely when we were in the middle. I pointed out a few things to Tina.

'With our friends from the south last night we were probably down to the right somewhere. I'd guess at the base of one of the old tower blocks. It makes sense. They can sit and watch West Beirut and monitor the phone lines and the radios. They probably never relinquished the post from 1982.'

'It smelled as though that was when it was last cleaned. Incidentally, I wanted to ask you, Henry. Do you think the old man has any reason to be worried about what the group is up to?'

We inched forward.

'No, I wasn't lying to him. Not at all. I think they have just put two and two together and made five. All of that stuff could be explained if Nickie or someone else was fiddling around with algae. But I wasn't going to explain to them what I'd been told by her.'

The gold-toothed Syrian soldier at the first checkpoint into West Beirut seemed to be uneasy about us. He checked our papers again and asked a superior officer before he gave us the go ahead.

'But slowly, slowly.'

I had been prepared for the change, but it still caught me off guard. The last few years had altered West Beirut far more than I could have imagined. Graffiti in Arabic in praise of Allah and Amal were everywhere as were posters of Khomeinei, Musa Sadr and Koranic verses. Headscarves on the women and the chequered keffiyah headdresses on the men were widespread. I wondered how long you'd last with either in East Beirut. Probably minutes.

The decay since I'd last been there was depressing. Cars were older, everything was shabbier and more squalid. The cats looked like they were having a hard time. I glimpsed what I was sure was a rat on one rubbish pile. It was dispiriting. Parts of Damascus aren't wonderful, but then they never were very good. These streets had once been like those of any crowded Mediterranean city of France or Italy. Now they looked like Cairo at its worst.

'Just look ahead. Don't catch anyone's eye.'

I turned carefully down a narrow road to Mousaitbe. There were just so many people and the prospect of running into someone or something was a nightmare. There was washing on every balcony. Stray wires ran off the lamp posts as people tried to cheat what was left of the state, or possibly resorted to desperate measures to repair what the electricity board couldn't. In some areas all the women and girls had headscarves and some wore half veils. All averted their gaze. At key junctions bored Syrian soldiers watched from behind sandbags and smoked and chewed and spat.

'The problem is to avoid going down any street where the traffic just gets snarled up, or where they are having a family dispute. Unlike East Beirut there is no single militia running everything. The Syrians act as a damper, but there's a lot going on that they can't control. By all accounts it was impossible before they returned.'

Tina just nodded and said nothing. I glanced at her to check she was all right. She was taking it all in, but she didn't look to be over the moon with delight about what she saw.

Then the buildings opened out a bit and there were a few old balconied houses with pine trees in their gardens, redolent of long gone Ottoman splendour. We skirted Sanniyah Gardens, battered and dirty and full of memories of the refugees in 1982.

'The Holiday Inn over there, a name to conjure with in the early days of the Civil War.' I gestured to the grey gutted whale of a building ahead.

We crossed the once glorious Hamra with the dirt and the potholes and kept going downhill. Then at last through a gap in the houses we could see the sea. I glanced again at Tina, who had visibly brightened at the sight and we drove down and onto the beginning of the Corniche. The perfect blue sea seemed to highlight the drab dirtiness of the town.

'Ras Beirut ahead. Where the headland turns the corner. The green is the American University of Beirut. Of happy memory. The shell is the old US Embassy and Rimmer's apartment is just here.'

I parked with one wheel in a rubbish pile and got out. There was no sign of life on the third floor of the old building, although the balcony doors were open suggesting that wherever the occupier was he was still in town. An old man, dark skinned and almost skeletal, came over and begged for alms and I dug out a few notes. The raging inflation had ended the day of the handful of coins. A cobbler opposite waved his hand at me in a beckoning gesture from within the dark recesses of his shop. I went over and assured him in the best Syrian Arabic I could muster that my car was not a bomb and that I was a friend of Professor Rimmer. That seemed to help.

Then with Tina close behind I went over to Charlie's block of flats. We climbed the three flights of stairs to find steel bars blocking access to the remaining two floors, unpleasantly reminiscent of the grid preventing our escape just an hour or so ago from Mrs Chehab's apartment. There was a string attached to a bell and I pulled it. There was a distant tinkling somewhere, but nothing happened. The silence persisted. I tried to hide my disappointment.

We walked slowly downstairs. The bottom flat had its

door open and inside a woman was mopping the floor. Seeing us she stood up and came over. She was apparently in late middle age and dressed in the black shapeless gown that is almost a uniform among Muslim women over thirty throughout the Middle East. I greeted her.

'*Salaam aleikum.*'

She smiled, showing broken and discoloured teeth. '*Wa aleikum i salaam. Meen baddak?*'

There was going to be no conversation in English here, or French for that matter. I kept going in Arabic. A Syrian accent would be no disadvantage here.

'We are looking for Professor Rimmer. The tall Englishman with white hair.'

'Come in, sit down, he is not here. He is gone out. Maybe an hour ago. Come, sit down, and wait.'

I looked at Tina, who looked tired and fragile. It wasn't a bad idea. It hadn't been an easy morning. I wondered, not for the first time, what price she was going to have to pay for getting Fuad out. *If* we could get Fuad out. It wouldn't hurt to wait for half an hour and then go up to the hospital to see if Ghassan was around.

'Thank you, sister. You are kind.'

She peered at Tina. 'Your wife?'

'My bride.'

Arabic, always more precise when it comes to family terms, has a special word for a newly-wed wife.

'Congratulations. Does she speak Arabic?'

I translated to Tina. She gave a fair impression of the Lebanese negative cluck, which was a good start.

So for half an hour we sat and drank tiny cups of sweetened coffee and two small children with brown eyes and runny noses came and stared at us in a worried manner until Tina made friends with them. It was good to see that she seemed to relax. We talked about the situation, and the economy and she said how that everyone was glad to have Professor Rimmer about because he reminded them of the old days. But it turned out that the old days hadn't been that good for her.

Hers was a Shiite family. They had had what she described as a farm, but sounded more like just fields in South Lebanon, south of Tyre. What with the Palestinians and Israelis battling all around, things had been bad for years. Then after the first Israeli invasion of '78 they – and it sounded a large family – had come to Beirut as refugees. Then they'd lived in the southern suburbs for a few years; 'not nice', but now they were here. Here they 'looked after' the flat for someone who had left to go abroad. The house was poorly furnished with a lot of bare wood, bare plaster and bare tile. It was, however, scrupulously neat. The sole wall decoration was, I noticed with a certain private amusement, a large, appalling picture of Mecca, dominated by iridescent reds and purples and surrounded by a baroque gilt frame.

Tina followed the story carefully as I translated it. Human interest always grabs her attention.

'Ask her if she hopes to go back to the south.'

No, she said, it was finished. Her son was working in Italy. She hoped she could join him there. *Inshallah*, God willing. Then she shook her head and looked very sad.

'*Ya haram Lubnaan!*'

' "*Ya haram Lubnaan*"; add it to your vocabulary and produce it regularly. It's not easy to translate; it's a lament for Lebanon. "Poor old Lebanon" but much stronger.'

Half an hour passed. I made our apologies, courteously thanking her for – but declining – the inevitable invitation to lunch. I said we would be back to see Professor Charles later. Then we walked up to the hospital. It was nearly midday and the sun was warm and bright and the red tiled roofs of the American University shone in the sun and brought back the past. I nudged Tina.

'So that was one of the fearsome Shiites of West Beirut. Scared you silly, didn't it?'

'She was a very nice, hospitable woman who'd had a rough deal out of life.'

'There's probably half a million of those here.'

212

The hospital, its white stone skinned walls pitted and locally poster-covered, was as busy as ever. The Syrians had restricted access with sandbags and we had to file past a red-bereted soldier chewing gum, who showed not the slightest interest in who we were.

The receptionist, whom I felt I vaguely remembered, put out a call for Ghassan, and a few minutes later a bulky figure in a white coat wove his way through the crowds of relatives in the foyer. We may have only met briefly before, but I got a kiss on both cheeks.

'Henry Stanwick! Welcome, my brother. An honour. Your wife?'

He looked at Tina affectionately. There was no denying that Ghassan Halibi wouldn't have won any prizes for beauty. In fact it was difficult to deny that he was downright ugly. The ears and the nose looked as though they had been issued by the same people who dished out Syrian army uniforms; they were too large and nothing matched. But it was a happy, caring face and when you knew him the nose and the ears didn't matter.

'Do you have a few minutes, Ghassan?'

He looked at the clock. 'Yes, I'm on duty in an hour, but let's have lunch. We get so few Westerners through these days, it's nice to see anybody.'

We queued for food among the doctors and nurses and then found a quiet table overlooking the street and Ghassan said grace in clear Arabic, loud enough for the neighbouring tables to hear. Having a dad who is big in the Syrian Army has its advantages. Then over meat and vegetable stew, rice and the inevitable hummus we brought each other up to date with the news. We both tried hard to explain points to make sure Tina didn't feel too much out of our strange world. Eventually, the reason for our visiting emerged and Ghassan shook his head.

'I've made enquiries and, to the best of the knowledge of the people on the checkpoint, no one resembling Fuad

Attiyah passed through. But you know our checkpoints. Some of the soldiers are fresh from farms in the Jezireh or Deir-ez-Zor. They may have been thinking about their favourite cows or goats when they waved him through. I also understand that we know of no one being held in the north, particularly anyone with an American residency. Sorry.'

It had always been a wild hope of Antoine's anyway.

'So it looks like Elias Daoud has him then. Know anything about him?'

Ghassan finished chewing a bit of meat, swallowed and wiped his mouth.

'Not much. I think Damascus is happy that he has promised not to talk to our friends in the south.' I caught Tina's eye so that she knew that he was talking code. 'And they in turn, are happy he is not talking to Fatah or some of the other Palestinian groups. So his condition is stable. But as you know, Henry, I have no taste for politics. Let the dead bury their dead.'

There was the sound of an ambulance siren. Something crossed my mind.

'Ghassan, does anybody here have contact with the hospital at Farayoun?'

He put his fork down. 'Yes, apparently they have a deal with us that we let them have photocopies of articles. Varouj takes them over to Jounieh and then they are passed on. It came up the other day. I was in the library and he was working on the photocopier. He said it was funny because they were a small hospital.'

This sounded encouraging. I wondered briefly what sort of thing they would be photocopying. I could think of a few topics that might interest the group as Nickie had described it. General genetic techniques perhaps, maybe things about reactions to pollutants.

'You wouldn't offhand know what sort of things they were interested in?'

'Well, that was an odd thing. Varouj said he was going to

214

stay clear of Farayoun. I said I'd heard it was healthy. He said that from these reprints it must be a very sick place. I asked him why and he said that every single reprint request for the last six months had been about viral diseases.'

I put my glass down slowly, trying not to spill the water. 'Of man?'

Ghassan looked at me strangely. 'We *are* a hospital, Henry.'

Another siren wailed outside, but I barely heard it. I was still reeling under Ghassan's extraordinarily disconcerting news. I was so taken aback that I nearly told him the conclusions that Zvi and his colleague had come to yesterday, but commonsense got the better of me. I glanced at Tina who looked equally stunned. I suddenly thought I'd better change the subject before Ghassan noticed something was wrong.

There was no need to because someone had come over to Ghassan, said a few words and moved on to another table. Ghassan was getting to his feet.

'I'm sorry; there has been trouble in Zarif. The first casualties are coming in. Come again here. Tina, you must visit Damascus and my family. God bless.'

There was another siren. As Ghassan left I looked at Tina.

'I now haven't a clue what's going on in Farayoun. I'm at an absolute loss.'

As we left the hospital another ambulance squealed in to the emergency entrance. It was becoming a bloody little afternoon in Zarif.

We set off down to Rimmer's flat and then I had a thought.

'Let's take the long way; we're not going to Farayoun tonight. It will only take an extra ten minutes.'

So we walked down through the grounds of the American University of Beirut, the last refuge of peace, tranquillity and vegetation in West Beirut and still, despite everything, one of the world's prettiest campuses. We strolled down and, with only the briefest of pauses, passed the Aleppo pines, the fine nineteenth-century, stone-built buildings and Malcom Kerr's memorial. Then we walked down past the sports field to the seafront entrance where the rotting sandbags still stood where the US Marines had hunkered down while everything went to pieces in '84. And I tried to confine myself to the sort of dry factual account that you might have got if AUB had been on the tourist routes, which it was once. But it was difficult because there seemed to be ghosts everywhere. Then we walked back along the corniche to Rimmer's house, past the old US Embassy. At length Tina spoke.

'Thanks, Henry. You told me a lot by what you said and what you didn't say. I can fill in the blanks. *Ya haram Lubnaan.*'

Then it was up the stairs and pulling on the string of the bell again.

After a few moments the door opened and a head of white hair stuck itself out and looked at us. Then the rest of the torso emerged, naked apart from a strategic bath towel. The pink mass stared.

'Professor Rimmer, I believe?'

Then the torso spoke. The voice was quite as remarkable as I remembered it, deep ringing tones with an accent more suited to an Oxford lecture theatre of the 1950s than West Beirut in the late 1980s.

'Good heavens above. It's Stanwick. With a woman. How perfectly charming. Welcome to the Abyss.'

25

We sat on the balcony watching the sea and trying to make out the details of Mount Lebanon, visible as a white mass through the haze, while Charlie got dressed. He said he needed something 'more suitable for the company of ladies'. An attractive Filipino girl, whom he had introduced as Maria and left us to guess whether she was a servant or a girlfriend or both, served us with cold drinks. The afternoon sun shone on the balcony and warmed us.

It would have been idyllic but for two things. The first was that it was already two o'clock and with darkness due in three hours we really needed to be going within an hour or so. The second, and related, problem was that there were suddenly problematic noises coming from over to the east. It wasn't hard to identify the noises. That wasn't the problem; the problem was that I didn't want to identify them. I said a little prayer that they would go away and pointed out some of the sights to Tina. A minute or two later Tina told me to be quiet and put her head on one side and listened. She looked up at me, eyes wide.

'Henry, what's that?'

It crossed my mind to pretend not to hear it, on the basis that it might suddenly stop. But it didn't.

'What's what?'

She looked vaguely irritated with me. 'The noise that sounds like machine gun fire.'

'Ah that. That noise.'

She gave me a severe glare. 'Yes, that noise. What is it?'

'Well, do you want the honest answer?'

The glare turned into a look of unhappiness. 'Of course, but I'm not going to like it, am I?'

She wasn't and I didn't blame her. The way this trip was going I was beginning to hope they were synthesising tranquillisers up in Farayoun. I tried to adopt the tone used to explain cricket to Americans.

'No, you see it's a local pastime. Sort of street fighting. Localised, probably about a mile and a half away. Only light weapons, small things, nothing really of battlefield calibre – well, not so far. If it stays like this then it's no big deal, we just take a longer route back. This sort of thing used to go on for weeks. The Syrians will probably roll in fairly soon and beat up both sides. My guess would be that the Zarif street party has got a bit out of hand and everybody's weighing in to settle old scores. Anyway, here comes our host.'

Charlie appeared from his bedroom dressed in flannels, a blazer and a cravat. Doubtless the last cravat in West Beirut. He had even combed his unruly hair.

'Just wonderful! May I join the party? I was so bored. I trust you will excuse me for bathing in the afternoon. It's the power cuts. One does so hate trying to get clean by candlelight. And it's been every night this week. "Lighten our darkness, we beseech thee, O Lord." ' He looked upwards.

'...And by thy great mercy defend us from all perils and dangers of this night.' Tina looked a little embarrassed.

Charlie looked at me with a wry pout.

'Well, the lady not only knows it, she sounds like she meant it.'

There was a burst of machine gun fire. It was a little nearer. If it kept on getting closer we might all be saying Amen to that soon.

'I did,' said Tina in a thin voice.

'She has this curious belief that prayers are a serious matter. I quite agree in fact.'

Charlie wriggled a little on his seat.

'Ah yes, one forgets these things. Sorry and all that. But, my dear Henry, how long has it been?'

'Years, long years, Charlie. I've followed your exploits from afar, but there isn't the coverage that there was.'

'No, the spotlight shines elsewhere these days. I wondered about arranging to have myself kidnapped and then to be released spectacularly after a few days, to see if anyone noticed. But it would have meant giving press conferences looking unshaven. One has to have a certain self-respect.'

He called Maria over and asked her for some orange juice. I looked carefully at him. On the surface there didn't seem to have been much change over the past few years. There was still the mischievous grin, but it seemed to be more sardonic than it had been. It was, I felt, almost as though in trying to keep grinning the smile was twisting into a cynical leer. Did he perhaps also seem slightly thinner in spirit? Were the mannerisms just that little bit more affected?

So for a few minutes we discussed what had happened and friends that had left and general tales of woe in Beirut. I kept wanting to look at my watch, but I daren't because, despite the impeccably English pose, Charlie had been here for twenty years and was an honorary Lebanese in many ways, so you just couldn't rush him. As we talked the rattles got a little nearer and in the shop along the street near the mosque there was a little cluster of people listening intently to the radio – which is one of those small things that registers a faint warning if you've lived in West Beirut.

'...so, anyway, what brings you here? Hardly a place for any world-besotted traveller, but then you always did try to be unworldly, didn't you, Henry?'

I recognised the quotation and decided to try to speed things up.

'Talking of Yeats,' he bowed his head to indicate I'd hit the mark, 'an old student of yours; author of *Orientalism in the Poetry of W B Yeats* no less, is being a slight nuisance. In short, he is holding a friend hostage.'

There was a further rattle of machine gun fire. Unmistakeably nearer this time and Tina squirmed uneasily. The handful of people at the shop began to disperse decisively towards their homes – which is another signal. On the military equivalent of the Beaufort Scale we had moved to a gale warning. If you're out in the open it's time to get home. Charlie seemed to ignore it, his face showing theatrical astonishment at my news.

'Good heavens! My old friend and distinguished pupil, the Czar of Farayoun, the last intellectual in Levantine politics, Elias Daoud? He's stooped to kidnapping?'

I nodded and he looked vaguely serious.

'I am profoundly dismayed, Henry. Shaken to the core.

219

Absolutely. I mean seriously, he's grabbed a fellow?'

'That's the case, Charlie. No ransom note yet, but it looks like Elias.'

'He's probably still trying to get the demand to scan. Well I'm blowed. But then he is a sheik and lord of a country – albeit a very small one. Perhaps he just wanted to have a hostage too. They are something of a status symbol. Is the chappie British?'

'No, Lebanese, but American residency. He's an old friend. In fact I was wondering if you could cast any light on it, or perhaps pull a string or two.'

There was the sound of further rattling and a few booms. Definitely nearer. Downstairs a woman's voice could be heard calling for her children to come in off the street. Time to batten down the hatches and bar the door, the old man with the scythe is on his rounds. The tension on the balcony edged a small notch upwards. Tina's hand trembled a little bit and she put her glass down noisily on the table. I glanced at Charlie. I noticed he was listening, but he made no comment about the fighting.

'Most odd business. Dashed odd. But a two part question there, young Stanwick. Second part first: of course I will put pen to paper for you. We're still pretty pally. I'll give you an introduction and ask him what the game is. You'd like that?'

I tried to restrain my enthusiasm.

'If you wouldn't mind; we're not certain he is holding this fellow, but it would be good if you could politely ask for all possible help, and give us an introduction. Thanks, Charlie.'

There was a loud, crisp bang. That sounded like a grenade of some sort and was definitely much nearer.

'In fact, Charlie, if you could do it now, I'd be greatly obliged because it sounds like there's a spot of bother locally.'

'Yes, I'd noticed the whizz bangs. Probably nothing. A shame, I was hoping that you'd be able to stay for supper. By candlelight of course,' and he gave a rather mocking grin at Tina, 'albeit of necessity rather than choice. But I take your point. I will do it this very minute.'

He downed his orange juice and went back into the apartment. I smiled at Tina who was looking distinctly uneasy. The nearest firing was still probably a mile away, but definitely more vigorous than it had been. There was now a fairly constant crackling of small arms fire which sounded like a pile of small twigs burning. Against that, isolated muffled blasts could be heard, but there was no trace of either the sharp edged explosion or the whistling and deeper boom that mark outgoing or incoming artillery shells respectively. I tried to encourage Tina.

'Good, that's excellent news. Our first concrete progress. We can have our letter and go.'

'That would be nice. Very nice.'

She jumped slightly as a louder blast echoed down the street.

'Are we all right, Henry?'

'The problem with you, my wife, is that you would be angry if I said anything other than the truth. We are sitting in West Beirut and there is small scale fighting going on nearby and spreading towards us. I suppose we are all right, but it is a rather limited sense of the word. Anyway, the traffic is still moving and the shops are still open. We could still leave. In a sense it's just a bit misleading; the place is generally pretty quiet. But at least you have the opportunity of hearing a little of what it can be like.'

Tina shook her head at me in mock amazement.

'I see. If I think of it as a privilege it's not so scaring. Henry, if I may make a generalisation, women don't find gunfire exciting. At least this woman doesn't.'

'I'll make a note of it. Anyway, one trick is to try to occupy the mind. Attack Charlie on his atheism or his dress sense. He'll love it.'

At that point the shutters on a nearby shop came down with a screech of metal. Then, following the signal, other shop owners began putting boxes inside and closing up.

Further shutters fell. The tension took another turn upwards. Tina looked at me.

'I suppose it's just early closing day, Henry?'

'Probably. Perhaps there's something good on television.' I looked at my watch. Three o'clock. Although the balcony looked broadly northwards it was at the western edge of the building and still got some oblique sun. But it was starting to get cool. The firing seemed definitely to be gaining in vigour, rather as though lots of other people were joining in. It was also getting closer.

There was a noise below and the traffic slowed and stopped on the corniche. Then, with a great whining and screaming of gears, they began to reverse backwards rapidly until there was enough space to do a three point turn. I glanced down the road towards the area of the hotels. In the distance men with guns were emerging from down a side street.

'My dear, time to adjourn indoors, as Charlie would say.'

She caught my glance and got up quickly. At that moment Charlie came over with an envelope. He was holding a glass of beer in his hand.

'What, getting cold outside?'

There was a burst of fire along the street. It had the rhythmic beat to it which I've always taken as giving a challenge rather than indicating any serious intent to kill. Doubtless it may do both. Charlie stood upright and put a hand to his ear.

'Ah, *au contraire*, warming up. Just like old times. Anyway, come in and I'll close up. Here's your letter.'

I glanced at it. From the envelope at least it looked exactly what was required with 'Sheik Elias Boulos Daoud, BA, MA' written clearly on the front and the name and signature of the sender scrawled across the back. I gave it to Tina who put it carefully in her handbag. We went in and sat down on the sofa.

Charlie closed the French window onto the balcony, came over and sat down in an easy chair facing us. More firing echoed down the street. I'd forgotten how loud it was.

'Looks like quite a little spot of bother down there. It may settle down, but I think you'd be advised to plan on leaving first thing tomorrow. The Syrians prefer to let them run out of steam and bullets and then crawl by at dawn.' He swallowed a mouthful of beer and adopted a reflective, gloomy look.

'But they can't control it. This place has swallowed the French, the Palestinians, the Israelis, the Americans. It will swallow them. It's insatiable.'

He caught Tina's expression. 'Don't be unduly alarmed, Mrs Stanwick. Not about this noise. 'Tis but a passing fancy. If they hit the car it will be a nuisance, but I don't think you are at risk here. One rarely gets bullets actually in the apartment.'

I looked around the room. When empty it would have been quite large, but it was full of twenty years of accumulated possessions. Bookshelves took up half the walls and seemed to extend into the hall and beyond. The remaining spaces were filled with prints of Lebanon, wall hangings and black and white photographs of old buildings. In a corner was a small plastic Christmas tree with a neglected air about it. It was the first artificial tree I'd seen that seemed to have suffered from acid rain. Charlie caught my glance.

'Yes, I still keep everything here. Some people have shipped it all out bit by bit. I don't think I could do that.'

'Why not?' Tina was speaking quietly.

' "Where your treasure is, there will be your heart also." I've seen it happen. People move their things out then something happens and they follow them.'

'Why do you stay?'

'Henry, your wife is full of deep questions. Why do I stay?'

He folded his long arms elegantly and looked at her. 'In part, sheer inertia. It would almost be more frightening to leave than to stay after all these years. I have a vain hope I suppose too that the old Beirut will all come back. It won't, of course. Also, in a strange way I'm secure. The clock has stopped here. I don't like the new things going on in English, I don't understand structuralism, I can't stand modern poetry. I don't care a hoot who won the Booker Prize. Here I've become an institution, in a small way. There are other attractions about Beirut. In some ways you feel close to the heart of things, close to the core of the world. I've actually come to admire the disintegration; perhaps I'm a frustrated vandal.'

He gave me a twisted grin and turned back to Tina.

'Even the language is disintegrating. For instance, the Arabic greeting *Marhaba* requires the response *Marhabtein*. Now when French speakers here say *Bonjour* people reply *Bonjourein*. See, it's linguistic collapse – the rules of grammar buckling and bending under the gravitational forces of the Black Hole of Lebanon. But you probably wouldn't find that compelling....'

There was more firing. Maria came out of the kitchen looking slightly perturbed. 'Charles, what eez happening?'

He threw his arms wide and shrugged.

'Sorry Maria, I don't know. I wonder if anybody knows. But there will be an extra two people for supper.'

Maria nodded, smiled at us and went back to the kitchen. Charles looked pensive.

'I'm working on a poem about it all at the moment. "The Garment." '

I was gratified to see Tina listening carefully as Charlie put on his declaiming voice.

'Here the fabric's torn, the thread's unravelled,
In these streets of rubbish, these barricades,
One by one the fibres unknit still further
With each bomb, each kidnapping, each and every death
Unpicking warp and woof, pattern and structure,
And throwing form into formlessness.

But who can repair it?
Who sew up again these tangled strands
Of culture, creed and class into a living pattern,

224

Indeed, prevent our unweaving from its final end –
A world exposed, unclothed and of comfort devoid.
No one, says the sound of boots on shattered glass.'

There was silence. I looked at Tina. I don't think she'd been expecting to get involved with literary criticism. She rose to the occasion, however.

'Yes, I'm intrigued by the metaphor. The last line reminds me of Eliot. "The Hollow Men", is it? Possibly too much.'

Charlie nodded approvingly at me. I was quite impressed myself, not so much by what she'd said, but that she had managed not to say it was pretty bad, even for a draft.

'Yes, too blunt an allusion at the moment. Just a draft, you understand. I have to maintain my reputation as poet of the abyss.'

Or the abysmal poet, I thought.

There was a further roar of machine gun fire. Our host seemed reminded of something by it.

'Ah yes, you asked me a question earlier. Could I shed light on your friend's disappearance? Not really, although I haven't seen Elias for six months. In truth I find getting to Farayoun a bit nerve-wracking these days – all those checkpoints. I'm getting old. Then last time he was a bit cool. He has got some funny friends, these days. Maybe some grand ideas too. There was an Armenian chappy, Har-out something-ian there too. Been in America, businessman, dressed well but just odd. Not Elias' sort of fellow at all – I wondered what the relationship was. Almost as though Elias owed him money. They do say that Elias is involved in the drugs business. He's a funny fellow.'

I let Tina ask the question.

'In what way?'

'He's "mad, bad and dangerous to know". Well not quite; at least not all the time. He's a mass of contradictions. I suppose he typifies Lebanon and Lebanon is the world. He lives in the twentieth century and he can talk to you at length about the world's problems, but he's a feudalist at heart.

He's an intellectual of sorts, or he could be – his thesis was his own work and his own choice incidentally, in case you were wondering – but he can be a genuine Mount Lebanon peasant; stubborn and suspicious of anyone beyond his own valley. He's brutal enough in administering what he considers justice, but he has never exacted revenge on those who killed his wife and child, although he knows who did it. He's a skilled administrator of the valley, but he refuses to allow any opposition, and likes to rule by decree. That's one reason the brother, Butros, is in France. Old Elias is happy to talk about truth and honesty in literature, but he is as corrupt as everybody else in his position. He's proud and arrogant, but totally insecure and introspective. He's a sceptic, but superstitious and mystical.'

Charlie seemed to chew over something in his mind.

'He's certainly no Christian, but even his rejection of that is complex. Part of him is pagan and goes back to the old Lebanon, perhaps even before the Maronites.'

The glass in the windows rattled as something exploded down the street. Tina looked at me with a pale, tense face. Charlie merely gave the windows a brief glance and then continued.

'Do you know Farayoun?'

I nodded. 'But not well.'

'It's an odd place. Cut off, isolated. If you are wandering in the hills above Daoud's house, or in the valley below the town, it can be strange. Numinous.'

He sipped his beer reflectively. ' "Numinous." Oh but it's splendid to use that word! The level of English round here has dropped very much. One tends to talk perpetually in Special English. Anyway, where was I? Yes, it's a weird place. Some people say that you see things – even before the drugs trade. That's in part why Elias took such a fancy to early Yeats. It's difficult to put into words unless you are in that league.'

He paused and stretched his legs out. 'Part of it is that although the valley is Maronite on the map, it's not and it never has been truly Christian. To be sure there has been the form of things on the surface, but it's a pagan place underneath and I suspect it always has been. The old shrines, that go back beyond the Romans to the Canaanites, still receive worship and honour of some sort. Flowers, articles of clothing and, for all I know, blood. So Elias is part pagan, yet he also sees himself I think as post-Christian as well. He's openly scornful of the church and has no time for the priests. The few who still survived in the old monastery along from his house he sent packing and they fled into the more orthodox heartland above Jounieh. He's now renovating the monastery, he tells me. Perhaps in Daoud the old and new pagans meet. Pagan and Neo-Pagan.'

It seemed a thorough assessment.

'Sounds like you've got him all sorted out.'

'I've been giving thought to a poem on him, but it's only notes. I could hardly publish it, could I?'

It was getting cold. Charlie got up and turned the gas heater on. Bursts of firing continued outside.

'I suspect the electricity will be off again tonight, so perhaps we should make up beds for you in the back room while we still have daylight.'

Tina must have made a face because Charlie smiled his half leer.

'Fortunately, because of the ridiculous way everyone built in this part of town, you have a window facing a solid wall about ten feet away, so you will be safe from all but the most freakish of ricochets there. You may even get some sleep.'

That evening is almost burned into my memory. The darkness of the main room was broken only by four candles and the red glow from the gas heater. We sat round the long table and, in the gloom, worked through a meal of soup, chicken, a rice and nuts dish, salad and fruit. The conversation was dominated by Charlie and me as we talked about the past and its moments of glory, laughter and tears. Tina and Maria

227

sat opposite each other and made polite conversation or just listened. Occasionally, Tina would enter our discussion, but she seemed ill at ease and talked a lot to Maria about the Philippines and cooking and everything except the situation.

In terms of impressions it was memorable. To look at it it was a homely, even romantic scene. The light of the gently flickering candles cast golden flecks in Charlie's white hair and caught the embossed titles on the spines of the books. There were odd moments when it even sounded cosy with the quiet female chatter overlain by Charlie's glorious voice with some story or joke of the past in a sort of concerto effect.

Then there would be a deafening gale of machine gun fire from the street and the conversation would stop for a moment until it was over. Or there would be a flash and the words would be held in mid-sentence until the windows had finished rattling and they could be released and heard. Once or twice I listened to the shooting and my stomach began to churn, but it seemed so dislocated and unrelated that it wasn't threatening. Once shrapnel of some sort clattered on the balcony after a particularly loud bang and Charlie merely expressed the solemn hope that his cactus hadn't been dismembered.

Tina and I drank only soft drinks while Charlie got out a bottle of wine or two and set to. After the meal we felt our way round to the comfortable chairs and sat and talked further in the gloom. Tina snuggled next to me on the sofa and we drank percolated coffee. If you could have taken away the offstage noises it would have been almost pleasant. After half an hour or so Maria made her apologies and left to go to her room.

Strange to say, if we'd gone to bed then ourselves, our memories of that night might almost have been happy ones, given the way the mind filters out momentary alarms and scares. That was not, however, to be the case, because what happened was horrid and shocking. Not that there was any bloodshed, but then some things are worse than spilled blood. In a way too it had nothing to do with the petty war going on outside.

All that happened was that we talked, but to say that would be a bit misleading. In fact I (or more rarely Tina) just triggered Charlie and he produced anecdote after anecdote. At first he told these clearly and loudly in his splendid voice, but as time wore on they became quieter and the words slightly slurred.

He was lamenting the loss of Western journalists in West Beirut. 'Now when I get to the Commodore it's all Turks and Yugoslavs and no one worth kidnapping. This place has not only become dull, but the cause of dullness in others.'

He poured himself another glass of wine and stared at us.

'I think it's one reason I came here, Henry old chap. In the sixties it was a vibrant, exciting, stimulating place. In its way it was one big long party. Good food, good manners and good conversation. Ah, Mrs Stanwick, if only you could have seen the place in its heyday. Everybody – ambassadors, White Russians, Red Russians, courtesans, men of letters, musicians, smugglers, revolutionaries. And the intrigues; spies, double agents, treble agents. You have no idea. An endless source of innocent merriment. A great long party.'

I ventured to intrude. 'And injustice.'

He sighed.

'And injustice. Anyway, that was until the sad and bloody year of '75. People started leaving the party then. Your husband came, I remember, towards the end of the first phase of the war. Many of the best guests had already left the party and the rest were looking at their watches. Some of those who were left might as well have gone too because they had become witless or boring. Then it all turned rather tasteless, as parties do – an unseemly squabbling for the last bottle of plonk.'

He drank heavily from his glass and sighed again.

'Now I seem to be left alone with the empty bottles, the bores who haven't yet fallen asleep, the stale cigarette smoke and all that's left on the table are dirty napkins and empty plates. The party's over and everybody's gone, Henry. Yours truly is left here with Maria who's charming and pretty, but probably thinks Keats is a plural noun. "Glory and loveliness have passed away." '

Tina spoke somewhat timorously. 'Was it ever that?'

There was the sound of a bottle being put down rather uncertainly on a tiled floor. The voice sounded tired.

'No, probably not. In my better moments I think your husband's right. It was rotten. To the core. But then that was part of the attraction. We always knew it was rotten, I think. We knew it couldn't last; that the wine would run out, the woodworm would get the floorboards; that there were rats in the cellar and that the perfume couldn't hide the smell of the sewers for ever.'

He paused. He was drinking far more than I'd ever seen him drink. I wondered if it was because tonight he knew that no one would call, that this night he could afford to drink. Or was there something else that disturbed and provoked him? Or had he simply become a man who needed a bottle or two in an evening? In a sense the drinking didn't bother me. What was new and horrible was the turn his conversation took and the way it exposed how the rot had finally gained a hold in Charlie's soul. There was a long silence as he seemed to review things.

'See, Henry and Tina, you know what this place is, don't you? This is the world's end. This is where we all go. Beirut today, Nairobi tomorrow, London the day after. Goodbye civilisation. "Look on my works ye mighty and despair." '

I held Tina's hand. I wondered how I could get him to snap out of it all. As I thought, he continued unsteadily.

'Listen. Let me recite you my favourite poem. Well, just the end. Arnold's "Dover Beach". Of course you Christian folk hate it, with its sneer about the sea of faith retreating.'

He pulled himself upright in his chair and began.

'Ah, love, let us be true
To one another! for the world, which seems
To lie before us like a land of dreams,
So various, so beautiful, so new,
Hath really neither joy, nor love, nor light,
Nor certitude, nor peace, nor help for pain;
And we are here as on a darkling plain
Swept with confused alarms of struggle and flight,
Where ignorant armies clash by night.'

His voice rolled round the room and died away. Outside, the gunfire continued. Charlie seemed to slouch back in his chair.

Tina spoke firmly and clearly. 'Just because it's fine words doesn't mean it's true.'

'Truth ends here, Mrs Stanwick. This is the end of the line. The end of all lines. I had a dream the other night, that Beirut was a plughole and all the world was flowing as if it were simply bath water. And I found myself pulled in and I couldn't swim out because of the currents. Then as the water started to curve round and round, down in the final spiral, I decided that I might as well surf on it. And so finally, gloriously, climactically, I surfed in – into the vortex and was gone.'

He seemed to lurch in his seat, steadied himself and took another gulp of wine. I wondered if I should interrupt and try to get him to stop drinking. As I thought about it I decided that if a man chooses to drink himself silly when he's in his own flat and he believes the world is meaningless and to all appearances he's correct, it's hardly right to try and stop him. In retrospect I wish I had, but it was already too late. He started speaking again, his voice lower, deeper in the pit.

'You know, Henry, I now know this of a fact, a certainty. All is disintegration and darkness ultimately. It's a joke, all the world's a stage and we all wait and the conjuror pulls the cloth away and, *voilà*, there is nothing. This is the void, the abyss. We have now come to the world's ending. The heart of it all. It's not anything, it's a void.'

He laughed, almost crazily. Tina shuddered and whispered to me, 'Can't you stop him, Henry?'

'I'll try. Look, Charlie, it's not like that really. There is meaning ultimately.'

Some wise guy with a machine gun let loose outside as if to mock my words.

'Sorry, Henry, let me finish.'

He got to his feet clutching glass and bottle and wandered unsteadily in the darkness towards the doors that led onto the balcony. I realised that if he was going to try and go out beyond them, I would have to stop him. He stopped just in front of the glass, then he spoke again. The voice was going now, the beautiful rounded modulations breaking up.

'There's nothing at the centre. Nothing at all. Just savagery and anarchy. Mistah Kerr – he dead.'

He lurched and dropped something; there was the sound of a glass breaking.

'Damn it all. Dropped the glass.'

He walked unevenly away from where it had fallen, but still broadly parallel to the window. He fell silent. Then there was a flash which showed him in eerie silhouette propped against the window with the bottle to his lips. There was a bubbling, uncontrollable sobbing laugh which was broken only by a great window-rattling blast.

'Stupid. Whole town, world's going to bits and I worry about a glass. Everything's going, gone. Ignorant armies clashing by night. Things fall apart...the centre cannot hold, the blood dimmed tide is.... No, that's wrong. Who cares anyway? Just words. Words are noise, noise is words. Gunfire and poetry are the same.'

Then he turned slowly and awkwardly to us and stretched out an arm as in some prophetic judgement. Then he began to shout, but now his voice was not neutral. It was saturated in fear. 'Look! There's nothing there!'

The fear turned to terror.

'Nothing! Nothing! Just darkness. Just a void. Nothing

at all! Nothing!'

With his last wild shout, the bottle dropped from his hand and smashed on the floor. Then, mumbling loudly but incoherently, he took two lumbering steps towards us before suddenly falling over as though struck from behind. He hit the floor in a great, sagging, fluid collapse and lay there without movement.

We checked him over as well as we could by torchlight and there seemed no serious damage. With the help of Maria we put him to bed and then went to bed ourselves in a suitably depressed state of mind. Eventually, despite the continuing gunfire, we slept and woke just after dawn. Outside, silence seemed to reign. I put my head round the door into Charlie's bedroom and he was snoring heavily and looked as though he'd live. A cautious examination from the balcony showed that the shopkeepers were already sweeping up some of the broken glass in the bright morning sun. As we watched, a Syrian lorry full of soldiers, guns at the ready, came driving slowly along. Behind them the morning sea was blue and mockingly innocent.

I got a piece of paper from Maria, and wrote a quick thank you note to Charlie. Then Tina took the sheet, paused for a moment and put across the bottom a single line.

'The Light shines in the darkness, but the darkness has not mastered it.'

I nodded approval. 'It's a good Christmas text.'

Then we got Maria to let us out and, walking carefully to avoid slipping on the spent cartridge cases, went over to the car. It was untouched and we slowly drove away.

After a silent half hour's driving we were back at Antoine's flat.

26

We had a quiet breakfast with Antoine and shared with him something of what had happened. Of the puzzling news from Ghassan about the interest of Farayoun in diseases I said nothing. Equally, I passed over Charlie Rimmer's disintegration into total despair. Yet in their way they were the two things that stuck in my mind, far more so than the chase or the fighting the night before. In particular, the shock of seeing Rimmer, so long apparently able to stand untouched above the anarchy of Beirut reduced in the end to crying in the dark, had been great.

Antoine had some news for us, although it was not what I had hoped for. There had still been no word about Fuad.

'As you noticed we have had a few more people looking after the building. Since then we have seen nothing of the blue BMW. Elie, for instance, was up all last night downstairs by the door. He volunteered. It was he who brought me this message for you. It was given him by a man in a car early this morning.'

He reached up onto a shelf and took down a simple white envelope. The front was addressed to us care of Antoine in English and Arabic. I weighed it carefully in my hand and held it up to the light. I'm not sure how small letter bombs can be these days, but Lebanon probably holds the record so I wasn't taking chances. It appeared to contain a single sheet of paper so I opened it cautiously, and unfolded the letter. It was dated '02:10, 28th December'. In a brief moment of consternation I looked at my watch. Yes, that was today; despite everything we had only been in Lebanon forty-eight hours. I read the rest of the letter quickly, noting that it was in a different hand to the address.

Hi Henry,
    We want you to get on up to Farayoun and try and get your
friend out as soon as possible. On the way north call in at what
these people say is the Kaslik Marina near Jounieh. They say
you'll know it. We are sitting on a big yacht called the 'Irene' of
Limassol. We have some information that may be of help and
we need to talk. I'll get some food laid on.
    Good wishes
    Jim Elweth

I passed it over to my wife. Tina read it carefully and looked
at me. She was looking tired and drawn, but seemed to be
doing her best not to let it show.
    'Genuine?'
    'As far as I can tell. The reference to food is a bit of a
telltale. Whoever wrote the main letter didn't write the
address, which is fine because I don't think Elweth has any
ability in Arabic. And Kaslik would be a good place to meet
up.'
    Out of courtesy, I showed it to Antoine. Trying to choose
my words carefully I explained that Elweth was an American intelligence officer involved in chasing up the group we
suspected were at Farayoun.
    'So why is he here? Because he too has learned something
about this place? Or because he is following you?'
    I thought hard. 'I think at first because he was following
me, but now he may have information. We will find out.'
    'But his interests are not really the release of Fuad?'
    I bit my lip.
    'They may be. I will try to persuade him of that.'
    Antoine simply nodded; his face, tired and slightly grey
in its pallor, showed no emotion.
    'So you should be in Farayoun this afternoon?'
    'At last.'
    'Count your blessings. To get your letter of introduction
in this time isn't bad. This is Beirut. Also, Henry, I realise

you believe that you are partly to blame for this event, but I
do thank you for the risks you have taken already.'

A little voice in my mind muttered, 'You ain't seen nothing yet,' and I tried to ignore it, but the thought wouldn't go
away. Indeed, all that we had done was get a letter of introduction and that had been hard enough. We still had to get to
Farayoun and get Fuad out.

Antoine's gaze caught my eye. He had a resolute look.

'Henry, I was thinking that I would come up to Farayoun
too – not today, but tomorrow – if you think that that would
not interfere with your plans.'

It was a difficult point from several angles. By all accounts
Antoine and Elias were not going to hit it off. There was a
good deal of risk to Antoine and it might just mean one more
hostage. However, if Elias was going to grant us any favours
it would probably have been by then.

'Yes, all right. That sounds fine to me. Hopefully we will
be out by then with Fuad. Incidentally, what's the weather
forecast?'

'Yes, that is another point. They say tomorrow evening
the rains will come and there will be snow on the mountains.'

He smiled wryly. 'So if we don't all get there tomorrow it
may be next year before we are able to get up.'

True enough, I thought, the roads could easily be closed
for two or three days. So we really had to aim at getting Fuad
out as soon as possible. Antoine spoke again.

'Tomorrow is Sunday. Tonight I will try to call Cyprus
and pass on the news. Then I will take the morning service
and Nabil can take the afternoon one.' He looked at Tina.
'I'm afraid that even in this relatively quiet part of town few
people, especially the elderly, want to be out when night
falls, so we have an afternoon service.'

Then he paused, and when he spoke again it was in a
lower, but no less firm, voice. 'I have also prepared for the
worst. I believe that it is possible I may be held too. Indeed,
if necessary, I would be happy to trade myself for Fuad. I

would have made the offer before, but I didn't know who to address it to. In that case Nabil and all the others know that no price is to be paid for me.'

A silence hung over the table. There was a lot I could have said, but nothing seemed to be worthy of following Antoine's statement. In particular I tried not to think of my part in triggering this sad affair. Antoine seemed to sense my feeling and smiled, clapping me on the shoulder.

'But being taken hostage is not my main worry. That I have already shared with you. Henry, I fear only one man in Lebanon.'

I thought I could guess, but I asked it all the same. 'Who?'

'Myself.'

An hour later, after making arrangements to send messages and packing up, we were on our way north. On the way to the rendezvous at Kaslik we ran over some things together. The priority was to get Fuad out, and in order to do that we would have to try to conceal, if at all possible, the news that the group Jim wanted so badly were probably in Farayoun. The kidnapping and the apparent research interest in diseases had quite badly shaken my faith in what Nickie had said about the group. Nevertheless, I had no interest in delivering them and their data into the hands of Elweth's masters for their own purposes. Equally, I certainly didn't want him or the Israelis messing about in Farayoun before we and Fuad were well clear. Related to that was the need to ensure that Jim didn't learn about my meeting with Nickie. Unfortunately that ruled out having a go at him about taping conversations. So it looked like being a tough meeting, especially as I didn't want to lie – partly because I didn't believe in it and partly because I was no longer any good at it. But I was going to do it if the only alternative was a far greater evil, and there looked to be plenty of those around.

It wasn't hard to find the 'Irene'. The yachting marina at Kaslik is the south-west edge of the semi-circle of Jounieh

Bay and only half a mile from where we had docked just two days earlier. There were a large number of expensive yachts in dock and the effect was that of a moderately luxurious yachting pool in the south of France. The man at the entrance took our names and the name of the boat and directed us to a large white yacht over in the far corner. He was insistent that we walk, so leaving the Peugeot we strolled slowly to the 'Irene'.

Given that it was Saturday, and that a few hundred miles away a big storm was heading in, it wasn't too surprising to find a lot of people on their yachts. Some were clearly just enjoying the sun and lolling around on deck. Others were performing those various peculiar acts and services that yachts demand. I did notice as we neared the 'Irene' that a number of the boats had rather more muscular young males than one might expect and that quite a few of those appeared to stare unsmilingly at us from behind the protection of sunglasses.

At the 'Irene' the security was very plain. A young man on the quay painting an already painted life raft called us over and asked us who we wanted in poor French. Then a few yards on, a man in a nylon anorak which badly concealed a bulge over the left part of the chest stopped us and asked for our papers in American English.

Just before we got to the vessel there was a cry of 'Henry!' and a figure that had been checking a coil of rope detached itself and came over. It was Jim Elweth, even taller and more long limbed than I remembered. He came and shook my hand as though we'd been at college together for years. I kept reminding myself of the necessity of putting Fuad's safety first so I politely introduced him to Tina and apologised for ruining his Christmas. Then I switched my brain into overdrive to try and answer the tricky questions that were bound to be coming.

'No sweat. We had the in-laws over from Denver and it was getting a bit much. Anyway, this is a really neat business. Boy, these Israelis are jumping up and down like you

238

wouldn't believe. Sounds like the thing has gone up to the very top, so we've got this meeting set up here. They've sent some really hot people up. There's this guy David from the airforce – looks like he's fresh out of school, but what he knows about airstrikes! All in his head. Fantastic.'

I looked at Tina. If they'd got an expert in bombing raids in then the whole thing had got totally out of control. Besides, I was going to have a great deal of difficulty being nice to someone from that particular branch of the armed services. But I didn't argue for several reasons. The first was I didn't want to rattle Jim and the second was I wanted to get on to Farayoun. Then Jim threw me the first question.

'Anyway, before we go meet these guys I need to know how come you are here?'

It was the one I'd expected and I had a prepared answer, which while not the whole truth, was about as much as I was prepared to trust Jim Elweth with. In fact, it was a lot more than I would have trusted him with.

'It's a long story, Jim. I should say, as I've said to the Israelis, I honestly don't know if this has anything to do with the other business.'

He looked disappointed. 'No kidding? I thought you'd just been telling them that, kinda leading them along. Well I was reckoning we'd pinned them down at last.'

A look of cunning crossed his face. He was not a man who found it easy to mask any emotion.

'So what's your link?'

'Well, you know I used to live here? I happened to suggest to my brother, who's based in Cyprus, an idea I had that somewhere up in these mountains you could do what you wanted and that this place would be ideal for some sort of secret project. I guess what you and I had talked about had made me think of it – with there being no government here and so on. It was a sort of stupid thing to do because he mentioned it to Fuad, his friend who was visiting, and Fuad must have asked a dumb question near where something was going on. So I'm here because I feel it's my responsibility.

239

It's not a thing anyone would do except for duty.'

He looked at me slightly sideways. 'So you never heard anything more of "Jezreel"?'

If he'd asked that question in almost any other way I'd have to have lied, and I'd probably have done it so badly that even he'd have spotted it. But the way he phrased it let me off.

'Honestly, Jim, I'd nearly forgotten about the name until the Israeli guy the other day started to get all worried about it. No one has used that word to me since Lemaire.'

I thought he was going to ask me another question, but to my surprise he said something else.

'Good, well take it from me, we are sure glad that you didn't tell these guys anything. It's appreciated by my boss too. My strict orders are not to tell them anything more than the time of day. Frankly, when we heard they'd got you we were worried. It was kinda my fault. I said for them to go ahead and pick you up off the top of my head. Then the boss pointed out we didn't want them to know too much but... it was too late.'

At first I could barely believe what I was hearing, then as he went on it became depressingly credible.

'See, Henry and er, Tina, I guess it's hard to explain to you guys, but we'd really rather they didn't know a thing about the group. I mean we're on the same side, sorta, but if they got their hands on it we'd have to buy all the data back. And it's our data. And then we couldn't know whether it was altered or not. It's even possible,' here he dropped his voice, 'that if these guys got hold of the project first then they might just not let us know at all. Sometimes we don't trust these people, so I've just told them that, yes, it's possible that Jezreel was a chemical or biological weapons project and yes, it's possible that it may have ended up here. So you keep quiet on what you know, and well done so far. You're smarter than I thought.'

It was all I could do not to laugh out loud. I wondered whether this show was classed as an 'Intelligence meeting

240

between Allies' because there were clear deficiencies in both intelligence and allied aspects.

Then there was an impatient wave from the yacht.

'Time for talking.'

It was a beautiful yacht. I know as much about them as I do about fast sports cars, and for the same financial reasons, but I think I can still appreciate them. This looked to have everything – space, style, equipment. I suppose it was a forty footer, perhaps longer. The only thing was that there was a sense of sterility about it, as though it hadn't actually been used much. It was so neat that it almost appeared to be a film set.

There were just five of us at the meeting, although the cabin was so large that we could have fitted a few more in. The five were Tina and myself, Elweth and two other people. The younger of the two was the David that Jim had raved about; a thin, dark, curly-haired, clean-shaven youth in new pressed jeans and a thin, expensive-looking woollen pullover. He was sitting fingering what looked to be a very expensive paperback-sized computer. He actually did look like he was little more than a student, either that or the latest violin virtuoso out of New York. His companion was a stiff-backed, heavy-jowled man in late middle age in a well-worn sports jacket who looked like an unemployed school-teacher. He was introduced as Nathan. I had a very strong suspicion that, anglicisation of the names and pronunciations apart, neither would have answered to these names at home. We shook hands coolly and formally as if it didn't mean anything, which it didn't. In fact I heartily wished all three could have been on some other boat somewhere else, preferably on a raft adrift in mid Pacific where they could do least harm.

Nathan started. Here, as yesterday, age seemed to equal rank. He had a cautious, steady voice with just a hint of a central European accent.

'This needs to be a quick meeting if we can manage it. Both David and I have work to do tomorrow and no wish to

241

be stuck in this boat when the weather changes.'

I wondered how they would get back to Tel Aviv and decided that they'd probably sail out and be transferred to an Israeli gunboat. They could then either cruise south overnight or even – if speed was essential – be picked up by helicopter. I was struck too by Nathan's very good command of English. It crossed my mind that maybe they had deliberately sent up very westernised men for this meeting in order to smooth it with Elweth, whose tolerance of foreignness was probably minimal.

Nathan picked up a sheet of typescript which looked to be in English. He had a furrowed brow and seemed ill at ease.

'I think the best thing to do is read you a rough, edited translation of the conclusions of an urgent meeting held yesterday in the Defence Ministry. In a fuller revised form it will be discussed by the cabinet tomorrow. Eventually, if necessary, it will be released to our allies.'

He cleared his throat. 'In the past forty-eight hours the State of Israel has been alerted to the existence of a threat to its security. This is the possibility that chemical and/or biological weaponry...' 'CBW,' Elweth whispered to me in tones that all could hear, 'is being produced in one of the territories in Lebanon not under the control of either the IDF, SLA or the Syrian Army. New analysis of data collected two years ago but overlooked,' here he shook his head in apparent reprimand, 'suggests the accumulation of equipment for the production of dangerous micro-organisms, possibly viral pathogens, in the area of Farayoun in north Lebanon. Information from other sources suggests the possibility of technical assistance from the West on this. Although the notional controller of the area, Elias Daoud, has shown no previous hostility to the State, it is considered possible that he, or an organisation working with his knowledge, is preparing the material for sale to a third party. The close proximity of Farayoun to a number of hostile elements is to be noted.'

Nathan coughed dryly and looked up from his notes very briefly to see if we were all listening. For what sounded like a badly written first draft of a government statement it was gripping reading.

'This situation presents the State with many problems. In the past it has been made clear to our neighbours that some military developments, including the development of biological weapons, would not be tolerated within the immediate regional geopolitical framework. All major parties in the area are aware that, in the event of them pursuing certain lines of research, the State is prepared to countenance the use of any appropriate military action to eliminate the threat. Without prior warning.' Nathan looked round at us to make sure that it registered and then continued. 'They have therefore, to the best of our knowledge, desisted.'

He took a sip from a glass of water.

'The problem that now arises is the possibility of the development of biological weapons within a non-State entity in the region. The likelihood of the use of biological weapons against the State of Israel has been considered minimal in the past because of the unpredictability and international repercussions of the use of such agents. However, the possibility of their use by terrorist groups cannot be ruled out. The small size of the State's population renders it particularly vulnerable to such agents. The incapacitation of even twenty per cent of the adult male population would make the successful defence of the State questionable.'

Nathan looked around. 'There is then a brief discussion in the original document of population levels at which the State of Israel would become unviable. That is untranslated and I omit it for security reasons. I shall move on to the conclusions of the discussion which are much as you would have expected.'

He bent down over the paper again.

'The potential threat posed by this operation is rated as

very high. Given the duration over which these facilities may have been in operation, the possibility that biological weapons have already been produced and stockpiled cannot be ruled out. Consequently, all possible efforts should be made to establish the threat posed by this operation as soon as possible. The need for precise details of the nature of the organisation and its goals should be subordinated to the necessity of the immediate, total elimination of the laboratory facilities and stockpiles. A working group with emergency priority and wartime powers is to be established to ensure the success of this operation. This elimination should be proceeded with as soon as confirmation of the threat is received and the precise locality of the laboratory or processing site known. The perceived risk is so great that even a large-scale operation with substantive spillover should be endorsed.'

I nearly snorted aloud at the term 'substantive spillover'. I've seen what they mean: kids with their arms blown off, flattened schools and mass graves. I just gripped the table and said nothing.

Nathan, however, was finishing. 'The political isolation of Daoud from all other parties in the region indicates that even the largest scale operation currently envisaged would have no lasting political repercussions.' There was a lingering something over the word 'currently' that caught my attention for a moment. Nathan turned to us. The document certainly explained his worried look.

'In essence that is the problem as we see it in a broad sense. Let me start to focus it: we have two specific problems. The first I will deal with. It is that we have to establish that Elias is in fact doing what we fear. He may be innocent.'

Here he looked around as if to see if the idea had any takers. I wasn't going to argue for that, not after what I knew about their bedtime reading in Farayoun. There was silence and Nathan continued.

'But he *is* up to something. One suggestion from our

244

biologists is that he is going to try to steal patented micro-organisms – I'm told they exist – and produce medical drugs from them. This fits with the fact that everything that can be faked is being faked in Lebanon. Technically they say it is feasible, although it's an odd way to make money. It's easier to print it. And for a lot of good reasons – moral, military and economic – we don't want to do something without the evidence.'

True enough, I thought. Flattening a neutral party's hospital without a good excuse is an expensive and effective way of generating propaganda for your enemies. Nathan coughed slightly again.

'Excuse me. So we must have some sort of confirmation that what is being planned in Farayoun is the production of disease causing micro-organisms. I should also clear something up. Suppose, you say, these things are being made but are not intended for us?'

That particular question wasn't bothering me, but what was causing me increasing concern was the thought that there was going to be a price tag on this fascinating glimpse into the workings of Israeli Intelligence. Nathan opened his arms in a gesture of innocence.

'After all, Elias has so many enemies that they may be intended for someone else. That, we have decided, is irrelevant. Farayoun is a mere sixty miles from our northernmost territories. At this season, and others, winds can blow from the north, so clearly even a laboratory accident could threaten us. Within hours. Equally, the Syrians could move into the area – a very undesirable situation. Therefore, the conclusion is simple. If this work exists it must be destroyed. Any dissension?'

I thought about it and decided I had to say something. I wasn't just going to rubber stamp an air raid.

'I'd like to say that I assume the phrase "this work must be destroyed" refers to the lab and the bugs, not the people.'

There was a nod from Tina. Nathan was silent for a

moment and then he waved a finger in agreement.

'An excellent point. Yes. David will discuss this precise issue with you in a moment.'

David just nodded quietly. Nathan shuffled his papers together.

'So the first problem is confirmation of the hazard. David, now over to you.'

David leaned forward on the table, arms in a semi-circle in front of him.

'First of all, may I say, Dr Stanwick, on behalf of the air-force, that having read your file I quite understand your sensitivities over, er, laxity in targeting accuracy. We have made improvements since your last, er, acquaintance. Although it was before my time.'

I suppose I tried to maintain a fixed smile. I'd never seen myself as being sensitive about laxity in targeting accuracy; I'd always thought that I just didn't like seeing the innocent killed.

Realising that I was going to make no comment David began again, this time with more force and fluency.

'Right. Our second problem is this: having found that Daoud is doing, or allowing, this terrible thing, how do we destroy it? And as Dr Stanwick has so rightly pointed out, with the need for the minimum civilian casualties.'

That definitely worried me. When people start praising your high moral tone, it's time to start looking for the rat.

'This is a difficult, very challenging technical problem, but we can do it.'

I noticed again the excellent English, this time with an American accent, coupled with all the enthusiasm and confidence of a post-graduate who thinks his thesis has overturned every bit of work in his field since Aristotle. It's no wonder that he had won Elweth's admiration.

David continued. 'So problem two is precise location of the hazard. This brings us into a difficult area. Allow me to show you a model.'

He reached back behind him and brought out a three-dimensional plastic model of a landscape, about a metre by a metre. It was not unlike some of the models you can get to show the features of glaciated regions, or the topography of the Lake District. This had been roughly painted in browns and greens and had small coloured blocks on it to show buildings.

'Farayoun. We have a computerised machine that makes these off aerial photographs. Much more useful than the photographs themselves and we can do it within a few hours of getting the images in. Some of our politicians have trouble with maps.'

Nathan frowned. I felt that hadn't been in the script. I looked carefully at the model. It was a fine piece of work; the features were so dramatic, especially the valley and the cliffs, that at first I thought the vertical scale had been exaggerated. But then I remembered how rugged the scenery was and decided that there was no distortion.

Elweth muttered something about it being real neat. I picked it up, rotated it and put my head down so that I could look up the valley towards Farayoun as though from the road. The effect seemed to be accurate. I put it down and Jim picked it up. Oblivious to everyone else he started to move his hand in a slow snake like fashion up inside the valley. To my dismay, I realised that his hand was meant to be a bomber flying in to attack. David caught his action and gave a quick smile.

'Er, excuse me, Jim, can I have it back? Thanks. Now we believe that the operation is centred in Farayoun itself. That would make strategic sense; Elias could keep control of it and it is very secure. Unfortunately, we have paid little attention to this area. That, of course, was not the airforce's decision.' He was given a brief glare from Nathan at this point, who clearly felt that this was another departure from the script. 'Anyway, for whatever reason, we have no very high resolution photographs. As we do not wish to alert Elias we would prefer not to do any low flying or use drones to produce it now. Such images are apparently unlikely to tell us anything anyway. It will all be indoors. We are currently running a series of analyses, at different wavebands, of the area.'

David looked around to be sure we were taking it all in. He gave the impression of a university lecturer giving a talk to sixth formers; having total mastery of his subject and without fear of criticism, but with a slight unease about exactly how low a level he should pitch the talk at. He looked at his watch, a large technical looking digital affair.

'The next reconnaissance flight should be overhead in thirty minutes. We are being careful not to alter existing patterns too obviously, but it's difficult at this time of year. The first detailed photographs and analyses were taken yesterday; we will do more today and more tomorrow. Then I'm afraid we are blind on most wavelengths for two, maybe three, days till the storm clears.'

He lined up the block model carefully. 'Now see the situation. A deep gorge with three cliffs – call them lower, middle and upper. Farayoun town rests on the lower and greatest cliff. Our interest lies in the area between the middle cliff and the final upper cliff which is the boundary to the valley here. This we consider is the target terrain. Above this middle cliff at Farayoun we have three potential sites; in fact the only three buildings above the town itself. It's a tight spot.'

David looked around at us, as if to make sure that he still held the attention of his class. He turned to one side. 'Jim, that's why we'll use F-16s; manoeuvrability even with full payload is unbeatable.'

Jim nodded earnestly and with evident attention. There was no doubt that they had him hooked.

'Now, we believe that the most likely centre of operations is the monastery, Deir Musa – although what Moses had to do with it.... Note, it's a tough target, I mean, well sited spot; you can see it backs up against a smaller cliff.'

He pointed with a thin finger to a small red block nestled against the hillside and extending outwards along a protuberance of rock above the gorge. What I found chilling was the knowledge that what I saw as scenery or geomorphological features he saw in terms of accessibility for bombing raids.

'It's been recently refurbished, has new power lines and lots of space inside. Apparently it is still being renovated, according to Elias. Eventually, he boasts, he is going to turn it into a college. So he claims. Six cars there yesterday at midday, so that's the hot favourite.'

He waved his finger over the block.

'Analysis of the buildings was disappointing. We were hoping to pick up some sort of thermal anomaly or, even better, noise from computers. We got nothing of note, but we were able to scan for only a few minutes.'

Then he moved his finger along the cliff edge to a small purple block close to the edge of the cliff, but not on such a rocky protrusion as the Deir.

'This is Elias Daoud's house. Large, and sprawling. About a mile from the Deir. Eight cars there yesterday. Well equipped for power. A possibility, but it does not have as much room as the Deir.'

Then he moved his finger to a yellow block, slightly up the hill and just to the west of the purple block so that the three points formed something of an asymmetrical triangle.

'This is the third spot. The Hotel Barakat, but it hasn't taken guests since 1975. However, yesterday's image shows a dozen cars. A 1920s structure and unlike the Deir and the house it is just off the road, or track over the mountain. Good power again.' We stared at the model.

There was another aside to Jim. 'Not apparently a well-built building and I would think that nothing special in the way of ordnance would be needed. Not ordinarily, but....'

He seemed to recollect his lines and stopped in mid-sentence. He jabbed at the model with his finger. As he pointed it out I noticed the track snaking upwards and over the edge of the model.

'Oh yes, Daoud has his own radio set up at the house and

a decent mast. He regularly communicates to Cyprus, and maybe elsewhere, by radio telephone. A Cyprus team is looking into that end of things, but provisionally it looks like there is digital as well as analog transmission. That is, he uses a computer and modem setup as well as talks. He's sending electronic mail, possibly telexes.'

Elweth spoke, 'You've been monitoring him, Dave?'

Nathan and David looked at each other with something like unease. It was the older man who spoke.

'No, Mr Elweth, we have not done so far. Since the collapse of the phone system almost everybody with money uses radios here. The wavebands are full. How can we tell signal from noise? Besides, we have concentrated our efforts on the south and in Syria. We are trying to listen from now on, but it could take months to know what messages were contained in Daoud's shopping lists.'

David broke in. 'Although even listening may be difficult. If he is using a very directional signal, and possibly transmitting short compressed messages, it will be hard to get anything.'

There was a moment of silence. These people clearly had a problem. Then David spoke again, looking at me.

'Incidentally, Dr Stanwick, we have no idea which of the three buildings might contain your friend. There is also a barracks of some sort in the centre of town. So he might be there.'

He paused and stared at the model. 'So this is our second problem. We do not know where the hazard is.'

Jim Elweth looked at him and scratched his head.

'How quickly can you move an agent in; or have you got one there already?'

David looked at Nathan for guidance. The older man rubbed his chin as if to play for time. Then he spoke.

'We are talking weeks in an optimum case for a preferred operative. Daoud is suspicious and hostile, has few friends and the hazard will be under deep cover. These three buildings are the only buildings above the middle cliff. Now we could probably get a man into Farayoun town fairly quickly. But above it? There is not much traffic on the road even in summer and in winter very little. Daoud has been a nobody in our books. We haven't bothered with him, we have enough problems. We are also a long way from home to mount an airborne operation. Mr Elweth, we have to admit it, we have an intelligence hole here. Beyond that I will say nothing of our plans.'

I was increasingly disliking the tone of the conversation. It was leading up to something and I didn't know what. I glanced at Tina and she was sitting tight lipped and clearly uneasy. David began again. 'The location of the hazard then is a problem, but it is a worse problem because of military difficulties. If you'll excuse me I will briefly discuss our military options.'

He looked around again and I felt he seemed to be more at ease. Clearly he was now in his element.

'Now this is a job for the airforce. We have no agents in place, a helicopter based operation is out of the question because of range. We would also have to do it under the guns of the Syrians.' He looked at Elweth. 'They've got three ZSU twentythree-fours near the top.'

'You don't say?'

I wasn't sure that Jim had a clue, but he was loving it. I had to admire how David was handling him. He may have been young, but he knew how to play Jim Elweth. David turned to me.

'Radar guided anti-aircraft guns. No real threat to our planes, but bad news for choppers. Anyway, they could in theory make trouble for a protracted operation and the co-operation of Damascus cannot be relied on. Also there is another factor.'

He paused for effect.

'Suppose these organisms exist and are stored. In the time it would take for us to land and launch an assault they could be released as a desperate final measure.'

There was no doubt about it; everyone was telling me

secrets. On the basis that there's no such thing as a free lunch I wondered again what the bill on this was going to be and how much Tina and I would be paying.

'Now, of course, the airforce has the potential to put several tons of a variety of ordnance on anywhere you care to name in Farayoun. There will be little if any opposition and even if the Syrians choose to fight, we doubt whether they can protect Daoud. So that's good news and makes up for the fact that there's not a lot of room to line up a good bombing run in the rather restricted space of the valley.'

Yes, I thought, open cities are so much better for that. But I couldn't see the technical problem. Just drop the bombs and go home.

David cleared his throat. 'This is, however, a special case. We cannot risk a situation in which all we have done is rupture the tanks or whatever vessels are containing these pathogens. It may even be that these things are in glassware.'

As he said it I saw their problem and began to have a very unpleasant feeling about what lay in store for us.

'Fortunately, we have a partial answer in that we have bombs that implode rather than explode. The effect of these would be to suck in the walls of the lab. If we followed up that within seconds by high temperature incendiaries we could virtually guarantee sterility. We are conducting further tests, but we are fairly confident.'

Elweth was grinning. 'That's neat. Real neat. Cook 'em with a cocktail.'

It came back to me now. They'd used a single implosion bomb in Beirut in '82 and pulled down an entire building in Bourj el Barajneh, with over a hundred fatalities.

David politely ignored Jim and continued. 'But even with that set up we need two things: precise location of the lab and precise delivery. For the location we must know where the hazard is to within ten metres. No more. For the delivery our boys can do it if they have perfect visibility and the best we can set up in weaponry.'

Then Tina spoke quietly but clearly.

'I hate to interrupt what is clearly an exciting conversation, and I'm probably totally naive, but can we return to what Henry said earlier? Assuming you do have to carry out this business, what about the people – some of whom may be innocent?'

David looked at Nathan as if to say, 'This one is yours.' Nathan smiled at Tina in what seemed a kindly fashion.

'Right, thank you, Mrs Stanwick. Yes, we are interested in minimising casualties. Very interested. It is, in fact, one reason we are talking to you. First, there will be a brief warning of about two minutes. It will be unmistakeable; either a drone or a practice attack. It will be enough time to get clear if they run, but not long enough for them to pocket any viruses. Does that satisfy you?'

Tina looked at me and then muttered, 'I see.'

I said nothing because I was still thinking over the answer. It might have been true, although I very much doubted it. But the straight answer should have been something along the lines of, 'Madam, we can't take chances and anyway they had it coming.' What Nathan had given was a carefully designed cosmetic answer. They wanted our cooperation. Tina sat silent, still clearly unhappy about something.

Meanwhile, on the other side of me, David was speaking in a low, confiding voice to Jim. What he was saying was all but incomprehensible, at least to me.

'I'll go over the provisional mission profile with you later, Jim. But we are planning a big show; "Belt and braces" as you say; just in case. Airborne C3 with RPVs, a high-level fighter screen with LDSD capability and ECM-ECCM cover. Munitions will be smart bombs, laser guided, fire-and-forget systems. Everything PGM; the whole works. And a few specials, maybe some of the new shaped charges if we need them. Anyway, we'll go over it later. There's actually a problem using PAVE TACK guidance; the valley is too steep and too narrow from some

253

angles. We may have to rewrite the textbook.'

The look on Jim's face told it all: there was total rapt attention. What I'd simply heard as the jargon and the acronyms of death had proved to be a magic spell. It was as though you were promising a hi-fi fanatic his dream system. He was entranced. Why were they being so nice to Elweth?

Then Tina spoke again. 'I just have one other question. Why are you telling us all this?'

That's my girl, I thought. Straight to the point. Elweth, apparently suddenly and cruelly woken from his dream of the better, bigger and smarter bang, looked at her in consternation. Nathan sipped from his glass of water and folded his hands and leaned his elbows onto the edge of the table.

'Excellent. It's about time we came to the point. As we have said, we have two problems and the answers to both lie in Farayoun. We cannot get into Farayoun for some time and at the moment we can't even come up with an excuse that would allow us to go knocking on Elias Daoud's door. And for a number of days we will not even be able to see into Farayoun. You, on the other hand, are going there this afternoon.'

He cleared his throat as though he were about to say something distasteful.

'So, quite simply, we want you to answer our questions for us.'

27

There was a silence, but I was too stunned to notice whether it was for a second or for a minute. Then I broke it with what I don't suppose was a very dignified performance.

'You are crazy! Absolutely out of your minds. You've got the wrong person to help you. You've read my folder. What do you think I was doing in the summer of '82 in Beirut? Plane spotting? I've been bombed by you people. I've seen what you did to the Palestinian camps – almost totally indiscriminately. I'm not going to line up an air raid for you or anybody.'

Jim Elweth at least looked discomfited. I think he was having serious doubts about whether this really was the right way to enlist someone's services. Nathan waited in impassive silence. When I finally stopped for breath he spoke quietly and slowly.

'Yes, we've read your folder. In fact we are asking you for help because we've read your folder.'

I ignored him. 'You make the whole thing sound as innocuous as ordering a Chinese take-away. "Hello, Tel Aviv, can you deliver two tons of number 57 on the monastery door? With lots of fried rice and don't skimp on the phosphorus." No way!'

David gave Nathan a curious glance. I think he was having his doubts as well. Tina seemed numbed into silence which was at least more dignified than my reaction. Nathan waited again, without hint of impatience or irritation.

'Let me repeat. We've read your folder. You are idealistic, honest and moralistic. You hate indiscriminate carnage. Bizarre as it sounds we trust you.'

This time he got through. I stopped muttering and listened. Nathan continued in a flat, almost soothing, voice. There was no doubt he was in charge.

'We want to explore a number of possible avenues with you, gently and slowly, with plenty of time for objections. We are talking morality, not politics here. At the outset though I must point something out to you. There are a number of options that are no longer open to you. Wheels have been set in motion. As you have heard, detailed military plans are being made. You cannot put the

255

clock back. What you *can* do is ensure that what is done
– if it has to be done – is with the maximum success and
the minimum of bloodshed. Also we say this: you will not
be communicating with us directly. As of the end of this
meeting you will contact us through a third party, so you
should not think in terms of working for us. As I shall
point out, it is in fact for a greater good and a larger
cause.'

Then he was silent again, allowing time for it all to sink
in.

'We want you to go up to Farayoun as planned. We
expect that Daoud will greet you as a friend of a friend.
Indeed, as the friend of one of the few friends he has left.
All we ask is that in Farayoun you simply keep your eyes
and ears open. All being well he will release your friend as a
favour to Charles Rimmer.'

Nathan sat back and looked slowly around the table.
'Now perhaps, let us call it Case One, you see nothing and
simply return. You pass on that information and we are no
worse off. But your negative report may have saved much.
You see, we are already putting other plans into operation,
but they will take time to mature. In the meantime....'

He paused and coughed gently. 'Ah, in the meantime,
perhaps some of the hotheads in the cabinet may say that
we should go ahead anyway. I do not need to name names,
but they might say, "Flatten everything, house, Deir and
hotel." Perhaps your negative report may stop that. So that
is Case One. Any comments?'

I had none. This had all the appearance of being a beautifully constructed and rehearsed trap.

'Very well. Consider Case Two. You find out that
Daoud is simply cloning insulin or human growth hor-
mone. Naughty, but neither here nor there to us. You
report it. If it fits with our other data then we do nothing,
and again you will have rendered all sides a service. The
planned raid will be cancelled and we will sleep a little
easier in our beds. That is Case Two. Do you have any

256

comments on that?'

I glanced at Tina, who looked utterly miserable, and shook my head. I felt annoyed, but I could appreciate the logic. I even had a glimmer of the argument for the remaining case.

'Case Three: you find that something terrible is being prepared; indeed, is standing ready for use. Some germ, some virus, some bacteria. Now remember what you accused us of? "Indiscriminate bombing" I think you said.'

He let the words sink in. Objectively, I could see that it was beautifully done. Nathan was barely recognisable as the dry schoolmaster reading the official document earlier. He seemed to bow his head, as if taking the guilt upon him like a heavy chain. 'Indiscriminate bombing. Yes. It cannot be denied I think. Things got out of control. Men in a hurry coupled with poor planning and poor intelligence. You see what happens.'

Then he looked hard at me and leaned forward with his eyes wide. It was not a menacing gesture; he was too smart for that. He began speaking slowly and solemnly, but with a carefully rising intensity.

'Indiscriminate. But how much more indiscriminate would this abomination be? Man and woman, civilian and soldier, Arab and Jew. In fact it would discriminate. Our soldiers we might be able to inoculate, but the sick, the old and the children?'

He shook his head. The atmosphere around the table was intense. I know politicians, and one or two preachers, who would have given their all for his verbal gifts. He only paused for a fraction of a moment and then began again.

'But of course that would not be the end of it. Supposing this horror, this abomination, were to be sent among us – even a mild form, merely crippling and incapacitating – the hawks in the cabinet would argue that we must strike a deadly blow, a killing blow, at our enemies lest they take advantage of us. At Damascus, at the camps. It would not be a well-timed, careful, precise strike. It would be a brutal, coarse slash, using everything we have and we would be heedless of who we hit.'

The words penetrated deep. There was the briefest of pauses before he continued in deep tones.

'And of course if it came to the worst, then there would be those who would remember Masada. And no one, no one for thirty generations, would inherit the land of Israel.'

There was total silence. Suddenly, as though they had been waiting offstage, a double boom announced the arrival overhead of the reconnaissance planes. Tina and I jumped and Elweth looked at his watch.

'You guys are a minute late.'

David smiled faintly at him. 'It is the Sabbath.'

Nathan cleared his throat again. 'So there too, in Case Three, your moral duty seems plain. To tell us where, precisely, accurately, these dreadful things are so that we can simply and quickly destroy them – maybe without any loss of life. They cannot bring peace to the region; they cannot bring justice.'

He looked at me with apparent compassion. 'I imagine you are tempted to refuse to co-operate at all, to do nothing. That would be very terrible. First, it is too late now – already you have started the machinery of war in motion. Secondly, I am certain I do not have to remind you how you would feel if these things were released and you had done nothing. Didn't one of your Englishmen say that "For evil to triumph it is simply enough that good men do nothing"?'

I was silent. I felt I was being pulverised. But Nathan continued, remorseless, unyielding in his attack. 'Consider finally, this. It is an argument I do not wish to bring in because the thought of it freezes my soul, but listen; if we are convinced that these things, these bacterial agents, these biohazards, are stored in Farayoun and we can get some proof of it, but we still do not know where exactly in these three buildings, within ten metres, they are housed, then we shall have to use the obvious solution.'

For a moment I didn't understand what he was talking about.

'The obvious solution. Indeed, the weapons which might almost have been specifically designed for this case: ones which produce a flame hotter than the sun. Small, clean ones.'

My ignorance fled as the dreadful words sank in one by one. He glanced searchingly at Tina and me.

'Yes, Dr Stanwick, we prize our security very dearly.'

There was a strangled silence. Then there was a little noise from Tina, a small gasp or a sigh. She was looking at me in something approaching despair and I think she was hoping that I would laugh it off, or call their bluff. I said nothing. In truth, I had nothing to say.

Elweth finally broke the silence. Even he sounded vaguely sobered. 'A nuke would sure fry any bugs.'

Then he paused and, I think, remembered who he was. 'But they sure wouldn't like it in Washington.'

I decided I needed some fresh air.

'Excuse me, I'm going to take a walk. Tina?'

She nodded faintly. Nathan looked around the table. 'We understand, but before you make a decision let me say that if you do decide to assist, then you report to Mr Elweth in Cyprus or the Cypriot captain of the yacht, which will be back here from tomorrow morning. You will not be working for us, we will keep no records of your involvement and once you return from Farayoun the matter will be forgotten.'

'I see,' I said, and walked out onto the deck and from there onto the quayside where I found a concrete wall, sat down on it and stared out over the sea. Tina sat nearby and was silent while I ran it all over in my mind. Every option was closed off. After a few minutes I turned to Tina. I could hear the bitterness in my voice.

'Neat, isn't it? They have me trapped. Incredible. They are going to have me working for them. I don't understand it. Is there no other option?'

259

She sighed. 'I see none at the moment. Maybe in Farayoun another way will open. Perhaps these people will be too clever for their own good. Perhaps it's what has to be done. I don't know.'

'So I say yes?'

'No, I suppose *we* say it.'

So I went back down into the shade of the cabin where they were getting a foil wrapped lunch out of insulated boxes. Nathan looked at me.

'We see no option but to say yes.'

My words sounded like a betrayal and they certainly felt like it. Nathan nodded. There was no elation in his eyes.

'Any conditions?'

'Can you do anything to help me get Fuad out?'

'We've thought about it and the answer is probably not. The only thing is that if you can get a message through to us we can pick you, or him, up almost anywhere along the coast. Preferably at night.'

Nathan looked at David, who said something very quietly in Hebrew. It struck me as an interesting reflection on how well planned the thing was that this was the first aside they had had to make to each other. Nathan spoke again.

'Yes, there is also another offer we make. Mr Elweth is going back to Cyprus tonight to be on standby. If you so wish, we can take your wife back, and guard her for the duration. Talk it over together during lunch.'

Elweth's promised meal was a brief one. Tina and I ate outside on the deck, although much of the food seemed to want to stick in my throat. She had said little since Nathan's offer and I had made no comment on it. As she had said to me once, 'There are some battles that you have to fight on your own.'

After a few minutes she spoke quietly, 'Henry, will you be angry with me if I say I am tempted by the offer?'

'No. In fact if it was the other way round I'm not sure how I would answer. Remember that this is the last get-off point. Next stop is Farayoun.'

She seemed not to have heard. 'It's just that I've had no chance to adjust to this place. I've only met Antoine and that Shiite woman who are even remotely normal. I'm just out of my depth and I'm frightened half the time. The trouble is I say to myself I have no need to be scared, but it seems I have. And I'm worried that I will get in the way. I haven't actually been much use so far, have I?'

I found it a hard question to answer without swaying her decision either one way or the other. In the end I just came out with the first platitude that came to mind.

'Well, I've enjoyed your company.'

'Yes, but if I had thought about what I was saying in front of the others, Zvi and the old man, we would simply have the problem of Fuad. Not trying to stop, or start, an air raid.'

'Hmm, you have an undeniable point there. There can rarely have been a more striking arrival in the Middle East. On some of the scenarios this morning you'd make Cleopatra look like a minor personality, but then we aren't sure what is really going on and you may have done us all a great service. These boys may be right that something horrible is brewing up there.'

She said nothing for a few minutes. The waves made a gentle lapping sound against the side of the boat and the rigging and flags fluttered softly. Far away there was the inevitable noise of traffic.

'Do you want me in Farayoun?'

It was a tricky question. 'Only if you want to come. This is a volunteers only mission.'

She fell silent for several minutes.

'Look, Henry, I think this thing is like riding on a roller coaster. The worst bit is standing outside and agonising about whether or not to take the risk, but once you're on it the only way off is to go through.'

'So?'

'So, I'll come, voluntarily and in fear and trembling, but

261

from now on no looking back.'

There wasn't much to say. As Elweth was tearing up half a chicken nearby I passed on kissing her, but I squeezed her hand hard. Then I whispered to her. 'Thanks. I'm not sure I'd entrust you to this particular shipping line anyway.'

After lunch there were the details to clear up. The basic idea was that we would report to either Elweth in Cyprus or the boat's captain as soon as we got out of the Asal Valley. However, a number of plans were laid in case of contingencies. The main one of these was that if we got stuck in Farayoun, due to snow or worse, we should try to communicate any results to Cyprus by either hand carried message or phone to a number they gave me. The phone message idea I didn't like. The idea of engaging Elweth in conversation from Farayoun, where at least some of the people would know his voice, wasn't attractive. It would also take a minute or two at the least to give the message clearly. I wondered too how accurate Jim would be at passing on any phone message. I supposed they'd have the line wired up to a recorder. That raised another point, as the record of that would be an unequivocal link between me and this dirty work. Something a bit more distancing would be useful, particularly in view of the ease with which Jim lost data. I had an idea.

'Jim, you've got a computer on-line in Cyprus?'

He nodded. 'Sure, of course.'

'So I could slip you a three-line report in a couple of seconds. All I'd need to do is borrow a machine for a couple of minutes up in Farayoun. It would give another option.'

Jim got a confirmatory nod from Nathan.

'OK, let me dig out the protocols for you. At least that won't wake me up in the middle of the night. Anyway, I'd prefer hard copy.'

He went along the boat in pursuit of his briefcase. Nathan looked up from perusing the model.

'Try to make contact within four days.'

'Why?' I asked.

Nathan spoke slowly, 'We have to allow for the fact that something might go wrong. Supposing they suspect and interrogate you. You might reveal something. Inadvertently of course. It is a risk we think is low. However, in that case we would not hear from you and we would assume the worst. So if you do not reply to here or Elweth in four days' time we will evaluate all other data and make a decision. Your loss, er, absence would be data.'

'And you'd go ahead anyway?'

'That is a cabinet decision. Unlike our neighbours, we are a democracy. I cannot predict the cabinet's vote. A silence from you might certainly throw the balance in favour of an all-out air strike where we waited for a wind blowing away from us, crossed our fingers and struck at all three buildings. Probably only with conventional weaponry. It depends if we felt lucky.'

'I see.' It came out as a pathetic answer, but then it was difficult to think of anything remotely adequate. Meanwhile, Jim came back with some numbers on a scrap of paper. Fortunately, they weren't too hard to remember: the phone number was only a digit away from the other one and the setup parameters were those I had on my own machine back in Grantforth. I memorised the number and crumpled the paper up and threw it into the pile of waste foil and napkins from lunch.

Then David spent some time clarifying terminology for the messages so that they wouldn't raise too much alarm on the remote chance of them being overheard or picked up by the casual listener. Rather elegantly the use of code was to be avoided, by couching the message in terms of an evaluation of the structure of the various buildings. Comments about soundness were reassuring, but identification of structural problems was an acknowledgement that a hazard existed and a recommendation for urgent treatment was an acknowledgement of an imminent threat. An evaluation of all three buildings was to be given if possible. At this point

Nathan took over and looked hard at Jim. 'Mr Elweth, you understand that there is to be no discussion on such a message. Nothing more than a bald statement that you confirm transmission or a request to retransmit. Then no further contact. At all.' The tone was very strict.

Jim stared back at him. For a brief moment he seemed to pause and I wondered if he was going to rebel. Then he shrugged.

'Well sure. This is your project – I'm told to give you full assistance. Whatever you say.'

Nathan gave just the faintest hint of a smile. 'Thank you. Thank you, Mr Elweth.'

After a slightly awkward silence David suggested what would be the likely result of a 'recommendation for urgent treatment'.

'In that case, the first day that the weather clears we will probably strike at the structure mentioned at the earliest opportunity. It will probably be early morning, just as soon as the shadows lift off the buildings and they get the sun on them.'

'Why then? You like the smell of napalm in the morning?'

There was a flicker of something across David's face, but it was covered quickly by a mask of blandness.

'Oh really, Dr Stanwick! No, in part because it may simply be the earliest we can do it. Given the twelve hours of darkness at this time of year there is a fifty per cent chance the weather will clear overnight. Also, we've learned from experience the light will be perfect then. Good strong shadows. They allow us to bomb with the precise accuracy that our critics sitting in their armchairs a thousand miles away so desire.'

Fair comment, I thought. Actually, David might never have smelled napalm. He was simply a glorified technician; a man who merely set up co-ordinates, ordnance types and mission profiles and who talked about payload delivery. He neither dropped the bombs nor saw the shed blood. He

264

dealt only in abstractions. David continued, back now in his lecturing tone. 'It also allows us a whole day to run follow up airphoto missions to determine the damage. Evening is useless. If we missed first time round then it would be twelve hours at this time of year before we got another try.'

I looked hard at him. 'You'd better get it first time.'

'Oh we will.'

'So if I do send out a recommendation for immediate action, we'd better not be around the hazard area on the first clear dawn after the storm has finished.'

David nodded firmly. I thought about this scenario, where they launched the attack on the basis of my phone call to Elweth.

'You're putting a lot of trust in me.'

David nodded again, but with less dogmatism.

'We are, but we will cross-check your evaluation. I won't say any more than that. And we won't be asleep during the bad weather. There are teams working on this in a number of places and their data has to be merged. We'll try and put a surveillance plane or a drone over the area during the storm. It won't be able to see anything on the visible waveband, but it will be able to circle overhead for a long time unnoticed. That may give us time so that we can get enough data from electronic noise from computers and machines to determine a hazard. It won't give us a precise location, but it may confirm the nature of the problem.'

Then that was it. They checked I knew the Cyprus phone numbers and the codewords and there was an odd moment where we just said goodbye to everybody and Nathan and David merely said good luck, and turned away.

Jim Elweth came with us some way to the car. Out of earshot of the boat he turned to me. He seemed troubled.

'Well, Henry, this whole thing seems to have snowballed. I guess we have to play it the Tel Aviv way. It'll be a shame if this is the base of the group and we get it all wiped

265

out. But my orders are to back these people. As my boss said on the phone yesterday, their real threat has priority over our imagined one. What can I say?'

I shrugged. 'Sorry, Jim, it's not my profession.'

After looking awkward for a moment Jim shook hands and made something approaching a little speech about 'it all being real impressive of us to go and be willing to do this kinda thing'. I wondered if he'd totally missed the nature of the conversation. Then he turned and went back to the yacht where I noticed that they were already unfastening the moorings.

We got into the car and just before I turned the ignition key I paused and turned to Tina.

'Ready to go?'

Her answer surprised me.

'Yes, very much. I've made my resolution and I'll stick by it. The only way home is through Farayoun.'

'You sound almost happy about it.'

'In a way I am. I've resolved my problem of commitment. Whether I like it or not this has to be done.'

I squeezed her hand. 'Well done. I'm proud of you.'

'Thanks, but I tell you what I would like after meeting with that lot.'

'What?'

'A nice bath with lots of soap and disinfectant.'

28

Then we drove northwards through Jounieh and along the coast road. For the first time there was some hint at the existence of patches of countryside rather than a continuous urban sprawl, but the banana plantations and the fields of polythene covered plants seemed threatened by the marinas, holiday homes and new apartment blocks. Still, away to the right up the steep sides of the mountains and along the flanks of the valleys, there was a glimpse of a purely rural, even forested, hillside. The coastal plain was so narrow and the hills rose so steeply up from it that it was impossible to see the tops of the mountains except in very brief glimpses up the deeper valleys. But even here there was no escape from the war, with continual reminders such as bullet holes in walls, partially infilled craters on the road and the universal political posters.

As we drove we talked of all sorts of things.

'Henry, do you trust those people at all?'

'Not in the slightest. What they said was for our, and Jim Elweth's, consumption. It had all been rehearsed beforehand. I'm afraid that if they had compelling evidence for what they fear tonight, Farayoun would be rubble tomorrow. You can forget your two minute warning as well, I'm afraid.'

'Why do you think Jim was there?'

'I think at first they thought they could pump him for information, but he wouldn't play. First sensible thing he's done in my opinion. Then he was simply a necessary evil. If they do have to flatten Farayoun in a hurry then it might be as well not to have annoyed the US over the issue. I think they also realised they could use him as an intermediary, a handler for us. That was smart; there's a small but significant psychological difference between calling him and calling them, and they know it.'

'You know, I feel sorry for Jim.'

I glanced at my wife. She was being serious.

'You do? There were two other people in that meeting that I felt sorrier for – you and me.'

'I know what you mean, but I feel he's a nice lad who just got corrupted by the system. Maybe it's not too late for him.'

'You mean he could still break out of it all? Maybe. But

it would cost him. Besides, he was lapping up Boy David's jargon. We will see.'

The traffic might have thinned out, but the road was not without its hazards. Just before Jbail an old truck pulled out straight in front of us, nearly forcing me into what would have been a ditch if it hadn't been filled with ten years' worth of car fragments and litter. It seemed to typify what was happening to my life. What had happened on that yacht had made me feel very unhappy.

'Tina, why am I so easily manipulated? These people remind me of Vaughan; setting me up like that.'

Tina shook her head. I glanced at her – she was smiling slightly.

'I've been thinking about that. In its way it's a compliment. You, and I suppose I, are predictable. Because we are predictable we are programmable. How do they make you do what they want you to do? Easy. Put you in a situation where there are only two options, then just make sure that the first one is morally unacceptable. You can be relied on to lock your teeth into the second option, however unpalatable it may be, and not to let go. That's all you need. Then they wind you up and let you go. Not many of us around today.'

I snorted. 'Too true. At this rate we will be extinct shortly. You make me feel like one of Boy David's smart bombs.'

But it was a good analysis all the same and we slipped into a brooding silence. After a few miles Tina spoke.

'Henry, I think we need to make one thing clear before we get into Farayoun.'

She sounded resolute and I wondered what was behind it.

'Fire away.'

'Well, it's one of the problems you have with me being along. I give them leverage over you.'

'You mean the "tell us the truth or your wife never plays the piano again" scenario?'

268

I didn't feel the slightest bit like joking about it, but if you start seriously thinking about the creative things these people can do to your loved ones you end up gibbering before they even start asking questions.

'Well, you have my instructions not to let that influence you. Do what you have to do.'

I tried not to think about it, but it was a good point to raise and I was glad it had come from her.

'And vice versa. But pray it doesn't come to that.'

We passed Jbail without stopping. There would either be lots of time to look at the archaeological sites later or else.... I preferred not to think about any other possibility. A few miles before Batroun I pulled in and we stopped and said a prayer.

We drove through the town and were waved through the last Lebanese Forces' checkpoint with only the briefest of questions. Then we rolled slowly across the bridge over the Nahr el Asal and turned immediately right down off the autostrade. Interestingly enough there was no longer even any sign to Farayoun. Then we drove up slowly to the checkpoint.

The size and scope of the fortifications caught me by surprise. It was actually quite a formidable military structure by Lebanese standards, with proper emplacements made out of sandbags and sand-filled oil drums. There was at least one manned heavy machine gun post. There was no way you would have driven through this checkpoint by accident; indeed there even looked to be lighting for nights. Somewhat more unnerving than the hardware was the fact that several militiamen stood around looking more or less alert. Most Lebanese militia posts I've come across have less vigilance and menace than the average Grantforth traffic warden on a hot Friday afternoon.

A further eye-catching feature was a number of big posters of Elias Daoud looking statesmanlike into the distance with the flag of Lebanon waving behind him. Some way behind, in fact. The slogan in French and Arabic was 'Forward with Hope and Unity.'

I slowed to a stop and spoke under my breath to Tina, 'Do everything slowly.'

A militiaman came over. He wore a tidy green uniform with the north-arrow cedar symbol on the chest and an apparently new AK-47 assault rifle held in both hands. At least the barrel wasn't pointed towards us. I glanced briefly around the post, noting two other militiamen standing around with hands on weapons and staring our way. This was one of the few militia outfits that I felt merited the term 'soldiers'. Things had changed in the years since I had last been here.

The militiaman by the car said nothing for a moment as he looked inside and at us. Then he spoke to me in uncompromising Arabic.

'Do you speak Arabic?'

It was curiously disconcerting, even after only a few days back in Lebanon, not to be given some sort of formal greeting. I tried the caring smile and the slow, painful Arabic.

'Hello. How are you? Yes, I do speak some Arabic.'

It came out so beautifully mangled that I felt confident he would identify me as an innocent foreigner rather than a spy.

'What do you want?'

I tried to remember who it was had said Elias was trying to run the valley on Albanian lines.

'I have come from Beirut. I have a message for Sheik Elias Daoud from Professor Charles Rimmer. Let me show you.'

I very slowly pulled the envelope out of an inside pocket of the anorak I had lying on the back seat. Without letting go of the letter I held it out so he could see it. He spelled out the English aloud, but didn't look convinced.

'Who is it from?'

'Professor Charles Rimmer of the American University.'

'Rimmer.' I think the name rang some sort of a bell.

270

'OK. Your papers.'

'Certainly.'

A lorry drew up behind us. To my surprise the militiaman waved us in off the road and told me to switch the engine off while the other two on duty checked out the truck and within minutes let it pass. As I pulled off he ordered two more men to search our car. I had no idea what they were looking for, but they did a thorough job and took over ten minutes to do it.

The chief of the checkpoint, who not only had some sort of rank but also insignia to prove it, kept us waiting there in the car for another twenty minutes while he talked to Farayoun on a radio. I think Tina began to have fond thoughts of Cyprus and I began to appreciate why the two on the boat – I preferred not even to think of them as Israelis – had been so keen to acquire my services. But I was beginning to doubt whether we would get very much further. At length our interrogator strode over, followed by another armed man.

'OK, you go straight up. One of my men, Khalil, will sit with you on the way.'

My heart sank. It wasn't quite being arrested, but it was nearly as bad. Driving with an armed man behind my neck is a pet loathing. No one who's had it happen to them ever complains about the mother-in-law in the back seat again. On rare occasions you can get your own back like making them carsick. I once played a Wagner tape to some Israelis. If that's in my folder it may explain a lot. This time I just forced a grin and Khalil clambered heavily into the back. I tried to make polite conversation in Arabic.

'Khalil, that is a good name. Like the poet Gibran, eh?'

'Gibran was from Bsharri. That's a dungheap. Drive on.'

So I started up gently, wondering what else we could talk about now that we had exhausted the arts. It turned out that Khalil didn't like conversation at all and he particularly didn't like it when I pointed out the scenery to Tina. So I stayed quiet and just hoped that Khalil had got his safety

271

catch on.

In places the road had deteriorated badly, although elsewhere there had been clear attempts to put down a new layer of asphalt. Along the steeper parts there were the vestiges of crash barriers, mostly buckled and torn metallic ribbons with patches where bullet holes had rendered them sievelike. Every so often, half hidden in the Aleppo pines, you would see sandbagged emplacements facing down the road. It looked as if Elias had learned from the Israeli debacle on much gentler terrain in the Chouf that with the right defences even an incursion with heavy armour can be made too costly.

As we wound up the road it was possible to see what a marvellously beautiful valley lay below and beyond us. The flanks of the valley showed flat areas of rich brown soil separated by steeper belts of bare grey rock. Trees, both evergreens and deciduous, occurred widely and every few kilometres a narrow muddy track would snake off to some farmhouse or other. Streams could be seen everywhere and there was an almost continuous sound of running water. Behind us I could catch a glimpse of the sea in the rear view mirror. It was now past four o'clock and the light was fading quickly. In the side valleys dusk was gathering and as we climbed through Mrebbine lights were on in some of the shops along the main street and there was a smell of wood smoke.

Beyond Mrebbine there was a clear view to the mountain crest still 5,000 feet above us, but only a dozen miles away. Ahead the snowfields were beginning to get a salmon hue as they mirrored the sunset. Along the roadside snow drifts started to occur and gradually the sound of running water disappeared as we climbed higher. As I turned the car heater on I glanced at Tina and saw that she was just staring around with interest and apparent appreciation. I hazarded a comment.

'Hard to believe that you are just an hour from the Green Line.'

She nodded in agreement.

Khalil's grunt of 'enough!' in the back was something of a deterrent to further conversation. Indeed it's hard to enjoy even the most beautiful scenery when you've got a man with a loaded automatic rifle sitting behind your head; especially when he seems to think you are a spy. And of course it's even harder when you know that that's exactly what you are.

So it was with pretty low morale that I drove carefully through the now freezing slush of the outskirts of Farayoun. At another checkpoint just before the centre of town we were stopped briefly before Khalil was recognised. By now the house lights were on almost everywhere and the shutters were being closed. In the newer shops the men were clustered round the gas heaters. In the older buildings you could see stoves in the middle of the rooms with pipes that went up to the ceiling. Farayoun seemed to have grown considerably since I had been there last, but then it had been very much an island of tranquillity by comparison to elsewhere in Lebanon. Indeed, war damage in the town seemed almost non-existent, although the older stone-built Lebanese buildings, which still predominated in the centre of Farayoun, are much more resistant to bullet hole damage than the newer breeze block and concrete-built modern varieties.

Then we began the steep ascent up to the middle ledge on which the hotel, the house and the monastery stood. As we took the bends, incised in places between snow drifts several feet thick, I could briefly look down into the great slash of the Asal gorge. Its bottom was now masked by purple grey mist and growing shadows which merged in the higher parts into the delicate pink of the snow fields. Tracing the gorge westward brought you to where the sun was setting in oranges and yellows over the headlands. Below in the town the lights were twinkling in the cold air.

And you could have wept for the contrast between the beauty of the world and the fouled up mess that had produced the situation we were in.

To my relief we were soon over the slippery ascent of the middle ledge and onto the gentler slope that led up towards the cedars beyond and then to the narrow summer road over the top. What we were on could hardly be dignified with the word 'plateau', being barely a mile wide at the broadest point between the lip of the rock ledge and the upper cliff that formed the northern wall to the entire valley.

No sooner were we over the top when we were stopped at another checkpoint. I braked gently to avoid skidding on the ice and the car came to rest safely. I looked up to catch the last rays of the setting sun on the highest points of the rock face to our left. Here the delay was again minimal; Khalil had simply to shout out who he was and we were waved through.

Although I knew exactly where the hotel and the monastery should have been from the model it was difficult to see either on account of the thick but patchy woods that occurred in the area. The lights of the house, however, were clearly visible through the branches of the trees to our right. Khalil spoke again. It was only his second full sentence since we had started. 'Turn down to the house.'

I obeyed and we slipped and slid off the main track down towards the large two-storied house half-hidden by walls and trees. Behind it the mass of the mountain loomed high and dark, and above that the stars were coming out.

Then we were stopped before large wrought iron gates set in a high wall and there were further sandbags and militiamen. A short way down to one side along the wall was an ugly concrete construction that was evidently a guard house. By it were a number of four-wheel drive vehicles, most in standard camouflage pattern. The militiamen here were heavily wrapped up in anoraks with fur hoods and a brazier was burning. In the shadows of the wall stood a small fir tree with several chains of twinkling electric Christmas lights over it.

'Stay here.'

Khalil got out of the car. As he did so a draught of pure cold air blew in causing an instant shivering fit. Here at over 5,000 feet it was already well below freezing point at sunset. But with Khalil's departure we could now at least talk.

'Well, Tina, welcome to Farayoun.'

'Henry, the valley is gorgeous. I had no idea.'

'Yes, magical.'

Part of me felt like saying, 'Yes, complete with ogres, witches and the worst sort of magic,' but I rejected it. They could, and probably would, come later. For this moment, at least, it was a beautiful and lovely place.

We waited for ten minutes while people came and went in the gloom and the car got colder and the sunset faded in the distance. Then someone drove up fast and the militiamen stopped chattering and stood silent and alert. A figure came over with Khalil behind him and stopped briefly at the car. He said something to Khalil who moved softly and opened the door.

'Get out.'

I moved to pick up my anorak only to have my arm grabbed roughly by Khalil.

'Out now.'

'As you wish,' I muttered, and climbed out. Although there was really little more than a breeze it felt like an icy gale. I regretted not having put on winter clothes earlier. The man with Khalil had moved over towards the pool of light by the guard house where he stood motionless as if a statue. Then he made a slow, beckoning motion with a finger. Into that one gesture he somehow managed to put an enormous menace. We walked over to the light and stood there shivering before him in the snow. The face that stared at us had no expression. It was a lean, middle-aged face with scars, lines and a misshaped nose. The staring eyes, sunk in shadows, seemed full of a cold malice. It was not a face to look at too hard so I looked away. Nothing

275

was said for a full minute.

Then he spoke slowly and coldly in poor English.

'I am the commander of the Sheik's Forces.'

It was a statement that demanded no response. It got none. There was a further silence. Then he spoke again.

'Stay there. Say nothing.'

Then he turned round and walked into the guard house, leaving us standing in the snow watched by Khalil. I was wondering what came next and whether I could get away with whispering to Tina and how long we could survive standing in this cold when beyond the light something happened. The gate opened slightly and a smallish figure moved through the gap. Hands were raised to hoods in salute and Khalil and the others fell back. The figure, in a smart black wool coat and scarf and wearing heavy gloves and a fur hat came over to the car. For a few seconds he stared at us, although I couldn't see his face because he was standing outside the circle of light. Finally he spoke in English, with what might be described as a hint of a slightly rusty British accent.

'Good evening.'

Then he came forward and the light fell on his face and I knew that at last we stood before Elias Daoud.

29

The figure extended a gloved hand.

'Dr and Mrs Stanwick. Welcome to Farayoun.'

The words were, however, cool, and the grasp limp. But it was still a very considerable improvement on any other welcome we'd had in his valley. The English greeting had caught me off balance and I had to struggle to dig up the formal Arabic I'd had stored away for some time.

'It is an honour to meet your excellency Sheik Elias. May I present my bride Tina.'

This seemed to surprise him. He replied with the appropriate responses and continued in Arabic, 'I was not aware you spoke Arabic. Harout did not tell me that. Perhaps he thought it was not an important thing. Does your bride speak it too?'

His Arabic was confident and precise; a thing not to be taken for granted among Maronites. But who was Harout?

'Not yet I'm afraid, Sheik.'

He smiled at Tina in a civil, Embassy party fashion. Then he returned to English.

'Your husband says that you have not yet mastered Arabic.'

'This is only my third day here.'

'I hope your stay will be much longer. Now please, it is cold and I see you are not dressed for our winter nights, especially for standing outside. Get your coats and follow me.'

I needed no further encouragement and ran to the car and pulled out both our anoraks. When we had put them on the Sheik spoke again.

'I will lead you to my house. Be careful, it is a little slippy... I'm sorry, is "slippy" correct? Or is it "slippery"?'

'I think either will do in spoken English, Sheik. "Slippery" is probably better in written English.'

'Good; you will excuse me. I have only limited practice in English these days.'

'It's very good. Professor Rimmer spoke highly of your ability yesterday.'

I had to remind myself as I said it that it was only yesterday we were eating in Ain Mreisse. To my surprise, and initial worry, Elias stopped suddenly in his tracks and I nearly collided with him.

'Charles? You spoke to him yesterday?'

277

'We ate at his house and slept there last night.'

It always pays not to skimp details of the relationship that you are trying to build on in this sort of context. Elias turned and stared me in the face. I'm not sure it was very helpful because it was extremely dark on the path.

'I know you were in West Beirut yesterday, but you went to see Professor Rimmer?'

The affiliation of the men in the blue BMW now seemed confirmed.

'Indeed, we are old friends. Not as old as you and he, but I taught with him, in a different department, in the years '81 to '83. So when I heard that he was a friend of yours I went to ask for a letter of introduction. Which I have.'

There was a slight pause and I began to wonder whether Rimmer was no longer a big friend. Then Elias turned round and continued walking.

'Interesting. I will see your letter. Now this is my home. It was built in the 1880s so it is not very old. There was an older house but, as is the Arab way, it was demolished rather than renovated. However, I have not demolished this house in turn.'

We both said how pleasant it looked, which was indeed the case. The house was built on an expansive scale out of cut white stone blocks with red roof tiles. Beneath the balconies of the upper floor vines, now brown, ran out on wires.

'You may be interested to know that in the Asal Valley I have made it an offence to tear down any building built before independence. I think this is unique in Lebanon.'

It crossed my mind to ask what the punishment was. I wouldn't have been surprised at anything from a ticking off by the magistrate to being buried alive under the rubble. Some people can take architectural conservation very seriously. I thought I'd leave finding out till later.

As we approached the house the door was opened by an African who looked like he might have been Sudanese. If he was, he was unusually short, but then I suspected Elias might not like servants who were taller than he was. The servant took Elias' coat, hat and gloves first and then – with a certain ceremony – our anoraks. I took out the letter to Elias.

In the light of the hallway I had my first chance to look properly at Elias Daoud. He was slightly built so that although only perhaps five foot four he was well proportioned and there was no tendency to the almost universal flab of urban Lebanese over thirty. Although I knew he was forty, he gave the impression of a man in his mid-thirties and his brown eyes were bright and alert. The straight brown hair was thinning but well trimmed and matched by a neat small moustache. The mouth was firm and tight and while not cruel did not look kindly. There was a definite bearing of dignity and importance about Elias, but it was very much more than an aristocratic air. It was the pose of one who habitually wields power alone. He was not the sort of person you would try to outstare, nor was it easy to imagine anyone laughing at him. It struck me that the face could easily have been that of some Lord or Duke out of the Middle Ages, once out a-riding with his squires and now preserved badly in a stained glass window.

'Is that your letter from Charles? May I read it please? Do please go on through into the room on the left.'

We walked in carefully. I suppose I might have been able to predict the room from the man. It was long and spacious but well filled. Three large leather sofas were arranged around a large, stone fire place. Above them hung an enormous cut glass chandelier. The lighting was however all done by spotlights. The walls were hung with prints and wall hangings and I caught a glimpse of what looked to be original Roberts' prints of Lebanon, some Eastern church icons and some expensive looking tapestries. The walls were lined with chests and tables. On them, and above on the walls, were family photographs. There were no books, indeed the only reading matter was a couple of magazines on a coffee table. At one end of the room sat one of those expensive hi-fi systems that gets design awards and the sum of whose controls are three buttons and a knob.

Along the side opposite to the fire two pairs of double doors opened onto a balcony. Unusually but sensibly, the original wooden doors had been replaced by double glazed glass doors so that you could look out through them. Heavy curtains hung either side and Elias went over and drew them. The central part of the floor was covered by a single massive Persian carpet. The whole effect was pleasing and, with the omission of the chandelier, would have merited a spread in some of the Western design magazines. For a second we stood by the door till Elias, still reading the letter, motioned us over to the sofas. I walked over the carpet hoping my shoes were clean.

Elias sat down and helped himself to a number of pistachios from a bowl on the table next to another bowl with the inevitable pile of cigarette packets. He gestured to them carelessly, still reading and rereading the letter thoughtfully. Then, having neatly flicked the shells into the fire, he looked at us over the piece of paper.

'How is my old teacher?'

A tricky question, but my maxim is, when in doubt, be honest. I looked at Tina who nodded at me to speak.

'In physical health well, or so it appears. In spirit, not so good. Yesterday was a bad day in Ain Mreisse; there was shooting. He got very depressed.'

I paused; Elias was still watching me carefully. 'It was very disturbing. He had a bit to drink, which didn't help. It was a very literate depression though – except towards the end when he was misquoting badly.'

'What was he misquoting?'

Fortunately I knew, having once liked the poem. 'Mostly your old friend Yeats; "The Second Coming." '

Elias nodded and folded the paper up carefully.

'That sadly sounds like an authentic experience these days. I am sorry to hear it, but the situation is getting to him at last. Is he alone in the flat?'

'He has a young Filipino lady – Maria, who cooks.'

Elias nodded again. 'I'm indeed sorry for him. I must have him to come up here again. Perhaps we can work further on our book. Now if you will excuse me I must make a phone call.'

He walked over to a phone in the corner and pressed a few buttons.

'Harout? Good. The Stanwicks are here.' He was speaking clearly in Arabic. 'They are friends of an old friend so tonight they will be staying with me.'

There was a pause, then he continued in a slightly sharper tone. 'No, I see no reason to doubt who they are. They will also be dining with me. We will not discuss business. I suggest you come round afterwards. At nine.'

He appeared to be on the point of putting the phone down when there was something said further that caught his attention. 'Really? Sent by a man in Jounieh? Who? Find out who.'

A brief pause.

'Harout, what do you mean by it's too late?'

There was the sound of something that might have been a long excuse on the other end of the phone. Elias appeared to be getting agitated and then interrupted abruptly. 'Enough, Harout! Enough! So Sammy overdid it again. I'll talk to him tomorrow. Both of you need reminding who runs this place. I will see you later.'

Then Elias appeared to have a final thought. I suppose I shouldn't have been listening, and certainly after what I heard next I wished I hadn't been.

'Oh, Harout. He's still recognisable, isn't he? Good. Well get the body dropped on the Jounieh Road tomorrow, with some note about it being a judgement on spies. Otherwise they might think it was a family feud.'

The effect of the words was akin to ice cold water down the spine. Was it Fuad they were talking about? I must have jumped because Tina looked at me in consternation. I could say nothing as Elias had put the phone down and was walking back to us. He sat down and looked at me and I think my expression of horror must have registered because a flash of something crossed his face.

'I'm sorry. I'd forgotten you understood. Don't worry, it wasn't Fuad – he is alive and well up at the hotel. You will see him tomorrow. Yes, we've had a problem today. Some time this morning someone tried to drive up to Farayoun through the checkpoint on the coast road. They didn't know him and he claimed he had relatives here. It was all a bit odd, so they had a chat with him and apparently he started to get nervous and kept looking at the car. So my men took it to pieces and found a radio transmitter hidden in a seat. According to orders they handed him over to Sammy. Sammy is the head of the Forces.'

I looked at Tina who shivered. Elias nodded.

'I gather you made his acquaintance. Anyway, Sammy got carried away. The man didn't tell us much other than he'd been recruited in Jounieh. Now it's too late. But it's an odd business; the radio was clearly Israeli. The whole thing just seems, what's the word, bodged. No, botched. As if they were in a hurry.'

As he was saying this he was looking intently at us, his eyes flicking from one to the other. Fortunately I think I had been so concerned that it might have been Fuad that I was briefly relieved to hear it was only an Israeli agent. Then I thought about my own status. By this time Tina was speaking.

'I'm sorry, this Sammy had this poor man tortured and killed?'

There was a battle going on in her voice between fear and outrage, but the outrage had won. That's Tina, I thought. Elias nodded, apparently taken slightly aback. Tina continued, 'But that's awful. Don't you set any standards here?'

I winced, scared that Elias would call in the dreadful Sammy, but I suppose she had a point; what were we supposed to do? Shake our heads and eat pistachios? Elias' face became pale and I thought he was going to shout at her. He put his hands together and his fingers intertwined with one another. In the end what came out was a string of words with pauses between that conveyed barely restrained anger.

'The situation is a little more complex than you think.'

He stopped for a moment, then continued in a slightly less impassioned voice.

'Now if you will excuse me for a moment I will ensure that the chef realises he is cooking for two more people.'

He got up, still pale, and walked out of the room. Tina looked at me.

'I'm sorry,' she whispered.

'It was a fair comment.'

Then we sat in silence for a minute before Elias returned. His colour had returned and he was all charm.

'I'm sorry; you are new to Lebanon, Mrs Stanwick. Let me try to clarify the situation. As Charles will have no doubt explained to you on his way to oblivion, we live on the edge of a sea of anarchy here. On the margins of that anarchy islands of stability can be maintained, but only by what I call firm rule and you would call despotic ruthlessness. And I am a despot.'

He paused and looked hard at Tina. I think she felt he was trying to intimidate her because she spoke out clearly.

'Well, you don't look like one.'

It was not a response I would have advised, but then if I'd wanted a tame wife I wouldn't have married Tina. Elias turned to me, with something of a mixture of annoyance and amusement on his face.

'Dr Stanwick, your wife is elegant and charming, but she seems curiously ignorant of the customs of the country. When a man here says he is a despot he does not want to be contradicted. If she wishes to have my despotism demonstrated I can soon arrange for a real head on a real platter. Don't you find travelling with her in this country a little dangerous?'

283

I had to guess how deep the amusement ran. My feeling was that it wasn't a vein that could be mined for long.

'Forgive her, Sheik, it was my fault. We were in something of a hurry and I failed to explain the complexities of the situation. Perhaps you would be able to do so. In the meantime, I trust you will accept her words as proof that she values truth above flattery. Besides, I assume you would have been more offended if she had said you did look like a despot.'

He looked at me. There was still a faint hint of levity, but it looked almost worked out.

'I see. Well, Mrs Stanwick, if you survive long enough to look around Farayoun you may see things that remind you of a liberal democracy. I have a dozen Muslim families in the valley and they have full rights to worship as they see fit. Indeed, I helped rebuild the mosque. I support education; I have built a hospital and a school, although we need another. I have banned the shooting of birds in the valley and encouraged reforestation. I have, as I already said, rigid planning rules. I do my best to ensure that wrongs are righted where possible and vengeance is restrained.'

He shrugged. 'Indeed, you may look at me and say that I do not appear to be a despot. True, I can still quote you whole chunks of poetry. True, I have a Belgian chef. True, I have one of the best collections of classical music in the country. But you would be making a sorry – even possibly fatal – mistake if you took me as being a gentle, or even a liberal man.'

Elias paused and looked at the fire.

'Harout tells me you are Christians. Then you may understand if I tell you that this is an Old Testament world here. Count yourself back in it. My name Elias Daoud is Elijah David in English. I am no prophet and just a little king. This is one of those little fringe semitic kingdoms that appears now and then in that book; the Hivites, the Amorites, the Daoudites; "lesser breeds without the law". Yet even within this valley with perhaps 40,000 people, there are a dozen clans. If my father, and now I, had not ruled firmly and effectively we would have destroyed each other in this valley in these dark days. Instead, we have stability and peace here and even our powerful neighbours prefer to leave us alone. But I cannot relax.'

He fixed Tina with a dark stare. He was not easily stoppable now. 'For instance, last year we had a murder. A nasty affair. If I had left it alone it would have become a clan feud with a dozen dead. We caught the killer and feeling was running high. There was no doubt of his guilt. Satisfaction must be made. I ordered that he run from Ras el Bourj to the monastery. He didn't make it; he was tied by a long rope to the back of a jeep that did a steady twenty-five kilometres an hour and didn't stop till it reached the monastery. Think about that, Mrs Stanwick.'

Tina visibly paled. Elias ignored her and turned to me.

'Incidentally, that was Sammy's idea, but I backed it, *pour discourager les autres*. I rely a lot on Sammy; he sees to it that my men are equipped and that the morale is good. He is a general worthy of a larger force. He is intelligent and loyal to me and indispensable. But on occasions he goes too far. Today was one. It might have been better to keep the man alive longer, but that is my only criticism.'

I could have added a few others, but I kept my mouth firmly closed. Then Elias looked at his watch. 'Forgive me. We shall eat at a quarter past seven. It is informal, but you may want to wash and change. I will get Malik to see you to your room.'

There was a slight pause.

'Harout wished you to be given rooms in the hotel, where Fuad is being well treated, but not by true hotel standards. I have overruled him, as you are friends. However, I would be grateful if you would not abuse the hospitality. In view of today's unpleasantness it would be as well if you did nothing that might give rise to suspicion. Besides, you would find nothing. Be down here at seven.'

It was difficult to complain about the standard of the accommodation, particularly as the room had a balcony overlooking the gorge. In fact, as I found out when I looked over the edge, it actually overhung the gorge. At this point the middle cliff upon which the house stood was close to the great lower face with the result that within a mile you dropped 2,000 feet. Although the temperature was so low as to be bone chilling I stayed outside for a few minutes looking into the blackness of the depths of the gorge, the glistening snow of the ridge and below, the lights of Farayoun. To the east, about a mile away, the monastery could be seen perched in a notch of rock. The moon's light was reflected off the roof and it seemed deserted. I wondered yet again what – if anything – was going on in there.

Shivering, I went back in to find Tina lying on the bed and staring at the ceiling. I lay down next to her, partly for comfort and partly because I didn't want to speak in anything more than a whisper.

'You OK?'

'Just undergoing adjustment to the circumstances, that's all. Like finding out Kubla Khan is really Genghis, and recovering from meeting Sammy. Actually, Henry, Sammy made me realise something.'

'That you shouldn't have come?'

'No. But you remember Elie, the kid we first met at Antoine's who gave me the jitters? I'm beginning to think he was actually a decent sort.'

'He was just an amateur psychopath, whereas Sammy is the professional. That's probably progress. It sounds like you may yet survive the trip.'

'I think so. I'm determined to.'

'I'm gratified to hear it. Whether I will, given any more of your gay repartee with the local tyrant, is another matter.'

'Sorry. But you can't let some things pass, can you?'

I thought about that and decided that she was probably right.

286

'No, I suppose not. I mean silence is implicit approval, but it's a dangerous path.'

'Exactly.'

'Incidentally, do you realise that the fact we are staying in Elias' house is encouraging? In this culture it would be very dishonourable to slay a guest.'

'I suggest you remind our host of that.'

We ate in the dining room. It was a long room with a proportionate table and rather more ornate than the other rooms we had so far seen in the house. Elias may not have demolished the house, but there were indications of extensive and costly refurbishment. The food was French – there may have been a Belgian influence, but my experience of haute cuisine was inadequate to judge. Anyway, the standard was well up to that of a good London restaurant. In general Elias steered the conversation away from any areas of difficulty and stayed in good spirits. I couldn't help but notice that he treated Malik as little more than a slave, with frequent cursings and rebukes. I thought at one point Tina was going to protest, but she evidently decided against it.

He spent a lot of time extolling the virtues of the place of his birth and how there was no place like it on earth. Most Lebanese do this and for once my agreement was more than simply good manners. As he spoke there was a definite impression of a different Elias; a man who liked to go walking for a whole day down the valley or to climb up above the monastery in summer to watch the dawn. An Elias who liked to go up to his cedars on a winter's day and sit under the snow laden branches. A man who liked to see the wind blowing the spray off the waterfall, to watch the eagles high over the cliffs and to stare up at the rock faces unchanged since his ancestors had arrived in this valley. Or, as he put it frequently, *his* valley. How much was reality and how much appearance was difficult to say. I wondered whether he was an aesthete forced to be a thug, a thug pretending to be an aesthete, or both at once. This being Lebanon I presumed the latter; that thug and aesthete coexisted.

He returned to talking about the cedars and as he did, his voice became distant and he seemed to be speaking from another world. 'You know, there, among those holy trees, I sometimes see things.'

Whether or not he saw the evident puzzlement on Tina's face I don't know; it is quite likely that at that moment he was only barely aware of us being at the table with him.

'I can't explain. Dream creatures, shapes, people. From the past. It's a strange place.'

I find I generally don't speak the same language as visionaries and mystics so I kept quiet. Besides, I'm especially cautious about visionary despots – next thing you know they're claiming to be God and demanding worship and shortly afterwards you are likely to be just so many lion sized bites. Anyway, he might well have seen something – even sceptical Rimmer had felt the place was peculiar. And the cedars could well be the oddest part of this whole odd valley where you felt at any minute the twentieth century was going to get up and go away in disgust.

Elias seemed to stare at something in silence, then he focused on me and appeared to snap out of his reverie. He spoke in a peevish tone.

'You know that's one thing I can't stand about Harout. The man has no soul. He's a technician.'

This time I had to ask. 'Sorry, Sheik, who is this Harout?'

'Ah yes. Harout Artemian. Harout is one of the head people of the group. I believe *the* head. He runs all the organisational side and is the one who deals with me. Yes, Harout.'

The final phrase strongly indicated that there was at best a mere working relationship and at worst a muted hatred between them. I remembered Charlie moaning about the Armenian in Elias' life.

'How did you get involved with the group?'

He looked at me. 'I promised to Harout I wouldn't talk

288

business, but breaking promises is a despot's privilege. Isn't that right, Mrs Stanwick?'

Tina smiled faintly at him. Very faintly. I understood her feeling entirely. Elias was fascinating to listen to and he would have been a natural for a television documentary, but physically sitting here in his house and realising that he held the power of life and death over us was a very different matter. One would have given a lot to be able to put him in a little glass box or, even better, to know you had the ability to switch him off and watch him fade into a little dot on the screen.

Elias took a sip of wine. He seemed to be an abstemious drinker. 'So you know something about the group then, Dr Stanwick?'

'A little from what I learned from Tim Vaughan and have heard since – the idea of the impending global threats and the development of a secret group to combat them.'

Elias appeared a little puzzled. 'But I gather you are not a member? Indeed Harout sometimes refers to you as a threat. I find this curious, but it can wait till later. It's a stupid question when you are at my mercy, but are you in fact an enemy of the group?'

It always happens, whether by accident or design. Just when you feel you have mastered the bowler and are nicely settled down to slog him all over the ground, he bowls a vicious bouncer targeted right on the middle stump. I tried to prod my brain into activity.

'An enemy of the group? Well, Sheik, the honest answer is no, not at the moment.' It was just about truthful.

'Why the last clause?'

'Because I don't know everything that's going on and therefore have insufficient data to judge. Some things give cause for concern. All I can say is that at the moment I am neutral on the group. If I can get Fuad back I may even be positive.' Especially, I thought, if I can be reassured over why these people are interested in viruses.

'But not positive enough to be a member?'

289

'I was put off.'

Elias slightly closed his eyes and gently nodded his head. 'Most interesting. I too have my problems. Anyway, we can perhaps discuss these things later. Instead, let me tell you about my involvement in the group. Now about four years ago Harout came up and had a long chat with me. He wanted a base to run his group from. He told me about it. The group had a diagnosis and a cure. I was broadly in agreement with the diagnosis. The political side of his group's thesis isn't a theory in Lebanon; it's a fact. Things do fall apart and the disintegration can be explosive. It's also catching. The ecological side is evident too. My father used to talk about hunting bear in the valley only thirty years ago. There used to be a Roman marker stone wall below Farayoun marking the limits of the cedar forest in those days. Soil erosion here is very bad too. So I believed his diagnosis.'

At this point the lights dimmed momentarily. To my surprise Elias shuddered. 'I hate that. It's very upsetting; I just find it like an intimation of mortality, to misquote. We don't get power cuts longer than a few minutes here so I shouldn't complain, but the hydroelectric station needs a massive overhaul. Of course we have a lot more demand now than when it was built. Everybody watches video, for example. So every so often the voltage drops. The state won't fix it of course. The group has its own stabilisers and standby generators, but it annoys them. Anyway, it makes the point. Things tend to disorder and the more complex the system the greater the tendency to a catastrophic disruption.'

Elias shook his head and banged the table gently with his fist. 'Do you realise that there was no mains electricity at all in Farayoun until 1962? Yet now if the power system really went we'd be in a catastrophe here. I'm not sure that 200 years of loyalty to the Daouds would survive my people not being able to watch *Rambo 3* or losing the contents of the deep freeze. Barely quarter of a century!'

He collected himself and then began to speak in a quieter manner. 'Anyway, the diagnosis was difficult to argue with. In fact I believe the analysis of the problem more than I do the cure. Sometimes I think that should the prophecy be fulfilled and lights go out over the world we would survive here. It would be cruel, but the valley is defensible as you have seen. It could even be self-supporting.'

This was the Elias Daoud of the 'Forward with Hope and Unity' poster, the dreamer of dreams, the leader staring into the troubled mists of the future. He chuckled slightly, but it was a cold sound.

'Sometimes too I think of the irony that that would be. If this part of Lebanon might outlast the West, the first casualty having become the last. Maybe we would survive as a last outpost of civilisation. A new Byzantium.'

Tina's voice disturbed the silence that followed. 'But you would not be Christian.'

The visionary look vanished abruptly to be replaced by one of great sorrow. 'I will tell you some other time of my separation from the church. It concerns the tragedy of my life. I do not tell it lightly.'

'I'm sorry. I didn't mean to touch on that....'

Elias shrugged. 'Anyway, back to Harout and the group. The cure he never defined clearly then. He's not much better now. However, it seemed like a worth-while thing to support and the terms were very good. Some of the long-term promises were very attractive. Most attractive to a beleaguered man.'

He looked at Tina with a rather wry smile. I think he'd decided that Tina baiting was a worthy sport.

'Everyone else was going into drugs and I've never been very keen on it. Only vaguely a matter of morality, but also too much money slips out into the wrong pockets. This deal allowed me to control a centralised economy.'

He finished his wine and toyed with the glass. He seemed to be talking to no one in particular.

'But at times I wonder if it's worth it. Sammy doesn't like

291

it, particularly since Harout has a few armed men of his own, and people come in and out. Harout vouches for them, but I don't know what they do and Sammy doesn't. All those boxes of equipment too. And I don't like having always to be nice to dull, soulless Harout with his bastard Arabic. I'm not even sure I trust him. Yes, I'm in charge of the valley, but Harout sometimes pulls the strings and that rankles.' The irritation was evident in his voice. 'Anyway, you'll met him in person later – meanwhile let's go back to the other room.'

There we sat round the fire on the sofas and Elias asked about the state of Britain. He revealed that he had been at a private school near Salisbury in the mid 1960s for a couple of years until his mother had been sufficiently disturbed by press reports of the breakdown of morality in Britain to have him brought back to Lebanon.

'For safety!' He shook his head very sadly.

He was beginning to discuss his hopes of travelling again beyond the valley when there was a knock at the door.

'Come in.'

The man who entered was about the same height as Elias but of a thicker build. I guessed he was in his late forties; his dark wiry hair was beginning to show white streaks and to recede markedly. Although the broad face was marked by a large nose, a feature highlighted by a bushy moustache, the thing that most struck you was the pair of large brown eyes. These seemed curiously prominent and again and again you would find yourself looking into them. It was an unmistakably Armenian face and the eyes excepted, he was a very ordinary man. Among the jewellers of Bourj Hammoud or in the camera shops of Hamra I wouldn't have given him a second glance, yet there was something about the face that was familiar. I just couldn't place it, but I was sure I'd seen it before, neither in Beirut nor Cyprus but somewhere further afield.

Introductions were made between the stranger and Tina and then myself. He held out a hand.

'Harout Artemian. We meet again, Dr Stanwick.'

'I'm sorry, I don't think we've met. Or have we?'

The face was indeed familiar, but not the voice.

'You saw me, but I did not see you. I was the man who met Tim Vaughan from the helicopter that fateful day in the pinnacles of Madagascar.'

I stared at him again. I was prepared to believe it was the same man; the man who had gone through with the charade of apparently killing Vaughan; the man whom Jim Elweth had wanted me to try and identify from his photographs. For a moment I couldn't think of anything to say.

'I see.'

Harout seated himself on the third sofa. It was interesting that he and Elias wouldn't sit together. There he sat and looked at the two of us with his big brown eyes. Then he reached over to the table and took a cigarette out of one of the packets in the bowl. He lit it fluently and sat back to stare at us again. Finally he spoke.

'What are we going to do with you, Dr Stanwick?'

30

I couldn't think of a good answer so I shrugged my shoulders and returned his gaze. He sighed.

'Maybe you start by telling us why Fuad Attiyah was overheard in Ras el Bourj asking whether our hospital was large enough to use the boxes of glassware that were being unloaded from the boat?'

The English was correct although there were vestiges of a thick Armenian accent.

'All right, I'll tell you. Nickie Hammond took me out for a meal.'

I was intrigued to notice the flash of cognisance between Elias and Harout when I mentioned the name. It crossed my mind she might be here.

'I noticed that her warm coat had an Arabic laundry mark. From that and a few other facts I deduced that she might well have been somewhere in Lebanon. Having spent some time here that intrigued me and I asked someone who knows what's happening in Lebanon today where the most likely spot would be to set up a secret, highly technical outfit. He had no hesitation in naming here. Unfortunately, my brother heard the conversation and, linking it with an earlier discussion on genetic engineering, decided you were doing fancy things up here. He then apparently mentioned it to Fuad, who was visiting Lebanon. He rather foolishly decided to find out a bit more.'

There were glances at each other. Harout spoke again, probing and testing. 'So why are *you* here?'

'Easy. We were already coming to Cyprus when Fuad was taken. As it was my carelessness that had caused the problem and also because I knew Charles Rimmer, an old friend of the Sheik's, I felt I should come.'

Harout looked at Elias who nodded faintly as though he was thinking about something else. He seemed vaguely bored by it all.

'So you bring your wife on a trip like this?'

'Cyprus was full of nosey people asking odd questions. Yours?'

'Ours. So that's all? Carelessness and coincidence?'

'Exactly so. For the carelessness I apologise. The coincidences are not in my department. I presume that what I have said matches Fuad's statement.'

The face was inscrutable and expressionless. It was impossible to know what was going on beneath the mask. There was something undefinable about Harout; something that I couldn't put my finger on. But it was odd. There was no obvious nastiness stamped on his face, unlike some of the people we had met in the past few days, such as Eduard and Sammy, but there was something rotten somewhere and whatever it was I didn't think I cared for it.

'So, Dr Stanwick, what do you want?'

'I want to be able to leave here tomorrow with Fuad. In return for that I promise to keep my mouth closed – rather, we promise to keep *our* mouths closed – as long as we are satisfied that you mean no harm, that is.'

I hadn't meant to put in the last bit. It had surfaced rather unwelcomingly. I'd been intending to have a no-strings-attached offer. Harout said nothing for a long time, but just stared at me. He reminded me of a pond with ice over it; underneath the impenetrable surface was a hint of chill, dark depths. Every so often he would shift his gaze briefly to Tina and then look back at me. Finally, he spoke to Elias.

'Sheik, let's go and talk.'

Elias glanced at him sideways and then looked at me. 'In a minute, Harout. I have my questions too. Why did Miss Hammond talk with you in the first place?'

I noticed that Harout's face bore the very slightest hint of unease.

'She wanted to recruit me to the project. The genetic engineering work on algae.'

'And you refused?'

I couldn't work out what was going on, but for once it didn't seem to be my problem.

'Yes, Sheik.'

The unease was definitely there in Harout's eyes, but he said nothing. Elias turned and looked at the Armenian with some suspicion and then back at me.

'Harout told me that no one had ever refused to work with the group.'

Harout spoke to Elias. His voice was smooth and unruffled. 'Dr Stanwick is the exception. His was always going to be an unlikely recruitment.'

Elias twisted his fingers together. He seemed to be very uneasy. 'Harout, I'm not happy about this. Not at all. You presented the project as being so attractive that there would be no objections, that essentially you could pick up whoever you wanted. You now tell me that at least one person couldn't be recruited.'

Harout stared at Elias with unblinking eyes. 'I would prefer to talk to you in private about it.'

There was a snort from Elias. 'You can say it here. As a consequence of your attempted recruitment your, our, tightly guarded secret is apparently being discussed in schools in Cyprus.'

Harout's gaze stayed immovably fixed on Elias. 'Project security is my business, Sheik.'

Elias began to pale and his fingers interlocked frantically. His voice began to rise.

'At times, Harout, I doubt your sense. You tell me that these programmes are valuable. You tell me that US Intelligence is trying to locate you. Today we find we may have had an Israeli spy in the valley. What happens if Damascus hears? Supposing we have an Israeli helicopter landing at night? Sammy's men are already stretched to the limit to provide you with security. I already have complaints from wives. My men work like mad to protect you. Yet you, you yourself, threaten everything by trying to recruit someone who cannot be recruited! I despair!'

Interestingly, Harout did not quail under the onslaught, but simply reached out and lit another cigarette. Then he spoke to Elias.

'I will talk to you about it later. We had our reasons.'

Elias threw his arms in the air and got up and walked over to the window. After a few seconds, having apparently cooled down, he came back and stood behind the sofa he'd sat on. He stared at Tina.

'Tell me, Mrs Stanwick, why your husband wouldn't join Harout's project to save the world.'

The response came rapidly. 'You can ask him.'

'I wanted to ask you. You speak bluntly.'

Tina coloured very slightly. 'I think we both say the truth. He wouldn't join because Nickie had denied ever having been in the Arab world while her coat showed she had. He felt that on that basis he couldn't trust the rest of the story. I agree with him.'

She glanced at me for confirmation and I nodded agreement. Elias looked at Harout with something like a smug look on his face.

'There we are, Harout; a bit more honesty in the right place might have saved a lot of trouble.'

Harout gave me a frosty look, then turned his eyes on Elias. 'I hadn't appreciated that was the problem. Sheik, as I have said, I think we should talk alone.' His tone of voice seemed somewhat different, somehow conciliatory and commanding at the same time.

Elias seemed slightly taken aback. 'Very well. Excuse us.'

They went into another room and closed the door.

I thought the room we were in might be bugged so I decided not to say anything of note to Tina.

'Interesting situation. I wonder how much Elias knows. Still, let's talk about the decor.'

After twenty minutes they both came back. Elias spoke. 'Harout has agreed to try and convince you of how worth while the whole thing is. So he'll tell you a bit tonight and tomorrow he'll show you round the monastery. In fact, all of us; I haven't been round for some time. This time it's going to be the truth.'

Harout nodded impassively. I realised that I'd have felt happier about him if under some lights he didn't look like Stalin.

Harout began to talk. He spoke in a dull tone, almost as if he wanted us to fall asleep.

'The Sheik wants me to tell you more about the project. Let me tell you a little about myself first; maybe you will understand something of the background better, perhaps be more sympathetic.'

He lit a cigarette and leaned back.

'The first five years of my life were in Italy. In Rome. Most of that time was during the Second World War. My father died in the fighting and after the war we went to Beirut to live with an uncle. He was the only survivor from a family of seven out of the Armenian genocide. So I grew up knowing that life was hard and that every time the world rolls over it crushes an Armenian. I did well at school, by work and intelligence, and got a physics degree. Yes, AUB.'

He drew on his cigarette. Even in recounting his tragic past he seemed passionless.

'Well, I have a few gifts and one of them is guessing trends. In the sixties I got involved in electronics and I soon had a company in Beirut and Amman. I lost the Amman offices in the fighting of September 1970. After that I moved to the States and started a branch there. So when I lost the Beirut office in '75 that was just a small catastrophe. In the States I married an American girl, started a family and got into defence work and computers. Then we got the backing to do the Jezreel Project computer set-up. At the time I didn't even know the name, or even that it was for the military. They just had a lot of money. I was the hardware man. We had just two software people then, Hendriksen and Leclerc.'

'Two?' I said, somewhat incredulous. 'You couldn't have set it up with just two.'

Harout puffed on his cigarette again; he didn't seem the slightest bit put out.

'Because of the security problems, we evolved a special technique. Hendriksen and Leclerc outlined a framework and got the different people in the project to commission lots of separate programs. They just made sure these modules were the same format and language. So at the end of the day the modules simply had to be integrated. The subcontractors had no idea of the whole, they just thought it was a one-off climate program, or a stand alone agricultural projection model. We also did basically the same with the hardware. We've kept the same principle ever since. Take a project, design it thoroughly, break it down into elements, sub-contract and only integrate at the final stage. So we only do planning, design and integration here.'

The scheme he outlined made a lot of sense in terms of logistics. I could also see how people working on a secret official project could easily shift into working on a secret unofficial project. Harout glanced at Elias briefly before looking at Tina and me.

'I hope you are noticing that I am giving you all the facts.'

He finished his cigarette and continued, 'Incidentally, the project cost me my marriage and the kids. So I was in on the project and I knew as well as anybody what the results were. I used to sit around talking to people like Tim and Duane and Mike, who all knew a bit about the hardware too. We'd talk about the conclusions and it was obvious that they were never going to be bought at the top. So we kicked around the idea of blowing the results to the press, but it wasn't all complete and anyway so what? Another six-day wonder. Then someone – I forget who – suggested we kept it running. Well, we laughed, but then I went home and thought about it.'

Harout paused and stared at me. Was there a fraction more passion here?

'You see, I sat down and went over my life. So many times I'd been squashed and each time I'd just been able to walk out of it unscathed. But I could look back and see that each time I'd escaped a whole lot of other people had been wiped out. That I was a well-off company president was a statistical fluke. By rights, I should have been selling chewing gum on the streets of East Beirut or be in an unmarked grave. So I knew the system was rotten. Now I had an opportunity to do something to make things better.

I had the money and I had a strong suspicion that somewhere in Lebanon I could find a secure base. I said, "Let's give this a go." So we had a long discussion and realised that the whole project was so secret we might get away with it. So we copied the software and the source code, borrowed the data and by the time they closed it down we'd duplicated everything except the hardware.'

He nodded at Elias.

'The Sheik was very useful. We developed a good working relationship and he has been our patron ever since. We were greatly helped by the fact that the authorities decided to delete all references to the project. So we ceased to exist. What else do you want to know?'

He looked at me. The question I wanted to ask was about the reprints on viral diseases, but this was probably not the time. I wanted to take the opportunity to look around the monastery without Harout having cleared everything away first.

'OK, funding. This is a big operation. Where does your money come from?'

Harout looked at Elias who smiled rather meanly.

'Tell him about the local arrangement, Harout. He may appreciate it.'

Harout shrugged. 'I gather Nickie told you about our investment programme; that works well. We also run a little sideline to top up our coffers. It demonstrates the sort of thing we do very well. We have some extremely good computer experts, as you know, and so we raid bank accounts.'

Tina and I exchanged puzzled glances. I interrupted, 'Sorry, Harout, stealing money by computer is just the same as any other stealing. It may be easier, but it's still wrong.'

Harout's face wrinkled into some primitive precursor of a smile and I noticed Elias was smirking. But on neither face was innocence or happiness present. Harout continued. 'Henry, you appreciate that there is a vast economy here built almost entirely on drug smuggling, piracy and kidnapping that cannot be taxed or touched? Well, these people now bank abroad. We are talking of many tens of millions of dollars. Simply, we have over the years accessed a number of these accounts and creamed off a substantial amount.'

At first I was stunned, then as the irony and even the justice of it got me I found myself laughing. Harout sneered.

'Of course, who can they complain to? The funny thing is that they all think that it's one of the others. Or Mossad. I'm told that one or two have even gone straight as a result. Of course the state should confiscate the funds, but in the absence of the state we are acting as a legal agency. What's neat is that their financial problems curtail their military ambitions and so we dampen down the situation here. Anyway, it's just a sideline, but I thought you'd find it interesting.'

I did, acknowledging mentally that there were a number of intriguing moral dilemmas raised by the technique. Doubtless, discussion with Tina would be able to shed some light on it all. Suddenly I was conscious of feeling tired and, looking at my watch, saw it was half ten. It had been a long day. Elias caught my glance and turned to Harout.

'Harout, the rest can wait till tomorrow, but I would like you to tell them about the political programme. I don't think they know about that.'

Harout looked at Elias carefully then gave a little dismissive shrug of the shoulders.

'OK, I'll make it brief. We have a science and a politics thrust. The science you know a bit about although there are other projects there. The political wing is very secret. Basically, we identify people who are sympathetic to what we stand for: fair, competent global management for our long-term goals of sustainability, stability and security. Good, intelligent, caring people who have the material for service in the media or political systems of their country. Often there are many people with such abilities, but they lack resources, training or even goals. When we identify suitable candidates then we back them through the system – often through different political parties. Nothing too right or too left. Backing in financial and other ways.'

I thought I caught a small but unmistakeable whiff of rat.

'What ways?'

Harout's big brown eyes stared at me. 'Training, backing, all through third parties. Foundations, scholarships, the rest. We give them hints. Tell them to expect the economy to overheat in six months. So they are already making speeches about it beforehand. Suggest they write a memo to the Prime Minister or the President pointing out hitherto unforeseen repercussions of the recent developments in the Middle East on oil prices. Then when their modest prophecies are fulfilled we make sure copies of the speech or the memo make it to the press and soon our people are "men of vision; people to watch". In time they will be policy makers. We just hope it is not too late for the world.' He paused. 'You will say it is wrong. Maybe. But I suggest you compare it to the other ways of selecting people for high office.'

He had a point. I used to know someone with ability and integrity who nearly went bust trying to get himself elected as an MP. Harout now spoke in a quieter, softer tone.

'But I am happy to talk about the ethics of it all with you. Perhaps you should come on board; maybe we need you. But whatever your criticisms Henry, and Tina, always remember this: we believe that unless we act in time there will be terrible things ahead. Something must be done.'

It was a curiously persuasive voice, and one that seemed to sweep aside all objections. I felt I'd said all I wanted to say and Tina looked tired. I decided it was time for bed.

'Well, thank you, Sheik Elias, and you, Harout. So we will see you in the morning? And you believe that it will be possible for Fuad to leave tomorrow?'

Elias looked at Harout briefly.

'Yes, we think so. With some guarantees.'

Before we got undressed I persuaded Tina to come out on the balcony. It was chillingly cold, but the sight alone repaid the shivering. The moon was nearly full, although riding low in the western sky and the cold clear light it cast picked out every detail of the landscape in shades of pewter and silver. Above the gorge the snow wrapped hills shone and glinted. It was incredibly clear and the moonlight was reflected off the ice of the waterfalls. The monastery lay quiet and massive and behind it it was possible to see the dark patch of the cedars surrounded by a white blankness of snow. Beyond them lay the great wall of Mount Lebanon. It seemed to mark the edge of the world, and in a sense it did. Above the whole scene, and in spite of the strong moonlight, the sky was shot through with thousands upon thousands of stars.

I whispered to Tina, 'I brought you out here partly for the view, but what do you think about what we've heard?'

Tina shivered. 'Lovely view, pity about the company.'

She looked around her urgently.

'I don't like Harout one bit. There is something wrong there.'

'Interesting. My sentiments entirely. But can you define it?'

She was silent for a long time. 'No, but I feel it's like us and dogs and sound. Sorry, I'm too tired to express myself properly. I just think that in some way, on a frequency I can only just hear, he is radiating something unpleasant.'

'I think I know exactly what you mean.'

She spoke again in a very low voice. 'Do you suppose the man they picked up and killed was one of the... Jim's friends' ways of obtaining more data?'

I whispered back, 'I'm afraid so, poor fellow. We may be their last hope. A nasty situation where they have to rely on us, but what do you make of the group itself?'

There was a moment's hesitation. 'Yes, interesting. Apart from my feelings about Harout it's just morally grey at the moment, but I wonder can you live in a grey area for very long without slipping into black? Still, at least it seems as if we may be able to get Fuad out.'

She looked at me, her face half in shadow. Then she spoke again.

'But, Henry, it's silly but....'

'But what, my dear?'

'Well, I feel it more than know it, and I'm tired. I just think that maybe we've been brought here for something more than getting Fuad out.'

I knew what she felt, but as usual she had articulated it more clearly.

'To blow a whistle maybe?'

She shivered. 'Time for bed before I get frostbite. Yes, to blow a whistle. Or maybe more.'

31

Despite the comfortable beds and the effective heating we woke early as the first rays of the rising sun found their way into the bedroom through a gap in the curtain. We dressed and went out onto the balcony. Stepping out onto it appeared at first to be a dreadful mistake. The brightness of the light was so dazzling that I had no alternative but to close my eyes tightly. Then I made the mistake of taking a deep breath, producing an agonising effect as the freezing air hit my lungs. It felt like being stabbed.

After a few moments I opened my streaming eyes and tried to focus them on the ground below. That simply produced a horrible impression that I was suspended hundreds of feet above the ground. Finally, when my vision was fully restored, I realised that this was no illusion. A dizzy 200 feet or so below us the cliff ended abruptly in a mass of snow draped scree and small trees. I hastily tried to concentrate on the wider view.

Even after several minutes the effect of the view seemed overpowering. The scale and the detail of the scene, and the intensity and character of the light were remarkable. Every detail of the landscape unfolded around us was crisp and clear, from the hard crusted snowdrifts on the heights to the soft pale brown fields in the valley bottom away to the west. We could see the tiles and telephone wires of Farayoun and make out people in the streets. Above us hung a deep blue sky. For several minutes the view absorbed our thoughts and our conversation. Then cold, hunger and duty got to us and we went downstairs for breakfast.

Elias was not present and a different Sudanese served us. We were just debating whether to have more coffee when there was the sound of a door opening and people talking. One of the voices was female and had a familiar English accent. Then Elias entered followed – at an appropriate distance – by Nickie Hammond. We rose to our feet. Elias made the introductions.

'No, please sit down. Miss Hammond, you've met Dr Stanwick, but I don't think you've met Mrs Stanwick.'

Tina shook hands. It was curious to see them together. Tina slightly taller and certainly thinner, Nickie the more formal and dressed in a style of expensive practicality. I wondered if she had a designer lab coat. I noticed that she'd cut down on the earring size and make-up compared to the Dales, but she still had the fine gold chain around her neck. Nickie came round and shook my hand. I looked in her face; the same blue eyes, but what emotion was it in them?

'Good morning, Nickie. I didn't expect to meet you here.'

She glanced at Elias who had sat down and was helping himself to coffee.

'No, Henry. I certainly didn't intend to extend an invitation. In fact when I heard you were coming I was very worried that everybody would think I had said too much. I gather it was the dry cleaners' mark?'

'That, and a few fortuitous deductions.'

Nickie shrugged. Our arrival seemed to be no great disaster for her.

'Still, nice that you could have brought your wife. It's a lovely place. I wish I could spend more time up here. Spring is the best time. Anyway, I've come over to take you to pick up Fuad. I gather he's being released this morning.'

She looked at Elias when she said it. He merely nodded and looked out of the window. She turned back to me.

'But you're not leaving till this afternoon, I gather?'

I glanced at Elias, who looked up.

'Ah yes, Dr Stanwick. Harout said he had some things to do this morning that couldn't be postponed and that he was going to show us around the monastery in the afternoon. I gather you will be able to leave straight after that.'

It was a bit of a blow. I would have liked to have been on the road by lunchtime, partly just to get out and partly to try to catch Antoine before he had to brave the checkpoints up to Farayoun. I wasn't going to argue though.

'Certainly, Sheik. The weather will hold to allow us to leave late this afternoon?'

'Yes, but I gather there will be snow this evening, so I wouldn't leave it too late. This morning I wondered if you would be interested in going up to the cedars with me. It is, perhaps, my way of celebrating Sunday. I shall be walking and it takes perhaps forty minutes to get there. I am an anomaly in Lebanon. I prefer to walk if I can.'

306

I thought of something.

'Excuse me, Sheik Elias, Fuad's father *Assis* Antoine Attiyah said he would try to drive up to Farayoun this afternoon. I should have mentioned it before, but I had thought that we might be out of the valley in time to catch him.'

Elias looked a little sourly at his coffee. 'I see. Very well, it will be better to let him come. I will instruct Sammy to get the checkpoints to let him through. After searching.'

He finished his coffee.

'I will go walking in an hour. I suggest you go and get your friend and bring him here. Miss Hammond will take you up.'

Elias paused and looked at me hard. 'Dr Stanwick, be aware that Harout has the right to change his mind. Should he do so I am not sure I can change it back again, or that I would wish to. By agreement the hotel is off limits to my men. However, once your friend is in my house I think we can guarantee his safety.'

I can take a hint like that. I also made another note that the relationship between Elias and Harout was very strained.

A few minutes later we were making our way up the gravel path towards the main entrance to the villa. We made conversation about the weather and the valley, then Tina and Nickie made the usual comments about how male dominated the culture seemed to be.

After a glance around, Nickie turned to Tina and spoke quietly, 'So you are staying with His Royal Highness, are you? Is he treating you all right?'

'Fine, but an interesting character.'

Nickie nearly snorted. 'I'll say. When you hear what he gets up to from the technicians who live in the town you get a different picture. Not that they say much – they are too scared of him.'

I joined in. 'He's tough, is he?'

'I should say, Henry. Anyway, I'll tell you more when we're past the Household Cavalry.'

I looked up to see that there were two militiamen on duty at the gate; they let us through with a brief exchange of courtesies in broken English. From there we took a gravel path up through the trees. Out of earshot of the gate Nickie continued.

'Actually, he's not a nice piece of work. I'm not just saying it because he can't bring himself to call me *Dr* Hammond, but he isn't. He builds roads, but they're for his troops, some of them are ecological disasters. The hospital modifications were all for his Forces. Compulsory military training for all children over twelve – that's really popular! The town stinks in places, he cut corners on getting new sewage lines in and he's failed to pay for the hydroelectric station to be maintained. Harout is mad about that. Ten per cent tax on everything and how much he creams off for his Swiss bank account no one knows. And Sammy!'

She looked over her shoulder.

'Sammy is the icing on the cake if you like. He gives you nightmares. He's a cross between a rabid Alsatian and a gorilla.'

Tina said quietly, 'We met him yesterday.'

'Probably ruined your day. The joke at the hotel is that if you play word association games with Sammy and say "Fingers" he responds "Break". No, it isn't very funny, is it? Unfortunately, he's bright with it. Well, he certainly scares the people in the valley. Everyone takes out insurance by becoming a party member, a *Daoudiste* and so then they get the party symbol sprayed above the door. Yuck!'

I knew the sort of thing she was talking about. 'And does the angel of death pass over if you get the sign above the door?'

Nickie grimaced. 'The only difference is supposed to be after Sammy has asked whether you are right or left handed. If you say "right" and you're a party member he only breaks the fingers on the left hand.'

I could see Tina starting to look unhappy. Then she seemed to shake herself and the look went. I was interested to hear what Nickie had said and found it all too credible. What I don't think she realised was that actually Elias was no worse than a lot of his neighbours and possibly a good deal better. However, I thought it was time to change the subject. I hoped it might also give me a chance to try and find out something more from Nickie about what was going on.

'By way of a breath of fresh air, how goes the algae, Nickie?'

'Just fine. It looks like it's feasible. It seems we can identify the gene for calcification and incorporate it into other algae. The problem is that it seems to weaken the organism. It's apparently a common enough phenomenon. We also suspect after a few generations it would probably shed the gene. So it's getting it in and making it stick. Anyway, it's going to take another year to get all the data in from the sub-projects on overall feasibility.'

'You're just working on single-celled plants here?'

'That's right. I think there are crop studies being done elsewhere, but that's no problem. It can be done in an open lab. We just do the things that the various protocols don't allow here. The whole idea of possibly releasing an altered organism into the environment would have the lab shut down in no time anywhere else. No excuses accepted. Certainly not an almost imperceptible increase in global CO_2 levels.'

I was dithering over whether I dare raise the question about the viral research, especially as we hadn't got Fuad out. First, I'd tell myself to postpone it, then I'd decide that this was the only place as we might never otherwise have the opportunity to talk alone. Then I'd go back again to being cautious and so on. Could I trust her? I think Tina caught my dilemma and tackled it her own way.

'Nickie, you just work on algae here?'

Tina got a slightly puzzled look.

'Correct. I can give you the full Latin names if you want. We're certainly not cloning His Highness if that's what you're worried about. Why did you ask?'

I thought of intervening, but decided Tina probably knew what she was doing.

'We were talking to a doctor friend of Henry's in Beirut and he said he'd heard that reprints of papers on viruses were going up here. But no one's working on viruses, are they?'

Nickie stopped in her tracks. 'Viruses? You must have misheard. No, not here. We are working on nothing of medical interest.'

The tone of her voice was slightly hesitant. She shook her head and set off walking again. I thought I'd better say something to keep the momentum going.

'We also heard that you'd had a negative pressure ventilation system delivered. That's a bit of a strong precaution for algae, isn't it?'

It was a stab in the dark and as I said it I realised that it was a dangerous one at that. Harout would know who it was had stopped that particular ship load and could probably surmise whom we had heard the story from. Nickie stood still.

'I don't have one. Marine algae aren't biohazards. If we were close to the sea I might have one in case the wrong bug got out. Anyway, I don't see that there is anywhere you could fit it. You'd be talking about a whole chamber. No, you've been misinformed. There's nothing like that in the monastery. Sounds like someone has been feeding you rubbish about us.'

There was a definitely hostile note at the end. I felt that we had probably reached the limits of her tolerance. Anything more and we might be felt to be unfairly knocking the whole project. Tina, however, had a final go.

'Sorry, Nickie, you see we want to be really sure there's

nothing nasty being brewed up here. We'd never forgive ourselves if we made a promise to Harout and he turned out to be cooking up some virus to wipe out Africa. I mean, can you guarantee that there is no viral or bacterial work here? With one hundred per cent certainty?'

Nickie pouted as she thought.

'Golly! You are paranoid, aren't you? No, I can't guarantee that. The longest that Shirley and our algal team is here for is three months at a time. The valley is a bit isolated and we aren't allowed out beyond it – not that I fancy shopping in Beirut. We do a lot of work, leave the cultures with the technician, then go conferencing or checking ideas. Then we meet up again and come back here – sort of three months on, three months off. It varies. The members of the original team tend to stay here longer – even with a new image and identity they prefer not to travel too widely.'

'So there's half the year when you're not here? And presumably the night shift? But would you know if anyone was working on viruses?'

Nickie gave a faint sigh of weariness.

'OK. I'm not one of the co-ordinating committee. I know very little about what's being done even in the other sub-committees. People keep themselves to themselves here. I don't know at all what one or two are doing. No one gives seminars. All I can say is that I do not believe any viral or bacterial work is going on.'

She hesitated, prodding some snow with her boot. It sounded as if she was giving a lot of thought to her answer.

'However, the original project selected loners and that's a trend that's been continued. Some of the guys are almost monkish. That's no loss, I don't fancy any of them anyway. Well, given the place of work it's appropriate. The level of dedication is very high too. Being a workaholic is the norm. So, yes in answer to your question; in theory, someone could be working on viruses, but I'd have two objections at least.'

311

Tina looked expectantly.

'The first and main thing is that we're limited on space; you couldn't hide viral work. You'd certainly need safeguards like your ventilation systems. But secondly, why would we tinker with a virus? Specially on this kind of a project. The world's got enough problems. Sorry.'

I admitted defeat. 'Thanks, Nickie. We are glad to hear it. Matter closed. I'd have asked Harout, but he was with Elias and those two don't really hit it off very well.'

We set off walking again and Nickie shook her head.

'So it seems. Elias is perfectly charming on the surface most of the time, but desperately short fused. Anyway, we don't see much of him. Thankfully.'

We walked on up the path between the trees. I couldn't think of anything else to say. We had arrived at a dead end, or so it seemed. Tina spoke.

'So you enjoy working here?'

Nickie thought about it.

'Mostly it's fine. Great climate. Curiously peaceful, although I don't think anyone would believe us. I'm not over the moon about the monastery as a lab.' There was an odd tone to her voice as she said the last words.

Tina picked her up on that. 'It's not convenient or what?'

'Technically it's just fine. It's just the monastery. Very few of us like working late there. Some people call it "the monstery". Crazy, isn't it? Leading edge technology and state-of-the-art computing and some of us get the jumps at night.' She tried to laugh, but it sounded rather forced.

I was interested to note that Tina seemed able to get more out of Nickie than I would have been.

Tina was thoughtful for a minute. 'Is it just feelings?'

'Yeah, just feelings I suppose. It's an old building and sometimes I think it's haunted, but I say to myself, "Nickie, you're a big girl now."'

I nearly asked what size had to do with haunting, but I resisted. Which was just as well because what she said next was interesting.

'Incidentally, don't mention that to Harout. He regularly works all night in his office. The great High Priest.'

The expression caught my attention.

'Curious phrase. Why do you use it?'

'You'll see this afternoon. Harout's office is where the altar would have been.'

'The east end presumably.'

'No, that's normal, isn't it? No, the north end. Against the cliff. Anyway, here we are at the hotel.'

The hotel, with a broad, rather plain, two-storey, balconied frontage, had originally been built to take advantage of the view. It was surrounded by trees on all sides except the front where a concrete patio apparently passed into a lawn on which plastic chairs stood forlornly in the snow. The hotel showed signs of hasty renovation with new aluminium frames built into window spaces which still had the old green shutters. There was other evidence that the place had undergone a purely functional restoration with few, if any, concessions to beauty. We went round the back where two arms extended northwards. There was a smell of cooking from one wing. Behind the hotel was a car park almost enclosed by conifers in which a variety of cars stood and from which a short track to the main road could be seen.

The door we entered by was the original main entrance to the hotel. In the foyer three muscular young men played cards around a low table and muttered in what I was certain was Armenian. On our appearance, one threw his cards down and got up quickly. He had a pistol in his belt. A glance at the others showed similar armaments.

The foyer was plainly decorated with two big posters. One was that of the visionary Elias we'd seen before. The other, facing it, was of a large whale, making me wonder if Elias saw himself as an endangered mammal. Nickie spoke to the young man who'd come over and who stood flexing his muscles and radiating toughness in front of her. It looked as if Harout had recruited his own bunch of Armenians to protect the group. That raised an interesting point. For all Harout's vision of a brave new world, when it came down to bodyguards he had behaved like everyone else in Lebanon and had picked up some boys from his own back street. Mind you, from the attitude this one clearly had towards Nickie, he wasn't too bothered about the prospect of diluting good Armenian genes. I had a sneaking feeling that doing jobs for her was one of the more sought after tasks in the hotel.

'Kevork, we've come to pick up Fuad. OK?'

Kevork shrugged. 'Mr Artemian says it's OK. I'll take you.'

We followed him down a corridor. One or two doors were open and we got a glimpse of what looked to be a cross between large hotel rooms and student bedrooms with shelves containing books and cassettes, posters, pads of paper. We passed a middle-aged man in the corridor carrying computer printout, who just nodded at Nickie. I wondered whether this was any of the ten names that Jim Elweth had given me of those whose deaths had been so prematurely announced.

We turned down one wing of the building and came into an area without evident life and with a vaguely stale smell. At the end we stopped in front of a very solid wood door. Kevork pulled out a complex key and unlocked it.

The room was small and stuffy with only a little barred window. Fuad was sitting on the bed reading. He got to his feet stiffly and spoke in Arabic, with a touch of strained humour in his voice. 'What is this? A party?'

In the cramped room he seemed even taller than I remembered him. His face showed evidence of tiredness, boredom and a lack of shaving facilities, but otherwise he looked well. Then he saw me and his face took on a perplexed expression.

'Welcome....'

The pause lengthened and he spoke again in what he likes to think of as English.

'You look sort of like an Englishman I know.'

'And you, Fuad Attiyah, are a blessed nuisance.'

Then we hugged and embraced and Fuad kissed me on both cheeks. I wished he'd been able to shave. I introduced Tina and Nickie who were in the corridor because that was the only place there was room for them. Then, mindful of Elias' warning, I told Fuad to pack his things quickly.

Nickie said she'd work to do and after giving us a firm injunction to go straight back, she left. We began to walk back down to the house with Fuad and on the way down exchanged news. Fuad had been tolerably well kept, but had been subjected to repeated questioning by Harout and someone who was clearly Sammy. They had not, however, been violent and as he had nothing to hide they had in the end given up.

'But when I mentioned Andy's name this guy Harout lit up. "Stanwick? Spell that." So I was real worried that they'd gone back to you and were giving you a hard time.'

'What, give me a hard time? Fuad, it's only my friends who do that.'

I slapped him on the back. It was very good to have him out. Very good indeed.

'Well, Fuad, that's probably that. Your dad's coming up this afternoon and we are heading out just as soon as Tina and I have seen round the monastery with Harout and Elias. They are trying to assure me that nothing nasty is going on. If they do that, we all promise to be good and to say nothing and that's the end of the matter.'

'I'll be so glad for that.'

He walked on a little unsteadily, then he turned to me and stared into my eyes.

'So you guys really reckon there is nothing rotten going on here?'

'Fuad, you must learn to stop asking awkward questions.' I glanced over my shoulder. There were trees all around. 'We're keeping an open mind, let's say.'

315

'If you find something nasty, then what?'

'Never you mind. It's not your business. We hope we don't. We want to go home too, Fuad. The main thing now though is that you stay in Elias' house until we are ready to leave. If you step outside then Harout may change his mind and grab you back.'

'OK. I've used too much initiative already. I'll stay out. But I don't like what's going on here. Really I don't. Although I don't know much about it, something stinks.'

I looked at Tina and caught her expression. Everybody seemed to agree; something was rotten in this part of the world. But what and where?

At the house we put Fuad in our room, and with further warnings about straying, prepared to go and find Elias. Fuad lay down on the bed and closed his eyes.

'I'll be happy here, very happy. And whatever happens, Henry and Tina, thanks for coming.'

32

We closed the door on Fuad and went downstairs. There was no sign of Elias, but we found Malik, who took us to what was a rather fine library. Three sides of the large room were occupied by well-filled bookshelves. Normally these would have caught my eye first, but here the fourth wall took precedence because it was largely window and the view was due east over the dazzling snows. The line of the great limestone cliff edge drew the eye to where, a mile or so away, the monastery protruded, and for the first time I was able to look at it properly. It was a solid, low, two-storey building with the ubiquitous red-tile roof. An archway in the middle of the side facing us suggested that it was of a rectangular plan with a central courtyard. The northern edge abutted against another set of crags so that the monastery was almost overhung by rock at that point. The southern edge of the monastery was also striking. Here stuck against the block of the main building was a three-storey square tower which seemed to have an oddly truncated top. Near the monastery were a number of trees and through them it was possible to see the track coming down to a car park just beside the main building. Behind the monastery the hills rose steeper and steeper, the only break being the cirque in which, guarded by a stone wall, the dozen or so great cedars stood.

Elias was sitting at a desk to the side of the window and turned as we came in. He got up and picked his way round a large paper-strewn table towards us.

'Welcome to my study and to my inspiration. Every time I think about leaving this place I look at the view. That over Farayoun is also good, but it reminds me that we live in a world of people and problems. This is more soothing. Now let us take our walk. The young man is safe I take it?'

'Thank you, Sheik, he appears to have been well treated.'

I wasn't being facetious, I was just comparing his treatment to the fate of the man taken – and dispatched – yesterday. I wondered whether to ask to phone Antoine with the good news, but decided that even if we could get through he would be at church. Anyway, Fuad was only halfway free. I personally wouldn't be totally happy until he was out of Elias' control and preferably back in Cyprus. However, despite it all, I felt good and even elated.

'Excellent, now let us hope everything will pass off satisfactorily today. Shall we go?'

On the way out I glanced again at the library. At least half of the volumes appeared to be what might be termed serious literature and literary criticism. There seemed to be little written in the last fifteen years and I wondered how much Elias' tastes had been influenced by his mentor. There was certainly a good poetry section. Another set of shelves appeared to contain works dealing with politics and administration. It crossed my mind that there probably weren't many modern, or even twentieth-century, books in those fields that would be of interest to Elias either.

We put on our outdoor clothes again and followed Elias out. He was dressed in an expensive outfit that suggested a recent shopping trip to London and he looked every bit the squire, even down to a walking stick and green rubberised boots. I had assumed it would be a cosy little walk with the three of us, but I had forgotten the realities of the situation. Two fit young men dressed in what looked to be a copy of NATO winter uniform were waiting outside in the garden. Both were armed with small but ugly submachine guns and had packs and binoculars with them. Elias went over to them and spoke a few words in quiet Arabic that I couldn't follow.

Then he came back to us.

'My men will accompany us at a distance: George in the front and Michel at the rear. I'm sorry, but these are difficult times. They are the best of the best – I have had them trained in the States. They also allow me to keep in radio contact should a crisis develop. Well, shall we go?'

George led the way through the garden and unlocked the steel gate. I noticed that as he left the garden he carefully looked all around him before allowing us to follow. Michel locked the gate behind us. We walked along a narrow, ill-defined path only twenty yards from the cliff edge with the two guards keeping a discreet distance just out of earshot ahead and behind us.

Elias seemed to be in good spirits, although he was more ready to speak than to listen. Every so often something triggered him into a pronouncement. Neither I nor Tina were in any particular mood to challenge him, especially knowing his volatility. The apparent success of getting

Fuad out lent a certain contentment to the proceedings and there seemed little point in risking any disruption by irritating the guardian of his safety.

Elias waved his stick towards the monastery.

'At one stage my father considered putting a road between the house and the monastery. I have no idea what possessed him. It is barely ten minutes' walk and if you want you can drive back to the main road and along past the hotel. This obsession with the motor car!'

Halfway to the monastery he stopped on a slight rise. 'I must seem to you like a man secure, mustn't I?'

I gave a half-nod, noting that George was using the opportunity to scan the route ahead thoroughly with binoculars, while Michel was using the radio.

'But you see all round these ridges lie my enemies. Just beyond the crest of the hill is a small Syrian post.'

He pointed to a slight depression on the crest from which one could just see the faint line of the road running down towards the cedars. Then he turned to the north and gestured to the savage rock faces of the upper cliff only two or three miles away.

'Beyond these cliffs here are further enemies. The same to the south. I am a king, but a hemmed in one. Still, we seem to have stability and the Syrians are courteous and are prepared to leave me alone. I am no threat to them. Indeed, sometimes I do them small favours. For example, I return to them people that have tried to flee.'

He leaned on the stick.

'But there are times when I feel trapped, imprisoned. There are moments when I hate this valley, when I feel it is Lebanon's largest prison.'

We walked on through the crisp snow for some way, finding it generally firm enough that we did not sink in. We were slowly climbing on a more or less direct line to the cedars and were already some way above the level of the monastery. The central courtyard was now plain and there was nothing to see of interest.

'You know, I am tempted sometimes to leave. To, what's the word, abdicate? Let my brother take over. But where could I go without one of my enemies finding me? I complain about Harout and his group, but they have given me false papers. Now, suitably disguised, I can leave the valley for up to a week. I become a common man. I was in Dublin last year. Oh marvellous! I'd never been before. Then I had to come back, in case they realised I was gone.'

He looked at me slyly. 'That is in part why I pretend to be the moody emperor and disappear for days or nights. I tell Sammy that I am in the tower and will not be disturbed.'

At this point he gestured to the curious appendage to the monastery.

'Sometimes I travel to Damascus over the top. They think I am a travelling merchant.'

He seemed puzzled. ' "Merchant?" That sounds terribly old fashioned, like the Arabian Nights. What do you say now?'

'How about tradesman, sales representative, or just businessman?'

'Hmm, leave it at merchant. Anyway, at the checkpoint we always laugh together about Elias Daoud, the one-valley warlord.'

He chuckled dryly. He might have made the joke, but I wouldn't have dared, not with George and Michel, the human Dobermans, hemming us in.

We now reached the dirt track that ran from the main road down to the monastery and crossing it continued on our straight course for the cedars. The snow was softer here and threatened to overflow into our boots. It certainly made for heavy going. When we stopped for breath at one point, Tina turned to me with a wry smile. I think she was finding herself able to relax a little.

'Anything about the limestone weathering of importance, Dr Stanwick, or are you on holiday?'

I looked around. 'I'll make a brief professional pronouncement. My last of the year. Not much to see. It's mostly been fairly rapid physical weathering, although there are some caves. Mostly along some of the joints and small faults which are very important here. The snow melts gently over spring and summer and the meltwater seeps slowly into the cracks and joints. The result is that even at the end of a long hot summer the springs and the rivers still flow, which is one reason why this area is so fertile. End of lecture.'

Elias gave a little nod. 'Very good. Perhaps I should get you to give a public talk.'

'Any time, Sheik, it would be an honour.'

Maybe, I thought, but if we get out of here with Fuad I don't think we will be interested in returning. At least, not with the merry trio of Harout, Elias and Sammy still around. It was curious that out of Elias and Harout it was the Armenian that I distrusted most. For all his complexities, tempers and contradictions Elias appeared at least comprehensible, if not exactly predictable, and his dangers seemed mappable. Harout, by contrast, appeared to be uncharted waters in which all sorts of things could lie underneath.

The gradient now became steeper and for some time there was no sound except heavy breathing. It was becoming warm work. Then faintly below we heard the pealing of bells. Elias stopped.

'I allow them ten minutes only – except to declare an emergency.'

A few minutes later they stopped.

'Good. I said I would tell you about my attitude to the church later. I will tell it this afternoon if this pastor comes. Then he may judge my case.'

Suddenly we reached the road from the hotel over the ridge. Elias stopped to draw breath and we were grateful to follow him. I suppose we were high enough for the thinner air to make a difference to our unacclimatised lungs. The two militiamen nodded to Elias and set off for the cedar grove. I continued to be impressed by the efficiency of Elias' military operation; these men were fit and competent and no chances were being taken on Elias being ambushed among the great trees. I looked at him. His thin face was slightly flushed, but he was clearly quite fit as we must have climbed several hundred feet and he had set the pace all the way.

I looked along the road. The snowplough had been along it after the last snowfall and stones and broken tarmac showed along its length. I traced it to the ridge and travelled it in my mind's eye – down over the watershed into the fertile flat Bekaa, past the now off-limits glories of Baalbek and the lesser ruins of Anjar, then up again over the Anti-Lebanon range and finally into Damascus. Some day perhaps we'd do it.

Elias broke the noise of our heavy breathing. 'I have this road cleared after every snow storm. Sammy keeps a post up the top with a dozen people in it and we like to keep it well supplied and the men rotated. We have good relations with the Syrians, but we make sure they'd have a job sneaking in.'

'How would you stop them?'

'We'd just blow the road. We have the holes drilled and the explosive ready. There is a practice every six months or so. It would take ten minutes. The road's been there since Roman times, if not earlier. It would take weeks to rebuild it and there's no other way over for vehicles. We have to maintain our vigilance. In addition to the military, there is always a little traffic between us and the Bekaa, although not so much hashish as people think.'

He grinned at Tina, showing a gold-capped molar.

'Mrs Stanwick, what do you think of a country where you have to disguise a scientific project as a drug smuggling and processing operation?'

Tina gave him a cool smile. 'I would say there was something badly wrong with the world.'

322

Elias turned his grin on me. 'Dr Stanwick, I think your wife and I agree on something at last!'

Elias looked up at the cedars.

'We have to wait here for a few minutes until Michel and George have done their checking. It would be fearfully romantic to be killed in the Cedars of Farayoun, but I would prefer to avoid it. It might even fan Charles Rimmer's waning poetic talents into a final flame.' There was a gesture from Michel. 'Ah, that is the all clear. Let us go.'

We began to walk the last few yards of the snow up to the cedars. As we got closer it was possible to see how majestic they were. They were by no means as large as those at Bcharri, and indeed I've seen individual cedars of comparable size in some English stately gardens, but these appeared to be all of classical proportions with the long, low branches spreading widely and their shape highlighted by the snow resting on them. The isolation of these trees in the whiteness, free from all taint of human presence apart from the simple wall, was impressive.

Just as we approached them there was the echoing double blast of two sonic booms. It was a sobering sound and much of my raised spirits had evaporated before the last echoes died away. I looked up. High above us in the deep blue sky, two silver pinpoints at the end of the long threads of cotton were swinging round and going southwards again. The point around which they were turning was directly overhead. If I had had any doubts about who we had been talking to the previous day, or their seriousness, this removed them at a stroke. These half-circles miles above us seemed to say, 'Don't forget. Here we are.' I looked down quickly, unwilling to draw Elias' attention to them. He didn't even bother to look up. The guards appeared to be equally unconcerned; I assumed that the planes regularly turned round over this area.

'Just the Israelis. They worry about the refugee camps at Tripoli. If it wasn't for their planes, sometimes you could forget there was a war on. Do you hate them too, Dr

323

Stanwick?'

Typical of Elias – the wild question out of nowhere. The safest answer would have been one of extreme Arab rhetoric about desiring to spit on their graves, but that wouldn't have been an honest answer.

'Hate them, Sheik? No, although I've been tempted to. They have done terrible things, but now I leave it to God to judge them. A Christian Palestinian friend of mine said it very well: "They have destroyed my country, my home and my family; these things I cannot keep. If I hate them then they will have destroyed my soul and that I do keep." '

The response was a silence followed by a quiet, reflective voice, 'Easy to say.'

Then I realised that he had lost a mother, wife and child at the hands of others.

'Yes, Sheik, easy for me to say.'

We walked on carefully towards the wall, against which the drifts must have been six or seven feet thick in places. We then scrambled over the stonework and were under the great trees. I noticed that the militiamen stayed outside the clump on guard.

Elias turned to Tina. 'In Arabic we call these trees "*El Arz er Rab*". It means the "Cedars of the Lord".'

'Why?'

'I don't know precisely. I think there is something in one of the Psalms about them being the "trees of the Lord". Anyway, we think that these trees, above all trees, are his; that he owns them.' There was a detached, almost awed tone in his voice.

We looked up at the vast branches and dark olive green needles and through to the great blueness of the sky above and smelled the clean smell and each of us fell silent. It was an awesome place. At first I thought it was simply because of the age of the trees and the fact that some of these trees might have been living things for fifteen centuries or more, but then I realised that it wasn't the age, it was something else, something deeper. It just seemed to me appropriate that Solomon should have used these cedars for his temple because of all trees these seemed inclined to make their own grand architecture. You almost didn't need to cut them to make them into a place of worship. In such a place even I could have been tempted to be a mystic.

How long we stayed there enjoying the sunlight, breathing the clean sharp air, revelling in the silence and watching the birds going from branch to branch I don't know. Eventually it was time to descend. Slowly, with damp feet and trousers, and guarded at front and rear by the faithful George and Michel we made our way back down to the house. Just on the road Elias stopped and looked slowly at the landscape.

'I love all this valley and I hate it. I am safe in it as long as I rule, as long as I take precautions like having these two men. But if I let go my rule, or if I slip, then that will be my end.' He sighed. 'Perhaps one day I will go and not come back, but they would hunt for me somewhere. And then too this valley cannot afford such a crisis, not surrounded by enemies. No, I am a hostage here, for my own safety and that of my people. This is both my refuge and my prison cell.'

33

The midday meal was substantial and Fuad joined us to make up a foursome. Elias was quiet and made only a small contribution to the conversation. I watched Fuad carefully. Although he ate little there appeared to be nothing wrong with him that a few days in Cyprus wouldn't cure. That could probably be said too of both Tina and me, although she now seemed to be in control of herself.

Towards the end of the meal something of Fuad's previously bubbly nature surfaced. He turned to Elias. 'Sheik, you know really why I came to this valley?'

Elias looked up from toying with a knife.

'No. I was told it was something about a school.'

I had a feeling of unease. I was very fond of Fuad and he had a lot of charm, but he was perfectly capable of rushing in where angels feared to tread. I tried to catch his eye. It was too late.

'Sure. George my boss was thinking of trying to start a school up north of Jounieh. Non-sectarian, independent, free from influence. We'd like, well, wondered whether a site in your valley might be a possibility. Near Mrebbine say.'

The way it was phrased there was no doubt that it was a request.

Elias looked at him in astonishment. For a moment I thought he was going to go into one of his furies and all the good work was about to be undone, but when he spoke it was in tones of annoyance rather than wrath.

'I don't believe it! You just escape with your life and you want to come back? You are asking me to let you build a church school in my valley?'

He turned to me. 'Dr Stanwick, if you must put your head into a lion's mouth, do not do so when you have companions who like jumping on his tail.'

I tried to smile and worked hard to come up with the soft answer that turneth away wrath. However, Elias had continued speaking in a tone that didn't entertain any sort of answer.

'The response you take back to Cyprus, young man, is simply no. I prefer my isolation. Besides, who would send their children into Elias Daoud's valley to be taught?'

He shook his head in disbelief and returned to playing with his fork. A moment later he looked up.

'However, I admire your courage and your zeal.'

326

Fuad made some gracious remarks and a few minutes later, after asking permission, left to return to his room.

The remaining three of us moved from the meal table to sit down in the other room. Elias, now in a brighter mood, showed off his collection of records, tapes and compact discs which was impressive. At first I thought it might just be a status symbol, or some prop to a reputation as the 'thinking man's warlord'. In fact it turned out that he not only took a genuine pleasure in classical music, but that he was very knowledgeable about it. He seemed especially keen on baroque music and was clearly fascinated by the idea of court orchestras and court composers. He hinted that should the day ever arrive when he could dispense with 'his Forces', he'd be happy to put the money into his own modest baroque ensemble. Whether he was entirely serious I don't know, but I wasn't going to be the one to tread on his dreams. In the meantime he had the problem of music supplies all sorted out.

'I get the *Gramophone* sent over every month from Cyprus. Then I go through it, make a list of what I want and send it over to my agent in Cyprus. I do it through a computer setup. That way nothing gets garbled over the radio phone. It's just like telex really. My agent is efficient, but he doesn't know one Bach from another. The same with books. So eventually the Montiverdi or the Handel makes its way over to Cyprus and gets brought over on Harout's yacht.'

Then, as he was explaining this, something happened which indelibly made the point that music has no ability to improve behaviour. Tina was lying back on a sofa, with her eyes half-closed, listening to the allegedly authentic Corelli. Elias suddenly noticed that Tina had a faint smile on her face. To my astonishment Elias stopped in sudden irritation and his hands began to interlock frantically together. He clearly thought the smile was directed at him. In a harmless way it may have been; indeed, there was something bizarre about the juxtaposition of technological and musical sophistication in this man who appeared to be

327

closer to Charlemagne than the Common Market in his politics. Whatever the cause he turned to me with his lips thin and bloodless.

'Dr Stanwick, your wife is beginning to relax in my presence. I trust she is not beginning to find me amusing. Perhaps she has forgotten who I am. I also use the computer to order the weaponry that Sammy persuades me we need, and also to check up with my agent on whether my brother is planning to get rid of me. I enjoy music, I enjoy poetry, but I am primarily interested in survival.'

The voice was chilly, even angry. Tina shot upright instantly on the sofa with her face pale. She spoke uncertainly, but with a hint of defiance.

'I'm very sorry, Sheik. I was just enjoying the music myself. No insult intended, I can assure you.'

Elias paused and seemed to collect himself.

'Very well, none taken. Not yet. But remember who you are with.'

It was an extraordinary outburst – apparently totally unprovoked. I think he genuinely felt there was a danger in having people relaxing around him. Any prospect of dropping to first name terms with him vanished completely.

Then, as suddenly as it had begun, his mood ended and his voice changed back to normal.

'That's another good point about the group. Without them I'd only be able to justify sending things over every month or so. Now there are generally trips every week. In fact the boat's due in today, Harout said, so that should have some things on.'

Mention of Harout brought a frown to his face.

'I do wish you hadn't turned up here. Fuad, you, your wife. All of you. Before you came I had no problems with Harout or the group. Perhaps a few technical and financial irritations. Now, maybe I have some doubts. Perhaps....'

He left the sentence hanging in the air for some time.

'You see I am just a patron in name of the group. What

they do I know only a little of. At times I wonder myself what is being hatched in that monastery. Then Harout pays me and I am able to keep Sammy and the Forces happy.'

He paused reflectively.

'So I do hope you are happy this afternoon with what you see, Dr Stanwick.'

'We hope so too, Sheik. Very much.'

There was a buzzing of the phone. Elias answered it and speaking in Arabic said, 'Bring him over.' He nodded at me, 'The father is here.'

Five minutes later Antoine Attiyah was shown into the room by Malik. He came in very diffidently, but his surprise and delight in seeing us was clear. There was, however, a searching look which suggested he had not yet heard news of his son. I gave him a quick thumbs-up gesture and relief flooded his face. He approached the Sheik and, shaking hands, made a very fine statement of the honour and the gratitude he felt that the Sheik was assisting in the case. I didn't follow all the ornamented Arabic, but it seemed elegant without going over the top and I detected nothing but sincerity in what he said.

Elias thanked him for his kind words and then motioned to me. 'Henry, if you would show Pastor Attiyah to his son, please?'

Antoine's face beamed. He gave Tina and me a large hug and then I took him upstairs. I opened the door just enough for him to get through and caught a glimpse of Fuad lying on the bed. As soon as Antoine was in the room I closed the door and went back downstairs. It was good that their reunion could be arranged privately; such things tend to get very emotional in the Arab world.

Ten minutes later Antoine came down. He stood before Elias, his eyes shining. He spoke in Arabic, but it was plain speaking.

'Sheik Elias, I wish to apologise to you and to ask your forgiveness. I have thought many bad things about you over the past week. One or two may have passed my lips. I would like to say that I am sorry. Your actions have disproved my words.'

It was a curious situation. In the rigid hierarchical system that has prevailed in the Middle East since before Abraham the situation was clear cut. Antoine, a man with no rights, was making an apology to one who held absolute power over him, yet it seemed to be Elias who was discomfited and who was ill at ease. For a moment he looked away, then he spoke quietly in Arabic.

'Your thoughts may not have been out of place, Pastor. I should have had him released earlier, but these are difficult times. Thank you for your apology, but it was unnecessary. Please sit down with us.'

Antoine sat down slowly and carefully on the sofa in between Elias and ourselves. Elias turned to him and, presumably mindful of Tina, spoke to him in English.

'I understand your son meant well. The action was misunderstood. He is, however, a credit to you. I would be tempted to think about discussing this idea of a school were it not for security considerations, but perhaps you think Elias Daoud is the wrong man to ask about such a school?'

That wasn't a loaded question so much as one primed, fused and with the trigger cocked. Antoine clearly recognised it as such. He paused, then spoke carefully and clearly.

'There is no doubt, Sheik, that your interest and ability in things of the mind is very high. There are, however, those who question whether you have such competence in things of the Spirit.'

Elias began to knit his fingers together. I hoped Antoine knew what he was doing, but with only a fraction of a second's pause he continued.

'I, however, say this: there is no shortage of judges in our country, but few of these judges have any sympathy or understanding of what they judge. I do not know your story in detail, so I will not judge you. I know only this about you: you have suffered.'

There was a long pause, then the knotted fingers fell apart. I felt I could start breathing again. Elias looked at us each in turn.

'Thank you. Let me tell you my story. It concerns the monastery that we are to visit shortly and it concerns my reputation.'

He sat back in the sofa and stared at a photograph on a chest. I glanced at it. It was of a pretty young mother and an infant.

'The problems go back a long way. My father married outside the Maronite church. My mother – God rest her soul – was a devout woman and she did much good, but the priests never liked her. They were formally polite. Then when the Civil War started there were great requests made to my father to supply men. "It is his spiritual duty," they said. He refused. That went down badly in Jounieh and with many around the Patriarch. When my father died the mourning was muted.'

He gave a shrug and a little, bitter laugh.

'Some of those who cried most were, I suspect, those who saw that I would be worse. I took my father's stand about the war and kept the militia here. However, I changed things in the valley. Privileges that belonged only to the priests I removed. I married a Greek Catholic girl from a good family near Tripoli. That again was frowned on. I became involved politically, I criticised Pierre and Bashir, I visited Syria and talked to Assad. There were rumours, and I have never denied them, that I talked with Arafat. The priests protested loudly. The joke became that Bashir had the Palestinians to fight and Elias his priests. The priests did not quite curse me to my face, but they did it in private.'

Then he stopped. He said nothing for a whole minute, his face filling with anguish.

'Then Nada, my mother and little Mary were killed by

331

a bomb which was placed on the roadside to be triggered when the car passed. That was a Tuesday.'

The grief was stamped over his face. 'I mourned for three days. On the fourth day I made enquiries and confirmed who it was that had ordered the bomb. Everybody knew. It was deliberately aimed at my family. It was a lesson, they said. So I called up the man who at that time held the highest office in the church. "*Abuna*, our Father, you know who did this thing?" I said. He would not deny it, so I asked him to denounce them publicly by name by Sunday evening. Then I rang off. Everybody from Tripoli to Tyre knew what I had asked. All day Sunday we listened to the radio. He gave his address and said nothing.'

He shook his head. 'On the Monday morning Sammy and a dozen of his loyalest men came with me to the monastery with a large truck. We gave the monks half an hour to get ready and loaded them on the truck at gunpoint. They were dropped off at Jounieh.'

He sighed. 'We cleaned out the monastery. The filth we found: drink, pornography, items of sorcery. Their library – library they called it – had a dozen books in it. I was tempted to let the Deir burn or leave it to fall down, to let the sun and the rain cleanse it and to give it back to Nature. Then Harout came. He seemed attracted by it, although he drove a hard bargain. I handed it over to him and he brought in his Egyptians to rebuild it.'

He shrugged and looked into the fire.

'So that is my story; why I will never be a Maronite saint.'

There was silence. Then Antoine's quiet voice broke the silence. '*I* do not condemn you.'

The emphasis was strongly on the first word of the sentence; leaving open the possibility – even probability – of other judgement. Elias continued to stare into the fire.

'Since then I have not entered a church, or said a prayer – at least not to that God.' He looked at Antoine as if to say 'so there', but there was no pride in it.

332

'I would only say, Sheik, that there is a foolishness in burning down a fruit tree because you ate a bad apple from it.'

'Perhaps.'

'I do not wish to defend the man, but from what I know he felt that everything he stood for was threatened. He did not dare denounce a man so powerful for this act. It could have destroyed his church. I think it would have been better if he had, but he felt that a little evil was better than a greater one. He went for safety.'

Elias turned to him. 'Pastor, that was no excuse!'

Antoine shrugged his shoulders. 'You are right, but which of us has not been tempted to take the safe road instead of the right one?'

He said it without any emphasis, in his usual quiet voice, yet the words seemed to be so strikingly appropriate to my own long-term concern about jobs that I looked up, expecting to see Antoine staring at me. But he had his hands clenched together and was staring at them. There was no answer from Elias.

After a long, hanging silence Antoine spoke again. 'Sheik, does what you have rejected leave a void?'

Elias shifted slightly on his sofa. 'I fill it with my dreams, Pastor.'

'Are they strong enough to stand on?'

Elias looked up into space. 'No, Pastor. Dreams never are. A man I studied once found that out. "Now that my ladder's gone, I must lie down where all ladders start, in the foul rag and bone shop of the heart." '

As he spoke I remembered the bitter cynicism of Yeats' last years. Antoine was now silent in turn. I thought at first that having his opponent concede a weakness he would have pushed harder, but he didn't. That wasn't his way. Then he spoke again in a slightly different tone.

'Sheik, can I ask why you were prepared to lose honour rather than take vengeance?'

Elias looked stiffly at him. I made a mental note never to

travel anywhere in Lebanon again with either Attiyah. To talk about 'losing honour' was risky ground indeed.

'I see where your son gets his boldness from! Dr Stanwick gave me a pretty answer earlier today about revenge. I wish I could echo it and tell you I had left it to God. But no. Partly I was afraid. They could have destroyed me and the valley. But partly, I'm afraid to say, Pastor, I still hope to live to get it.'

Antoine nodded, as if it was what he expected. 'But if I am not mistaken, at least one of your enemies is dead.'

'Indeed so, struck down at a moment of glory. Perhaps I should see the judgement of God on that, but Pastor, I say to you sadly but honestly that I am not satisfied. I still have scores to settle.'

'And when they are settled, will you then have peace of mind?'

Elias stared at Antoine, then turned away to stare silently at the fire. I felt he was trapped.

Then the phone rang, which was probably as well. Elias got up to answer it and then came back to us.

'Harout is here with a vehicle. Let us go. Pastor, would you too like to come and see what we have done with the Deir?'

Antoine stood to his feet. 'My son will be safe here?'

'My word of honour.'

There was a moment's hesitation on the tired face. I felt sure that part of him wanted to refuse and stay with his son, but something else, perhaps curiosity or more probably duty, drove him on. He spoke firmly.

'Thank you, Sheik, I would be very interested.'

34

We pulled on outdoor clothes and went out along the path up to the gateway with Elias leading the way. Looking down the valley I noticed that to the west an immense wall of thick dark grey cloud was draped over the sea. The threatened front was on its way in. Antoine was behind me and I turned to him. His lined face looked thinner than ever with the thick coat he was wearing. I gestured westwards.

'The storm is coming in, Antoine. I hope we can get out in time.'

To my surprise he stopped in his tracks. He spoke thoughtfully. 'Yes, a storm is coming, Henry. We should indeed be gone. I wish we were already. But....'

I waited, uncertain of what was causing his hesitancy. He shivered and seemed to speak mostly to himself.

'No, we can only go if we have done everything we were sent to this place for. And have we? Have we, Henry?'

I stared at him. His tone was odd and faraway and behind his thick lenses his eyes seemed to be fixed on the billowing clouds. I wondered whether the valley was getting to him. I tried to think through his question.

'No, you are right, Antoine. Not yet. I am glad you are coming. We may need another pair of eyes.'

He shook his head. 'Eyes? I may be no good there. But, Henry, I tell you this: I feel, I know with my heart, that there is more here than visible things. It is not just the weather, there is something horrible in this valley.'

I wondered what exactly he had in mind and was going to ask him when there was a shout from the gate and I

335

took Antoine's thin arm and motioned him onwards. If he felt like that, then all the more reason to get this visit over and done with and leave. Beyond the gate Harout was standing a few yards away from the Range Rover smoking. Elias, in his dark coat and wool hat, called Antoine over to introduce him to Harout. I merely nodded at the Armenian and went over to the vehicle, mindful of the need to speed up the proceedings so that we could get out before the storm broke. My recollection of such storms was that you would get blizzards well below the height we were at and the prospect of driving down 3,000 feet of snow-covered bad road in minimal visibility wasn't appealing. So I wasn't close enough to hear what was said between Harout and Antoine. Whatever it was Harout turned rapidly on his heels and walked to the driver's seat. As he passed I noticed his look was expressionless apart from the eyes. In them there appeared to be some intense emotion, either hatred, or fear, or both. Antoine walked slowly behind him, his face pale and grim. He came up to me and gripped my arm. In the grasp there seemed to be a hunger to hold flesh and blood. Elias followed, looking perplexed.

Harout drove angrily, grinding the gears and sliding and skidding the wheels on ice. He said nothing. We drove westwards to the main road and then back up past the hotel before turning off down to the monastery on the track. It crossed my mind for a moment that Harout was just going to accelerate onwards and launch us into space over the sheer rock face. In the event he slewed to a sudden halt next to a dozen other cars in the gravel and snow of the car park at the edge of the monastery.

This close, the Deir looked imposing with its solid walls and small barred and shuttered windows. The fact that the walls ran out of a sixty-foot-high overhanging limestone cliff added to the impression of something hewn out of rock. Beyond, on the southern edge of the monastery, there were a few trees and then, as the promontory ended

336

with a 200–foot drop, nothing. Two miles away, across the valley, more cliffs faced us with sheer rock faces, scree and snow patches.

Harout got out of the car quickly and the rest of us followed. I whispered in Tina's ear, 'Keep your eyes open.'

She whispered back, 'Don't worry.'

I glanced at Antoine, who seemed to be huddled into his coat. He shook himself and followed as we were led in through the archway. I noticed that the two framing stone columns looked Roman and concluded that they were doubtless recycled as so much of Middle Eastern architecture is. A glance around showed large pale limestone blocks with beautiful knife sharp edges distributed around some of the lower parts of the walls which looked to be of a similar origin. I wondered if they'd carried them up from the temple of Adonis below. Behind the archway were open double doors apparently made out of wood. The hinges were massive and the bolts solid metal bars. Trying to mimic carelessness I gave a door a push. It barely moved; there was clearly steel underneath the wood. From the archway we were led into a small anteroom where there were three monitor screens, a microphone and a battery of switches, indicator lights and speakers. Nearby stood one of Harout's muscular Armenians from the hotel carrying one of the new fancy lightweight compact submachine guns. Harout rotated a switch and a number of images appeared on a screen in succession: a laboratory, a corridor, a library, a study. Most images had one or two people in them. Harout muttered irritably.

'Can't see her. Let's call her up.'

He pressed the microphone button and summoned Nickie to the gate. Harout turned around and spoke in a vaguely aggrieved tone. Under the ice something seemed to be swirling. He seemed to be trying to avoid Antoine's eyes.

'She'll be here soon.'

He looked around and continued talking in a dry, dull tone as if this was the thousandth tour of the week. 'This

337

is the gatehouse. We just have standard security systems installed. The location is so secure, thanks to the Sheik, it's a bit unnecessary, but we couple it with fire sensors.' He gestured to another array. 'In fact most of these alarms are duplicated at the hotel. Ah, here she is.'

Nickie hurried over, face slightly flushed.

'Sorry. You were so late I'd given up and was making myself a sandwich.'

Harout grunted at her. 'The boat is late at Ras el Bourj and they are a bit worried about the weather. The skipper wanted to turn back to Cyprus.'

Then he looked around. 'Now please follow me. Feel free to ask questions of myself and Nickie. Please don't touch anything or stray away. Not that there is anything to hide, but we aren't adjusted for tourists and there are a variety of hazards around.'

The whole thing had such an air of unreality about it that it crossed my mind to try to ease the atmosphere by making some banal joke such as asking if we could buy brochures, but the thought died as quickly as it came. There was too much tension on all sides. Only Elias and Nickie looked even vaguely at ease. I glanced at Antoine's grey face and wondered what was troubling him.

For the next hour we were shown around the whole of the monastery. In one sense there was nothing to see. Indeed, as secret operations go it was remarkably dull. We went round anti-clockwise starting from the middle of the western side. In some ways the monastery reminded me of an Oxford college, say, Christ Church. Smaller and cruder, but the same combination of wood or stone floored corridors, narrow stairs, bare stone walls, poor lighting and sheer weight of years. We were shown every room, albeit briefly. Some of the rooms were occupied by people who were not introduced, but who nodded and smiled at Harout and then bent down again over keyboards, screens or pads of paper. Other rooms were unoccupied, with just empty desks and filing cabinets and books. In some places there were arrays of rooms which appeared devoted to a theme. The first one we came across was four adjacent rooms filled with people whose bookshelves indicated an interest in populations. Their walls were covered with graphs about infant mortality and fecundity and global population projections. Along from them in a symmetry that Malthus would have liked, was a sequence of rooms concerned with agriculture and food supplies. So it went on.

About half the rooms appeared to have people in, but whole sections appeared to be currently uninhabited. A suite of rooms that clearly belonged to the political group, and another set that were owned by the pollutants team, were all empty. Nickie explained that different groups spent different amounts of time at the Deir. The questions we asked were answered with fairness and I detected no hint of any deception in Nickie's responses. There were a number of questions she couldn't answer and passed them on to Harout. His answers were gruff and minimal. In fact he spent a lot of time staring at walls and apparently trying to keep as far away as he could from Antoine. Clearly some extraordinarily violent reaction of personal chemistry had occurred between them. I assumed it was to do with the fact that Harout had been the prime mover in the kidnapping of Fuad. Antoine himself said nothing, but just looked around. At times he seemed almost like a man in a dream and I had to hurry him along in case he got left behind.

The only zone we were moved through with anything like haste was one of a few uninhabited rooms where the books on the shelves were all about finance, banking and bank security systems. The haste seemed reasonable and anyway there was little here to interest me. One or two rooms were totally empty as if awaiting new projects and some had been little modified from the original monastic cells.

Nowhere in all that we saw was there any evidence of any space that could have hidden a laboratory of more than broom cupboard size. I didn't exactly tap walls, but I kept an eye open for any discrepancies between rooms and I found none. Given that we knew that any such chamber had required a ventilation system it was presumably at least the size of an average bedroom. Furthermore, the fans must emerge somewhere.

As I went over everything I felt that all in all it was a convincing set-up. There was no doubt in my mind that this was a genuine research unit; it was like many an academic set-up I'd seen, but this had a good deal more urgency. No one seemed to be hanging around corridors moaning about government policy or students. The fact that here there weren't either might have contributed to the apparently intense atmosphere of hard work.

Eventually, having done both floors of the west and south wings, we came to what had been the nave of the monastery chapel. This ran along the whole length of the eastern side from the tower to the upper cliff wall. As we looked into it it was difficult to see it as a nave any more. It was just a long hall that had been separated into three sections. All had false ceilings, but it was possible to see above them from an open staircase at the southern end and there was nothing but space up to the wooden beams of the roof.

The most southerly of these was Nickie's lab. The conversion had been done very well and the result was a clean elegant laboratory with an air of sterility about it. Four people were working, but we were not introduced to any of them. I glanced around with what I hoped was taken to be merely polite interest. There was lots of equipment, all of it apparently of the latest vintage. In addition to the microscopes, centrifuges, fridges, flasks and anonymous white vats I also noted some of the fancy machines for sequencing DNA that you see advertised in *Nature* and that bankrupt even the universities that don't have ill conceived business ventures. All the papers and books I could see were on genetics and algae and on the walls there was a series of large black and white plates of curious sculptured discs like lunatic designs for winter tyres.

Tina nodded at them. 'What are those?'

For once I knew. 'Those are scanning electron microscope photographs of coccoliths. They're the little plates of calcium carbonate that occur in some algae. They're what the chalk is made of. Just billions and billions of them.'

Nickie overheard and turned to Tina with a faint smile.

'If we can get more algae to produce things like that we can keep using the internal combustion engine into the twenty-second century. If not, better invest in boats before the icecaps melt.'

I had my problems with Nickie about her having lied to me, but I liked the way she rarely seemed to get full of doom and gloom about such things. I supposed it probably wasn't encouraged in the group. After all, once you've identified a problem the best thing is to go and tackle it, not sit around moaning. Here she seemed more confident than earlier. I think she felt that now we had seen her laboratory we couldn't possibly doubt the innocence of what she was doing.

I continued to look around. Along one side there were tanks with lights glowing over them and in one corner there was a large tank with a tap and a sign saying 'Sterile Seawater'. I tried to fix it all in my memory while searching for anything out of place.

There was nothing. It rang no alarm bells. It was either a stunningly good cover up or the real thing. There were no fancy fan arrangements, and the laboratory door we entered by was sealed tight but not hermetically. There were no warning notices and no signs of blood or blood testing equipment. There was no evidence of anything like the sort of precautions you would have to have taken if you were dealing with disease causing organisms. Yet Harout didn't know – couldn't have known – the specific

341

things we were looking for. In fact he was apparently forced into allowing this visit only twenty-four hours ago. It was all very puzzling.

After a few minutes we left. I caught Tina's eye and she bent towards me and whispered under her breath, 'Not at all medical.'

That was interesting. Tina spent a lot of her time discussing hospital equipment requirements and the fact that she recognised nothing fitted with my evaluation of the laboratory.

The middle section of the nave was a seminar room with screens, projector stands and a long central table. It was unremarkable and empty.

The third section was Harout's office. This, I thought to myself, was where the High Priest served. In all respects but one there was little to catch the eye. It was a spacious room with a desk of American boardroom proportions, filing cabinets, bookshelves, easy chairs and a thick carpet. On the east side there was a small arched window with plain leaded glass which looked towards the ridge. On the west side there was a second door.

On the north wall there was no trace of any altar. Instead, on it hung a large painting that ran from floor to ceiling. It was this painting, perhaps eight feet wide, that caught my eye and held it.

It is difficult to describe the painting, or at least to convey its potency, but basically it was a vivid jungle scene, a green tormented jungle overflowing with detailed life. It owed a little – a very little – to Henri Rousseau, but there was no naivety in it. That was the last thing that came to mind. Technically it was of high quality and many of the effects were almost photographic in their realism. It was a stylised scene because Old and New World animals met in it. Yet there was more to it than a simple jungle scene.

As I stared at it I felt troubled. I looked at Tina, who reached her hand out to mine and held it tightly. She evidently felt the same. There was something about the painting that was wrong. Maybe several things, because it was difficult to isolate the problem. The eye was caught by one aspect then another. What was it that was wrong? Certainly the greens were too lurid, almost putrid. Also there were no people, at least no living people. In a corner a tiger, red muzzled, was looking up from eating something; something half-hidden by the grass, but which might have had a human form. Under a tree elsewhere there was something white that might have been bone. There were also other elements that you felt were unwholesome. In the shadows there were fungi: sick, grey, soggy, corpse-like things. All over the picture there were flies: large, fat, black and reminding you unmistakeably of their relationship with maggots. On the leafmould of the forest floor there were holes filled with darkness, in which you felt you ought to see eyes.

Near the centre of the picture a yellow jaundiced snake hung out of the branches of a prominent tree. The snake's large fanged head had eyes that seemed to follow you. The tree containing the snake was strangely familiar and had a brown wrinkled fruit. In fact when you looked at it carefully you wondered if it wasn't an apple tree. Possibly the tree and the snake were the focus of the picture, possibly they weren't. It was the sort of picture that seemed to have no centre. Indeed, as you looked at it you realised that the proportions of the picture were totally wrong. It was altogether the stuff of nightmares. Indeed, I have dreamed of it since and woken up sweating. I wasn't sure whether the artist needed psychotherapy or exorcism.

Yet as I looked at it in mounting revulsion and horror I felt a curious sense of satisfaction. Because I knew then, as surely as Tina held my hand, that what we had come to was evil. If this was what hung in Harout's office then I personally needed to know nothing else about the group. I didn't know what they were up to. I didn't need to. All the seeds of doubt that had been sowed in my mind from Nickie's first conversation onwards had instantly

343

flowered. If I could have set fire to the place there and then I would have done so. Behind me Antoine muttered something quietly in Arabic. He switched to English.

'Wicked, a detestable thing.'

Harout, who obviously caught the meaning, if not the precise wording, avoided his gaze and spoke loudly. 'Symbolic. I saw something similar in New York and commissioned this. Well, we must move on. Let me show you the computer facilities.'

We left the room through the other door and came straight into the north wing. I noticed Antoine had stopped behind and I turned to fetch him. He was staring at the painting with a fixed almost manic look.

'Come on, Antoine. I know how you feel. We've got to look at the computers.'

He didn't look at me. His face was grey and he seemed to be perspiring. 'Henry, you know I have no sympathy with altars, but that thing alone is an evil painting and to put it where an altar would have stood is dreadful. Whoever did that is capable of the most terrible things.'

Then he followed me, shaking his head.

The computer set-up occupied most of the ground floor of the northern wing of the Deir. I suppose I should have paid more attention to it; it was after all the program it was running that had caused all the trouble. Instead, I found my mind full of the painting. What I actually saw of the computer set-up was impressive. In an immaculately clean room there was a series of small linked mainframes with lots of monitors, keyboards, cables and printers. It extended over several rooms and wiring ducts were punched through the old walls. The roofs in these rooms were lower than in the comparable rooms and I asked why.

Harout answered, 'We have put a lot of screening above the computers. These machines radiate a lot of radio interference. In theory it could be picked up by monitoring aircraft so we mask it out. The position against the cliff is also critical.'

On this mention of monitoring aircraft I decided not to ask any further questions and just looked around. But of all man's machines, computers are the most inscrutable so we passed on quickly. Above the rooms with the computers was the library. It was imposing, even allowing for the fact that the monastery was merely an integrating centre. Clearly there was no budget shortage here. I tried not to look too curious as I scanned along the shelves. There appeared to be no large section on viral diseases, but what did that prove? There were filing cabinets apparently filled with microfiche. The virus data might all be hidden in there. Anyway, even an absence might simply indicate that the papers were being held elsewhere.

Then there were a few small rooms and that was that. We walked back along the west wing to the door. I felt defeated. True, I knew for certain that what was going on was evil, but where, and what was it? They were questions I had to answer. Harout looked at his watch.

'Well, that's it. Nothing more. Of course we have a lot of work going on in other countries, but here you have seen everything.'

He was lying, I was absolutely sure, but I couldn't prove it.

'Now I must go and check up on this problem with the boat. I may have to go down to Ras el Bourj, but I hope not. I trust you have found nothing to disturb you?'

There was an embarrassing silence.

'Except perhaps my taste in art.'

At this point he smiled, but it was not a happy smile. I looked around. Only Nickie's face showed any emotion. She just seemed impatient to get back to work. I decided I had to say something.

'No, just that. Everything else is most interesting.'

Tina nodded in agreement, followed by Antoine.

Harout looked slightly happier.

'Good, well that appears to be the end of the matter. If you, Sheik Elias, would look after everybody and sort out with them the nature of the confidentiality we expect, I would be obliged. Perhaps you can show them your tower if they are interested? Thank you all. Goodbye.'

Elias nodded. Harout made a little bow and left to go back to his office.

We walked out of the courtyard. It had become darker. The sun was beginning to be occluded by fine high haze and below it to the west a towering dense mass of dark cloud was bearing down on us. The breeze was picking up slowly and it felt cold with the sun's rays dimmed. We had an hour, maybe two, before the snow would come.

Elias turned to us. 'You may as well come and see my tower. It will not take long.'

Nickie, who had clearly been thinking of going back to her lab, gave me a look of amused intrigue. As we followed Elias round the side of the monastery she whispered to me, 'I'm not missing this. An unheard of privilege.'

At the foot of the structure, Elias stopped.

'It apparently used to be a bell tower, but was destroyed by Muslims in the thirteenth century. So the tale goes, but no one knows for certain. It was certainly rebuilt, without the bell, some time after that.'

There was little to see here either. There had been a single large room on each floor. The ground floor was empty, the first floor had been partitioned into cooking and bathroom facilities and the second floor was a single combined study and bedroom. This top floor had shuttered windows on all four sides and I went over to the one overlooking the monastery. Elias threw it open for me. I looked out. There were no vents in the red tiles, no secret extensions. Nothing unusual at all.

Elias peered over my shoulder. 'I don't use this tower very much, but it's sometimes just nice to be here. Poetic.'

I had a vague recollection that Yeats had had a tower somewhere, and of course there was the Martello Tower in 'Ulysses'. I supposed for a petty despot into Irish Literature it was an essential possession. Elias pointed out of the window.

'There is a track up to the cedars from here. It's not easy to see, it runs up along the cliff. I used to take it as a child; it saves a long walk up the track.'

He traced it with his finger and I could see it. It started just by the car park and wound its way up the crags above the north end of the monastery, finally cresting them high above the nave.

I looked again over the monastery in gnawing disappointment. All the alarm bells were ringing in my mind, but it was agonising not to know what was going on. Or where. Yet I was certain there was something we hadn't seen.

We complimented Elias on his taste in towers and climbed down. Nickie and I were first out. She bent towards me.

'A bit of an anti-climax really. Still, it's the first time I've ever heard of anybody entering His Highness' inner chambers.'

I turned to Nickie. 'Nickie, that picture in Harout's office. You like it?'

She shook her head. 'I think it's rotten, but then I never was much good at art and they told me at school not to criticise what I didn't understand. Actually, it gives me the creeps.'

That was interesting; the negative opinion was apparently widespread.

I was about to talk to Tina as Antoine and then Elias emerged and the door to the tower was locked. The Sheik called out to us.

'Five minutes and then we leave, all right?'

I nodded. There seemed no point in staying. I didn't even know what I was looking for and in ten minutes' time we would be off down out of the valley and away. I'd expected to see something and I hadn't seen anything. Tina came over to me as Elias and Nickie walked over to the Range Rover talking together. Antoine wandered away on his own, deep in thought or prayer. I spoke to Tina quietly as we stood alone.

'Weird. Apart from that picture I saw nothing wrong. I may be a Philistine, but it's going a bit far to call up an airstrike just because I don't like a bit of art. Did you see any hard evidence?'

'No, none at all. No trace of any laboratory. But that painting was ghastly. It deserves an implosion bomb of its own. What does Antoine think?'

Antoine was now staring at the monastery. I called him over.'*Assis* Antoine, what do you think?'

He came over and shook his head. 'I was just wishing I could stand by those pillars and be Samson, but I suppose I'd only take a part of that place with me. It stinks of death, Henry. Death and worse.'

'Sorry to sound dull, but what evidence do we have?'

He shook his head. 'None. An old man's intuition. A loathsome painting. An Armenian who makes my hair stand on end – and that's odd because as a race I'm fond of them. I let my son work for George Roumian. You are right, Henry, there is no evidence, but this place is not good. It always had a bad reputation, even a hundred years ago. I've read the books. There is, however, one other thing. Did you notice what was missing?'

'Sorry, I didn't notice anything missing particularly.'

'Well, there is not a trace of anything to do with this place's origins. There are no crucifixes, no statues, no inscriptions. Nothing. I find that very curious. The Ommayid Mosque in Damascus has not been a church for twelve centuries, but they have not been as thorough as Harout has in four years in eradicating the evidences of Christianity.'

He looked at the monastery again and seemed to shiver.

I turned to Tina. 'This is stupid. There must be an answer. I know in my heart that it's all wrong, but I can't prove it. Let me think for a moment.'

That's the trouble with experiences. As I had looked at that painting I knew that what it stood for was totally evil, but here out in the open air a little voice seemed to say, 'But how can you be so sure?' and I had to say that I couldn't be. I needed facts. In my consternation I decided I wanted to look over the cliff, so we walked towards the lip of the promontory. Cautiously, I looked over. It was a long, almost sheer drop. If the monks had been given to drunkenness or sleepwalking then they would have done well to keep clear of here. I idly wondered if their bones lay down below at the bottom of the cliff. Tina followed in silence and looked over as well and by unspoken agreement we both stepped back clear of the edge. I began to think we ought to go back to the Range Rover and then go home after fulfilling our obligations in Jounieh. I turned to go.

As I did I kicked something and looked down to see what it was. Emerging from the snow was a hard, white object that had a finely porous texture. I gave a little start. Tina looked at me.

'What is it?'

'Nothing, I thought it was bone. It's just tufa.'

'Which is what?'

I wasn't really thinking about what she was saying. It was time to go, time to call it a day, make our promises and leave.

'Oh, it's the redeposited calcium carbonate you get on spring mouths or caves.'

'There's a lot of it about. What's it doing here?'

I hardly ever get irritated with Tina, but I was feeling somewhat annoyed with the situation and this was not the time or place to discuss limestone weathering, especially as Elias was gesturing us over to the vehicle.

'My dear, it's here because this is all limestone.'

'But where is the cave or the spring?'

I looked down. There was indeed a lot of it. There was even a broken stalactite.

In an instant it clicked. I said a little prayer of thanks.

'Mrs Stanwick, sometimes you ask stupid questions. That was not one of them. There *is* a cave. Within the past few years it has been cleaned out and most of the debris thrown over the cliff. This is what failed to make it. Now where is the cave?'

I looked at the cliffs behind the monastery and the flat surface between us and it. There could be no doubt. None at all.

I caught my breath. I should have guessed it earlier.

I spoke quietly to Tina. I didn't even want Antoine to hear at this stage.

'Tina, don't point and don't stare too hard, but look over the end of the hall – the nave, I suppose it should be. See the joint in the cliff?'

'You mean the narrow dark line, the fracture.'

'Exactly. Notice how you can trace the same line just to our right almost under Elias' tower and how the cliff edge we are standing on is weathered back along it. Now if you look elsewhere along the valley these large joints are often where caves form. Now extrapolate that line into the building and tell me where it goes.'

'Actually, that's a coincidence – it bisects the nave. It would run down behind the middle of Harout's room. It's too neat.'

A gust of wind caught us. It was time to go. The black swirling clouds were speeding towards us.

'Let's move. It's no coincidence at all. There was probably a shrine or a grotto or even a temple at a cave here before the Deir. When they built this monastery, maybe 500 AD, they just built over it. Which is why the altar faces north.'

'A cave? That would fit nicely. So what do we do?'

'That's a good question, but unfortunately – very unfortunately – I do not believe that we can now drive on back to East Beirut. No, I'm afraid we are going to have to have a long discussion with the Sheik.'

350

We strolled back slowly. I went close to Tina and spoke in a low voice.

'And, Tina, if we talk to the Sheik – and we've got to – I don't know what will happen.'

35

We got into the back of the Range Rover and Elias bounced off up the track. He half turned over his shoulder to me.

'You must leave quickly if you are to miss the snow. I will just drop Miss Hammond off at the hotel and then take you down to the house. You can be on your way in ten minutes.'

I looked at Tina, who mouthed, 'Yes, go on,' at me. I took a deep breath.

'Sheik Elias, my wife and I wish to talk to you first. We are not happy about what is going on at the Deir. We think, in fact we know, that Harout did not show us everything.'

Nickie, sitting in front of me, began to protest, but Elias started to speak and she stopped in mid-word. She knew her place.

'Ah, so you found what you were looking for, Dr Stanwick? Very well, you had better talk. I was afraid you would.' It was vaguely bitter in tone, but there was no note of surprise.

Antoine spoke in his clear, quiet tones. 'Why afraid, Sheik? You are the head of this valley. If Harout is indeed doing something wrong then you should know. I suspect you already know in your heart that he is up to no good.'

I think if Elias could have locked his hands together in

agitation while still dodging holes and ice, he would have. From where I was sitting he looked very uncomfortable. Nickie turned to Elias and addressed him in irritated tones.

'Sheik, I would like to hear these allegations. I know something of what they suspect and do not believe them. We did see everything. There can be nothing else there.'

Elias nodded. 'Very well, you will. Come down to the house. Now, *Assis* Antoine, you who are my conscience, you will be leaving?'

I looked past Tina at Antoine, with his chin jutting out, the veins visible through the spare flesh. I thought he was going to make no answer. Then he spoke so quietly that I could barely hear him. 'Sheik, you know that tonight I would wish to be back in my own house with my son, yet what can I say? I know less than Henry about this place, but it seems to me that there is indeed something wrong – very wrong – there. So I wish to stay. I think you also are going to have some hard decisions to make. I would like to help if I can.'

Given the last part of his comment, I half expected the Sheik to throw Antoine out on the spot. In fact he merely grunted. 'Huh. Very well, if you must. But I warn you, you may not be able to leave for some time now. If Harout finds you here I do not know what he will do. Anyway, we will all go to the house and then meet together.'

Twenty minutes later we were sitting downstairs on the sofas in Elias' house. In one way it was a cosy little group; Elias and Nickie sat together (although it seemed that Nickie was sitting as far away as she could without falling off the sofa), Tina and I faced them and on the third sofa, in between us and facing the fire, sat Antoine and Fuad. Fuad was very quiet and I have no recollection of him saying anything during our discussion. There was in fact little that was cosy about our meeting. Outside the light was fading rapidly as the clouds quickly moved over us and the gloom seemed to be spreading into the room. There was also a palpable tension present and Nickie in particular seemed very annoyed.

Elias crossed his legs and picked up a handful of pistachios. 'I suggest Dr Stanwick makes his case first.'

I paused for a moment. Once I started there would be no return. As I tried to think about a strategy it struck me that with Elias' temperament it was going to be like a dash through a minefield. I decided to start gently.

'Sheik, when Harout rebuilt the monastery, were you around?'

He threw some shells into the fire. 'No, it was part of the conditions. He showed me the plans beforehand and I checked them. I made a number of stipulations: no alteration to the outside of the Deir, nothing to be done that could not later be incorporated in a school or college building. It became obvious early on that Harout could be trusted to keep these, so I left him alone. The mess of the building work annoyed me and having all the Egyptian labourers around was a nuisance, so I moved down to a villa near Mrebbine for a couple of months.'

I'd successfully got a long way into the minefield. 'The reason I ask is that there is a lot of waste rock on the edge of the cliff. Some of it is the sort of rock you get inside a cave. Do you know where it might have come from?'

Elias looked hard at me. 'A cave? But there are none there. I know this part of the valley better than anybody. There are no caves near the monastery.'

I breathed a sigh of relief. If he'd been able to give another origin for the tufa I'd have been really stuck. I'd made further progress through the minefield.

'Well, Sheik, I think there is a cave. I think that it is probably behind Harout's office. I think you will find the picture pulls or slides out to reveal a door.'

There was a little exclamation of satisfaction from my right. I didn't have to look to see who'd made it. Antoine didn't need convincing.

Elias had a nonplussed expression on his face. 'Behind the old altar? But surely....'

I could see him trying to visualise it and I gave him a moment before continuing. 'Do you have any records of the history of the monastery? On what it was built?'

He indicated in the negative with a Levantine bob of his head. 'There may be something in the books I collected from the monastery, but I lent those to Harout. Anyway, the oldest ones were in Syriac and it's hard to find anyone who understands that these days. It has certainly been suggested that it was built on an earlier site of worship. You saw the Roman columns?'

I nodded and decided to keep pressing. So far I'd got through the minefield very nicely, although Nickie looked extremely unhappy, her emotions apparently rotating between disbelief, annoyance and fear.

'So why shouldn't the early site have been built around a cave or crevasse? Baalbek is supposed to have been.'

Elias stroked his chin. I don't think he liked the way the conversation was going. He was, however, too smart to ignore unpleasant data, especially when it affected him. 'Springs and caves here are very special. The one at the source of Nahr Ibrahim, for instance.' He looked at Antoine, 'Special, to the common people, the uneducated, that is.'

Suddenly something came to him. 'But you remind me of a thing I did once read in a very old book, that although the name of the monastery has always been Deir Musa, the house of Moses, there was an ancient tale which said it had once been known as Deir Mot, which would have been suggestive.'

He looked again at Antoine, whose face seemed to have acquired a strange, intensely foreboding look. Elias' comment made little sense to me. To call anywhere 'the House of Death' was a grim joke in any language. Antoine answered slowly and thoughtfully.

'I see, Sheik. You think that it might refer to the old

Canaanite god? The place of Mot, the God of Death and Infertility, who lived in the underworld and whose name persists in Arabic and, I believe, Hebrew when we use the word "death". Yes, why not? People have long memories here. Too long by far. And any temple to Mot would have involved a cave, of that I am sure.'

He stopped abruptly, as though taken with a thought too serious to allow further conversation, and stared into the flames.

The shadows were thick in the room now and outside, the sky was a dark looming blackness. There was the noise of wind from the balcony and in the distance I could hear voices shouting as people closed shutters. I wondered why Elias didn't put the lights on.

With Antoine sunk into silence, Elias looked at me again. 'So you suggest that in the course of his renovations Harout found a cave of some sort? But what has he done in it?'

'I don't know, but this is the other point. We have heard that he has been getting papers sent up from the American University Hospital on viral diseases.'

Elias' fingers began to wrap themselves around each other. This looked ominous. He rose to his feet and stared at me.

'Viruses! In *my* valley? Such a thing?'

It was genuine surprise. Elias was no actor; not in that sense. I got the feeling that his agitation was such that if Harout had been here, the Sheik's mobile fingers might have found themselves round a windpipe. He walked over to the windows and stared out into the blackness. There was a distant rumble. Antoine stirred and we caught each other's glance.

He spoke quietly, 'No, not artillery, not this time. Thunder.'

Elias turned and walked slowly back to the sofa. 'Yes, the snow has started.' He turned to Nickie. 'Miss Hammond, tell me what you think.'

She gave a little start. I noticed that her hostility had turned into gloom. 'Sheik, what can I say? I have worked on this project for three years. I feel insulted by this story. I wish I could disprove Henry's idea. I mean, Harout can't be working on diseases. He's an odd man, that's true, but he is sincere, he believes in the group and this doesn't fit. Anyway, the others of the co-ordinating committee, well, at least some, would have to be in with him on this. I just say that I can't believe it.'

Her statement came out all dislocated; half defensive, half fearful.

Elias looked hard at her. 'You can explain this report of an interest in viruses, though, can't you?' There was a rough edge to his voice.

Her eyes scanned all of us. There was a bright flash of lightning. 'I just don't want to say anything more. I can't believe this.'

Elias shook his head in annoyance and began to speak. The peal of thunder interrupted him and he had to start again. His voice was filled with poorly suppressed anger. 'Answer me, girl. Can you deny this?'

Nickie began to tremble. At this point Antoine spoke in stern tones. 'Sheik, have mercy on her. She is seeing what she has believed in for years disintegrate. You will gain nothing by pushing her.'

Elias glared at him for a moment and then seemed to collapse. 'Very well. I apologise, Miss, I mean Dr, Hammond.'

Tina pushed me along the sofa and motioned for Nickie to come alongside. She got up and sat down heavily next to Tina. She seemed on the point of tears and rubbed her eyes. Tina put her arm round her. Outside there was a dramatic multiple flash that left us blinking and then a great rolling and reverberating blast of thunder which died away slowly. No one said anything. Elias got up and switched on the lights, drew the curtains closed, then sat down. Finally, Nickie spoke. She was trying hard to conceal her emotions, but her voice was shaky.

'I don't know why I am saying this, but there have been odd things. Harout is very tight on chemicals. We have to put in an order for them and one of his staff hands them out. He says it's because of the difficulties of getting new supplies, but once I was in a hurry and got some enzyme direct from the stores. I saw exactly how many more bottles we had. Then a few weeks later he said we were out of it. I couldn't believe it.'

I tried to speak as gently as I could. 'It was an enzyme for working with DNA?'

She dabbed her eyes and nodded. I felt I had made the case. Suddenly I noticed everyone was staring at Elias. I suppose it's an occupational hazard of being a despot; total power brings total responsibility. He was plainly unhappy to the point of misery. To my surprise he turned to Antoine.

'My conscience, what do you advise?'

Antoine looked him in the face. It struck me that he alone of us had absolutely no fear of Elias, Sammy or Harout.

'If I understand what has been said, then you must do something. Henry says that he thinks this thing lies behind that horrible painting. I think I agree, although my reasons are not so scientific. Can you look behind it, Sheik?'

Elias looked ill at ease.

'Pastor, Harout pays me a lot of money. In fact, five million dollars a year.' There were some faint murmurs. Actually, I wasn't surprised; Harout had money to burn, none of it his. Elias went on. 'For that price he has sole possession of the monastery and the hotel. I have access to the tower alone. I cannot get into the Deir and certainly not into Harout's office. I do not have either the keys or the combinations for the door locks.'

He looked at Nickie as if to suggest that it was her problem. Tears were running down her face. To my surprise Antoine leaned over and gently wiped her cheek with a large white handkerchief. 'You've made your make-up run,' he whispered. For me it was a moving gesture; in the sort of Lebanese church in which Antoine was involved, make-up is universally held to be wicked. I once heard it denounced from the pulpit, with the rumble of shellfire in the background, suggesting a bizarre set of priorities. But then maybe they feel make-up is an evil they can handle. Nickie thanked him and gradually seemed to regain some sort of composure.

She turned to Elias. 'I can get into the Deir, but I cannot get into Harout's office either.'

Elias spoke quickly. 'Fine, then it must be by force. I will call up Sammy. He will enjoy it.'

I nearly shouted at him. A typical Lebanese reaction; shoot the lock off rather than find a spare key. Fortunately, my exclamation coincided with a clap of thunder so that its effect was somewhat overshadowed.

'No! There must be no weapons. We don't know what is stored there. If anything is released then we could all be in terrible trouble.'

Elias stared at me. I could see him doing mental overtime.'I see your point. Yes. I suppose also I would prefer to test your theory first. It may be wiser to leave no trace. That way I can see what is there, and plan a strategy.'

I could see exactly the way his mind was now working. As lord of the valley he had to know what was going on, but he wanted to try and keep his business deal intact at all costs. Perhaps there wasn't anything really important going on in this alleged secret chamber, maybe it was just a little virus, maybe he could slip a biohazard clause into his next contract with Harout and make it ten million per annum. Elias turned to Nickie.

'Miss...Dr Hammond, if you let us into the monastery could we break in?'

There was no hesitancy in her reply. 'No. The locks to both doors to Harout's office are complex combination locks. Both corridors are watched by television which is connected to the hotel. There are vibration sensors all over. I think infra-red beams in the corridors too.' She paused. 'Also, when I enter, the computer notes it and again when I leave. If you do make a break in I believe you will be discovered instantly. And even with your protection I'd rather you didn't do it under my name.'

That seemed to be the end of that bright idea. With people like Harout's group around you don't suddenly find doors with keys in them or locks that yield to credit cards. I think everyone else felt we had come to a dead end. The only thing was that the high security suggested that there was indeed something of more than ordinary value there.

Nickie spoke again. 'Besides, Harout might be there. Or some of the computer people or technicians. Terry works late a lot. There's often a night shift too.'

There was a brilliant flash and a deafening rumble of thunder only a second later. Tina jumped. The thunder echoed round and round the valley.

'Normally.'

It was Nickie's voice. Elias turned from staring into the fire. 'Normally?'

Nickie looked thoughtful. 'But not tonight. With the weather the track will soon be blocked until the snowplough goes down. There was a car accident one year or something, so there is no work at the Deir until the snow is cleared. Harout had ordered everyone out back to the hotel by five today. Even the guards.'

Antoine nodded his head as though he had heard some expected news. 'How interesting. Sheik, it seems you are being given an opportunity.'

Elias rubbed his chin in thought. 'Perhaps. Is there another way into the office? Perhaps the window?'

I joined in. 'It was just big enough to get through and it didn't look too strong. There are probably no monitor cameras in his office.'

Elias shook his head. 'Ah no, it will not work. I have remembered something. Unfortunately, as Miss Ham-

359

mond said, the window – in fact all the windows – are wired up with very sensitive vibration sensors. Harout does love his technology.'

Nickie abruptly turned to Antoine with an expression of curiosity and even awe. 'No, the pastor is right, there is an opportunity. Harout overdid it with them. They are too sensitive. They have to be turned off during storms. They won't be on tonight.'

Elias shook his head as if in disbelief. He stood up, walked to the window, opened a curtain and stared out. After a moment, he turned on his heel abruptly and faced us. He had made his mind up.

'In my way I am superstitious, maybe fatalistic, but as the pastor has said, there is an opportunity to test Dr Stanwick's idea. I have never failed to take advantage of circumstances and I will not do so tonight. Tonight, at midnight, we will go and see.'

It was the tone of a definitive, final pronouncement.

So the plans were drawn up. At midnight those who wanted to go with Elias would walk the mile to the monastery, go round to the north-east corner and push the window in. All being well, by the time the damage to the window had been found, Elias would know what to do. If we couldn't get beyond the painting, or if whatever we found was not important, then there was a fair hope that the broken window would simply be attributed to storm damage of some sort.

Some way would hopefully be found to try to get round the picture and into whatever was behind it. I wasn't terribly optimistic, but then Sammy had probably ensured that burglary wasn't too common in this part of Farayoun and security – once you penetrated Harout's office – might be quite lax. With regard to people, in the end it was decided that everyone but Fuad would go. Rather to my surprise Antoine insisted on coming. He said quietly to me, 'This is something that I must do.' Nickie insisted on coming, but gave no reason. I think she hoped to have her beliefs vindicated at the last, but whatever happened, she wanted to see the truth with her own eyes. Tina refused to be parted from me. Fuad we felt we couldn't take. In the event of our being disturbed by guards his position would be very desperate. He protested only feebly. There was a brief discussion about taking George and Michel, or even Sammy, but Elias vetoed it. 'The fewer we take, the better,' he said, but whether his real concern was security or the weakening of any subsequent bargaining position was unclear.

The decision made, Elias allocated bedrooms to Fuad, Antoine and Nickie and ordered Malik to have them prepared. Then we sat around waiting for the meal. Outside, the storm was in full force and the windows rattled every few minutes with the thunder. Tina and I had drawn back a curtain and were looking out. It was extraordinarily dramatic as flash after flash occurred across the valley illuminating, for a fraction of a second, moving sheets of near horizontal snow. On the balcony the snow accumulated and piled up against the windows like a rising tide.

Antoine joined us.

'Do you like this, Tina?'

She turned to him in some puzzlement. 'Like it, Antoine? I'm impressed by it, awed by it, but it's a bit frightening.'

He nodded. 'If you'll forgive me for the sermon, but the subject came up earlier in an indirect manner. The Canaanites' chief deity was Baal Haddad, who seems to have been the thunder god. Certainly the Romans made his temples into those for Jupiter, but if you read Psalm 29 it describes exactly such a storm as this running over Lebanon, even breaking the cedars and dying out in Syria. Very Canaanite, up to a point. But the difference – and it's a big one – is that it is the Lord's storm from beginning to end. So tonight. This storm is on our side, Tina.'

Tina looked at him gravely. 'Thank you, Antoine. Now you say it I remember it. It's a pity my father is not here to

361

see the storm.'

It was curious to hear mention of that other world. Alec and Viv, Abie and Grantforth seemed so very far away. I wondered how much Tina missed them all. In one way I would have given a lot to be back. Yet in another I was glad to be here. This seemed to be no chance meeting, but one summoned for a purpose. Things were moving to a head and this was where I should be. Yet as I thought about it, it seemed a daunting and even unnerving prospect. The issues and powers involved seemed so immense.

We returned to the fireplace. Even with the curtains closed, the central heating on and the fire roaring, the house seemed chill and bleak.

Over the meal Antoine and Elias sat and talked together at one end of the table and snatches of their conversation drifted down to where the rest of us ate quietly or engaged in desultory talk. Something Antoine said stuck in my mind.

'See, Sheik, my heart grieves for the Christians here. That is why I came back. For twelve centuries we Arab Christians have taken refuge under Mount Lebanon and sat here, trembling for our safety. We have huddled together in these valleys under this mountain like sheep under a rock. Our churches have become like old men, afraid of heights and danger in the streets. Secure in our traditions, but the traditions have become our shrouds. We should have been light yet we have become darkness – as your own tale demonstrates. Yet it is my belief that things will turn here, although I do not believe I will see it....'

After the meal Antoine rose, made his apologies and asked to be excused. 'I will be resting in my room. Call me please in time.'

Then he spoke a quiet word in Arabic to Fuad. 'My son, come and see me before you go to your room.'

He left quietly. Elias looked at me. 'When this is over I

will ask the pastor to come and visit. If I had met him earlier, perhaps....' Then he switched moods abruptly and threw a dark glance at me. ' "When this is over!" If you are right – and as the pastor prophesied, my heart tells me you are – then I do not like to think about the future. If I have to throw out Harout I will have so many problems.'

He turned away and in a troubled silence stared at the fire.

At midnight we gathered downstairs. It was largely a sombre gathering. Tina was withdrawn and silent and occupied with helping Nickie who seemed to be having doubts about whether or not she wanted to go. Personally I felt extremely anxious about the entire breaking and entering business, although there seemed to be no other way. My own preference would have been simply to call Cyprus, ask for several tons of high explosive on the Deir, and then – blizzard or no – to drive out of this valley. But that didn't seem to be a viable option and when the Lord removes the guards and switches off the alarms for you, it does seem a bit silly to refuse the offer. By contrast to my depressed spirits, Elias seemed almost cheerful. Looking resolute and business-like, he had found a number of torches and issued those to everyone. He also had a hammer and a chisel which he put in a coat pocket.

He motioned me aside. 'Henry.' It was the first time he had used my first name. 'I am taking a gun. Do you want one?'

It took me a second to refuse; normally I'd have turned it down straightaway, but tonight I felt frightened. Then I realised there wasn't much point.

'Thank you, Sheik, but no. I would just make matters worse. I fear I would probably shoot my friends.'

Antoine must have detected my unhappiness because he came over to my side. He looked almost bird-like with his narrow face and bright eyes. What he felt in his heart, I couldn't detect; he exuded nothing but determination. He whispered to me.

'Courage, Henry. I know how you feel, but we've done our running already. Now we must stand.'

I squeezed his arm. 'Amen, Pastor.'

Then we were ready, gloves on, faces muffled up. Elias checked us over.

'Remember, we just want to see and come back. If there is trouble we must try to get back here. In my garden Harout will not touch us. But keep to the path. Now stay together. We will stop only at the foot of the tower. You will obey me unless I order otherwise.' Then he opened the door and we followed into the gale.

For the first minute I thought we were going to have to turn back. The cold was knife edged and progressively numbing, and the wind found every crack in the clothing. The snow was not so much falling as being flung at us. To add to it all we were in the middle of a thunderstorm. I tried to remind myself it was on our side, but that was little consolation. In between the blinding lightning flashes everything was pitch black except for the yellow circle of torchlight, blurred by the driving snow.

Elias took the lead, followed by Antoine and Nickie with Tina and I bringing up the rear. Fortunately we were going eastwards and so the snow was at our backs. It was coming down, or along, so thickly that I could only see the third torch ahead. A layer of snow had soon built up all over our backs. Every so often the lightning would flash and I would be able to see all four people ahead for an instant before the gloom descended again. The noise from the wind and the echoing and re-echoing thunder was so loud I could hear nothing else. Very rapidly the whole venture seemed unreal, but just when I was convinced it was all a dream, I found that I wanted to wipe my nose and my handkerchief was under two layers of clothing. That was reality. But of course we were in Lebanon where normality in any real sense had evaporated in spring '75 and a certain deranged reality was par for the course.

Yet the cold too reminded me it was real and it also helped to remember that only twenty or so yards away was the great drop off the edge into the valley. Despite it all I had to admit with Antoine that it was a perfect night for the job. The blowing snow had begun to fill in Tina's footprints before I had reached them. We could have passed only fifty feet away from alert sentries with dogs and gone totally undetected, torches and all.

I suppose we were only walking for twenty minutes. It could have been twice as long. Elias seemed to know the way, although there was little obvious to guide him except snow-draped bushes. We kept sinking into the soft snow and in places it was already well above the level of my boots. I wondered how Antoine was doing and marvelled again at what drove him.

Suddenly there was a very bright flash and there, silhouetted black ahead of us, was a wall of the Deir. Then it was gone and the merest instant later a great roaring rumble of thunder rolled over us. A minute more and we were clambering inside the Sheik's tower. Together, Elias and I closed the door against the blowing snow and the roaring wind.

A sort of peace descended.

Then the light came on. Four white figures faced me in piles of snow. Elias, recognisable only by his shorter stature, removed a scarf from his face. 'Everyone all right so far?'

There were nods and gasps and people brushed and stamped snow off one another. I glanced quickly at Tina, who seemed to be fine, and then went over to Antoine, who was leaning against a stone wall trying to wipe his glasses.

'Antoine, are you OK?'

He nodded and took a breath. I tried to brush the snow off him.

'Thank you, Henry.' He put his hands on his knees and bent like an athlete after a race. Then he looked up.

365

'A thought occurred to me as we were walking over. I wonder how many people could have made your deduction about that bit of rock?'

It was a strange question.

'I suppose now no more than three people in this country. Why?'

'It just struck me that it might be for that purpose, if no other, you had been brought here.' It was an interesting idea. He didn't stop there though.

'Indeed, if this thing turns out to be as big as I fear, one could almost argue that it was for this day's work you were drawn into your field of study.'

This raised a number of points that my brain didn't seem warmed up enough to address.

'I must confess, Antoine, that I hadn't seen today as being the most fulfilling of my career, or even the fulfilment of my career, but I take your point.'

Elias motioned me over. He spoke in a low voice. 'We must move on. I will leave this door unlocked so that if we have to flee we can use it as a temporary refuge. But, Henry, it can only be temporary. If anything should happen, get the girls out to my house and get Malik to alert the guards. Let us go.'

We pulled our scarves tight. Elias checked everybody then spoke in clear, firm tones. 'Keep close to the wall. The cliff edge is nearby here. As for the window, Henry will force it open. Make no noise when we are in until I say so.'

It struck me that although he might have been merely a hereditary ruler and small both in stature and domains, he had a great deal of personal authority. It also occurred to me that it was a definite shame he'd never really played his role on the national scene. But then he might just have become a larger despot, reliant on an army of Michels, Georges and Sammys.

Then he switched the light out and unlatched the door. It blew open suddenly, spilling snow inside. We filed out and together he and I pulled the door shut behind. For a few moments as I looked westwards the snow blew into my eyes and I was briefly blinded. Then I turned away, wiped my face and followed Tina.

Along the east side of the wall things improved. The wind here was not direct. However, wild gusts swung down over the roof and even up from over the cliff, bringing with them great flurries of snow. Then Tina suddenly stopped and I realised we were at the window. I walked carefully past the girls until I came to Antoine and Elias, who parted to let me in between them. Being the tallest, dealing with the window was my job.

I examined the window carefully. It started at about five feet above the ground and had a leaded frame in which were set perhaps a dozen small panes of glass. It was just going to be big enough to get in and out of. By the torchlight I could just see the glint of fine vertical and horizontal wires behind the glass. It was going to be difficult to make the breakage look like an accident, but I felt I'd give it a try. I looked around. I remembered that the jagged cliff at this northern end of the monastery here overhung us and a few yards to the east virtually merged with the lower cliff. It was not totally improbable that a rock dislodged from the top in the storm might have bounced outwards from the cliff and in against the window, or even that a freak gust might have burst it. Hopefully though we would not need any such excuse.

I went over to the foot of the cliff and, digging in the snow, found a rock the size of a small loaf of bread. I carried it to the wall and Elias and Antoine pointed their torches on the window. Then, turning my face away, I smashed the rock into the glass.

There was so much wind noise and I was so muffled up I hardly heard it. I took my torch and checked. It had taken out enough glass for us to get through, the wires were broken and I could hear no alarm. I pointed the torch into the room. It was empty. The light glinted off something in the picture and I shivered.

I stood back and motioned Elias forward. Rank has its duties as well as its privileges so I cupped my gloves to give him a hand up. He scrambled through and one by one the others followed. I noted that Nickie was clearly the heaviest by at least twenty pounds. With Tina through, I pulled myself up and in.

Elias had already checked the room out. He was putting a chair against the door. It wouldn't hold it long against force, but it would give us some warning.

Then everyone shook the snow off themselves and pulled down hoods and cautiously took off gloves. Despite the gaping window, through which a small cloud of snowflakes blew in, the room was quite warm. Tina shook her hair to get rid of some last bits of snow and came over and stood by me, clutching my arm.

Elias called out, 'Henry, I'm going to switch the light on.'

'Go ahead.'

The fluorescent lights slowly came on. I blinked and looked around. Elias did the same and I noticed he had his right hand in his pocket. There was no sign of a television camera or any other sensors. I hoped any underfloor vibration detectors were switched off. Both doors were closed and seemed locked. The possible significance, indeed necessity, of the two separate doors now occurred to me. They gave the curious a ready reason why Harout might disappear from his office without being seen to do so.

I averted my gaze from the picture and went and looked at the frame. Suddenly Elias reached out and snatched my hand away, speaking in hushed but urgent tones.

'Henry, careful! It may be booby trapped.'

I stepped back and closed my eyes. It was of course perfectly possible in Lebanon – home of so much innovative explosive technology – that the frame could have an anti-handling device. I turned to Elias.

368

'I think it's unlikely, especially if what's beyond it could be released by an explosion. But get everybody back against the wall. I'll try it with gloves.'

I was wondering, not for the first time in my life, about my compulsive volunteering, when Antoine pressed forward and spoke in a low voice.

'If you will excuse me, Henry, this is my country. Both you and the Sheik may have other things to do.'

To my surprise I accepted and stood back, but then Antoine, like Elias, had his own brand of unarguable authority.

Antoine gently pushed the central part of the picture. It was canvas and moved back a centimetre or two and stopped. Then he hit the same spot again with a fist. There was a dull hollow sound that was very satisfying. With this particular painting the sound of ripping canvas would have been even more so, but at least we knew that there was a space behind the painting. Antoine put his gloves back on and felt along the left-hand side of the frame. 'It's a very firm solid mounting. No obvious catch.'

He pulled and pushed. Nothing happened. I tried to think. There could be a number of ways of opening the door. However, they would have to be ways that couldn't be triggered by accident, perhaps by cleaners or the curious. The safest way of doing that was a double switch operation.

I took the torch, went over to Harout's desk and shone the torch underneath the lip. There was a small rocker switch.

'Antoine, stand back a second. Let me press this.'

I just hoped it wasn't an alarm and pressed. Nothing happened. 'Now try.'

Antoine slid his hand up behind the edge of the frame. He seemed to feel something and stopped, slid his hand down again and pressed. Then he stepped back quickly. There was a faint, brief noise of metal sliding against metal and then in near silence the picture swung slowly outwards away from the wall along a vertical hinge. As it did so, yellow fluorescent lights came on behind it. At an angle of forty-five degrees from the wall it came silently to rest, showing that it was mounted on a metal panel about two inches thick with three retracted bolts mounted along the edge.

The tension and expectancy were horrible. I think I stopped breathing as the door opened. The act of opening by itself was so eerie that you almost expected something to come out from behind it. I noticed that Elias had pulled out his pistol, which seemed to me an eminently satisfactory idea. But nothing happened and we started to breathe again.

Antoine swallowed, his voice sounded faint. 'Full marks, Henry. Better come and see.'

I walked over carefully and looked into the chamber behind the door. My mind was a blank, I felt there could have been anything there and it wouldn't have surprised me. The chamber was in fact a short corridor about twenty feet long. At the other end of it was a dull grey steel door set in a solid frame. On it was a very large swingdown handle that looked as if it needed two hands to operate. There was no doubt about two functions of the door. It was both shockproof and airtight.

Elias elbowed past me and stepped into the corridor. He was silent for a moment, merely shaking his head in disbelief. Then he turned to us, speaking in low, astonished tones. 'Incredible! But what has Harout got behind that door?'

36

One by one we stepped slowly into the corridor. On Elias' suggestion we partly shut the picture door behind us, preventing its total closure by a book from Harout's shelves.

Elias pulled the handle up on the far door. It swung open slowly and silently away from us. I made a mental note that it was designed more to prevent something from escaping outwards than to stop anything from entering it. It also seemed that we had got beyond all the security measures because here there were no locks. For a moment we could see nothing beyond the opening door but darkness. Then fluorescent tubes flickered on reluctantly. Apart from a faint hum of equipment, there was silence. The air coming out smelled vaguely unpleasant, stale and slightly antiseptic. Elias, holding his gun ahead of him, moved out of the doorway and I followed. We walked forward a few feet and gradually the remaining three came alongside us. Together we looked at what the lights revealed.

The door had opened into a cave of oval cross-section. I can best describe it by saying that it was the size and apparent length of two railway carriages put one on top of the other. The similarity extended further because the cave had been subdivided into an upper and lower level by a steel mesh platform. The door we had come in by was near the floor level of the upper platform and steps and a ramp ran down to an entrance to the lower level. The roof looked to be that of the original cave with lighting strung along it. The wall of the cave through which we had come was made of concrete. At the far end of the cave there was another wall, partially concealed, but also apparently made of concrete.

It was the lower level that caught the eye first. Almost the whole length of it appeared to be taken up by a sealed cabin unit. An entrance door protruded curiously and had a number of yellow signs around it. Either side of the door were oval perspex windows through which equipment could be seen. Next to the door was a series of tall, thin metal lockers.

Nickie pushed past me and looked down at the cabin. Then she spoke, her voice almost shaking with anger. 'I'll kill Harout! The liar!'

She sounded like she meant it. I was conscious of Antoine moving towards her. He spoke gently.

'Peace, Nickie. Do not add to the evil here.'

Elias spoke, his voice was deadpan. 'What is this, Nickie?'

She turned round to him. 'It looks like a very secure facility for doing work on dangerous micro-organisms.' The voice was just bitter now.

Nickie spoke again, this time sharply. 'No one, absolutely no one, should touch anything down there. I'll take a look in a minute. And, Sheik, please put that wretched gun away, we don't want holes in anything here.'

Elias stared at her and then tucked it away. Nickie shook her head again and stared at the lower chamber with an unfathomable expression on her face.

The upper floor now caught my attention. It was a long narrow office suite with bookshelves, computers and paper-covered desks. I turned to Elias.

'I think we should concentrate on going through everything up here. We may be able to find out what is going on.'

Part of me wanted to say that now we had seen it we should just clear out. But now, apparently so close to finding so many answers, I was reluctant to go back. I had suffered a lot at the hands of Harout's people and I wanted very much to know what was behind it. Elias nodded. 'Let us do that, but we should try to replace everything as we found it and leave no trace.'

So for half an hour we leafed through books, folders and sheets of paper. We puzzled over graphs, illegible notes and pads of printout. We were helped by the fact that nothing was locked away. Here, finally, they had felt no need to be careful. For the first time since Vaughan had introduced to me the idea of a secret project I felt certain that what I was now looking at was genuine. We had penetrated the last of the many levels of deception and stood at the heart of what the group was doing. We were hindered by the fact that much of the data was incomprehensible and in some cases only one word on a page made any sense. We were also unwilling to switch on the computers which would have almost certainly recorded our doing so. After twenty minutes Nickie and I went downstairs. The thin metal cabinets were not locked, and inside were hung thin nylon and plastic protective suits. We cautiously peered through the perspex at the containers with glowing thermostat lights and the fancy automatic analytical machinery. We were not surprised to see that the one thermostat we could read from outside registered 37°C. Then we went back and saw the others and in a few minutes more it was agreed that we had seen all we needed to see.

We stood around and talked briefly, in hushed voices, about what we'd seen and there was no dissension. What was going on was plain. The details were obscure and the timing was imprecise, but it was evident what the goals were. Once we knew what they were they seemed obvious and I almost felt I'd known about them for a long time. It slotted in neatly with all their other projects and indeed made sense of them.

The key bits of data were on one set of bookshelves. There was a series of thick commissioned reports from a number of different institutes on various causes of human infertility. Further reports, apparently dated later in time, concentrated more specifically on areas of the female reproductive system and on how they were disrupted by disease. A further focusing down seemed to be represented in a three-foot thickness of reprints stored in a series of boxfiles with the overall title of 'Viral induced blockages of the fallopian tubes'. Some of the strange virus names in those papers appeared again on another desk. This seemed to take the story still further with more diagrams and charts detailing specific aspects of some of these viruses. All the commissioned studies were medical; many had been conducted by reputable institutions for a variety of vague trusts and charitable bodies. I wondered how many really existed. But it was terribly plain that the work here was not targeted to the elimination of these diseases.

In fact, as other desks indicated, it was not even directed to the production of these diseases. Rather the aim was to identify and isolate the portions of the genetic code that produced the effects of these viruses and insert them into the genes for other viruses. It paralleled, in its deadly way, what Nickie was seeking to do with her algae. The final goal was something as contagious as influenza, but with a single side-effect, that of blocking permanently any hope of natural fertilisation.

Elias wondered aloud if they wanted the human race to become extinct. Tina pointed out, with no diminution of disgust in her voice, that it could be circumvented by two means. A vaccine could be given, but if the disease spread rapidly there might be no time to develop one. Or if the infection and damage had occurred, an egg could still be extracted and fertilisation brought about outside the womb and the embryo reimplanted. I realised as she said it that I was glad we had brought Tina and Nickie with us. Although the whole stratagem seemed monstrous, it was particularly directed against women. As such it was appropriate, as we looked at the evidence, that they should be represented. Tina ended by looking around in something like horror.

'So they'd reduce the human population initially very rapidly. Although eventually, I suppose, there would be a resistance developed. It's an almost unbelievable concept for population control. It's ecology gone mad.'

Perhaps surprisingly it was Antoine who answered her and who added the final chill to the discussion in a thin, dry voice, 'Yes, it could be overcome, but you're making a mistake in thinking of it as being an ecological tool alone. Its effects could only be overcome by those who had access to the vaccine or the hospital. It would be the ultimate reward for the faithful, the party members, the elect. Only they could have children. The group would be able to select who they wanted to reproduce. The poor and the powerless would perish.'

He stopped, his voice failing, as he thought about it.

'The ultimate political tool. So with this they would reduce the world's population at a stroke. I saw a target figure of a hundred million somewhere; instead of – what is it now – six billion? Then on that reduced figure they would impose their new order.'

When he spoke of those population figures I understood something more of that painting and knew why there were no people in it.

I do not know even now how far they had got. The evidence we saw then indicated they were trying a number of virus options; that much preparatory work, all innocuous in itself, had already been done throughout the world was clear. Here was where everything was being brought together, and whether that required months or years of more work was unclear. Some results seemed to indicate there to be a long road ahead, but there were other chillingly bland notes about imminent 'field testing of strains' in Africa and Asia.

I have since talked to people about what they were trying to do using deliberately vague, hypothetical ideas. I talked to some who believe that viruses are simply the product of chance processes operating over millions of years and billions of generations. I talked to others who believe that these things too are the product of an all-wise and sovereign Creator. Both agreed that, although midway between life and non-life, even the simplest virus is a marvellously fine-tuned and stripped-down invasion machine and both doubted, from their different perspectives, whether any virus modified by man would retain its potency for more than a few of its generations. I hope they are right.

But doubts remain. Harout's group had access to almost unlimited funds; they had some good people – and some who were the best; they had the place to put it all together and they had the motivation.

Perhaps with time they could have done it. Perhaps they already had. I do not think we will now know.

After a few moments' silence Elias spoke. 'Very well, we have seen all there is to be seen. I think it is time to leave.'

He said it in a curiously cool, flat way. The horror that had all but drowned us seemed to have left him unscathed. Antoine seemed to sense it.

'A moment! Sheik, you will see to it that this place is destroyed. As soon as possible.'

My first thought was that Antoine had been careless in making a question sound like a command. Then I realised that there was no carelessness. It *was* a command.

Elias trembled and instantly I saw the problem. He had not, indeed I suspect he could not, identify himself with the poor and the powerless whom the virus would have affected. He, after all, was Sheik Elias Boulos Daoud; if it needed money to get the vaccine or the fertilisation he had it and if it needed influence he had that too. I think he may even have been rather taken by the idea of a virus that spared the rich and kicked those who were already down. After all, both the Lebanese economy and the Civil War have long worked on the same principle. Whatever was going through his mind he turned on Antoine in freezing tones.

'Pastor, I am Sheik even here. I will decide. I alone.'

Antoine looked at him in deep sorrow. 'I see. Very well. But before we go, Sheik, I would point out to you that there is a further door at the end of this room.'

We looked at each other and then stared down at the other end where a green drapery hid the lower part of the far wall of the chamber. Antoine alone had lifted the curtain. Elias looked at his watch.

'Two o'clock. OK, but we must be brief.'

Lifting the curtain revealed another thick steel door set in a concrete wall. Elias swung the handle up and pulled inwards and the door opened onto a steel landing and darkness. The only light came from behind us and for a number of seconds we could see nothing at all. There was an inrush of damp air, cool and with a curious indefinably organic smell. It seemed to bring to mind gardens and woodlands, cut grass and soil with their air of growth and life. At first I thought it was pleasant and then I felt that there was an aura of decomposition about it and it no longer seemed to smell of the making of life, but rather the undoing of it. I realised that it reminded me of the picture on the wall and I shuddered. With it was a distant but powerful rushing noise. Then after several seconds a single faint strip light flickered hesitantly on overhead.

The light showed that running down from the platform was a metal stairway. We went out cautiously through the door and stood on the landing where there was just enough room for us all. Looking around it was clear that we were now back in the natural cave and it seemed at the foot of the stairway Harout's works ended. Below us, running out of the concrete wall, were the exit points for two fan systems. Beyond the stairway's end a narrow path seemed to run away along the foot of the cavern into a zone where the cave was restricted in width and height. As the roof of the cave sloped overhead it was impossible to see where, and how far, it ran to. Antoine climbed slowly down the stairway until he was on the next to bottom step and peered forward. He waved me down and I came down just behind him. From where we stood it was possible to look where the path led.

At first it was difficult to see anything because the only light was above us, but gradually it became plain that twenty yards or so ahead the cave floor seemed to vanish into a black pit. Above the edge of the pit something shining fell, or flowed, down from roof to floor in a pale vertical line. Slowly the eye comprehended the moving shape and it was possible to see that it was a column of water plunging down into the depths far below. It was this that made the rushing noise. How far it fell below our feet was impossible to say because there was only the faintest hint of any sound of it striking the ground. Equally, it was impossible to see whether the crevasse continued beyond the waterfall. It was an impressive and unsettling sight. I felt a strong urge to leave. The laboratory had been horrible, but here was no better. In fact, here there seemed to be a less tangible, but in its way more menacing, evil.

Antoine pointed with his hand to the side of the crevasse ahead of us.

'Henry, look at the blocks.'

His voice was muted as though he too felt in the presence of something. I saw what he was pointing to in the gloom. Just ahead of us, both sides of the path were lined by two levels of immaculately dressed stone slabs. The blocks lay perfectly flush upon each other.

'Roman work, Antoine?'

He remained staring ahead, his white head nodding slightly in response. 'Your temple, Henry, but it goes back well before Rome. We would probably find an altar by the waterfall, if we had the time.' He paused. 'Or the inclination.'

Indeed, as I looked I thought I could see a flat-topped stubby column in the darkness near the pit. It made me

378

shiver. It was no wonder that this cave had been a site of worship. In spring when the meltwater came roaring down it must have been awesome. I wondered about the strange coincidence - if indeed it was – that this place had been a shrine to a deity of infertility.

I traced the stonework walls again with my eye and wondered if there was any trace of it along the path nearer to us. As I looked I saw something. Either side of the path just in front of the bottom step that Antoine stood on were two small black boxes, almost invisible in the shadows. I called out.

'Antoine! Don't go a step further. There is what looks like an alarm set up just below you.'

He bent down and peered at them, then looked up at me. 'Thank you, I had not seen it. Anyway, it is time to go.'

At that point something happened.

Precisely what remains unclear. I cannot rule out some sort of collective hysteria as we were all tired and very tense. That is the simplest hypothesis. Yet in view of what Abie had dreamed of all those months ago and what happened later, I have my own view. All I can say is what seemed to me to occur.

Abruptly the light above us went out.

My own impression was that something passed in front of it first and Tina says that was what she felt too, but that she could have been mistaken. With the sudden descent of darkness there seemed to come the waft of a most horrible atmosphere of corruption and decay; an odour that seemed actively to press down on me.

I heard a gasp of horror behind; Elias and the girls scrambled back in panic. It was contagious – all I wanted to do was to get back and get out. I turned to go. In the patch of yellow light that was the doorway I could see the silhouette of Tina at the top of the steps. She was calling my name. Elias and Nickie seemed to be already inside the door. I took a step up and realised that Antoine was still below. As I turned to him I saw, or felt I saw, in the faint

379

light from the doorway what I can only describe as a moving darkness swirling around him and creeping like a mist up to me. I froze.

Suddenly an awful feeling of terror came over me. I call it a feeling because I cannot call it anything else, yet it was more than an emotion. Every sense organ I had suddenly told me I was falling. The roof had become the floor, everything seemed to be rotating wildly about several axes and I knew for certain that I was spinning downwards. I closed my eyes, trying to avoid panicking. It didn't help. I clung onto the steel railing, but it seemed to have vanished. Everything had gone; there was nothing but darkness, space and the eternal void. I longed to hit the ground, however hard, just to end the falling sensation. I tried to pray, but the void snatched the words away. Everything was black. 'I'm fainting,' I thought for a brief moment, but it didn't feel like fainting. It seemed as if I had been plucked from the earth and dropped spinning down through the universe itself.

Then a compulsion grew in my mind. The only way to stop myself from falling was to unclench my right hand and throw myself forward. Part of me knew it was a bad idea, but I couldn't remember why. Just as I was about to yield to the desire I was suddenly conscious of Antoine's voice shouting in Arabic.

'Unclean spirit, your time is finished! The Light has come and will come!'

The awful spinning seemed to cease abruptly as though it had never been. I was not even dizzy. I opened my eyes. I was still on the steps and holding onto the railing. Above me the strip light had suddenly come back on.

I glanced down to see that just below me Antoine was balanced unsteadily on the bottom step. It appeared to me that the dark was ebbing away downwards, but that in the process it was pooling about his legs. As it did so it seemed to be pulling him over. I reached out for him. He cried again, 'Go, in the name of Jesus the Messiah!'

At the moment he said it the living darkness about him vanished completely, but he was already falling.

I lunged forward to steady him, but I was too late.

Too late to catch him and too late to stop him from breaking the infra-red beam, because as I stepped down to reach for him, far away beyond the doors an alarm bell had already begun to ring wildly.

37

I leaped over Antoine towards one small black box, half hidden on the wall. I found the wires underneath and jerked hard. One pulled out and a tiny red light went out, but the bell continued to ring. I turned to Antoine, who was getting to his feet slowly and painfully. Even in the gloom I could see that he was deathly white. I grabbed him by the shoulders and began to carry him up the steps.

'No, I can manage. Just.'

I was certain that he couldn't, but I put him down.

'We must go, Antoine. I'm afraid you broke the beam.'

He struggled up a few steps and halted. 'Did you feel it? Whatever it was tried to pull me over.'

I beckoned Elias, who hesitated and then bounded down. The rungs vibrated in the empty cave. I noticed dimly that the foul organic smell seemed to have gone.

'Sheik, give me a hand with Antoine.'

Together we got him up the stairs and through the door. He stood up for a moment and then stumbled, but Nickie caught him. I pushed the door closed and swung the lever shut. I had had a vague hope that the bell would turn off with the shutting of the door. Unfortunately it was still ringing; indeed here it seemed louder than ever. Presumably it was sounding in the hotel and even now Kevork and his friends would be on their way. I just hoped they were very heavy sleepers, but I doubted it.

I tried to think.

'How long have we got, Sheik?'

I looked at him; he was pale but appeared in control. He had his pistol out. That didn't give me much hope given what Harout's tough guys would be armed with.

'Ten minutes I would say.'

I put my arm around Antoine.

'We may do it; help me with the pastor.'

Antoine was in a bad way. Even if we could have put him straightaway into a bed I think I'd have still liked it if someone could have watched over him all night. In crude mechanical terms, his limbs seemed to have seized up.

In the end we had no option but to carry him out of the cavern and along into the corridor. He was not in fact very heavy. Elias shut the steel door behind us. Then we pushed the picture door open and were back in Harout's room. There was a thick pile of snow now under the window and further flurries kept blowing in.

I stopped for a moment and listened; the alarm was louder here, but I could hear nothing else. No running feet or car engines. Not yet. I let Antoine slip gently to the floor as Elias removed the book and pushed the picture back. A spasm of despair wrung me, but I tried to throw it off; there was too much to do. Harout's people would be here in minutes and would know we knew everything. There could be no mercy now. Yet the horror that was there had to be destroyed. There was a further problem: unless precisely targeted, even a heavy direct airstrike on the Deir might do little to what lay in the cave – except perhaps release it.

I ran to the desk and pressed the rocker switch back to where it had been. Then I went back to Antoine who was speaking in an alert, if frail, voice. 'Sheik. You and Henry and the women must flee. I cannot.'

382

He paused and gasped. He seemed out of breath although we had carried him for the last hundred yards.

'Let them find me, otherwise they may kill you all and, Sheik, you have much to do. Destroy this place. Let the light in.'

I looked at Elias, who seemed frozen in thought. I turned to Tina.

'Tina and Nickie, go back to the house as fast as you can. We may follow. Go!'

For a second the girls did nothing then Nickie went over to the window and began to scramble out. Tina seemed to be about to come over to me. I repeated the order brusquely. It hurt.

'Go. I'll follow. You promised to jump if I said so.'

She looked at me blankly, nodded and then turned to the window and began to climb out. Elias suddenly turned to me; he appeared to have snapped out of his indecision.

'The pastor is right. I will go to the tower and as soon as they come, go out to meet them. I will tell them that I chose tonight to sleep in the tower and heard the alarm. I will encourage them to believe that Antoine acted alone. I do not believe they will harm a pastor. You must go and ensure the women get back. Do not stop. I will call you at the house as soon as I have been able to get Antoine out.'

Of all the evils around this sounded the least. I grabbed Antoine's hand.

'See you later, Pastor.'

He spoke in Arabic. 'God be with you, Henry, and your bride.'

I went to the window. There was a flash of lightning and a deafening crack of thunder. Elias stood by him.

'Pastor, I will be back.'

'Go, Elias Daoud. In God's name, go.'

I tumbled out of the window, vaguely conscious of the freezing wind and the snow tearing at me. However, the sickness and tiredness of heart I felt seemed more important than the cold. Elias followed me. I just prayed we had done the right thing. I found my torch and switched it on; in its light the faint outline of footprints showed up ahead. The snow was already filling them in. Rounding the corner of the building I turned full into the teeth of the blizzard. There was another flash of lightning. I felt the wind might have lessened a little, but it was still bitterly cold and visibility was only a few yards with the torch. I desperately hoped that Tina and Nickie would stay safely on course for the house.

The bulk of the tower was suddenly straight ahead of me. Elias came up to me and shouted over the wind. 'Go straight to the house now, Henry; try to catch the women. I'll go round to the gate. I can still hear the bell.'

He was right, it was still ringing. I nodded and set off. Faint tracks were still to be seen in the light of the torch and they appeared to be continuing in the right direction. I took my own orientation off the corner of the tower and set off. In a few seconds Elias and the tower vanished in the murky darkness and I was on my own in the snow. A thousand emotions fought to dominate my mind, but I forced myself to concentrate on going in a straight line. If once I went off at an angle there would be no hope. Unfortunately, the tracks appeared to have vanished already. In a few minutes I would be sufficiently clear of the Deir to try shouting for the girls.

Then I heard the ringing stop; someone must have got to the main switch. Harout's men had arrived. The wind briefly lessened and I kept on as fast as I dared in my little circle of light. After a few minutes I called out Tina's name. There was nothing. I tried not to think of the cliff and walked on, noting that there was now no sign of tracks at all. Just smooth white snow. I called again. Nothing. The snow piled up around my face and inside my hood. I kept going, but there was still no sign of the others. Perhaps I was going in circles? I felt sure that I should have overtaken them by now. Then there was a flash of lightning and a wall appeared in front of me. As the thunder boomed overhead I had the horrible thought that it was the monastery and that I had indeed gone in circles. Then I realised it was the garden wall. I walked cautiously down to the left in case I was already below the gate and close to the cliff edge.

The gate suddenly appeared in the midst of the swirling snow and I ran to it. There I stopped and called. There was a noise somewhere. I shouted again and then through the snow the tired, white forms of Tina and Nickie emerged. I hugged Tina and got a face full of snow for my pains. It was all I could do not to cry.

We opened the gate and a few minutes later were in the hallway of the house. Tina pulled her hood off, looked at me and began to shake, and then suddenly started crying. I nearly did the same, but I didn't want Harout to arrive and find us here at three in the morning wearing snow-covered outdoor gear. Nickie just sat on a chair with her face in her hands, oblivious to the snow starting to melt off her.

I patted her gently on the back for want of anything better to say or do and went to help Tina out of her anorak. Just then a phone rang somewhere.

There was the sound of heavy footsteps and a voice in oddly accented Arabic. It must be Malik. Something was said and he put the phone down with a crash. Then he ran along the corridor above our heads. I stopped what I was doing and leapt up the stairs, my heart heavy with foreboding.

Malik was hammering on Fuad's door and shouting in Arabic.

'Fuad, Fuad, come on, get up quickly! Your father is shot. Quickly, Fuad, he is dying.'

Fuad raced out of his room. I don't think he had been sleeping; he was half-dressed already. His face was ashen.

'Henry! Is this true?'

I didn't answer and grabbed the phone.

'Who is it?'

'Ah, Dr Stanwick, this is Sheik Elias.' The voice was strained. 'I'm sorry to have woken you but there's been an accident. Pastor Attiyah has been shot in the monastery.'

Above the grief I realised he was being careful in what he said. I could find no words to say. Elias continued. 'No, I don't understand either. He's very bad. I'm sorry. Get Fuad and go to the gatehouse. I'll call them and get them to drive you over. Sorry. You'd better hurry.'

Hurry we did. I managed to speak briefly to the grief-stricken Fuad as he was pulling on his anorak.

'Fuad, you were right, there is something horrible going on, but we must not reveal that we know of it. Elias is trying to imply your father acted on his own.'

He nodded. I think it registered.

Quarter of an hour later we were back at the monastery after a nightmare trip in a four wheel drive vehicle along invisible roads in a full blizzard. Tina had insisted on coming. Nickie, for whom everything had now seemingly fallen apart, had fled to her room in tears where she had locked herself in. I looked at Tina, who seemed to be strained almost to breaking point, yet there was still resolve and determination in her exhausted, drawn face. I wondered how I looked.

There were two vehicles at the monastery. One was in Elias' militia camouflage and there were a handful of men inside it keeping the engine running. Our driver said that Sammy had already arrived. It was further evidence that Elias was trying to maintain the initiative. As I noted it, half of me asked what it mattered now that Antoine was dying. Yet I realised that what we had seen earlier, the knowledge apparently bought at such a cost, must be preserved.

Elias was waiting in the guardroom. He looked profoundly agitated and almost in pain. One of Harout's men and one of his own were standing around eyeing each

386

other uneasily. He walked hastily over to Fuad and made profuse apologies; it was 'unprecedented, an awful tragedy, a terrible accident'. Then he led him hastily along the corridor to Harout's office and we hurried behind. Another of Harout's men appeared and followed us closely.

Half numbed by the tragedy I couldn't help but notice how cool Elias was, at least on one level. As we followed him quickly down the corridor he shifted into loud, agitated English, presumably to allow Tina some understanding of what was going on.

'I was sleeping in the tower. I heard the alarm and then shots. I called my men to drive here and went in to see what had happened. At first I thought it was the Israeliens.'

You fox, I thought, that's the one excuse which allows an Arab to do almost anything.

He continued, 'I couldn't believe it. Your father was in Harout's office. He must have got in through the window. Why, I don't know. I said to Harout how he hated the picture. Perhaps. That animal Kevork shot him twice. What is the world coming to? It is the worst thing to happen here in years.'

Then we came into the room. I see it now, fixed indelibly in my mind's eye as some sort of tableau. The light was on. A coat had been stuffed into the window to try to stop the snow coming in, but it was too small and above it small gusts of snowflakes drifted in. In the corner furthest away from the window Harout and Kevork stood, talking together nervously and quietly. As we came in they looked guilty and, turning their gaze to the foot of the picture, fell silent.

Below the picture Antoine was lying under an anorak, his legs stuck out awkwardly. A figure in a white combat jacket was kneeling over him taking his pulse. At his side lay a machine pistol. I recognised him as Sammy, but the thought held no fear. He turned a bleak face towards us

387

and nodded perfunctorily in acknowledgement to Elias. There was no emotion in his face. Fuad ran past and knelt down by his father. Sammy stood up and stepped to one side, letting a blood-soaked cloth fall from his hand, and retreated to stand by Elias. From the quantity of blood around the body there was indeed no hope of recovery. Fuad started talking quietly to his father who seemed barely to be conscious. Rather to my surprise Tina brushed past. I raised a hand to stop her, but let it fall. No female Henson could have done otherwise. They'd all done First Aid courses and anyway they just couldn't help it. She knelt next to Antoine, lifted the coat briefly and then lowered it as gently as she could, her face showing so little emotion it could have been carved. She stroked his hand a moment, then got up and walked over to me and buried her head in my shoulder.

It was curious how quiet the room was. Most incidents involving casualties that I've had the misfortune to witness in Lebanon seem to result in everybody running around, screaming and shouting at each other. This static quietness was different. I suppose everyone knew that there was nothing that could be done. Nothing at all.

Elias stood to one side and watched the whole affair with evident great distress. Mutterings came out every so often and some of them sounded like reproaches to himself or to others. Once or twice I caught a look of pure hatred pass between him and Harout. Sammy stood by him and said little – he'd seen it all before. I overheard him say at one point in a slow, flat voice to Elias, 'The priest talked to Kevork and forgave him,' and they shook their heads together.

In fact amid the waves of sorrow for Antoine and Fuad I found myself feeling a strange pity for Kevork. He looked totally miserable and avoided my gaze. I think however hardened in street warfare, and however nominal in religion – and Kevork looked to be both – to find you have shot a man of God in a monastery must be a horrible thing.

Then it came over me dully that in its way this was all my fault, that I was the guilty party in bringing Fuad here and setting everything in motion. Briefly I wondered whether I had ever done anything worse in my life. Then I looked at Harout and from him to the picture and I realised that we had been right to do what we had done.

Fuad looked round, tears streaming from his face, and waved Elias and me over. I gently disentangled myself from Tina and went to him.

Antoine's face was pale and his eyes seemed to stare at the ceiling. His glasses were lying broken some feet away.

'Elias, are you there?' He spoke in Arabic, his voice almost a whisper.

'Yes, Pastor.'

'This is not the way. You know what should be done.'

There was a pause. 'Yes, Pastor.'

A stab of pain crossed Antoine's face. He began again quietly: 'Elias Daoud is a good name. Now live up to it.'

I saw his hands hold Fuad's tightly.

'Henry?'

I could only mumble an affirmative.

'Thank you for coming back to Lebanon. See that your work is finished.'

'Pastor, I promise.'

There was silence. Then he spoke again slowly and painfully, but as I looked at his face there seemed to be relief in his eyes.

'Thank you for your prayers too. They are answered. I will not run away now.'

He fell silent and I thought for a moment he was gone. Then he spoke quietly. At first I didn't recognise the words because they were in classical Arabic. Then I knew them: 'Surely goodness and love will follow me all the days of my life, and I will dwell in the house of the Lord for ever.'

He spoke no more and a few minutes later his breathing ceased. I got up slowly, vaguely noting Kevork, Sammy and Elias crossing themselves, and walked out of the room. Tina followed at a distance and then we stood and hugged each other in sorrow and grief.

38

There wasn't much left of the night. We were driven back to the house by Elias. Fuad and his father's body were following with Sammy. The Sheik said very little, or at least little that was coherent, and I was in no mood to talk. I dully noted that he seemed to be a man in a mental torment. Finally we got to bed and eventually sheer exhaustion overcame grief and brought sleep.

It was late morning when I woke up, or so my watch said. The room was very dark and little light came in from outside. There was still some thunder around. I lay in bed as the weight of all that had happened gathered like a great cloud and hung terribly over me. Antoine was dead.

Then I reminded myself of what I'd mentally assented to for a number of years, but firmly believed in for only some eighteen months: that there are a lot worse things than death. However, a few moments later I began again to feel guilty about what had happened, yet as I thought it through I realised that I had no basis for that. In fact how could we have expected to penetrate so far without cost? Then too I wondered whether the thing, the spirit, or whatever it had been that had caused Antoine to fall across the beam, had triumphed. Thinking of the body resting against the foot of the picture it wasn't hard to see the scene as evil triumphant. But that idea vanished too. There were too many precedents – and one in particular – for evil over-reaching itself in such a manner. But I knew now what Abie Gvirtzman had dreamed of.

The way ahead was thorny. I could call up Elweth, but he and his friends left a nasty taste in my mouth. I've been in air raids and I've seen what happens, even in allegedly precisely targeted airstrikes. As the Lebanese say, they call it 'surgical precision' because it keeps the surgeons busy. Besides, I didn't trust Elweth and his boss one little bit. Calling them up, I felt, had to be the last option. No, hopefully Elias would kick Harout out and we would be able to dismantle the facilities. Nickie would know how to sterilise that laboratory; it should be possible. I could then call Elweth up and say that everything was under control. 'No sweat, Jim. Keep the planes at home.' Perhaps in that case we would be able to leave soon.

Yet there were so many imponderables. Did Harout really believe that it had been a one man operation last night? Would Elias really pull the plug on his source of finance? I did the only thing I could, and prayed.

Eventually I went over to the window and peered out beyond the curtains. We were surrounded by thick dark clouds and the snow was still falling heavily. Every so often there would be a flash of lightning and an echoing peal of thunder. I dressed and woke Tina gently. I didn't want her to wake up and find me gone. That done I went downstairs.

Fuad was sitting at the table staring out of the window. I sat down with him and we talked about his father a lot. Gradually I told him in brief what was going on in the monastery and the circumstances that had led to his father's death. Fuad said little and just listened, his eyes bright and moist. At the end he spoke slowly.

'Henry, oh, I shall miss him.'

'Me too, Fuad. All of us.'

It turned out that Fuad had seen Elias an hour or so earlier and that he was organising a snowplough to allow Fuad to leave with his father's body. Fuad paused and looked at me hard.

391

'Henry, I want to say something to you, something that I told my father before the end. For me the death of my father has sorted something out. He told you perhaps that he and Mama wanted me to be a pastor too? I refused and tried to be a doctor. That failed and I became a biology teacher. I think I was in some ways afraid of what being an *Assis* would cost. "In time," I said. That time is now. I will resign from the school and go to train, then I will come back here as my father did.'

There wasn't much I could say, which was probably as well as I felt almost too choked up with emotion to say it. I shook his hand.

'Fuad, every blessing.'

Tina came down a bit later looking pale and drained of life and with eyes that had been crying. She was very subdued, but said she'd seen Nickie who was staying in her room. Tina said little about what had clearly been a protracted private conversation, but it seemed that for Nickie the events of the previous day had been especially traumatic. In fact there was barely any area of her life that was not now in ruins. Tina shook her head.

'I think for the first time she has realised that there is good and evil. But, Henry, she too wants that place destroyed.'

A little later Elias came in. The events of the previous day had not improved him. He was nervous, jumpy and apparently racked by guilt and remorse. His swings of temperament seemed even more rapid and extreme than before. He was also unshaven. He muttered to himself a lot and in general had the air of a man brutally trapped by circumstances totally outside his control.

He announced that the snow plough was ready and a driver available to take a station wagon down to Beirut with Antoine's body. However, he wanted Tina and me to stay; there were things, he said, that we had to discuss. While that was doubtless true I also felt that he was explicitly denying us the freedom to leave. In fact, although he didn't say so, we were now being held by him. I wondered why and rather reluctantly agreed to stay for as long as he needed us. I wasn't going to complain because I couldn't leave anyway without making sure that my promise to Antoine was going to be fulfilled.

We bade our farewells to Fuad and I told him to tell George we were fine and would, all being well, be on our way back shortly. I just hoped it was true. He kissed Tina and me, shook Elias' hand in a formal fashion and left on his sad journey south.

Then we were on our own with Elias Daoud. I sat down on a sofa. He paled and snapped at me, his fingers twitching.

'Don't sit there! Pastor Antoine sat there yesterday.'

I moved onto the other sofa and Tina sat next to me. Elias was still shaking. He spoke half to himself and half to us in a mixture of Arabic and English.

'A priest, a pastor killed in my monastery. And where? On the steps of the altar. I swear to God I would have done anything to prevent it. He was a good man, a believer. I'm under judgement. I must be cursed now. I let that monster and his dogs in here. His blood is upon me. And that shadow that Harout has unlocked – death itself – in this Christian valley. What am I going to do?'

Every so often he would look at the sofa where Antoine had sat and weave his fingers together in anxiety.

'He sat there. I can see him now; he was my guest. Dead on the altar.'

After a bit he became quiet. In fact he sat in a miserable silence for so long that I began to feel quite sorry for him. Then he seemed to snap out of it. As last night he was not totally unmanned by events and he uttered a series of abrupt phrases.

'I've told them Nickie decided to stay with you last night because of the storm and that she will be up later.'

I said nothing. I was waiting for him to come to the big issue.

'I've told Harout that regardless of the circumstances Kevork went too far. I want him. I will not send my men in after him, but they are by the Deir and if Kevork leaves it they will seize him. He did a horrible thing. I've told them that if they catch him they are simply to throw him over the cliff. That blood must be paid for.'

I protested loudly. 'Sheik, no! Do you think that Pastor Antoine would have wanted that? Anyway, Kevork's crime is not the point. The real problem, Sheik Elias Daoud, is what you are going to do about Harout's project.'

There was no answer. I was going to repeat the question, but Elias looked at his watch.

'Let us eat now. Afterwards, only afterwards, will we talk about that.'

It was a miserable lunch. Elias picked at his food and cursed himself and at least a dozen other people most thoroughly. Tina and I didn't feel particularly hungry either. Nickie stayed in her room and the food taken up to her was returned uneaten.

After the meal we moved to Elias' study. I think he wanted somewhere where he could get away from the memory of Antoine. The window showed no view today, only a moving greyness of snow blowing in gusts around the house. Possibly the storm was easing off, but the snow was still falling heavily. Elias sat in his chair by the window looking very upset. I felt I had to push him.

'Sheik, the issue is whether you are going to order Harout out of the valley. For all you know he could be loading up viruses now.'

He looked at me irritably. 'Not for a few days at least — it was difficult enough to persuade the drivers to go down today with a snowplough.'

I had understood his haste in getting rid of Antoine's

remains, but I think he'd found, as others have, that removal of a body doesn't result in the removal of guilt. I gave him a straight question this time.

'Sheik, are you going to get rid of Harout?'

He squirmed a little.

'Maybe we were too hasty. Perhaps what he's up to isn't that bad.'

He didn't believe it of course. It was just a first line of defence. There was a snort of anger from next to me and I turned to try to appease Tina, but it was too late. She half rose to her feet and glared at Elias.

'You listen to me! What was there was wicked by any standard. Even yours. You know it and what is more Pastor Antoine commanded you to get rid of it. The only thing you have to decide is how you are going to do it.'

Then she sat down straightaway, apparently on the sudden realisation of what she'd said and to whom she'd said it. Elias fumed and glared at her, but he didn't say anything. Tina having paved the way, I thought I'd tighten the screws still further.

'Sheik, his last words to you were to do what should be done.'

He didn't like that. He reached in his desk and pulled out a set of worry beads and began to fumble with them.

'It's not easy, Dr Stanwick. Not easy.'

'Why not?'

He looked very shifty at this point and his hands scrabbled on the beads. 'The money for one thing. Without it I would be in trouble.'

'Sheik, you aren't telling me that you can be bought with money? I thought you were a man of principle and honour.'

That got him annoyed, but there wasn't anything he could do.

'No, of course not. It's just that Harout made promises to me. Precious promises.'

I realised we were on to something. 'Such as?'

He sighed and looked at a map on the wall. It was of Lebanon. Two areas were highlighted; one, in solid green, was the tiny strip of territory that he held, but there was a larger area extending far to the south and a slight way to the north shaded in green cross-hatching. He spoke slowly, running the beads through his hand.

'In due time, and I swear to God, Henry, that I didn't know how he was going to do it, Harout said he would reward me. Not with money – I scorn that – but with the mountain. The whole mountain, the whole of Christian Lebanon apart from the southern villages. From Beirut to Tripoli I would rule.'

He had lost his unease now; the dream, doubtless endlessly rehearsed in his mind, had taken over. 'Maybe beyond. I, Elias Boulos Daoud, not the Gemayels, or the Frangiehs, or the Chamouns, or some little general, would rule. And in that I would have my revenge. In due time that would be mine; I would be secure. They would guarantee my borders. The group would give it me.'

'When they came in their kingdom?' said Tina's voice beside me. So that was what lay behind his reluctance to have Harout thrown out. Not only the money but a heady promise of power, vengeance and security. No wonder with that and the payments Harout felt secure. Elias turned to me. 'I would do a good job in running the mountain.'

'That's neither here nor there. What are you going to do about the group?'

He slammed his hand down on the desk in irritation. 'I don't have to do anything. I can leave the valley. Run. Let my plotting brother Butros have it. Let him deal with Harout.'

I was beginning to get annoyed with his refusal to do anything.

'This is your job. Get the group out!'

He fiddled with the beads and a look of cunning came into his eyes. 'Anyway, I can't now. I'd like to, but it's too risky. See, last night Harout reinforced the Deir. There are six men there at least; all with weapons. It's very strong, Henry. What am I to do? Lose thirty men? Perhaps Harout would release those viruses.'

I said nothing and he went on. 'Of course I have some artillery. I could shell the monastery if you wanted.'

He knew my answer to that of course – which was why he had suggested it.

Tina nudged me. 'Henry, can I have a word with you?'

I made an apology to Elias and went with Tina into the corridor.

'Why not tell him we have friends who can do it?'

'He'd probably leap for my throat if he thought I was in league with those people.' I nodded southwards. 'Besides I don't like involving them.'

'Tell him you know a man who knows them. That was the idea anyway.'

I agreed with a great deal of reluctance. There now seemed no other course.

We went back in and I spoke to him again, choosing my words carefully.

'Sheik, supposing there was some way of destroying it completely and safely at a stroke.'

'How?'

Here goes, I thought. 'Look, I have an American friend. He has told me that the Israelis suspect there is work with viruses going on here. They are very scared by that idea.'

He stared at me with anger, his fingers twisting furiously. 'I will do no deals with them. Not at all. I have always stood against that. Let others make treaties with them.'

I wasn't surprised at his rhetoric. With the co-ordinates for his house probably chalked on every piece of Syrian artillery for miles around, he didn't have much choice. He fumbled with his beads. He was thinking very rapidly.

'Anyway, it's in the cave. Could they do it?'

I'd wondered that.

'I think so, if we gave my friend, my American friend, the precise location. They have bombs that suck in when they explode; I suppose implode. If they got one into the cave entrance its effects would be very powerful. Then they would use high temperature bombs.'

He sat silently. 'It would be a massive airstrike, yes? Fire and flame. The end of the Deir totally? My tower with it I suppose?'

He juggled his beads some more. I've always found it an enormously irritating habit and never more than then. I wondered what was going through his mind; his protestations notwithstanding, he seemed to be toying with the idea of calling up the Israelis.

'When would they do this thing?'

'If I made contact today and expressed an urgent desire, they would probably try as soon as the weather cleared.'

'Yes, that would make sense. Not even they can fly in this.' He gestured out to the whirling snow outside the window. 'So maybe tomorrow evening or Wednesday morning.' He spoke quietly. There was a long pause while he thought.

'I am intrigued. Leave me alone for a few minutes, I wish to think about it. I will meet with you in the other room.'

In the room with the sofas we sat down together.

Tina looked at me. 'Do you think he'll go for it, Henry?'

'He may do, but, Tina, I don't trust him one bit. Despite Antoine's words it is obvious where his interests lie. He's probably checking up to see if he could claim on the insurance.' Then I decided to change the subject. There was no shortage of things to talk about. We talked about Antoine for a long time before eventually passing on to Fuad and his plans. That was going to be further bad news for George Roumian, who was now going to be badly squeezed in Cyprus. I commented that he would just have to move James Erickson back into biology. Then we moved back to the facilities and plans that we had seen in the cave.

Tina shook her head ruefully. 'I suppose it's what you end up with when you start on a "no holds barred" policy. You go down a slippery slope very quickly. Poor Nickie.'

Then we returned to the most pressing problem: the removal of the facilities in the cave.

'Tina, I'm not leaving this valley until it's done. That laboratory has to be destroyed. I promised Antoine.'

She looked sorrowful and simply said, 'Me neither, it must be done. Even if it costs us what it cost him.'

It was a grim thought and I didn't like to think about how we were going to do it if Elias refused to let us go or talk to Elweth.

After what was more like an hour Elias came in. He seemed to be in a better mood; in fact a suspiciously better mood.

'On reconsideration I think that your suggestion might be interesting. Of course I would not be linked to it, would I?'

'No, the way I would do it would be to use your computer set-up here to send a message to my friend's machine in Cyprus. A few lines of text would be all that was needed.'

That seemed to please him.

'No long phone messages that might be intercepted?'

'That's the advantage.'

'Well write your message and I will send it, Dr Stanwick.'

I paused. There was something in his eyes and it wasn't the milk of human kindness.

'I'd prefer to send it myself.'

He objected to that and eventually we came to a compromise. He'd type up the message, I'd insert the codewords at the front and then I'd send it. Life gets complex when you can't trust anybody.

We went upstairs to a narrow windowless room with

his radio telephone set-up and a computer. It was what they call an 'industry standard' model and perfectly familiar. I took a pad of paper and drafted out the message to Jim. I didn't write the codewords down at all. They were going to stay in my brain until the last minute and after the message had gone off I was going to take care that the machine hadn't saved a copy of either the phone numbers or the codes.

When I'd finished writing, the message ran as follows:

Jim,
    After thorough evaluation severe structural problems have been noted in the Deir. These are particularly major in the north-east corner due to the existence of a north trending fissure extending back some way into the hillside. Priority should be given to cleaning this out to a distance of some thirty metres. This will be difficult due to some obstructions near the mouth. The problems are major and require substantial immediate remedial work as soon as possible. Conventional techniques should be adequate. Request immediate action on this.
    Best wishes,
    H.

I must admit I was quite proud of all the woolly verbiage, but I suppose the original idea was someone else's. I passed it to Tina who read it through carefully.

'You should add a note to the effect that the house and hotel are sound.'

It was a good point. I added an extra line and marked where it was to go.

'Have examined house and this is sound. Less detailed study of hotel suggests similar status to the house.'

I passed it to Elias, who looked at it very carefully. He seemed pleased.

'Excellent. Very subtle.'

He pulled an office chair over to the computer and sat down. I noticed it was kept switched on, presumably to

400

allow it to take any incoming messages from his Cyprus agent. He loaded the communications program, which turned out to be one I'd used before and typed in the message with two fingers. I stood behind him watching the screen. He seemed to be making a careful copy of the text. At the end he went back to the top of the document. 'Now, Henry, add your codewords to the top and send it.'

Then he got up from his chair and went over to near the door from where he could see neither the screen nor the keyboard. I felt very uneasy, but I couldn't put my finger on why I felt that way. I tried to shrug it off, saying to myself that it was just unhappiness at the whole idea of calling up these people. I filled in the codewords, I hit the appropriate keys and a window on the screen came up asking me for all the details of the number I wanted to dial. So I filled that in and pressed the return key.

The message 'Dialling.....' appeared along the bottom of the screen. As I waited for an answer it crossed my mind that perhaps I should sign it with something more distinctive than just 'H', so I scrolled the text up the screen so I could look at the end part. There was the sound of electronic chattering and the text message changed to 'Logged on. To transmit, press return key.' My finger hovered above the return key. One gentle touch and the message, with all its implications, would go off.

But something was wrong. What?

Then I noticed the last line. Instead of reading '....study of hotel suggests similar status to the house', it read, '...study of hotel suggests similar status to the Deir'.

I gasped. That was an awful slip. I stared at Elias.

'There's a mistake here!'

Then I caught the look on his face. It wasn't a mistake at all.

'What are you playing at? You want them to bomb the hotel as well?'

He smiled a rather sick smile and then gave me a defiant look. 'Yes, in case Harout and his men are not in the Deir.'

For a moment it didn't register, then I saw it. He wasn't just interested in eliminating the laboratory, he wanted to get rid of everything, especially the people. Tina, clearly puzzled by the conversation, came over and glanced at the screen and then stared at me, before turning on Elias with a look of pure fury. She stood there quivering at him. It scared me and I'm her husband. She didn't say a lot, but every syllable oozed contempt.

' "Sheik?" You're nothing of the sort; you're simply a cheap, two-faced, nasty little crook.'

I nearly told him what I thought of him as well, but in the end it was rather watered down. 'No deal, Elias.' (Tina was right: forget the 'Sheik' nonsense.) 'We've had death enough. I'm not going to be your executioner. There are people in the hotel.'

'Like Nickie,' snapped Tina, fixing him with a stare of ferocious revulsion that suggested she had firmly come round to the 'Elias is a maggot' school of thought.

He looked unhappy, but said nothing and I moved my fingers to the key combination that would reset the entire computer. I wasn't going to send any message and was going to make sure that he wasn't going to be able to either. The whole thing stunk to high heaven. We'd have to find another way. As I found the keys I saw movement out of the corner of my eye. There was a gasp from Tina. I looked up and saw Elias had his pistol out and was pointing it at her.

'Don't touch the keyboard, Dr Stanwick. Just move away.' There was a nasty tone in his voice.

I moved the chair back against the wall. Elias advanced on me keeping the gun pointed at Tina, but I couldn't let him send the message. He moved over slowly. All he had to do was press the return key and keep us locked up, then it was goodbye to the hotel, the monastery and all the people. Should I risk jumping him? I felt I had to, although there was very little hope that he was bluffing. This was Lebanon. I braced my hand against the wall to give me the push to leap up at him.

It closed on a cable. A cable! I glanced at it; it led where I thought it did. My hand closed around it and I pulled hard. Elias' hand was above the keyboard. He spun round and snarled at me, then turned and hit the return key.

It was too late; the screen was already fading. Inside the data would already be vanishing off the memory chips.

'Sorry, Elias. You've just had a power cut.'

He cocked the gun and pointed it at me, and I was just beginning to wonder how smart I'd been in switching the machine off when he seemed to have a better idea. He moved to the door, opened it and shouted sideways through it. The gun didn't waver.

'Malik! Quickly.'

'Yes, Sheik,' shouted a distant voice.

'Malik, call the guard. And get Sammy. Quickly!'

'Yes sir!'

There was the sound of a door being slammed. He turned to me. 'Now, Dr Stanwick, type it in again, or else I shoot your wife.'

I said a little prayer that I'd assessed him right. 'You wouldn't, Elias Daoud. A guest in your own house? You wouldn't be able to hide it.'

The gun wavered a little. I tried to hit a suitably prophetic tone. 'Judgement would surely come upon you. A pastor at the altar and an unarmed woman, a guest in your own home. Where is your honour? The world would know.'

He was sweating and the gun wobbled a lot. I thought the situation allowed for a slight relaxation in theological truth.

'She'd come back and haunt you, Sheik.'

He looked very worried.

Tina clearly had a tighter hold on her theology, 'Actually, I'd have better things to do, but don't do it, Henry. He mustn't have those codes. We agreed.' She was still angry.

It was stalemate. For a long time it seemed like nothing happened. The tension in the room was horrible. Then Elias pushed Tina over to me and I caught her.

'Sorry.'

He didn't sound it.

There was the sound of rushing feet in the corridor and on the stairs. The door swung wildly open and two militiamen burst into the room with sub-machine guns at the ready. Behind them there were slower footsteps and the scarred face of Sammy suddenly appeared. Elias turned to them and spoke in Arabic.

'Thank you. That was fast. I've just found these two trying to use the radio. Take them to the guard-house please, while I decide what to do with them. They were trying to call the Israelis.'

39

I thought about resisting, but there wasn't much point. For one thing, I was totally bewildered about what was going on and what Elias was up to. For another thing, in Lebanon there is not a lot of mileage in making a break for it, running out into the street and shouting for the police. There aren't any in the accepted sense of the word and the proliferation of automatic weapons means that you have to run pretty fast.

So they had a fairly easy job marching us through the snow to the guard-house, still with its Christmas tree. There they threw us into a small, evil smelling little room with some very nasty marks on the wall. I tried to comfort Tina who now wasn't really very happy at all. I couldn't blame her, as recent experience suggested that suspected

Israeli agents didn't go down too well with Sammy.

Twenty minutes later Sammy came in. He said nothing for some time and just stared at us, his sunken light brown eyes radiating intense hostility. He looked us over as though making a mental catalogue of which parts to tear, punch or break first. He was the sort of man whose hands would ball themselves up into fists at the slightest sort of opportunity. He was an undeniably frightening person and it gave me little amusement to note that his short greying hair was badly cut, as though the barber's hands had been shaking at the time. He looked very much on guard and extremely shrewd. A hint of stupidity in his manner would have been a redeeming feature; there was none. The only encouragement was that he looked disappointed, and that he didn't actually do anything. After several minutes he said in a matter-of-fact tone: 'You know we are going to kill you?'

Curiously enough, I didn't feel as afraid as I thought I would. Tina said nothing, although she had her eyes half closed and looked to be biting her lip. Sammy looked from one of us to the other. I think he had been hoping for more response. In the guardroom a phone rang, which seemed to make him irritated.

'But not yet. You, Mrs, we take to the hotel. You, Mister, we take to the Deir. There is no room in the hotel for two. Not a good hotel, eh?'

He stuck his face close to mine as if willing me to hit him. I declined the offer to remodel his nose further. I wasn't going to give him the excuse.

So they separated us, which was cruel, but it was by no means the cruellest thing they could have done and we knew it. An unhappy ten minutes later I was at the doorway to the Deir where Harout was waiting to meet me. At first glance he looked vaguely amused by the whole thing, but then you saw his eyes were full to overflowing with malice.

'So you finally annoyed the Sheik too, eh? Well fortunately I have a spare room that will do for you.'

So with a little help from one of Kevork's friends they led me along the corridor to a room on the south part of the ground floor. I vaguely remembered having looked into it and assumed it was a better sort of monastic cell that had not yet been converted into an office. In fact it had required little modification to make a prison cell – just a collapsible bed and some blankets. It even had a tiny washroom and shower. The door, however, was solid and lockable and the window firmly barred.

Harout pushed me in and then followed, closing the door behind him.

'The reason why you are here is simple. I had my suspicions about you and asked Elias not to let you go. And now he has discovered what I suspected: you have been spying. He doesn't want you to talk to anybody, so he's turned you over to me. It's a kind of peace offering too. He has decided that he needs me, so we are going to sort out something concerning you in the next few days, but in the meantime you are a guest here. Our choices are either to trade you or kill you. As the second option rules out the first we are currently keeping you alive. I'll try to get you what you need: food and some clean clothes for tomorrow. I mean, we wouldn't want any health hazards here, would we?'

As it happened I was thinking about something else at the time, more precisely someone else, so I didn't react to his comment as he'd hoped. I suspected he knew that I was aware of everything anyway. He stared at me with his bland face and deep round eyes. Then he shrugged.

'Elias says I'm not to interrogate you yet. Anyway, I've a lot to do. Your troublesome pastor friend left a lot of problems behind. You are now basically unimportant.' He spoke without passion. As always it was impossible to fathom what was going on underneath.

He turned as if to go. 'Oh, by the way; don't try and escape. We've made it harder by splitting you up. If either

406

of you does escape the instructions are to eliminate the other one as soon as possible. You understand?'

I nodded. I was beginning to understand why Antoine had found him so objectionable; it was nothing you could really firmly isolate, but there was just a general atmosphere of something unwholesome. You wouldn't have left children alone in a room with him. Knowing his tastes in art didn't make him any more likeable either.

So he left me alone with my thoughts. At first I lay down on the bed and felt sorry for myself and sorry for Tina. That did very little good at all, but then I've never known self-pity to help much anyway. Then I prayed, which is what I should have done first, but at the end of that I had to end with 'Thy will be done'. Still, it helped put me in a better frame of mind.

Then I examined the cell, looking for possible ways of escape. At first I went over it foot by foot, then again inch by inch. I tested every bar on the window, tried to prise up every flagstone on the floor and stood on a chair to examine the wooden beamed ceiling. There was no way out. I thought about making myself a nuisance by fusing the lights or clogging the drains, but the local threshold of tolerance seemed so low that I thought they might get nasty.

After that I sat down and tried to work out what was going on and whether I could drive a useful rift between Harout and Elias. That didn't seem on – my presence here seemed to indicate that they were now on good terms again. Besides, if one did want to spite the other they were as likely to kill us as release us. I could only presume that Elias, finding his attempts to get a third party to eliminate the group root and branch frustrated, had decided to throw his lot in with them.

Again and again I went over why I hadn't let the message to Elweth be sent. All logic said I should have gone ahead and tried to send it in the original form, but Elias would then clearly have done his best to make sure Harout was in the Deir. I also wondered where we would have fitted into those plans. Would he have let us go? As I thought about it I questioned what Elias would have done to us if I had sent the message. There was something odd about the speed at which his men had been able to run into the house. It crossed my mind that even if I had sent it he might still have got rid of us. After all, what Arab leader could afford to have living witnesses of a pact with those considered to be evil incarnate?

But I hadn't sent the message and unless I talked Elias wasn't going to be able to either, however much he wanted to. I thought that over carefully: without the numbers to dial or the codes he was helpless and when the plug had been pulled on the computer they had gone for ever. Only I had the numbers and codes now.

I looked out of the little window again and noted that the snow seemed now to be lessening, although the clouds were still thick and grey. They would probably break tomorrow and the day after the sky would be clear. I spent some time thinking about a possible, even probable, airstrike and the thoughts were not conducive to happiness. The extent to which the Israelis would effectively destroy the hidden facilities was clearly open to question. However, I had less uncertainty about the odds on my own survival, but in the end I decided to put further thoughts about that off limits. No, the situation looked pretty black and was remarkably short on any silver linings. The worst thing of all was that it looked like all our efforts, and Antoine's death, might have been in vain. Yet I couldn't believe that.

So I tried to make myself comfortable and sung some hymns badly which got me a reprimand from someone outside the door. The Armenians sing extremely well and rank way above the Welsh in prizing their choral traditions, so it's not surprising that the guard found it offensive. Then I waited for something to happen.

In fact very little did. I was given a rather basic evening

meal and that was it for the night. Eventually I took a shower and went to sleep. Oddly enough I slept long and fairly well.

Next morning there was breakfast delivered without conversation and I spent a lot of time trying to think of ever more imaginative ways to get out of the cell. None of them was very feasible and most required a string of near miracles. Even then you ended up with a five mile trek over the ridge in thick snow before you made it to the Syrian lines. It would have been nice to have had an angel unlock the door for me and lead me out, but they don't seem to go in for that much these days. The only break in the day was a silent midday meal.

As the day wore on the flurries of snow ended and the thick cloud lifted. By evening I could see clear over the valley in all its glory and the setting sun made a great fiery patch on my wall as it shone through the broken cloud. It should have provided cheer, but it didn't. It just confirmed that the skies would be cloudless tomorrow. I now felt certain that some sort of raid would occur in the morning. In the afternoon I spent a lot of time thinking about what the group hoped to do and how and where they were wrong. Or perhaps how they had gone wrong. I even struggled with alternative ideas.

The evening meal came without conversation, interrogation or anything. I could hear distant voices and footsteps overhead, but that was all. In fact it seemed as if the monastery was unusually quiet. Perhaps they took New Year's Eve off. I began to get bored and occasionally very depressed, but I fought hard against it and by and large won. When I felt bad I recited all the Bible verses I knew and that seemed to lift things. Towards evening I realised that it was the 31st of December. Tonight was certainly going to be a memorable New Year's Eve, although the probability of ever being able to reminisce about it with anybody seemed slim.

Eventually I went to bed, but slept only fitfully. I kept the curtains open to avoid the remote chance of oversleeping. There was just a faint chance that I might be able to kick the door down and make a break for it if my guard fled in instant terror on the promised practice run or warning. If there was one, which I doubted. So I wanted to be dressed and ready early. Besides, as I was well aware from previous experience, there is something peculiarly unpleasant about being bombed in your underwear.

At midnight I was woken up by the brief tolling of the church bells. Unusually there was no celebratory shooting to commemorate the start of the New Year. Then I remembered what a tight rein Elias Daoud kept on his valley. However, after this I couldn't get to sleep again so I dressed and put my shoes on and did some exercises to get the blood flowing. I looked out of the window at the stars shining in all their brilliance in the clear mountain air and for a moment I felt like banging and screaming on the cell door to be let out. But that passed. In fact I was by no means totally depressed. On occasions I even felt a little light-hearted. There was something richly ironic about my apparently impending fate. It was rough enough for me to suffer for being an Israeli spy, but for it to result in being bombed by their own airforce was a bit much. Well, I think Abie would have found it funny. There was probably a Yiddish word for it. It was just a pity I wasn't going to be able to tell him about it.

But such moments of levity were rare and I realised that I ought to prepare for the worst and I went over in my mind everyone I could think of who had been rotten to me and I forgave them. It actually didn't take a lot of time, although I had awful trouble with Harout and Elias Daoud. Oddly enough it was Elias who I had the biggest problem with. He had so nearly been on our side that it was hard not to feel bitter about it all. In the end I felt I'd managed to forgive him. Of course the reciprocal duty of asking forgiveness for everyone I'd been rotten to took a lot longer.

Time passed. There were few sounds in the Deir apart from the occasional footsteps of the guards and a few words of Armenian chatter in the distance. I lay on my bed and prayed for all the people I could think of. Some like the Hensons, Abie, Fuad and Laurent were easy; others less so, and again Harout and Elias proved difficult.

Suddenly it was six o'clock. The raid could take place in two hours' time. By then the Deir would be in full sunlight.

Then I heard the sound of a car arriving at the monastery and feet hurrying towards the door. Perhaps it was a reprieve? But the door opened and it was Harout with a guard behind him. He motioned the guard away, switched the light on and shut the door.

He went over to the bare table and sat on it heavily, staring at me all the time.

'You're awake? Good. We need to talk.'

He was unshaven and looked ill. However, his eyes, so dominating, still burned brightly.

'I've had a message from Daoud, indirectly. He says there will be an Israeli airstrike against here just after dawn. It must be stopped.'

The voice was gruff and assertive. His news brought a savage mixture of emotions: fear, puzzlement – even hope.

'I've talked to your wife. She doesn't have the codes, she says. I believe her. You seem to have a contact with these people. You can get it stopped. Even now.'

I was grateful for the news that she was alive, but how had Elias known? He couldn't have called up Elweth. Still, I could worry about that later.

'Maybe I could, Harout, but I won't.'

Of course as I said it I realised that I didn't make life easy for myself. He seemed to ignore my comment for the moment.

'I have a telephone in my office, any machine you need. Help us.'

I supposed a message to Elweth even at this stage might cause the raid to be aborted, especially if it said the material had been moved, but I wasn't going to do it.

'Harout, to use a phrase, no deal.'

It occurred to me that I should try to keep him here. In the two hours or more remaining he could do a lot of harm. However, he didn't seem to be in a hurry. Maybe he felt I had a hotline to the chief of the airforce. He sighed.

'I'm no fool, Henry. Let me tell you why we persisted with you. You see you are not alone. We have had other people object to our plans. People who despite our best efforts and finest offers will not support us. They cry "immoral" and "unethical", although the words have no meaning, and they refuse our advances. They are few, but they pose problems; many of them are in the United States and a number hold high office. Our marketing people have been worried.'

He paused. 'May I smoke? It is your bedroom.'

I've always had a weakness for the ironic. 'Given what's probably going to happen here in a couple of hours I'll let you off. Try not to set fire to the place though.'

He flexed his lips into a semblance of a smile and lit a cigarette.

'You came to our attention of course with the tragic affair of Vaughan. There were aspects of that which worried us profoundly. In particular you failed to act as you should have. You proved unpredictable. Then the business with Elweth came up, so we wondered what to do and persuaded Nickie to see if she could get you on board. She could genuinely have used you, but the real reason we came back to you was to see if we could persuade you at all. You were to be a prototype, a test case, an experiment. If we could have sold ourselves to you, then using the same strategy we could have moved much more quickly, more openly, elsewhere.'

He drew on the cigarette deeply and then exhaled slowly. He seemed to have all the time in the world. He put his head to one side and looked at me. 'You may derive some satisfaction from the fact that we found you impossible to work with. You have been very resistant. It has been very sobering dealing with you. Not only have you proved unusable, but in your own stupid, blundering way you became a threat to us. You and especially the people you brought with you. You have been a catalyst.'

He drew on the cigarette again. 'That is simply to explain why I am not going to threaten either you or your wife in order to make you co-operate. It would be a waste and even counter-productive. Equally, I will make no promises as I have done to that fool Elias. Strange to say you probably could not be bought even with the promise of England or Madagascar.'

'I gather much of Lebanon is spoken for?'

'Was. Let me continue. You see, Henry, if we are attacked today then this is the end of the project. We have elements elsewhere and a lot of the data is duplicated, but here is the core project and here is the financial centre. You know, I think, of the core project? The infertility programme? Yes, I thought so. The penetration of our defences was more than that old fool's work. Anyway, we could partially survive the blow, but not rebuild to what we are. What is more the chances of such a group as us arising again are most unlikely. We had a fortunate combination here: timing, people, place. It will not happen again – not until it is too late. So unless you abort this raid this will be the end of us.'

He stood up, walked to the window and stared out. Beyond him the darkness of night was beginning to pale. Then he turned round abruptly, dropped his cigarette butt on the floor and ground it in with his heel. Then he stared coldly at me.

'And with us, the world.'

Now something strange happened – not that I noticed it at the time. His voice seemed to take on a different tone, less harsh, more pleading, even congenial. He seemed a very different man, one wise and compassionate. His big eyes softened and caught my attention, emphasising in their depth his concern and understanding. As he spoke it was almost as though there was a background of music, with the notes highlighting his words and bringing depth and pathos to them. Recounting the bare phrases carries as much of what he made me feel as Schiller's 'Ode to Joy' conveys of the finale of Beethoven Nine.

'You see, Henry, you must choose what you want. Look out of these windows, see the slopes ravaged by erosion, the hills covered by soldiers, the skies filled with the vapour trails of warplanes. Go down to the sea and look at the rubbish that pollutes it. Go to Beirut and see the slums and the squalor, the drug addiction, the armies facing each other and killing for no reason; see the children in misery and hopelessness because of disease; touch the futility they feel and know. Feel the fear they have of being dragged away and murdered at any time just because of who they are. I have known all this. You too in a lesser way have seen it. Is this what you want?'

Of course not. How could I disagree? There was a pause. The eyes – those compelling eyes – seemed almost to fill with tears.

'Henry, if you let this happen you are condemning millions to suffering and fear. The homeless, the refugees, the sick, the poor, those weary of war. You will let the world rot and it will perish in dust and flame. I cannot believe you, you above all people, would wish it.'

The effect of his words was extraordinary. When he talked of refugees it was not simply a noun that I heard. Rather I saw them: the glazed, hopeless eyes, the skin loose over bone, the gathering flies and I could smell the scent of dust and death. When he spoke of war I heard the terrible sound of artillery and the awful space between the noise of the firing and the incoming final whine. I felt the explosion, smelled the dust of the rubble and heard the screams of children. All was despair and utter misery and

I wanted to weep.

Then his tone changed; there was hope and enthusiasm. Now the music was playing in a major key. 'In time, Henry, we can achieve our goal. We can still. The core project would give the world a breathing space, a chance to solve its problems. In that time we could move and change the political systems permanently for good. A stable, sustainable, secure world order. Within our lifetime we could see a new world. There will be no more gloom. A great light would dawn. It would give rise to a new age of government and peace that would have no end. There would be a new system upheld and established with justice and righteousness. Henry, we could remake the world!'

They seemed to me then glorious words. The note changed again. 'This is our vision, Henry, a new world, a fertile garden, not a slum or a desert. A world of hope not of fear, a world free from disease, a world of plenty. A world secure and at peace, a world finally redeemed.'

His words came as great echoing chords, throbbing with majesty from deepest bass to highest treble, a glorious mighty fanfare. Then there was silence. Out of it he spoke quietly and irresistibly.

'Which do you choose?'

It lay before me: the two choices. He spoke again gently. 'Call it off, Henry, call it off. Please.'

How could I refuse? All logic, all compassion led that way. How could I refuse this gentle, intelligent caring man? The vision was so compelling. It must be the only way. How could I have made such a great mistake? No, the raid must be stopped at all costs.

The strange thing is that I was conscious that if I had yielded then it would be a final decision. It was a once and for all choice. I would have bowed my will to Harout and the group, and I would have got up and left with him and typed the message or made the phone call and sent it off.

I was about to open my mouth and the word 'Yes' was already on the tip of my tongue when an image came to me. It was of a broken, bloody man lying on the ground. At first I thought it was Antoine and then I was not so sure. And he seemed as nothing, an irrelevance compared with the dreams and plans I had been shown. One dead man in millions. Statistically insignificant. I tried to brush the image aside and answer Harout, but it wouldn't go. It persisted, and as it did I realised that my loyalty, my promise lay there. It had already been given.

As I became aware of that everything became plain and I was aware of what lay behind the fine words. And as the impact and power of Harout's speech ebbed away I seemed to see that behind the broken man in my vision was a painting. 'So it was Antoine,' I said to myself. But it was different from the horror in the office; now there was a centre to it and it was the tree. But it had changed; the snake had gone, the trunk was vertical and there were just two branches and they were horizontal. And the horror had gone. Then as the focus seemed to shift again I saw that the dead man had gone, and where he had lain flowers blossomed.

And I knew there was hope.

Then at once everything cleared and I simply saw an ordinary, middle-aged man staring at me with large, tired eyes and an anxious expression. He seemed to be waiting for me to speak, and for once I knew what I had to say and had the words to say it.

'No, Harout, yours is not the way. I defy your very diagnosis. The disaster is only inevitable if we allow it. Your equations and algorithms left me out and, more fatally for you, Laurent and Antoine. I have that on your own admission. You have left out much else. Greed, selfishness and stupidity are not invincible. Indeed this world is, like our bodies, doomed to final decay. But that end may not be for a thousand generations yet, and even then, Harout, we know that as our bodies, it will be remade by him who made it. In the meantime we must hope and build and restore as we can, whatever it may cost us. There's no

416

easy way, no magic virus. Yours would be the cheap victory.'

As I spoke he seemed to crumple slightly, as if he were under judgement. It was almost as though he were being drained. 'Besides, your answer would never work, it would be no solution. You have taken no account of the fact that men are themselves corrupted and need restoring first. Your project has carried its seeds of destruction from the beginning. You started by trading away truth for security and your plans became twisted. You have now demonstrated where you are by killing the innocent and you stand judged. Your kingdom would become a global tyranny; nothing would stand in its way. We need saving from you. God willing, we will be.'

There was silence for a minute. Then he stood up slowly and brushed a fragment of ash off his trousers. The confrontation was over. He seemed very ordinary now; drained of all potency, all hidden depths, simply a quiet but ruffled man woken up early in the morning by a problem at work. He walked to the door and opened it slightly, then he turned back to me.

'I see. You put it very clearly. Well it was probably too late anyway.' He looked slightly puzzled. 'You see there was a lot of trouble over that man's death. Nickie made a dreadful fuss over it. In fact some of the team are leaving already.'

The tone was of a bored, flat bemusement, almost as though the whole thing now was of no interest. He shook his head in vague, almost dreamy disbelief.

'Already disintegrating! Who would have thought it?'

I had to ask something. 'Harout, I have one question. Why did you choose this place?'

A vaguely queasy smile came over him. 'I came to see Elias, and I walked in here with my dreams. I knew – I just knew – it was right. Something told me it was. Then we found the cave and the shrine in the renovation. A wonderful place. You wouldn't believe the inspiration I got

417

there. It was there I finally saw what had to be done with the world. To build the laboratory. The encouragement, all so helpful. Quite influential in its way.'

Then his face twisted as though something had snapped inside him. 'No. I must go. It's too late now, and I'm told the hotel is to be hit too. I'm afraid your wife is there. Anyway, I must leave. I want to transfer the funds to my own account, then I will leave the monastery. I shall at least receive my investment back and live out my years in comfort. We all have to survive.'

Then he went out of the door, closed it firmly, turned the key and his footsteps disappeared away.

I went to the window. Above the mountain the sky was turning from purple to a glorious red. Dawn was beginning to break. A lightning conductor indeed!

I spoke out loud.

'Well, Antoine, I kept my promise. We've won.'

40

I opened the window and breathed the fresh sharp air and stared out through the bars. The sky was becoming yellowish over the ridge to the east. I tried to imagine what was now going on a hundred miles to the south. I had images of pilots undergoing their final briefing, navigators checking maps and routes, engineers flicking test switches and armourers loading weapons. Perhaps the rescue helicopters were already beginning their slow offshore journey northwards in case they were needed. Maybe the co-ordinating planes with their radar and electronics to control the coming attack were at this very moment gaining altitude over the sea. For the pilots of the fighters and the ground attack aircraft, even on a cautious routing it was only a quarter of an hour's flight. Time for a last cup of coffee for them.

I looked at my watch: seven forty-five. Perhaps fifteen minutes, maybe half an hour, and they would be here. Already some of the hills towards the coast had caught the first rays of the sun, but here, in the shadow of the mountain, it would be another twenty or thirty minutes before the sun shone on us.

I vaguely wondered how Elias knew what was happening, but soon gave up; there were too many imponderables. It didn't matter much anyway. The main thing was that this place was going to be destroyed. Curiously, I felt at peace and almost in a dream-like state. I'd done all I had to do. There was much to be thankful for.

I just wished Tina were here.

Then there was the distant sound of a vehicle skidding to a stop and faint shouting. A few seconds later a siren went off, a tremendous wail of noise, echoing and re-echoing round the monastery. There was the clattering of feet in the corridor and the sound of footsteps running away from my door with the sort of speed normally associated with air raid alerts.

It took me several seconds to snap out of my frame of mind. Perhaps I wasn't going to die immediately. I felt almost cheated. I ran over and started pulling and kicking on the door. It didn't move at all. Then there was the noise of feet running towards me and a key was thrust into the lock and turned. The door flew open.

It was Elias Daoud.

His face was urgent, but without agitation; in a strange way it even looked calm. His voice was firm and decisive. 'Get out quickly, we've got twenty minutes.'

He held the door open for me to get out. I didn't need much encouragement.

'Where's Tina?'

We were running down the corridor now. There was

419

shouting ahead in bad Arabic.

'Safe I hope; on her way up to the cedars with Nickie. But careful! What's going on here?'

We rounded the corner into the west wing and stopped dead. Ahead Kevork was waving a sub-machine gun down the archway towards the car park and shouting. The gist of it seemed to be for someone to get out of a car quickly. Elias started to move quietly along the corridor again, but Kevork heard him and swung his gun round. Elias flung himself into a doorway and I leapt back round the corner. There was a burst of firing, deafening in the confined space, and bullets started to ricochet around off the stone walls. Even round the corner seemed exposed. There was an open door opposite so I ran over and stumbled inside.

It was the financial operations centre. The reason why the door was open was plain; Harout was there tapping at a keyboard. I jumped and looked for a weapon of some sort. To my surprise he just stared at me for a second and then turned back to the screen.

'Oh, you're out, are you? I thought I heard Elias.'

The voice was devoid of all emotion. It took me a few moments to get over the shock of seeing him.

'Harout, you've only got minutes.'

He shook his head as though it were a matter of declining a lunch invitation.

'I have to transfer these funds. I'm having trouble. I've pulled them out, but at the moment they are stuck in a temporary account. The machine is refusing to transmit. I think they are jamming the signal.'

That wasn't surprising if there was a raid due. I remembered vaguely that David had mentioned electronic counter-measures. They were presumably taking effect already. Outside there was further firing, although it didn't seem to be in our direction.

'It's the planes, Harout. Time to get out.'

'No, I'll keep trying. The jamming may weaken. I must try. It's all I have now.'

420

He spoke distractedly and hammered a key again. Outside there was a shout from Elias.

I didn't even say goodbye.

Kevork seemed to have gone and Elias was waving me on from the archway. Outside the monastery there was the sound of a car engine roaring and then, with tyres screaming, it was gone. I raced up to join Elias, but he had already run out into the car park. I followed him out, screwing my eyes up against the glare of the sunlight on the snow. The shadow of the mountain that hid us was retreating rapidly as the sun rose. Already the sun's rays were glistening off trees twenty yards away. Up the hill a Range Rover was skidding away up towards the main road.

In the car park Elias was stooping over a body. I ran towards him and he turned to me, his face sorrowful. 'Sammy.'

I looked and wished I hadn't. I suppose it *was* Sammy, but you couldn't tell from what was left of the face. He was dead already.

Elias muttered, 'Sorry, Sammy. Sorry.'

Then he turned to me. 'I'm afraid we've lost the car. Your friend Jim says eight-fifteen so we have less than fifteen minutes. Follow me up the track to the cedars. We must stay off the road.'

I was going to ask how he knew the time of the raid, but it could wait. There were a lot more questions. In particular I wanted to be certain that Tina was safe. I wasn't too happy with Elias' word alone, but there wasn't anything I could do about it. I looked at the track Elias was pointing out as it climbed the cliffs above the monastery. It was hard to see with the snow covering it almost entirely. In one or two places rock emerged, although even that appeared to be ice-covered. I turned to the west where the boundary between the brilliant sunlit snow and the mountain's shadow had swept nearer. Indeed as you looked you felt you could see it move.

421

Then I heard the noise: a faint hum, almost inaudible, but high above. I looked up into the deep brilliant blue sky and my blood turned to ice. There, vertically above us, the sun was glinting off two tiny silver planes moving slowly in broad, menacing circles in a scene of malevolent beauty. I felt as the mouse must feel about hovering kestrels; I trembled and wanted to hide. It was a paralysing sight full of all manner of menace. To me, they seemed for all the world the epitome of ruthless malignity, the very embodiment of death. I shivered.

Elias caught my glance and looked up. 'The first planes. Like Yeats' falcons in a gyre. Let's go. The rough beast slouches from Bethlehem.'

Rimmer would have been proud of him. We ran through the heavy, thick snow to the foot of the cliff. Elias stopped for a moment, then began to move with surprising agility up a narrow goat or sheep track. I followed as fast as I could, but I was feeling cold and stiff. I was also having problems finding the places to put my feet. Elias had made footprints, but walking in them wasn't easy as the compressed snow made them slippery. In summer it would have been a simple track, but with its covering of ice and snow it was treacherous. After a minute or so of scrambling I paused and looked down. We were now half-way across the cliff and already high above the monastery. The unstoppable sun was shining over the car park and touching the south-west tip of the monastery roof. Time was running out. There was no sign of Harout; in fact it was difficult to imagine that he would be able to tear himself away at all. I took a deep breath and started climbing again.

At one point I looked up to see that the sun was glinting off more wings. The planes were gathering. I kept moving as fast as I could, but I had the wrong shoes on and my feet kept slipping; not severely, but enough to ensure I walked and scrambled on all fours rather than ran. Elias was some way in front of me, but now the track was beginning to flatten out and the crest was immediately ahead. Above that we could make good progress.

I glanced back. The retreating shadow of Mount Lebanon was covering only half the roof of the Deir now. My legs ached, but I ignored them. I concentrated on the path. On this last stretch I had to go on all fours for most of the time, but I was nearly there.

Just before reaching the top of the hill the path crossed a narrow gully and it swung inwards round its edge. I realised that this corresponded to the line of the joint that had alerted me to the location of the cave and that directly below me must be the entrance. Indeed, as I looked down I could see the roof of the nave below. To my relief it was still in shadow. As I swung along the track into the gully I noted that Elias was out of sight, presumably already over the lip of the cliff and running up in the snow towards the road, the cedars and safety. In a few moments I'd be safe too. Over the sound of my laboured breathing I could hear that the air was droning and buzzing with distant faint noises, almost like insects on a warm summer's afternoon. I forced myself on. In the gully my foot slipped on a patch of ice. I stumbled, put out my hands, recovered my balance and breathed a sigh of relief.

Then from nowhere panic struck in a great tidal wave. Everything turned over, the sky rolled underneath dizzily and then climbed above me again. For a moment the Deir seemed to be hanging high over my head. I closed my eyes tight and hung on giddily. I was overwhelmed, inundated, flooded by fear. I was terribly aware of the drop below, the sixty or so feet above the snow-covered roof that the sun was creeping over. My hands trembled. Then I felt certain that I was slipping, indeed that my feet were already sliding to the brink and that I was on the point of rolling over and falling downwards. I told myself it was a lie and clung on, trying to pray.

Then the panic seemed to be replaced by an all-pervading sense of futility and complete despair. It seemed as if I

423

were under judgement. A voice inside seemed to say that I had no right to escape the coming fire, that I was as guilty as the rest and that all I could do was to let go and slip to my just fate. Time ceased as the struggle raged. Surely my feet were already skidding on the ice, my hands losing their grip on the rocks? I was going. I knew I was. My judgement was deserved and hell awaited. My foot was slipping. I must fall.

Then I became aware that something – someone – was deceiving me, trying to trick me into letting myself fall. Something so impotent, so defeated that it could do nothing but cast shadows on the mind. As I realised that, a verse came to me: 'And the one who trusts in him will never be put to shame.' And I knew I stood then and for ever not in my own strength or my own righteousness, but in that of another. And at that thought the panic and the despair fled.

I opened my eyes and saw that what I had felt was indeed not true. My hands still clutched onto the rock, my foot had not slipped. I stood secure on firm ground.

But I had lost minutes.

As fast as I could I completed the passage of the gully and scrambled to the top of the track. I stood up and looked towards the monastery for the last time. The sun was now shining over all of it and the roofs shone with a fresh sparkling brilliance. I looked away and fixed my eyes on the clump of cedars nearly a mile off. A hundred yards away Elias was looking towards me. He shouted something and then turned and began running up to the road.

As I followed him it seemed that there were more noises in the air: beatings and whisperings, twitterings and rattlings as of a gathering of terrible winged creatures. Suddenly something dark and brooding flashed overhead, casting a fleeting shadow across the snow. I glanced up in a new fear to see something too small and too quiet to be a warplane. As I fled on uphill in frantic desperation it registered as a drone, probing and decoying for missiles and radar. There could only be moments left.

I continued running. Terror was abroad. I slipped and slithered, bouncing off bushes and rocks, desperately trying to put as much distance as I could between me and the monastery. At least now I was running at a marked angle away from the line of the cave, but I had no idea how far I had to be away to be safe. The great trees were the only safe place. My lungs ached in agony and my legs screamed, but I pressed on through the thick, dragging snow. Sweat poured off me. Once I half fell and the temptation just to lie there in the marvellous cool whiteness descended over me, but I rose and staggered on. I floundered at another point in drifts up to my knees, but I clawed and pulled myself free and reeled on. I had to. Above my gasps for breath the chorus of noises in the air seemed to be growing with murmurs and whistlings running above and below the limits of hearing. It sounded like a demonic chorus, the very host of hell.

I ran on, on and upwards.

Then finally it came. I heard what I had been awaiting and dreading. The sound that must be the most terrible in the world: that of a jet diving on full power. It came from the south straight down at me. The faint whistling rose through a hideous rattling whine into a deafening, shrieking, heart-stopping roar. At the climax of the crescendo I flung myself forward down into the snow and braced myself, putting my hands over my ears and closing my eyes tight.

In the next second or so there was a cacophony of noises: the first jet – released from its burden – roaring skywards overhead, a second machine starting another dive, and above both a rising whistle which turned into the sound of something punching through roofs, walls, doors and burying itself deep and ... there was light.

The ground hit me and every cell of my body seemed to be punched, squeezed and vibrated in an immense blow. I suppose there was a noise, but that wasn't what was important. Ears were superfluous. The force registered directly, on skin, on muscle, on bone, on every nerve. It was as if a great door had slammed shut in heaven itself. I felt I was being swung by a giant against the hillside, then tossed into the air. Suddenly the hammering and thudding turned into a great roaring, juddering, thundering blast and air raced past me – not the hot air I'd expected but cold air screaming downhill into the blast.

Implosion.

Snow tore at my face, a seething wind ripped at my clothes.

For a fraction of a second things seemed to be settling down when I was dully conscious of the second plane racing away just overhead of me and something else whistling and smashing down through into the ground.

It was a repeat performance. Light flashed again, brighter this time. I was smashed against the ground again in another great upheaval as though trapped between hammer and anvil. There was a great throbbing, vibrating noise as if a train were passing within an inch of my head. Then the roaring seemed to wane and there was the sound of things falling around me. A great sucking wind full of snow rose to a gale and whipped over me before dying away slowly into a hissing whisper.

My mind kept muttering, 'After the wind the flame,' and I knew I must keep going. I tried to stand up and fell onto all fours. I got up again and started running, although I was still shaking all over and the snow seemed to be dragging me down. But the road was just ahead.

There were more planes coming in. I could barely keep on my feet, but managed to keep staggering onwards, all but oblivious of terrible clouds of smoke and dust drifting past. Then the diving noise began again and I threw myself into a snow drift just below the road.

A vast multiple rippling series of explosions occurred – less shaking than the first blasts but still awesome – this time with white and yellow flashes that didn't die away but lingered and grew. Then there came a foul scorching blast that roared over me like the breath of a dragon. I stayed down and tried not to breathe, although all around there was the smell of burning and of choking acrid smoke. There were hisses and spitting noises as things fell into the snow either side of me.

Then there appeared to be something of a respite, the only sound being that of a roaring and crackling noise from behind. I got to my feet and ran uphill and the light was all wrong, but I didn't dare look back to where there was an enormous sizzling and bubbling sound. As I ran forward I saw that I was casting two shadows.

Then I fell over a bank onto a flat surface that was free of snow and extended either side of me, and I realised it was the road. I lay for a moment, peacefully watching a fragment of ash drifting across the road and getting my breath back.

Then Elias was alongside. He was red-faced and panting.

'Come on up to the trees. Quickly, remember the road's not safe.'

I staggered to my feet and looked back. A foaming, billowing torch of flame was roaring up hundreds of feet into the air over the monastery. At its heart the flame was so brilliant that you had to look away and on the edges it turned to a dirty white and yellow colour. The heat was tangible. An envelope of oily smoke hung over it all and rose high into the sky. The eddies seemed to be carrying charred debris high into the air in turbulent spirals. It appeared that the flames extended into the cliff from the monastery; the cavern had apparently been breached all along its length.

I turned away and hurried up the hill, the after image of the fire still in my eyes. Wisps of evil-smelling smoke drifted past and I could feel the glow of the heat on my back. There were planes still around. I could hear further explosions away to the west.

The trees were only twenty yards away. I kept stagger-ing onwards; everything ached terribly. I just wanted to lie down. Then there was the sound of more planes racing in low and the whooshing noise of rockets being fired. A chain of explosions followed. Out of the corner of my eye I saw a great black shape racing down the road and passing almost overhead, its shadow blocking the sun for a moment, and an enormous roar following in its wake. As it went there was a furious shrieking, chattering noise, and an answering roar of explosions down the road. It vaguely registered on my numbed brain as rapid cannon fire. As I stumbled onwards I realised it had been aimed down the road. The road that Tina and Nickie had been on.

I tried not to think about it and staggered on, knowing that collapse was imminent. Everything – legs, arms, ears, eyes, lungs – ached or stung. Suddenly through my blur-ring vision I saw that I had come to the wall. Here the snow was thick and soft and climbing the piled stones took all my last strength. Gasping and sobbing for breath I scrambled over the wall to fall down into the snow beyond. I picked myself up and looked for Tina, but I was having trouble focusing.

Nickie was there, but....

Then Tina ran towards me and I stood up, and as she held me I fell over into the thick snow under the blessed cover of the trees.

'Are you all right?'

I was too busy breathing to answer. I could feel the cuts and bruises now. I couldn't speak. Rumbles and thunder-ings continued away below us and echoed round the val-ley.

'Yes,' I panted, 'just.'

The branches swam overhead in the sunlight. Above, the sky was immense and blue.

'Tina,' I gasped. 'Sorry for the delay.' I paused again, conscious of a burning sensation in my lungs. 'I nearly joined Lot's wife.'

I suddenly felt light-headed and half sat up against her.

'Tina, can we go somewhere else for Christmas next year?'

But no sooner were the words out of my mouth when the horror and terror and enormity of it all hit me and I found myself clinging to her, shaking like a leaf and incapable of all speech.

41

Twenty or so minutes later I had more or less recovered, although my ears were still ringing. I sat on a borrowed anorak under the cedars. All around there were large fresh piles of snow that had been shaken down by the blasts. A few yards away Nickie was leaning against a cedar tree looking miserable. Elias was down at the edge of the trees peering out over the smoking ruins of the monastery and the hotel. Every so often he would shout a warning as another plane flew low over the road. Tina huddled against me. She seemed to be in good spirits, although she was clearly slightly shaken. I asked her how the last few days had been.

'Tough, but I learned a lot. A lot, Henry.'

She had a curious determined look which, while encouraging, was somewhat daunting. The planes still flew around and several swung low over the cedars. Elias waved us down.

'Keep down. Jim warned us to keep off the road.'

That raised one of a number of questions. Just then something that I thought was an F-16 dived in and delivered a new round of incendiaries on the monastery. Further snow tumbled off the branches as the blast rolled around us. Another plane circled low overhead and then flew down the road so low that you could see the blue and white Star of David on the fuselage. I turned to Tina. 'I suppose they will all be happy about this in Tel Aviv.'

She was thoughtful. 'Yes, but it crossed my mind that in a way the project might have tempted them.'

That hadn't occurred to me, but she had a point and I took up her idea.

'You mean that if they had known what it was all about someone might have been inclined to let it proceed? True, they of all nations would have benefited most from it. At least at first. But I don't suppose the new world order would have found much of a place for them. Or probably for us. Oh well, they can't be tempted now.'

Elias walked back to us and then turned to look mournfully at the view.

'What a mess. Sammy dead as well. I think they've shot up the house too.'

There was a lot I wanted to ask him. At the moment he seemed distracted, staring over the ruins of so much of his life. Then he turned towards me rather hesitantly. I decided to satisfy my curiosity.

'Sheik, I believe you have some explanations?'

He looked at me. It was a funny look. He seemed a different sort of person. I couldn't pin it down. In one sense he appeared weaker, more human and yet there seemed to be more strength to him, as though he was more a Sheik, or even a king.

'Yes, and many apologies; but not complete explanations. Some strange things have happened that I do not fully understand. Maybe I never will.'

Then he looked rather ashamed, but it seemed to be with an open, even humble sort of shame. I was wondering whether this was the same Elias we had known before. He motioned to Nickie who came over slowly and stiffly.

'First though, I want to make the apologies. I have done some very bad things. Some of the worst of them,' here he looked at Tina and me, 'I have been able to stop. However, I will tell the story. I must shortly return to the house to direct operations, but I'm afraid these people seem intent on eliminating everything that moves. Fortunately, they seem to have spared both these trees and the car. But we are safer here for the moment.'

I looked around. Nickie, pale faced, sat down against a nearby tree trunk. Tina looked up at me and hugged me tighter. Elias began slowly as if recounting a dream.

'I think I can start where you first mentioned the possibility of this raid, Henry. Well a raid, not this particular one. I must take the responsibility for how this developed. You see, as I thought about it I realised that it would be an ideal opportunity for me to do what I had been considering for some time. That is to leave here once and for all. I think I mentioned this to you?'

I nodded.

'Of course I knew the way that the original members of the group had done vanishing acts and that had always attracted me. To go and leave no trace. To start a new life. But this sort of raid,' here he gestured to the still billowing smoke and flame over the monastery, 'offered an ideal opportunity – especially if I knew when it would happen. I had the false papers already, the money in the bank accounts abroad – everything. It would have all worked very neatly. I would have been free of Harout; I would have been sadly mourned, my brother would have taken over and Elias Daoud would have slipped out of history. And into the South of France.'

A plane came in low and fired rockets down onto the road by the hotel. It seemed to hit something because there was an orange fireball and an oily flame. Elias intertwined his fingers.

'Those people! We did the best thing, Henry, by walking up. Kevork's chances of getting away are very low. But I now have no wish to catch him myself.'

He shook his head. 'Anyway, where was I? Ah yes, so I

was very interested in the airstrike idea. It would have fulfilled my promise to Pastor Antoine and ensured that the group were eliminated.'

He looked unhappy. 'But I'm afraid I was wrong, very wrong, Henry, to try to add to your message and get the hotel destroyed. When you apparently erased the message I was very angry, but in fact I remembered as Sammy took you away that it was not lost.'

I stared at him. That had been one of the very few things that I had been confident of.

'But Sheik, I pulled the plug out; the screen went blank.'

'Call me Elias from now on. Well, at least in private. Ah very clever, Henry, but not clever enough. We have our power failures here. Harout had put me a board in the computer which backs up the memory during a power failure. You lose the screen image of course, but the data is safe. Batteries.'

I felt like banging my head against the tree trunk. 'Of course! How stupid! Here you'd have to have such a system. You'd never use it in the UK. So you just plugged it back in and sent the message?'

'Well actually I emphasised the hotel a bit more. Don't forget, Harout knew my new passport identity....'

Something clicked and I began to feel annoyed.

'But you put us in the hotel and the monastery. You were signing our death warrants!'

Elias rubbed his hands together briefly and looked very embarrassed. 'There's no denying it or excusing it. I planned to let you be killed. But let me finish first.'

I nodded for him to continue.

'So I made provisional plans to go to Damascus last night after having told one or two people I would be sleeping in the tower. My plans were hardened by the fact that I got a return message from a man called Jim which said, "08.15 on the first with no warning. Keep off the road." '

I was astonished and a little ashamed. Tina nudged me and gave me a smile. I spoke quietly, 'He wasn't supposed

432

to say that. That was quite against orders. They'll bust him for breach of security.'

Elias shrugged. 'You'd better be grateful. I might not have got you out in time otherwise.'

Tina and I looked at each other. I felt rather small. 'Elias, I misjudged that fellow. I'll have to get in touch with him and thank him and buy him a proper meal.'

'Buy him one from me too.'

He'd like that. Elias continued: 'So I should have been in Damascus by now. It was all arranged. Anyway, last night Nickie came round. Nickie, I've said enough for the moment. You talk.'

Nickie stirred herself slightly. She had pulled her gold chain free of her pullover and was twisting it hard. I half expected it to fly apart. When she spoke it was in awkward, almost traumatised tones.

'Me? Well if you insist. It's actually very simple, in one way. When I got back to the hotel on Monday night I called a meeting with everyone including Harout for Tuesday afternoon. I asked him to explain why the pastor was dead in his office. It was a weird meeting; he answered badly. He was normally so good at that sort of thing, I mean sorting out problems, making people see things his way.'

She looked at me. 'I suppose he's dead?'

'I'm sorry, I tried to get him out, but he was on the computer, trying to transfer....'

'Data?'

I paused. 'Of a sort.'

Nickie just shook her head and slowly continued: 'Then everything got out of hand. There was a lot of shouting and other things came up: all the problems we'd hidden because we believed in the project. It all came out. It was like the business with Antoine had acted as the trigger. In the end I said, "Harout, I'm leaving." He said I couldn't, so I asked whether he was going to have Kevork shoot me too. That got him mad so I just walked out, grabbed a bag

433

of things and ran down to the Sheik's – to Elias' – house. I knew that was the only place I'd be safe from him. I couldn't drive out of Farayoun without a car, could I? So that's my story. I think the rest Elias can tell himself. I don't understand what has happened. I need a holiday to get myself back together.' She sat back and stared up at the trees as if seeking comfort in them.

I saw her point; the whole thing was very strange. I couldn't understand why Elias wasn't in Damascus.

Elias looked over the valley. The planes seemed to be going home now and the flames were dying down over the monastery, but there was still a lot of smoke. On the hillside above it there was a great brown and grey zone where the snow had melted. The hotel appeared still to be burning fiercely. In the distance the bells were beginning to toll in the town. He began to speak again.

'Yes, Nickie turned up as I was in the middle of packing, so I didn't know what to do. In the end I offered her a ride to Damascus as long as she kept quiet. In fact I thought it would help my plans. I didn't tell her about what was going to happen here. She can't be blamed for that. So I told Sammy I would be at the tower last night. I dismissed the guards from watching for Kevork as well. I didn't want them killed. Of course in the morning it would be assumed I had perished and there would be no body.'

I looked at the smoke over the monastery. With the temperatures that had been present there I doubted if there would be anything organic left within a fifty-yard radius of what had been Harout's office, let alone any identifiable body.

Elias continued: 'The other thing that I thought was clever,' and here he looked ashamed, 'was that it could never be proved I'd actually ordered the attack. The rest was simple. I told Sammy that Nickie was going to Damascus, got him to clear the road with the snowplough and made him promise to ensure that she could leave and pass the hotel at two in the morning. He did that and she

434

waited for me here.'

'I nearly froze,' Nickie shivered at the memory.

'Anyway, I arrived here just after that by walking up from the tower – on the road, Henry. That track we took is too dangerous at night. We were just going to drive on. I was to put on my disguise and be a merchant travelling at night to avoid people noticing my companion. It would all have fitted.'

He shook his head faintly and began to speak again, but now his words were softer. 'But it didn't work out like that, did it? I wanted to say goodbye to the valley and so I walked up to these cedars. I stood just there, I think.' He pointed nearby. 'I looked over the valley in the starlight, one last time.'

A curious hesitancy came into his voice at this point and he seemed to be a sorry man.

'I told myself to rejoice. At a stroke I was destroying this evil thing and freeing myself from the curse of this valley. The world was mine. I had done it all so elegantly, so cleverly.'

He paused. 'And yet I could not rejoice. I had no peace; indeed, I felt a little ashamed already. And I couldn't get Pastor Antoine's words out of my mind. He had said how this was not the way. That rather irritated me because I realised that I had nothing really to be proud of. Indeed, much to feel guilty about. I realised that even with my new name and my new identity I couldn't leave my conscience behind in the valley. And I couldn't get Antoine out of my mind. Then I thought how he'd said about my name: "Elias Daoud; a good name, live up to it." So I said aloud – as if to him, "Old man, I have indeed been Elias. I've called down fire from heaven. This will make Mount Carmel look like nothing tomorrow. Won't that please you?" '

Tina and I exchanged glances. I hadn't seen it this way before. Elias continued in bitter tones. 'But that didn't seem to satisfy him, as it were. Or me. So I stood here and

435

I felt very sad and guilty. And it seemed a moment of great sorrow rather than triumph, because I felt very unclean. And I wondered what was the way if this was not. Then suddenly I knew that there was someone behind me. I thought it was Nickie, then I realised that it wasn't and I wished I had brought George or Michel because this must be an assassin. Then I thought that it didn't matter because I deserved death. It was a man.'

I noticed Nickie glancing over her shoulder with a look of unease. Elias ignored her but stopped for a moment and stared at me.

'I suppose you will understand, your wife too. You see I felt I knew who he was. He is the one who owns these trees, indeed planted them. He told me everything that I ever did. And it seemed that we talked a lot and I realised what I had done wrong and I shed many tears. And I knew what I must do. Then he left me, and I remembered Antoine's words again about my name and I realised that I must be Daoud too. I hope I will be a better David than I was Elijah, my friends.'

Tina and I stared at each other in bewilderment and wonder. Such things happen, but to Elias Daoud? Yet it rang true, right down to the last word 'friends', a phrase that Elias could never have used before. I glanced at Nickie whose face showed a stubborn bewilderment.

After a moment Elias spoke again. 'So I came down here like a man in a dream and I realised how little time I had left because it was now after six and dawn would soon be here. So I told Nickie what I had planned.'

She shook her head slowly in disbelief. 'I was appalled, Henry, Tina. I couldn't believe it. I had no idea what he had planned. I assumed you'd left with Fuad, until Elias told me.' She gave up and looked at Elias with a curious mixture of emotions in her face. He took over again.

'We drove down fast to the hotel. Nickie was to go and get everybody out of there while I went to the house and warned all my people to get down into town. I was worried they would be on the road or be in the house if it was hit. I think in fact they have machine gunned it. Also I did not wish to meet Harout, at least not without someone like Sammy beside me. So I organised that. After a few minutes at the house I drove back up to the hotel with Sammy following to protect me against Harout. When we got there we found he had gone to the Deir and not told anyone. I should have thought of that. So we had to raise the alarm. Nickie, you tell what happened. Please.'

I think from her face Nickie would have preferred not to, but she relented. 'If I must. I decided I would have to do my bit and get everybody out. So I woke Harout up first and told him. He was very clever and he said we should get Tina out first, so he took his keys and went down to her. He questioned her about stopping the raid. I wondered what he was up to – then he just pushed me over and locked the door on us.' She stopped suddenly, apparently overwhelmed, and nodded faintly at Tina to continue.

'So we yelled and shouted, but it was the end of the stores wing. No one heard us. I thought we were going to die.'

Nickie burst out, 'I'm sorry, I'm glad he's dead!'

I felt Tina stiffen against me, but then she reached out and held Nickie's hand. After a minute Tina continued quietly.

'It wasn't very pleasant, although I suppose I'd decided I was as good as dead anyway. But quarter of an hour later Elias came in with Sammy and let us out. He told us to take the car and go up here and to take shelter under the trees. So here we are. I wanted to go down and help get you out, but he said he and Sammy would do it and that I couldn't be of much help.'

I nodded. It was all becoming plain. It was as well Tina hadn't come down. Kevork could have easily shot her as well as Sammy.

Elias began again. 'I think a lot of people got out of the

hotel in time. The rest you know. Sammy and I drove down to the Deir and hit the alarm. All Harout's people fled, but left Kevork behind. He took my Range Rover and killed Sammy in the process. Poor Sammy; many years of loyal service. Yet I suppose it may be for the best. He will not be mourned and I would rather not have him around now. You say Harout is dead too?'

I sighed. 'Yes, I'm afraid so. In the end his vision left him and he seemed to become concerned only about the money. He tried to transfer it to his own account on the computer, but everything was being jammed. He said he'd got as far as putting in a temporary account somewhere. Where it will remain I suppose. It was a sad end.'

Nickie shook her head, but Elias nodded sadly as if in understanding.

The flames had died away now and there had been no noise of aircraft for some time. It was time to talk of the future.

'Elias, if I may ask: what happens now?'

'Well, I have a question first: do you both forgive me?'

Tina spoke quietly, 'I think the first question is do you yourself now forgive your enemies?'

There was a pause, then Elias spoke slowly. 'Yes, I think so. There is a pain there still, but yes, I do. Or at least I believe I can. After all, I believe I have been forgiven.'

Tina looked at me. 'So of course we do, Sheik.'

'Elias.'

'I agree with my wife. Most of the time anyway, and certainly on this.'

There was a look of relief on his face.

'Thank you. That is a great comfort, but I thought you would.'

He stood up and shook the snow off himself. Then he went and stared over at his valley.

'I think it is plain what I must do, although I am afraid. I must go back down and rule in a better manner. To rule more as David. There is a lot to be done in this valley, and much that is wrong here is due to me. Despite my boasting I have not been a good ruler. Can it be done, Henry?'

I thought hard.

'Yes, I have faith it can be done with God's help. I would say this, though, Elias – that evil cannot be eliminated by bombing raids. We have broken that particular wickedness by the grace of God, but other evils are still around. You must not do what the old monks did and just wall it up and forget about it. It must be fought and destroyed. It will help if you can replace it with good, but doing that will be slower and harder than calling an air raid.'

He seemed to weigh the words. 'What you say is what I have begun to think too. It will not be easy. Maybe too the time has come for me to look beyond the valley, to our own sad Maronite community. That will be difficult, but Pastor Antoine seemed to think that there was hope.'

He paused, deep in thought. 'Then beyond that is our nation. And there are still wider horizons.'

I felt I had to warn him. 'I should say, Elias, that the path you are choosing is right, but that it will be very hard and dangerous.'

He turned on me. There was a faint hint of the old temper in his eyes.

'Henry, I have learned this much. I've played for security for the last half-dozen years, maybe all my life. I would have played it till my death. Yet it is the highest foolishness. We seek to hold life in our hands and it flows out anyway like water. I know the risks. I saw what it cost Antoine. But we cannot keep life, not this life. Now let us go to the car. I need to get my things out. There is work to do.'

I looked at Tina, and Elias must have caught my puzzlement.

'Nickie wishes to go on to Damascus and home. I have work to do. Perhaps if you would drive her?'

A nice idea, but there were a few problems.

'We have no papers or anything, Elias.'

He looked slightly awkward.

'Curiously enough you have. I'm afraid I took your passports and your money. I reasoned you wouldn't be needing them. The passports are worth something on the black market and I'm not the only one who travels, or who used to travel, under false papers. So they are in the car. Plus some extra money which will see you all home. I will sort out with Fuad about the two cars that may or may not still be there. There is an address in Damascus to leave this car at. I think that should do you. Oh yes, there are also full papers to see you through into Syria, but don't stop near Baalbek.'

We walked down to the car in silence. The whole thing was so extraordinary that I could barely take it in. Elias went to the boot and pulled out a holdall which he put on the ground. Then he stood upright.

'Farewell time I'm afraid.'

He went over to Nickie and gave her a hug and a kiss on the cheek. It was the first gesture of affection I'd seen him give anyone. At first she froze, then gave him a cold embrace.

Then he came over and hugged and kissed us and it seemed that there were tears in his eyes. So we made our farewells and he set off, a lonely figure, down the long road to where the bells were ringing.

And we got into the car and drove out of the valley to Damascus.

But not quite. Because as he walked away Tina caught me by the shoulder and spoke urgently. At first I couldn't believe my ears and protested, but she continued and I remembered that she had promised to spring surprises. I didn't at all care for what she said, but as she spoke I knew it was right. Everything now fitted. Everything from the moment Vaughan had got in touch with me, and from even before that. It had all now come together.

So I ran after Elias shouting for him to stop and Tina followed after me and caught up with us as I was speaking.

'Elias, will you now let the school be built?'

He thought briefly. 'If I knew who was running it, but Fuad is going to do something else I hear.'

That confirmed it. I looked at Tina. There were indeed no cheap victories.

'Would you let us come and run it?'

He gave the first genuinely happy smile I'd seen him give. 'You would trust me? You are welcome. But....' His face darkened slightly. 'Look, Henry and Tina, I have now a rather uncertain future. I can promise you little.'

'Not even security?'

He caught the amusement in my voice and laughed. 'That least of all. But you already have the only sort you can have. Go! But come back soon and stay.'

And we did just that.